"This whimsical and enchanting tale, filled with poisonous injustice and seductively forbidden romance, will sink its claws into you and have you falling for the monsters."

—NICOLE FIORINA, AUTHOR, THE STAY WITH ME SERIES

". . . a fast-paced adventure story about prejudice and its consequences, the beauty of trust, and forbidden love."

—NATALIE MURRAY, AUTHOR, EMMIE & THE TUDOR KING

"A dash of darkness, a seductive romance, and a quest that promises death. A Cursed Kiss is a one-of-a-kind adventure in a mystical world you won't want to come back from."

—GOODREADS STARRED REVIEW

A CURSED KISS

Myths of Airren

Book One

Jenny Hickman

Midnight Tide
PUBLISHING

Publisher's Note: This is a work of fiction. Names, characters, places, and incidents are a product of the author's imagination. Locales and public names are sometimes used for atmospheric purposes. Any resemblances to actual people, living or dead, or to businesses, companies, events, institutions, or locales is completely coincidental.

Published by Midnight Tide Publishing.

www.midnighttidepublishing.com

Book Title/ Jenny Hickman- 1st ed.

Paperback ISBN: 978-1-953238-49-8

Hardcover ISBN: 978-1-953238-48-1

Cover design by Cover Dungeon

AUTHOR'S NOTE

This book has scenes depicting grief and loss, violence, sexual assault, and contains some sexual content. I have done my best to handle these elements sensitively, but if these issues could be considered triggering for you, please take note.

Pronunciation Guide

Gancanagh-(*gan•cawn•ah*)

Padraig- (*pa•drec*)

Tadhg- (*tie•g*)

Rían- (*ree•un*)

Fiadh- (*fee•ah*)

Ruairi- (*ror•ee*)

Áine- (*awn•ya*)

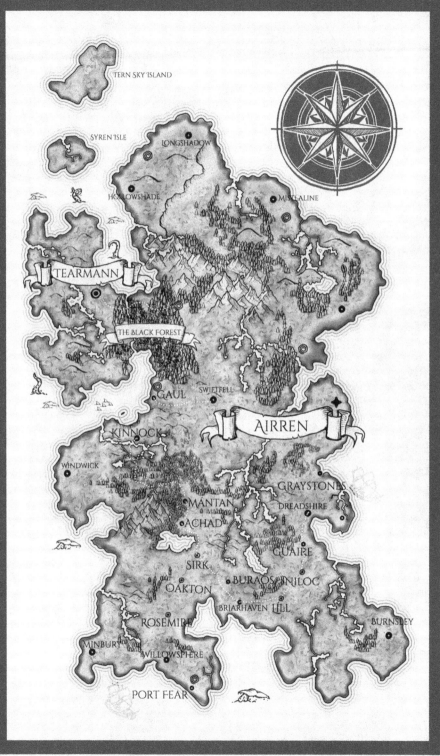

For my fellow
Romantasy lovers
Seeking an escape

1

MY DYING HEART ACHED INSIDE MY CHEST, SHRINKING AND withering until only an empty husk remained.

My hands shook as I clutched my skirts. It was all I could do to keep from dropping to my knees in the secluded alcove and begging my sister to call off her betrothal. "You said you weren't going to marry him. You swore you'd fix this."

"Keelynn, please keep your voice down." Aveen huffed and pinched the bridge of her nose. Exasperation left her shoulders slumping inside her sparkling blue ballgown. "I *will* fix it, but you have to be patient."

If we didn't act now, it'd be too late. "Father announced your betrothal two weeks ago, and you've done *nothing*." Nothing except pick out dresses for her trousseau, flowers for the ceremony, and a destination for the honeymoon.

A wrinkle formed between her perfectly arched eyebrows. "Delicate matters take time to resolve," she insisted, slapping me with the exasperated tone she typically reserved for our father.

Time had run out.

It was now or never.

"I'm the one who loves Robert." The harsh whisper tore

through my chapped lips. Licking them did little to relieve the dryness. "I've always loved him." Ever since he had rescued me from that rogue wave when I was fourteen, he'd been my courageous Prince Charming, saving me from the monotony of life on this cursed island.

Not anymore.

Now he was to be my sister's husband.

I dashed my hands against the traitorous tears tumbling through my lashes. Crying wasn't going to help. "Why didn't you tell Father to pair him with me?"

Aveen hated Robert almost as much as Robert hated her. And I was helpless, destined to watch as the two people I loved most in this world wedded each other.

What about *me*? Where was *my* happily-ever-after?

Aveen had suitors calling at the door every day. Why couldn't our father have chosen one of them as her husband and left Robert for me? As the eldest, she was expected to wed first, but that didn't mean she had to marry *him*.

Aveen rested her cold hands on the tufted pink sleeves of my lace and chiffon gown. "You have to trust me," she said, giving my shoulders a reassuring squeeze. "Have I ever let you down?"

The loose curls framing my face tickled my cheeks when I shook my head. "Not yet."

Aveen had been the steady shore to my shifting sea since our mother had passed away eight years earlier. She never failed to put my needs above hers.

Until she agreed to marry Robert.

"Lady Aveen?" a nasally voice called. It sounded like Sir Henry Withel, a knight from the neighboring island of Vellana. "I believe I have the next dance."

Aveen scanned the full dance card dangling from her wrist and swore. When she looked back at me, her blue eyes glistened. "I love you, Keelynn. No matter what happens, please remember that."

I couldn't find it in my hollow heart to return the sentiment. I *did* love her. But at the moment, I wanted to lock her away until after the wedding. *I* wanted to wear the ivory wedding gown that had arrived this morning. *I* wanted to walk down the aisle in the parish church and exchange vows with the man *I* loved.

She left me behind the thick velvet drapes and crossed the glossy parquet floor of our ballroom to offer a gloved hand to Sir Henry. Together, the two of them made their way to the dance floor.

I could do this. I could survive. I could plaster on a smile and feign happiness for a few more hours.

My mother's pearl necklace felt heavy against my throat as I took a deep breath, brushed my dark curls behind my rigid shoulders, and emerged into the ballroom.

Hundreds of candles cast the space in a rich, amber glow. The three-tiered chandeliers hanging from the vaulted coffered ceiling shimmered like moonlight on the sea.

A servant dressed in black swept past carrying fluted glasses of golden champagne. I snagged one and brought it to the line of chairs along the paneled wall. The only free seat was between Lady Gore, an elderly Marchioness who suffered from gout, and Miss Gina Fahey, the milliner's eldest daughter who was pushing thirty and had yet to secure a husband.

Music from the stringed quartet harmonized with the murmuring crowd, clinking glasses, and stomping heels. Skirts and coattails spun as couples danced in dizzying circles. Around and around and around, mimicking the dark thoughts spinning through my mind.

Aveen's golden hair flew across her flushed cheeks as Sir Henry spun her in a reel. Her betrothed watched from the fireplace with an impassive expression, surrounded by his three older brothers and a few other lads from our town.

I twisted the delicate stem between my fingers before lifting the fluted glass to my lips. Champagne bubbles tickled my tongue.

In three swallows, the drink was gone. If I was to survive this night, I would need more. A lot more.

Glass after glass, I drowned my sorrow, waiting for the alcohol to douse the fire of betrayal blazing beneath my skin. Searching for the blessed numbness hiding at the bottom of each glass.

A pair of polished black boots stopped in front of me. The boots led to a pair of muscular thighs encased in fine black breeches belonging to a man wearing a cocky smile.

Edward DeWarn, the new Vellanian Ambassador, was conventionally attractive, with a square chin and sharp cheekbones. His expensive black coat had been tailored to his thin frame. But what most caught my attention was the thin golden ring around his cerulean blue eyes.

"What are you doing tucked away in a corner all by yourself?" he asked, the light from a chandelier illuminating his brown curls like a halo.

"All this excitement is overwhelming." I fanned my face to make the lie more believable. "It's not every day one's only sister gets engaged."

Arching his eyebrows, he gestured toward the dancing couples. "Which means you should be on the floor, celebrating."

"Tonight, I prefer drinking to dancing," I said, my nail clinking against the glass in time with the waltz.

One-two-three

Clink-clink-clink

"That's brilliant news for me." He leaned forward to whisper, "I'm a terrible dancer," as if we were old friends. We'd only spoken a handful of times since he'd moved to Airren two months earlier. "Would you like some company?"

I glanced around at the now-empty chairs. When had Lady Gore and Miss Fahey left? No matter. They were dullards anyway. The ambassador didn't look like a dullard. He looked dark and distracting. "These seats are reserved, I'm afraid."

Edward straightened and made a point of sweeping the busy crowd paying us no attention whatsoever. "Reserved for whom?"

Shaking my empty glass, I let slip a conspiratorial smile. "The next man to bring me champagne."

The ambassador whirled and dashed around Regina Stapelton and her twin sister Brida, whose matching purple gowns reminded me of plump grapes. A moment later, he returned with two glasses, handed one to me, and sank onto the chair to my right.

"To betrothals," he said, holding his drink aloft.

My smile faltered, but only for a split second. "To drinking."

Our glasses met with a delicate *tink*.

Robert glowered at us from between jovial guests. I could almost hear his teeth grinding when Edward's hand fell to my knee.

Robert had no right to be jealous.

He could have stopped this.

All he had to do was call off this sham.

"Do you know what?" I set my glass on the windowsill. I had lost count of how many I'd finished, but from the fuzziness clouding my vision, it had likely been too many. "I think I *do* want to dance."

The ambassador shot to his feet and extended his hand. "If you care not for your toes, then I would be honored to be your partner."

I didn't care about my toes. At the moment, I didn't care about anything.

My hand slipped into his, and he took most of my weight as he helped me to my feet. It took a moment for the world to stop swaying, but when it did, I found myself in Edward's steady embrace.

A giggle escaped as we crossed to the dance floor and wedged ourselves between two couples. The musicians began a slow, whimsical waltz, and Edward's hand slid to the small of my back.

The dark look on Robert's face left me closing the gap between us until Edward's chest brushed mine and I could smell the alcohol on his breath.

One-two-three

Two-two-three

Had waltzing always taken this much concentration? Edward didn't seem to be having any trouble.

"I don't care for liars," I said with a laugh.

Edward drew back a fraction, his eyebrows pulling together as he searched my face. "And what do you mean by that?"

"You claimed to be a terrible dancer and yet you haven't stepped on my toes once."

He grinned and went out of his way to give me a light kick on the shin. "Better?"

"Much."

When the music ended, the ambassador asked for a second dance. I agreed. If he wanted to dance every last song with me, I'd let him. What was a party without a good scandal? It wasn't as if I had any other partners waiting in the wings.

By the end of the sweeping tune, his hand had drifted below my hip, and the gap between us was almost nothing.

Robert slammed his glass onto the mantle, his neck red beneath the collar.

"This ballroom is rather stuffy, wouldn't you agree?" Edward whispered against the shell of my ear. Delicious longing pooled in the pit of my stomach.

"It is rather stuffy," I said, my tone matching his. My coy smile felt as false as the words.

"Perhaps there is somewhere more private where we could retire for another drink." He slid one of the dark curls framing my face through his fingers and let it fall against my collarbone.

A chill of anticipation slithered up my spine. Distracting myself with him was exactly what I needed to turn this night around. "Go into the hallway and wait for me." The last thing we needed was for someone to see us leaving together.

He caught my gloved hand and lifted it to his lips, and I felt . . . nothing. Why couldn't I love someone like Edward? He was handsome, he was well off, he wasn't engaged to my bloody sister. If only I hadn't given my heart to a faithless lout.

Edward let me go and strolled confidently toward the arched doorway leading to the hall, nodding to couples as he passed.

I swayed slightly, floating on a sea of champagne as I meandered around the perimeter.

"Did you hear about Samuel Quinton?" Lady Gore asked in her haughty voice, layers of jewels decorating her ample chest. The cane in her gnarled right hand wobbled under the strain of her considerable weight.

"No, I didn't." Miss Fahey clutched the single strand of pearls at her throat as she stepped closer. "Do tell."

As anxious as I was to escape, I paused and pretended to retie the ribbon across my waist. Samuel Quinton had used to leave bouquets of wildflowers for me in the stables when we were children. He'd moved away a few years earlier, and I hadn't heard from him since.

Lady Gore crooked her finger, and Miss Fahey leaned in. My curiosity got the better of me, and I found myself drifting closer.

"I heard from a reliable source that he was murdered by a pooka this Tuesday just gone." She sniffed. Beads of perspiration rolled down her cheeks, leaving streaks in her white makeup. "All that was left of him was his coat and purse."

Miss Fahey sucked in a breath. "So tragic." Her hand shook as she sipped her wine.

"So tragic," Lady Gore agreed.

Neither of them sounded the least bit affected. Rumors of attacks were becoming more widespread. Only last month, a faerie had disguised himself as Lady Stapleton's husband and tricked her into bed with him.

The creatures plaguing this island were getting out of control.

A hand clamped around my elbow and dragged me toward the open balcony doors. "What the hell has gotten into you?" a familiar voice snarled.

My breathing hitched and all thoughts of the vile creatures scattered.

Robert.

"Unless you want a scandal, I suggest you let me go," I hissed, smacking his fingers where they dug into my skin. Couldn't he see the couples beside the dessert table staring at us?

His grip tightened. "So you can continue making a fool of yourself?"

Chilly night air hit my cheeks as we slipped onto the balcony. The moon watched like a silvery eye peering through a hole in the heavens. I jerked free and whirled. What was he thinking, bringing me out here like this where everyone could see?

"Worry about your *fiancée*, not me."

Robert stalked away from the door, tucking himself into the shadows. "*My fiancée* isn't letting men paw at her in the middle of a bloody crowd!"

"You have a point. Perhaps I should have asked Edward to meet me in the gardens and let him paw at me there. You know how much I love a good romp in the gardens, don't you Robert?"

The moon reflected in Robert's blazing eyes. "You will not let him touch you again. You're *mine*."

My skirts swished as I stomped after him. I had been his, body and soul. Clinging to him like the ivy climbing these old stone walls. "Not. Anymore."

He lunged. My back slammed against the gritty stones. Familiar lips crashed against mine. Bruising. Conquering. Tasting like mead and desire.

Damn the consequences of getting caught. It'd be worth it. *He* was worth it.

I poured myself into the kiss. Perhaps he'd forgotten what we'd had. Perhaps I could make him remember. If only these infernal garments separating us would disappear and I could show him again how much I loved him.

He consumed my senses, stole my rational mind. I loved him with every fiber of my being.

And yet I hadn't been enough.

"No," I gasped, turning my face away. "I won't do this to Aveen." He had chosen a side, and it hadn't been mine.

"What would you have me do?" Robert groaned. His hands tangled in my curls, tugging my head back, exposing my throat to his hungry mouth. "If I don't marry her, my father will cut me off."

A spark of hope ignited in my hollow chest. "We don't need his money." I cupped his smooth jaw and brought his face back to mine. "My dowry would be enough to support us." We weren't the wealthiest family in Graystones, but we were still fairly well off.

With his mouth pressed into a disapproving line, Robert's hands fell away. "Your dowry is a pittance compared to Aveen's."

In eight words, he'd stolen the stars from my sky and squashed them beneath his fine black boots. Aveen would inherit our father's estate—or, rather, her husband would. I would inherit nothing. "So that's it. You're just going to marry my sister for an *inheritance*? I slept with you, *Robert*." I spat his name like the curse it was and shoved against his chest. I had been nervous and scared and had tried backing out. But then he'd told me he loved me, and I'd given myself to him because I'd loved him too.

"Do you have no honor? Did you ever love me at all?" If only I were strong enough to throw him over the bloody railing.

His eyes fell closed and he pinched the bridge of his nose. "Keelynn—"

"Save your breath, you worthless cad. I never want to speak to you again." His lies chased me to the open doors. The ballroom was too loud. Too bright. Too crowded.

Aveen stood by the dessert table, laughing at whatever her friend Lady Marissa was saying.

The darkness waiting in the hallway called to me, an escape tugging me forward. Unquenched desire swirled in my belly, dancing with the sloshing champagne.

I skirted around a group of elderly men discussing a recent merrow sighting over glasses of port and cut straight through a line of young maidens staring longingly at the full dance floor.

A figure waited in the moonlight drifting through the wide bay window outside my father's study.

"I thought you'd changed your mind," Edward said with a knowing smile, drawing a finger along the golden drape's tassels. Two flutes of champagne waited on the windowsill behind him.

"Not tonight," I murmured, wrapping my arms around his neck and pressing my lips to his.

He tasted like champagne and cherries. When I tried to deepen the kiss, he pulled away, gasping for breath.

"You're so beautiful." His throaty whisper tickled my cheek as he dotted kisses along my jaw.

"Liar." Aveen was the beautiful one, with her round face, pert nose, and big blue eyes full of hope and optimism. My face was too thin, my cheekbones too pronounced. And Robert had once said my gray eyes were as cutting as a steel blade.

Edward smiled against my neck.

I imagined they were Robert's lips. Robert's hands sliding up and down my arms. My back. My hips.

Robert. This was Robert.

Only it didn't *feel* like him.

Robert was strong and insistent and passionate. Edward was too slow. Too careful. Too hesitant.

What was I doing? I didn't want this. Didn't want him.

His lips grazed my ear when I twisted my head away. "I've changed my mind. I want to go back," I said, pushing against his toned chest. The hands resting on my shoulders felt too heavy. I tried shrugging him off, but he didn't let go.

"One minute." He tugged on my sleeve, exposing my shoulder.

"What are you doing?" I shoved against his chest, but he didn't budge.

"I said give me a damned minute." Edward cursed when I pushed him again. "Stop hitting me. My cufflink—"

I drove my elbow into his stomach, sending him stumbling

from the enclave. The sound of ripping fabric echoed through the darkness. A cold draft tickled against my exposed breast.

Edward swore and yanked harder, struggling to free his cufflink from the lace at the top of my gown. "I'm so sorry," he blurted, tugging harder. "I didn't mean for this to happen. I'm so—"

"Ambassador?" My father's voice rang through the hall, accompanied by heavy footfalls. "I've been hoping to speak with you regarding—*Keelynn?*"

"Father . . . " Hot, shameful tears streamed down my cheeks. Clutching my torn dress to cover myself, my eyes darted to Edward's pale face. "I . . . We . . . "

My father's dark mustache twitched, and recognition sparked in his blue eyes. "*What is the meaning of this?*"

"It's not what it looks like, sir." Edward held up his wrist, flashing the offending gold cufflink. "This caught on her dress and—"

My father lunged, grabbing Edward by the collar. I had to do something. Had to stop him.

"You *dare* come into my home and accost *my daughter?*" A vein in his forehead bulged and his face darkened to a sickly shade of purple.

Do something, dammit!

My eyes darted to where Edward lifted his trembling hands in surrender.

"It was an accident. I swear," he said.

An accident. Yes. This was all an accident. A silly accident soon to be forgotten. One day we would laugh about it.

"What good is the word of a scheming bastard who lured an innocent young woman into the shadows without a chaperone?" my father snarled, lips curled back from his teeth.

"Father, please. This is all a misunderstanding."

Edward's panicked blue gaze landed on me. Something akin to relief washed over his features. "It's true sir," he said, nodding emphatically. "A simple misunderstanding."

My father let him go with a shove. "I misunderstand nothing."

The ambassador stumbled against the far wall, breaths sawing in and out, clutching his chest.

Stepping forward, I grabbed my father's coat sleeve. Surely I could make him see reason. "My dress ripped and . . . " And what? *Think, Keelynn. Think.* "And the ambassador was offering me his coat until I could change. That's all. Father, please. You must believe me. I'm telling the truth."

"*The truth?*" He pressed his hands to his temples and swore. "You think that matters in these situations?" When he dropped his hands, he refused to look at me, settling instead on glaring at Edward. "When people hear about this, she will be ruined. No one will want her."

Why did it matter? If I couldn't marry Robert, I didn't want to marry anyone.

Edward straightened his shoulders and tugged on the ends of his waistcoat, his worry shifting to resolve. "I understand how this unfortunate situation could affect Keelynn's prospects for a husband. I am happy to make this right."

Make it right?

Prospects for a husband?

Surely, he wasn't suggesting the two of us get *married.*

I didn't even know the man. And after this debacle, I was fairly certain I didn't like him either.

"That's madness," I cried, pain blossoming in my chest like what was left of my withered heart was breaking. "No one saw us. No one has to know."

My father loosened my fingers and turned his back to me.

He had done the same thing the day I'd begged him to reconsider Aveen's betrothal. Dismissing me as though I was nothing. As though I didn't matter.

The two of them disappeared into the study to decide a fate in which I had no say, leaving me standing in the hollow hallway, clutching my dress to my chest.

There had to be some way to get out of this. Some way to

escape.

Aveen.

She would know what to do.

I flew through the hall to the curved staircase. My hand slid down the smooth mahogany banister before catching at the very end where the newel post had been reattached. It had been my idea to slide down the staircase on a sled, but Aveen had taken the fall for it. All the terrible ideas from our youth had been mine.

The footman at the door startled when he saw me. "Milady—"

"I need a coat. It's an emergency."

He dashed into the cloakroom and returned with my favorite gray cloak. I thanked him, wrapped the soft wool around my shoulders, and fastened the clasp at my neck, concealing my disheveled state.

The torches lining our long, gravel drive lit the way as I raced to the rear of our home. My slippers slid in the damp grass as I crossed to the gardens. Wide stone stairs climbed to the balcony where music drifted into the night. How would I get her attention without letting people see me?

A peal of laughter echoed from deep within garden.

A laugh I would recognize anywhere.

Aveen was outside. It was the first bit of good luck I'd had all night.

My footsteps crunched on the stone path until there was another giggle followed by a deep male chuckle.

I froze.

Aveen wasn't alone.

Was she out here with Robert? *Oh god.* I wouldn't survive seeing them together.

I tiptoed forward to peer around a fragrant boxwood hedge. Aveen's sky-blue ballgown glittered in the moonlight. A cloaked figure sat across from her, toying with a lock of her golden curls.

He wasn't Robert.

The mysterious figure was slimmer, not as broad across the shoulders. I strained to hear what the man was saying.

Aveen straightened her spine and shook her head. "But Rían—"

The man pressed a finger to her lips and murmured something too low to hear.

Aveen nodded. The man, Rían, dropped his hand. She leaned forward, closed her eyes and pressed her lips to his.

My sister had a lover and had never told me.

We shared all of our secrets.

Or, at least, I shared mine.

A strange gurgling sound broke the silence.

The color drained from Aveen's face. She slumped forward and would have fallen off the bench if the man hadn't caught her in his arms.

An invisible boulder slammed against my chest.

My withered heart spasmed.

I opened my mouth to cry out but no sound emerged.

My legs had turned to stone and all I could do was watch the man lay her on the bench. Caress her cheek. And vanish.

"Aveen!" My stone legs finally lurched forward. Sharp, stinging pain shot through me when they met the gravel.

Vacant blue eyes stared back. Unblinking. Glassy. Dull.

"No . . . no . . . no."

No warmth.

No pulse.

No breathing.

No no no!

"Please . . . wake up . . ."

A banshee's piercing wail sliced the night.

She was only twenty.

She was too young.

"Aveen!"

Unmoving.

Unblinking.

Unchanged.

Until her white lips darkened to black.

There was only one creature on this cursed island who could have done this. A monster who preyed on innocent maidens and killed them with his poisoned lips.

The Gancanagh had murdered my sister.

2

Funerals weren't held for the family.

They were for the spectators whose lives hadn't been broken apart by death's cold, unforgiving hand. Whose worlds hadn't been shattered. Useless ceremonies to make those who were still whole feel less guilty about being around those of us with missing pieces. Condolences and handshakes and nods and tears did nothing for the ones experiencing a loss so deep that the wound would never heal.

As I stared through my black veil toward the casket at the bottom of the deep hole, my mind drifted to a different casket. A different grave.

If I turned my head, I would see the high cross atop my sister's headstone.

She had died four months ago.

Sixteen weeks.

One hundred and twelve days.

I had tried to emerge from the depths of despair. I changed my diet, took long walks, took short walks, spent time with friends, spent time alone, and even begged the village apothecary for something, *anything* to make me feel like living again.

None of it worked. I couldn't get past losing her.

And now these witnesses were back to watch me bury my husband.

Edward and I had been hastily married two days after Aveen's funeral.

I had gotten to wear my sister's ivory dress after all.

Once, I had dreamed of a big wedding overflowing with hydrangeas and music and fanfare. A loveless marriage hadn't deserved any of those things.

An unforgiving wind ripped at my veil, swirling my black skirts about my ankles. The other graveside mourners had their heads bowed. A stray magpie landed on a statue of an angel with her face upturned to the dark sky.

My father settled a heavy hand on my shoulder. He was the only family I had left, just as I was his.

And I couldn't find it in my shriveled heart to care.

I shrugged him off and stepped closer to my coachman. Padraig kneaded his black wool cap with gnarled hands and shifted uncomfortably from one foot to the other. His poor bowed legs must've been aching from standing for so long.

When the priest finally concluded the service, he led the procession of mourners from the graveyard.

Padraig's calluses scraped my hands when he gave them a tender squeeze. "I'll wait fer ye in the carriage, milady. Take as long as ye need." He hobbled toward the line of black carriages stretching along the lane.

My father pulled me in for a hug. His shirt smelled like tobacco and vanilla. A combination I had once loved and now loathed. "I'm so sorry, Keelynn. So very, very sorry."

My arms remained pinned to my sides. I only accepted the token of affection because railing and screaming would have been unbecoming of a lady of my station.

But I refused to say it was all right.

Because it wasn't.

He had forced me to marry against my will.

He had taken away my choice.

And for what? So that I could be miserable and alone only a few months later? What had been the point of any of this?

My father moved on to speak to some folks by the falling wooden fence surrounding the town graveyard. None of them looked the least bit sorry about Edward's passing.

Lord Trench stopped, his four sons behind him. All blond. All handsome. But the most handsome of them waited at the end of the line, his eyes pinned on me.

Robert.

"Sorry for your loss."

"Sorry for your loss."

"Sorry for your loss."

"Sorry for your loss."

All lies. They weren't sorry. They weren't affected. They didn't care.

"Lady Keelynn, I am so dreadfully sorry for what has happened," Robert said, his voice laced with quiet sadness.

I clenched my jaw and glared at the man I'd once loved.

Love. What a bloody curse.

Robert's hair fluttered in the wind. Hazel eyes searched mine. He lifted a hand to touch my cheek, thought better of it, and offered a tight nod instead. "If you ever need to escape, you know where I am."

If only there was a way to stop the fluttering in my stomach. "If I ever need to escape, I certainly won't be looking for you."

Robert's pained wince brought the first spark of joy I'd felt in four months.

More mourners crying false tears came and went.

They hadn't known Edward. And if they had, they wouldn't be crying over him. He'd been standoffish and irritable, nothing like the charming gentleman I'd kissed at the ball. But who could blame him after being forced to marry me?

There was only one person in the lot who seemed genuinely upset.

Whose tears I believed.

They belonged to my maid.

I wasn't sure when Sylvia's affair with my husband had started. It hadn't been long after the wedding. The day I'd witnessed them together in our parlor, I hadn't felt even a hint of anger.

I'd felt relieved.

It wasn't as if the sham had been a real marriage. The only times he'd touched me were while we exchanged vows, hand in hand, and then to press a kiss to my cheek at the end of the ceremony. He was constantly traveling to Vellana, so I only saw him a handful of days in those four months. Any time he came home, he insisted on keeping to his own chambers. And I hadn't complained.

I escaped the smell of fresh earth and made my way between weathered headstones to my sister's final resting place.

Grass had already claimed the patch of ground beneath the shadow of her headstone.

A name.

A date.

Beloved daughter and sister.

Words reminding the world that Aveen had never gotten to be a wife. A mother.

She could have been anything.

And now she was nothing.

Guilt tinged every inhale. Every exhale. Every beat of my unworthy heart.

I had done everything wrong, and Aveen had done everything right.

So why was I still here?

A sniffling sound drew me from my misery.

Sylvia and another woman had returned to Edward's grave. My maid clutched a balled-up handkerchief against her eyes. Her shoulders hunched as she sobbed. The other woman wrapped her in a fierce hug. "You're sure the witch can't bring him back?" she asked Sylvia.

Witch?

I'd heard tales of a witch living in the forests beyond our town but had dismissed them as hearsay. People were paranoid and loved nothing more than a bit of juicy gossip. But could the stories be true?

"N-no." Sylvia shook her head. "The bitch said I didn't have anything she wanted. He's gone, Liddy. He's really gone."

He's gone.

She obviously meant Edward.

Bring him back from where though? The dead? That was impossible . . . Wasn't it?

Everyone knew the creatures living on this island possessed magic, but I had never heard of magic raising anyone from the dead.

Aveen's headstone scratched my fingertips. If there was a witch, could she resurrect my sister instead?

"Excuse me?" I waved toward Sylvia and her friend. Both of them looked at me with wide, startled eyes. "I couldn't help but overhear your conversation," I said, not feeling the least bit repentant for eavesdropping. They had been discussing my husband, after all. "Did you say you'd been to see a witch?"

Sylvia dabbed at the corners of her eyes again as she nodded. "Y-yes, milady."

A chill slithered down my back. She'd met a witch. A real witch.

I stopped at the other side of Edward's grave, accidentally knocking a clump of dirt over the edge. It landed with a hollow *thump* against the casket at the bottom. "And where does this witch live?"

Sylvia and her friend exchanged worried glances. If word got out that either of them had conferred with a witch, they could lose their jobs. But if this witch found out they were speaking ill of her, they could lose their lives.

"I won't tell anyone," I assured them. "I promise."

The other woman settled a hand on Sylvia's slight shoulder

and said, "Fiadh lives in a small cottage in the forest north of Graystones."

The witch hadn't helped Sylvia, but would she help me?

There was only one way to find out.

I thanked them and spun on my heel, hurrying to where Padraig waited on the bench at the front of the carriage. When he saw me, he dropped the reins and made to climb down.

"Don't trouble yourself," I said, waving him back to his perch, "I can open my own door."

His wool flat cap slipped when he bobbed his head. "Thank ye, milady. These old bones aren't what they used to be." He settled himself back onto the seat and reached for the whip. The horses shook their massive heads and stamped their hooves in the mud, anxious to be on the way. "Will I bring ye to yer father's estate or the townhouse?"

"Neither," I said, throwing open the carriage door, a new sense of purpose filling my cold soul. "Take me to the north woods."

The witch's stacked stone cottage sat at the end of a lonely road cutting through a forest of twisted trees. A cow lazily munched a path through the overgrown lawn, staring vacantly toward a rusted iron gate sagging on its hinges.

Gnarled brown vines from barren ivy forced their way between the beige and brown stones. Green smoke lifting from the chimney in the center of the slate roof was the only indication that the cottage wasn't abandoned.

I had been taught that magic was darkness.

But I was already in the dark.

The creatures who wielded it couldn't be trusted.

But at this point, I didn't have much of a choice.

My clenched fist connected with the arched black door. The

light breeze rustling the overgrown grass stilled, and the door creaked open.

Hollow bits of bronze dangling from the interior handle jingled as I pushed the door aside. Stepping across the threshold, I ducked beneath bundles of drying herbs hanging from the low ceiling beams.

"Hello? Is anyone here?" The curtains were drawn so tightly, the only light in the room came from the open doorway and a mass of black candles flickering on a crude wooden table.

Long shelves lined the back walls, containing fluted glasses labeled "dreams" in warm, honeyed hues with cork stoppers. Jars of swirling black marked "nightmares" bore tin lids weighted down with large stones.

Bile rose in my throat when I found glasses of what looked like entrails displayed on a knotted wood mantle across a wide fireplace. I quickly looked away, focusing instead on a copper cauldron steaming over an empty fire grate.

"I'm looking for Fiadh." My voice echoed like the shadows were whispering back. *Fee-ah. Fee-ah. Fee-ah.* "I was told this was where she lived."

A rusty nail jutting from the uneven plank floor snagged the hem of my skirt. I bent to free myself, carefully so as not to damage the cloth. It wasn't that I had any particular fondness for the dress. But of all my mourning attire, this one was the least hideous.

I called for her once more.

The only response was the slight jangle of the chimes from an errant breeze

With hope leaking from my chest, I turned back to the door. The witch probably wouldn't have helped me anyway.

Tap

Tap

Tap

My legs locked into place, refusing to budge. My mind could've been playing tricks on me, but I swore I heard—

Tap

Tap

There it was again. Short and shrill like nails on glass.

Someone—or something—was here with me.

The hairs on my arms stood on end. My heart threatened to burst from my chest and land in one of the empty jars.

"*There once was a girl from Graystones, seeking a cure for death. She met a witch and begged for help but instead drew her last breath.*"

The high, sing-song voice appeared to be coming from the trembling shadows. "H-how do you know what I want?" I asked, backing toward the exit.

Coming here had been a mistake. A terrible, terrible mistake.

One of the stones on top of the nightmares rattled against the metal lid. The black liquid sparked as it spun faster and faster. The stone vibrated to the edge. Dropped onto the floor. Rolled toward my boot. And stopped.

Glass exploded. A black cloud shot toward me.

I clambered for the door.

It swung shut with a *bang*.

The candles on the table shuddered and went out.

Engulfed in darkness, I felt for the handle, praying it wasn't locked. The cloying scent of magic filled my nostrils. When I gasped, sickeningly sweet air slipped past my lips, flooding my throat with the force of a rushing river. My lungs burned as they expanded and I slumped to the floor.

Then a voice whispered in my ear, "*I know what everyone wants.*"

Eyes, hundreds of them, glowing and green, appeared in the darkness.

Surrounding me on all sides.

Waiting. *Watching.*

I screwed my eyes shut, praying the monsters would go away.

When I opened them again, the monsters had been replaced by something far worse.

It was a vision of my sister sitting on that bench in our garden, beneath the fuchsia she loved so much.

Panic raked its claws across my chest, dragging me *down down down*.

"*Please*." I scrubbed at my chest in vain. The pressure was unbearable. "*Help me*."

A frigid breeze swirled around me, tearing at my hair, freeing it from its pins, whipping the dark strands across my cheeks. I made one final grab for the handle, and my fingers met cold brass. The chimes clanged when I threw open the door. I sucked in a ragged breath, and another.

Cloud-filtered sunlight drove the nightmare into the shadowy recesses beneath the table. Before me now stood a striking woman in a flowing green dress with an open jar in her hand.

My likeness reflected in the hellish depths of her obsidian eyes. A paltry human, powerless, cowering on the floor.

Her raven hair, snagged with leaves and twigs, dragged along the wooden planks as she stepped toward me, muttering in a strange language. The nightmare flew from its hiding place and into the jar. With a wave of her hand, the caged terror disappeared.

"You're *sure* it was him?" she asked in a voice as sultry as her full, bloodred lips.

"What do you mean?" I hated the tremor distorting my words. Hated that my fear was so obvious. Hated that all it would take for her to end my life was a wave of her cursed hand.

The witch dropped to her knees and grabbed me, her sharp nails cutting into the flesh at my wrist. "The Gancanagh," she hissed, eyes wide, searching. "Are you certain the Prince of Seduction claimed her life?"

The Gancanagh wasn't a bloody prince of anything. He was a monster.

"I saw him."

As quickly as she had grabbed me, she let go and shot to her feet. "What would you give in exchange for her resurrection?" Her head tilted at an inhuman angle, like a bird's, as she watched me push away from the door and stand on unsteady legs.

What would anyone give to bring back the person she loved most in the world?

"Anything." All Fiadh had to do was say the word, and it was hers. If my purse full of silver wasn't enough, I would go to my father for a loan. I would sell everything I owned; I would sell my shattered soul . . .

The witch paced between the fireplace and the door, tapping a pointed black nail against her lips. "The universe will demand balance. A life for a life."

A life for a life.

"Whose life?" I didn't want to die. Surely she had a spell or potion that could bring Aveen back to this world without ending my own.

"A true immortal's."

"True immortals cannot be killed." Creatures could live for centuries, but true immortals lived forever. It was an impossible task befitting an impossible reward.

Fiadh's dark eyebrows arched toward her peaked hairline. "*Anyone* can be killed"—the witch withdrew a small silver dagger from a sheath at her waist—"if you have an enchanted blade."

The large emerald in its hilt glowed in the dim light.

I took a halting step closer. It was like staring into the canopy of an endless forest in the height of summer.

The witch tapped a black nail against the jewel. There was no way I could afford such a weapon.

"Once you slay the Gancanagh . . ."

The words rattled through my head.

Slay the Gancanagh?

"You expect *me* to kill the Gancanagh?" The only thing I had ever murdered before was my own embroidery.

She jerked forward, and I could feel the sting of her sweet breath against my cheek when she asked, "Don't you want revenge? Don't you want him to pay for what he's stolen from you? Don't you want justice?"

I wanted all of those things. But this monster had been killing women for centuries.

"An immortal's life force is eternal," she explained, turning the hilt over and over in her hand. "With the Gancanagh's blood on the blade and his life force trapped in the jewel, you can transfer it with a simple prick." She pressed the tip to her finger, drawing a bead of deep red.

Was it true?

Creatures like this witch were born liars. Still, what had been the point of coming here if I wasn't going to believe her?

This was Aveen. If I had a chance to resurrect her, I'd be a fool to pass it up.

"If I decide to do this, how will I lure him close enough to kill him?"

It was rumored that the Gancanagh's castle was on the other side of the island, guarded by creatures, protected by ancient wards. Even if I made it past all the obstacles, what would draw the monster to me?

The witch's skirts swirled as she spun toward the shelves to collect a small black box with a dusty lid. Inside was an emerald set in a knotted gold band.

"Once he learns you have this, *he* will find *you*." The ring disappeared in her clenched fist. "Trust no one and guard this with your life. Do you hear me? *Your life*."

The witch was willing to hand over the dagger *and* the ring?

None of this fit with what I knew about witches. They never did something out of the goodness of their hearts—they had no hearts.

"How much do you want for both?" Despite the fear churning in my stomach, darkness swelled within me, reveling in the idea of bringing the villain to justice. Even if the witch was lying, if I couldn't bring Aveen back, at least the vile monster would be no more. "I have some silver," I said, reaching for the purse beneath my cloak.

"I don't want your coins," she sneered, knocking my hand away. "I want your lies."

She was turning down money for lies? "What does that mean?"

"Once our bargain is struck, you'll only be able to tell the truth. It's an insurance policy of sorts." The strained smile she gave me didn't reach her eyes. "I've dealt with my fair share of liars through the years and want to ensure you'll do as you say." She opened her fingers; the ring trembled in her palm.

It seemed a small price to pay for a chance to bring back Aveen. "Then we have a bargain," I said, offering a hand to seal our agreement. "You give me what I need, and I'll kill the Gancanagh to resurrect my sister."

Her cold palm struck my lips. Magic forced its way into my nostrils, cutting off the air. I didn't want to breathe but my lungs were *burning burning burning.*

"Don't fight it," she crooned. "Accept the curse."

Curse? What curse? I hadn't agreed to a bloody curse.

The moment I inhaled, my lips felt like they'd been melted with a branding iron.

The witch removed her hand and passed me the dagger, her lips lifting into a mocking smile. "It's time for you to slay a monster."

3

KEEPING TO THE SHADOWS, I SEARCHED THE ROWS OF BUILDINGS
on either side of a dark, empty street. The place had to be here
somewhere. It had been two days since I'd met with Fiadh, and
my lips still ached. Instead of wallowing in self-pity over what
could've been the biggest mistake of my life, I'd thrown myself
into devising a plan to complete the monumental task in front
of me.

A plan that led me to Dreadshire, a village crawling with
unseemly characters.

The innkeeper living on the outskirts of the village had been
hesitant to give me directions to what he called, "a den of vipers."
Once he realized my mind couldn't be changed, he'd reluctantly
told me what I needed to know. Padraig was busy in the stables, so
he hadn't noticed me slip away.

If only I could find the blasted—

There. Up ahead was a wooden sign with a snake scorched into
the plank.

The Green Serpent looked the same as every other seedy pub
on this side of the village: grime-blackened stone walls, a moldy
thatched roof, a crooked chimney releasing smoke into ever-damp

air. Two lanterns bolted on either side of a black door flickered in the darkness.

Beside me, the river carried away the filth leaking from the cobbled streets. Clutching my wool cape closed over my mourning dress, I reached for the dented brass knob.

Inside, heat from the turf fire beckoned for me to remove my cloak. But the stench of sweat, body odor, and stale alcohol from the scarred men bent over their flagons forced me deeper into the lavender-scented material.

The mumbled conversations in the room fell silent. All eyes— and a few eye-patches—were trained on me.

My heart thudded against my ribs.

RunRun

RunRun

RunRun

Adrenaline surged, hot and chaotic, as I continued toward the rows of dark liquor bottles on the back wall. A table of men with braids and beads woven into their scraggly beards placed coins next to a pile of severed claws. My stomach twisted at the sight of yellowed tendons and blood.

I shouldn't have eaten that fish pie for dinner.

These were exactly the types of men I knew I'd be dealing with. Mercenaries. Killers for hire. The scum of the earth, willing to trade their skills and knowledge of Airren's dark underbelly for coin.

Humans with no qualms when it came to murder.

Hunters and slayers of monsters.

Something grazed my backside and squeezed.

I stumbled out of reach and twisted to find a man with a gold tooth smirking from his stool. He gestured toward his breeches and spat an offer that left my face burning.

Men could touch what they wanted—*take* what they wanted— and never taste the bitterness of consequences. If I spoke up, it would be my fault. I was the one who had walked in here wearing a skirt. I was the one who had been born a woman.

I kept my mouth shut like a proper lady and continued through a gauntlet of catcalls and greedy, grimy hands.

A wooden bar carved with profanity and male genitalia separated the liquor from the questionable clientele. An elderly woman with deep wrinkles and a scar across her sunken left eye emerged from a door at the back. When she saw me, her eye widened.

"I wonder if you might be able to help me," I said, resting my elbows on the bar and forcing a smile. "You see, I'm looking for a man—"

"Pet, I've been lookin' fer a man in this pub fer forty years," she drawled, hobbling closer and snagging a rag from a bucket, "and haven't found an honest one yet."

It was a good thing the man I sought wasn't the honest sort.

"A man to help me get to Tearmann," I finished.

The scar across her eye pulled when her eyebrows lifted. She made no attempt to hide her perusal from my hood to my trembling hands. "Why would someone like ye want to go there?"

There would be no point lying, even if the witch's curse weren't forcing me to tell the truth. The person I hired needed to have no qualms about traveling to the north to find the monstrous "Prince."

"I need to find the Gancanagh."

The woman's black-toothed smile shifted to a grimace as she began to scrub the stains from the bar. "These men will rob ye blind," she ground out. "Best be gone with ye and get the foolish notion of findin' the Gancanagh outta yer 'ead." Her eye flicked nervously toward a table of three men in the corner.

The first man had thinning gray hair, a snout-shaped nose, and drink-swollen cheeks swallowing his dark, beady eyes. To his left was a white-haired man face-down on the table.

The third man didn't look much older than I was, early twenties at most, with unruly dark hair spilling across his forehead. He wore a wrinkled white shirt with no cravat and a dark waistcoat. For some reason, his eyes had been smeared with black, like a badger's. But the oddest thing about him was that he was reading. In a pub. Filled with murderers.

"Please," I said, prepared to beg. "Surely, you can recommend *someone*. It's a matter of life and death."

A wave of vicious swearing erupted. Two men tumbled across the floor, splintering the wooden tables and stools and shattering glasses as they rolled. The man on top battered the one pinned to the floorboards, splattering blood all over my new boots.

"Get outside and wait." The woman jabbed a finger toward the door. "I'll see what I can do."

"Thank you. Thank you so much." I handed her a piece of silver and started for the door.

The unconscious man lying in a pool of blood looked familiar.

Hold on.

He was the fool who had grabbed me.

I rammed the toe of my boot into his ribs. Twice.

Cheering exploded as I made my way to the exit. The sweaty smell from inside was replaced by the stench of urine and filth clinging to the street.

Leaning against the cold wall, I waited for someone to emerge from the pub.

The door flew open, and my stomach tightened when the snouted man from the corner table stumbled out.

"Did the barmaid send you?" I asked from the shadows.

"Bleedin' hell, girl," the man rasped, clutching his chest, "yer gonna give a man a heart attack comin' at 'im like that."

"I apologize for startling you, but I'm looking for someone to help me."

His tiny black eyes swallowed the lamplight. "Help ye what?"

The truth sprang forth, unbidden. "Get to Tearmann."

The man's thin mouth flattened, and he wrestled with the end of his worn woollen overcoat. The width of his belly put the buttons under serious pressure. "Ye dinna have enough gold to get my arse to cross into that cursed territory."

Perhaps he wasn't the one the woman had sent.

"But . . ." The man's tongue flicked over his lips as his beady eyes widened. "I have a *friend* named Tadhg who might be able to help."

The way he said "friend" made it sound like the two weren't friends at all. Like he didn't like this Tadhg fellow one bit.

"Fer five pieces of silver, I'll bring ye to 'im."

It seemed like a lot for an introduction. But it would take a special type of mercenary to be willing to cross the border into the lawless territory ruled by mythical monsters.

"All right." I nodded. "Five coins it is."

"Come with me." He stepped into an unlit alley between the pub and a blacksmith's shop.

Should I follow a strange man into a dark alley?

Definitely not.

Did I have a choice though?

I could tell him to have this Tadhg fellow meet me here, in the murky light. Would it be any different? If a man wanted to attack me, he could. Lamplight or not. And it would be *my* fault for being on this side of the village at this ungodly hour.

The witch's dagger pressed against my spine from its hiding place beneath my cloak.

If I had to use it, I would.

"Are ye comin' or not?" the man called from out of sight.

I wrapped my fingers around the hilt and followed him into the gloom.

The reek of rot and feces wafted from behind broken barrels. Glittering shards of glass crunched under the heels of my boots. We ended up on the back side of the building, close enough to the rushing river to feel its damp spray against my cheeks.

The rear of the building was a mirror image of the pub at the front, only instead of being black, the door was green.

The man cleared his throat from the doorway. "That'll be six pieces of silver."

Six? That wasn't right. "You mean five."

Thick eyebrows slammed down over pinpoint eyes as he nodded his chin toward the door. "I agreed to bring ye where yer man is fer five. It's an additional coin to let ye inside."

This wasn't the time or place for an argument I couldn't win. Scowling, I reached into my purse and withdrew six coins. They disappeared into his coat pocket the moment they landed in his palm.

He sneered and pushed the door aside.

Tendrils of heat wrapped around my exposed hands, drawing me forward. Instead of smelling like turf and sweat, a sickly-sweet tang clung to the air.

Keeping my breathing short and shallow, I made my way into a room half the size of the one in front—and silent as a shadow. Candles dripped wax in nooks notched into the walls. Green halos encircled the steady flames.

As in the first pub, wooden stools with stubby legs surrounded the low tables. But the bar at the back shined with fresh lacquer, and the bottles on the shelves were green and black.

The only two patrons were a white-haired man passed out on the table and a younger man with kohl-smudged eyes reading a book.

The same men from the pub in front.

How were they in both rooms at once?

Of all the ridiculous notions . . . Being in two places at once was impossible. They must've taken a shortcut through one of the doors behind the bar.

Paper rustled when the younger man turned the page.

The white-haired man lifted his head, revealing milky-white eyes. "I hear yer lookin' fer the Gancanagh," the man, whom I assumed was Tadhg, said in a strangled whisper.

I threw back my shoulders and straightened my spine. The more apparent my fear, the more likely he'd take advantage of me like the goon at the door. "That's right."

Tadhg's wispy white eyebrows rose, but his face remained

33

slack. "Dare I ask what business a girl like ye has with a faerie famous fer seducing young maids?"

Girl? I was no *girl*. I was a woman on a mission. If only I could lie about what that mission was.

"I need to . . ." *speak to him.* Pain lanced through my skull like a bolt of lightning, burning the lie to ash. "I need to kill him."

Tadhg's expression remained blank, but the young man looked up from his book.

Never in my nineteen years had I seen anything as green as his piercing eyes. Even the island's fields couldn't compare. The black paint only made them more enchanting. The nerves in my stomach buzzed in warning.

"Afraid I'm not interested in murder today," Tadhg said in his pained voice.

I tore my gaze from the young man, freed my purse, and dropped it onto the table with a *thump*. "I'll pay you."

Bringing so much money to this side of the village had been risky. Still, Tadhg needed to know I was serious. That mine was an offer he couldn't refuse. "Half now. Half when we arrive at his castle."

The man who had escorted me shifted from his post at the door.

Sweet air smelling faintly of almonds tickled my nostrils. I covered my nose to keep the swell from consuming me. One of them possessed magic, I was sure of it. But which one?

"I need more silver like this island needs more rain," Tadhg muttered.

The younger man's gaze roved brazenly down my body, like he could see through the layers to what was hidden beneath.

"Fine." I yanked my cloak back into place. "If you won't help, then I'll find someone else."

I would visit every corner of this bloody island if I had to. All I needed was one person willing to help me get to the Gananagh's castle. I would do the rest myself.

Tadhg's veiny hand shot out, clutching the purse. "What makes ye think ye can get close enough to kill him?"

A fair question—and one I had to answer carefully, thanks to Fiadh. "I have something he wants." Again, my gaze slipped to the unusual young man. The buzzing in my stomach spread to my chest.

"Yer fair enough," the old man said, smiling and revealing a black gap where his front teeth should've been, "but the Prince of Tearmann could have his pick of any woman."

My nails dug into my palms when I tightened my fists. I may have been a fool around men in the past, but not anymore. "Not *me*."

"Go on then. Tell us what it is."

Gold—

Silver—

Information—

Bloody hell. My head felt like it was going to explode. "A ring."

The white-haired man's forehead smacked against the table. His body went limp.

"An *emerald* ring?" the younger man asked in a clear, melodic voice, his lilt caressing each word.

My hand flew to the ring concealed against my stuttering heart. There was no way he could have seen it. "How did you know?"

The book snapped shut, flew across the space, and landed on the bar. "I've changed my mind," he said. "I'll do it."

My stomach dropped to my toes. "*You're* Tadhg?"

"I am." The young man's head tilted, sending dark hair falling across his forehead. "Is that going to be a problem?"

Yes, it was a problem.

A *big* problem.

Not only did Tadhg possess magic, but the tips of his ears peeking through his hair weren't rounded but pointed.

Tadhg wasn't human.

Tadhg was one of the monsters.

I couldn't trust him to bring me safely to the inn let alone across the country to kill one of his own.

Tamping down my rising panic, I gestured toward the old man. "Why can't he bring me?" He didn't make me feel unsteady on my feet. He didn't make my pulse hum or my breath catch.

He wasn't a monster.

Chuckling softly, Tadhg kicked the old man's foot with his boot. The man didn't budge. "He doesn't seem up to the task at present."

"Then I'll ask someone else." *Anyone else.*

Watching me through narrowed eyes, Tadhg crossed his arms over his chest. "Suit yourself. Although, no mercenary can get through the Black Forest alive, let alone into Tearmann. And the Gancanagh's castle?" He shook his head and laughed. "Not a hope."

The territory surrounding Tearmann had been gifted to the monsters after the great war. Even with their magic, they had been no match for the human armies with their ash and iron weapons. When they surrendered, the king had given them the small swath of land to appease their leaders and maintain peace.

That land was cut off from the rest of the island by the Black Forest—a cursed place spoken about in hushed whispers. The forest was rumored to be ruled by the Phantom Queen—a being that survived by consuming human souls.

"I suppose you know how to get me through the Black Forest," I said, dread seeping into my stomach.

Tadhg's lips curled into a wicked smile, all teeth and empty promises. "I know how to get you through the Black Forest."

4

THE GAMEY SMELL OF LAMB STEW MADE ITS WAY THROUGH THE uneven floorboards in my rented room. From the mountain of black garments on the unmade bed, I found a bombazine dress with a high collar, long sleeves, and a tapered skirt.

After sliding the witch's dagger to the back of my belt, I tucked the chain holding the ring under my dress and shift.

Using a cracked mirror on the windowsill, I tried to fix my hair the way my sister used to. Aveen could turn my dark, unruly waves into glossy curls with a few strokes and twists of a brush.

All I managed to do was make it look like I'd been too long in the wind.

If only I had appreciated everything Aveen had done for me. If only I had thanked her and told her how much she meant to me instead of taking her for granted. If only I had told her I loved her instead of spending our last few hours together wallowing in self-pity and drowning myself in champagne.

I launched the thing at the wall. These regrets were as useless as that damned brush.

My fingers caught in the tangled strands, and I gathered and twisted them into a tight knot at the top of my head. I jammed in pin after pin, hissing every time one of the infernal things scraped my scalp. The style made my face look too harsh and angular, but I didn't care. It wasn't like I was trying to impress anyone.

The Dreadshire inn sat across gray cobblestones from a towering gray limestone cathedral whose spire pierced the persistent gray clouds.

Gray. Gray. *Gray*.

The color of my eyes.

The color of Aveen's skin when they'd taken her body away.

The color of her tombstone.

A patchwork of brilliant green fields waited in the distance.

The color of the emeralds in the ring and the dagger.

The color of the eyes that had haunted my dreams last night.

The color of magic and monsters.

I shook away the images threatening to overwhelm me and finished getting ready. After paying my tab, I offered the innkeeper a few extra coins to bring my trunk to my waiting carriage.

Outside, I found a market of crude wooden stalls and hand carts. Most of the vendors had already packed up and left for the day, but the fishmonger still had two salmon that smelled like they had been too long in the heat, and a pig farmer was trying to rid himself of a squealing pink runt.

Stepping over flattened streaks of manure, I made my way to Padraig as he limped toward me. The damp weather wreaked havoc on his arthritis and this summer had been particularly rainy.

"No sign of yer man, milady?" Padraig's words were a breathless wheeze from too many years smoking a pipe.

I followed his gaze to the looming clocktower in the square. If we left now, we would be able to make it to Mántan by nightfall. In my own town, being out after dark wasn't quite as dangerous as it used to be. But we weren't in my town, and I wasn't taking any chances.

"He will be here soon." *Hopefully*. The only thing worse than Tadhg showing up would be if he *didn't* show up.

Running a hand over the white hairs at the back of his neck,

Padraig glanced around at the nearly abandoned market. "I'm not tellin' ye yer business, but are ye sure ye know what yer doin'?"

I hadn't a clue. But if I thought about how out of my depth I was or what lay ahead, I would turn tail and run back to where I was safe and secure but drowning in memories of what should have been. "I'm following the instructions I was given."

That earned an incoherent mumble. Padraig had already tried deterring me from this "hair-brained plan." When he realized it was impossible, he told me he wasn't letting me go alone.

A cool, cleansing mist descended on us, sending me deeper into my cloak.

"Will ye wait inside the carriage at least?" Padraig opened the door. "Be no good if ye caught yer death."

A bit of rain was the least of my problems.

"You needn't worry about me. I'll be fine."

Padraig closed the door and went to check the two gray geldings stamping their hooves at the front of the carriage. The stragglers in the market dispersed until it was only myself and the now-pigless pig farmer.

A dark figure emerged from between a vacant butchery and a pink bakery with a wedding cake displayed in the window.

The memory of how devilishly handsome Tadhg had been last night couldn't compare to the reality of seeing him in the fading light, with a layer of stubble accentuating the strong line of his jaw and dark brown hair falling into his kohl-smeared eyes.

Tadhg seemed unconcerned by the way the mist clung to his black overcoat, strolling across the cobblestones like he owned time itself.

The strap on his leather satchel cut across his chest, and the chartreuse cravat spilling from his breast pocket seemed like an afterthought. Despite his mud-stained black breeches and dull black boots, he was the most attractive being I had ever seen—which irritated me more than the fact that he was late.

The more handsome the man, the bigger the let-down.

And I couldn't afford for Tadhg to let me down.

"What time do you call this?" I asked. He had told me he was busy this morning and couldn't leave until four. It was almost five. "And where is your horse?" Hopefully, it was stabled nearby. We were already late enough.

Tadhg brushed raindrops from his sleeve and adjusted his bag. The kohl around his eyes was beginning to drip down his cheeks. "I don't have a horse," he said in his lilting accent.

If he didn't have a horse, then how did he expect to get to Tearmann?

As if he'd heard my question, he looked past me toward the waiting carriage.

"You think I'm going to let you ride with me?" The very idea made my stomach tighten. The two of us . . . all but alone . . . for ten days of travel. He could kill me or curse me or do something far worse. *Not. Happening.*

Tadhg's dark eyebrows disappeared beneath his disheveled hair. "I can always stay here and let you find the Gancanagh on your own if you'd prefer." His low, musical voice slid along my skin like an unwelcome caress, making me shudder with revulsion.

I glanced at the carriage, wishing it were bigger or filled with other people or open-topped so I wouldn't be trapped inside with a bloody creature. I'd known this journey would have its hardships but didn't think I'd have to face them from day one.

I inhaled a deep, steadying breath. I could do this. A few days in discomfort was worth the reward of bringing back my sister. "I suppose there's enough room for the both of us."

He bent at the waist in a mocking bow and his hair fell forward, uncovering his ears. "You're too kind."

His sarcastic tone made me want to kick him in the shin. I *was* being kind. I could've told him to sit in the rain with Padraig.

My faithful coachman watched us from his perch with a grimace on his weathered face. His poor bones must have been aching something fierce. If only I could let Tadhg drive the carriage and bring Padraig inside with me.

A resigned sigh escaped me as I climbed inside and settled myself on the bench, trying to get a handle on my irritation.

This was a minor setback. I had endured worse.

Tadhg folded himself through the door, and his open overcoat brushed my knees. Although he was only a hand taller than me, he seemed to take up a good deal more room inside the carriage than out of it.

Instead of sitting on the bench next to me, Tadhg sat sideways on my trunk, facing the door. After unhooking his satchel, he removed his overcoat, revealing a missing button in the center of his waistcoat. It smelled like he had rolled around in a field—and from the grass stains on his white shirt, it looked like it as well.

"Where to, milady?" Padraig may have spoken to me, but he was scowling at Tadhg from the open door.

"We need to go to Guaire," Tadhg said, shoving his sleeves to his elbows, exposing muscular forearms far too tan for a person living on this island.

If the sun decided to grace us with its presence, it was usually hidden by clouds an hour later. I could count the number of proper sunny days there had been this summer on one hand.

Tadhg's coloring reminded me of the sailors from Iodale who docked their ships in the port near my town.

"*Milady?*" Padraig's blue eyes darted to me.

I offered my coachman a tight smile, then turned to Tadhg. How hard could it be to handle one irritable creature?

In my most diplomatic voice, I said, "We need to head northwest." Guaire was to the south.

"We travel to Guaire," Tadhg insisted, his tone matching mine and chin jutting forward.

Padraig must have sensed the impending argument and retreated.

"Is the Gancanagh *in* Guaire?" Tightness spread through my core. If he was close, then it may only be a matter of days before I could resurrect Aveen.

Tadhg folded his arms over his chest. The muscles in his thighs flexed as he stretched his legs toward the door. "Not at present. But I have some business to attend to before we travel to his castle."

What did he think this was? Some sort of hired coach? We were here for one thing, and one thing only—and it had nothing to do with his bloody business. "What sort of business could you possibly have that cannot wait?"

He looked like a pirate without a ship, or a rogue street performer. His "business" couldn't be more important than my own.

Tadhg pulled a silver flask from his bag, opened it, and took a slow drink. His eyes fixed on me, and then he smiled. "The type of business that's none of yours."

Brilliant.

Just bloody brilliant.

I was going to be cooped up for the next ten days with an insufferable ass. Although I was used to men dismissing me, the sheer arrogance in Tadhg's response made me want to claw out his eyes.

To make things worse, if I refused to take him to Guaire, he could refuse to bring me to the Gancanagh. It seemed I was destined to be powerless, and the victorious smirk on Tadhg's face told me he knew it.

I asked Padraig to head south, silently vowing to allow Tadhg one day to complete whatever "business" he had.

Padraig nodded, his mouth a grim line when he closed and latched the door. The carriage rocked slightly as he climbed to his bench behind the two horses.

Leaning back in my seat, I kept my eyes trained on the scenery rolling past. Colorful houses blurred into a pastel rainbow as we traded the village for the countryside. The rich, green landscape was beautiful but with darkness looming, it was also dangerous.

There was no telling what manner of monsters lurked on the other side of the hedges.

Pooka—shapeshifters who feasted on human flesh.

Banshee—wraiths who reveled in sending their victims to the underworld.

The Dullahan—a headless being that used a human spine as a whip and drew out souls simply by calling a person's name.

The sluagh—hosts of the unforgiven dead.

Malevolent merrow, wicked faeries, evil elves . . .

Why humans had come to this cursed island in the first place, I would never understand.

Tadhg brushed his fingers along the edge of the blue damask curtains. Back and forth. Back and forth. "I'm not sure if you realize this," he said, "but you never gave me your name."

I hadn't given him my name because I had expected our interactions to be minimal. Him on a horse trailing the carriage, me inside relaxing with a novel. Arriving at the Gancanagh's castle, exchanging coins, and going our separate ways.

"You may call me Lady Keelynn," I told him reluctantly

"Keelynn." He drew out the syllables as if savoring each one.

My stomach clenched in disgust. I did *not* like the way he said it.

"Slender and fair," he murmured to the curtain. "I suppose it would suit if you weren't planning on committing a heinous murder."

Killing a murderer wasn't murder. It was an act of heroism. Not that I expected someone like him to understand the concept of heroism. I'd read enough stories, heard enough tales, to know creatures like him were all villains.

"I suppose it's a good thing I'm not paying you for your opinion," I shot back.

A muscle in his jaw feathered, and his hand dropped to his lap. "Maiden Death."

Maiden Death? What is he on about? "Excuse me?"

His hypnotic gaze pinned me to the seat. "I've decided I'm going to call you Maiden Death."

"You will not."

"Mmmm . . . I think I will. Yes, Maiden Death is the perfect name for you."

My hands flexed into fists. I forced them open and inhaled a steadying breath. Tadhg could call me whatever he wanted, but it didn't mean I had to respond. We could spend the next ten days in silence for all I cared.

Not ten days.

It would be twelve days, at least, since he insisted on going a day the wrong bloody direction.

His gaze slid from my face to my flexed fingers. "I see you're married."

The ring on my left hand had felt heavy since the day Edward had slipped it onto my finger, like it was made of lead instead of gold. "I *was* married. My husband passed away."

As he stared at me, unblinking, a smile tugged at the corner of his lips. "Did you kill him too?"

He couldn't be serious. "I didn't *kill* anyone," I said, refusing to turn away in case he mistook it as a sign of guilt. "Edward fell off his horse."

At least that's what the missive from Vellana had said. It must've been a terrible accident because the coroner had insisted on a closed casket at the church.

Tadhg's head tilted as he rubbed a hand along his stubbled jaw. "Make it look like an accident. Very smart."

I refused to be baited, refused to say a word to him as long as he kept making terrible and unfounded accusations.

"Unfortunately, you'll have to come up with a different plan to murder the Prince of Tearmann. I've heard he prefers riding women over horses—and rarely falls off." Tadhg chuckled to himself, as if this was all some sort of sick joke.

My sister's life—*my* life—depended on my success.

"Allow me to make something perfectly clear," I said, lacing my fingers together to keep from slapping his smug face, "you cannot shock me with lewd and inappropriate comments."

Aveen and I had used to hang around the stables with Padraig when we were younger. The banter we'd heard between the stable boys had been shameless.

"That sounds like a challenge." Black shadows swirled in Tadhg's eyes, like the nightmare in the witch's jar. That's what Tadhg was: a nightmare disguised as a dream. For all I knew, he was as dangerous as the witch . . . or worse.

"Why don't we agree to keep our conversations civil and to a minimum?" I suggested. "It would make the journey easier for us both."

He'd keep his vulgar comments to himself, and I'd bite my tongue when he did something to irritate me.

Tadhg huffed a laugh before gulping from his flask and wiping his mouth on his sleeve. When he looked back at me, his eyes were narrowed, but the shadows had dissipated. "I'll consider it *if* you tell me what Fiadh took in exchange for the ring."

Hearing the witch's name brought back the clawing pain in my chest. "You know Fiadh?"

Long fingers drummed against the flask. "Everyone in my world knows Fiadh."

His world. A world of myths and monsters. In my world they existed; in his world they thrived.

"What she took is no concern of yours." The less we spoke about my bargain, the better.

Tadhg's knuckles, wrapped around the flask, turned white. "I can *see* the black curse living on your lips, so I know she took *something*."

He could see it? *Oh god.* Could everyone see it or just him? My hand flew to cover my mouth. And it was *black*? Was it as unsightly as it felt?

"Was it your truth?" Green eyes narrowed. "Or your *lies*?"

I flinched.

"Of all the foolish, naïve . . ." He raked a hand through his hair, uncovering the tips of his ears. "Bargaining with a feckin' witch. What were you thinking?"

"I had nothing left to lose."

Tadhg's brow furrowed as he studied me. "Everyone has something to lose."

Not me. Not anymore.

"How did you know about the ring and the curse?" Did he know about the dagger as well? The hilt jabbed into my spine when I shifted on the bench.

Tadhg drew a fingertip across the skin beneath his eyes and held a kohl-smeared finger toward me. "This allows me to see glamours and curses."

Fascinating. Something like that would be handy to have on my mission. "Where did you get it?"

Sighing, he dropped his head back against the wall. The trunk beneath him creaked when the carriage rocked. "I bargained with Fiadh."

We reached the outskirts of Guaire in time to catch the moon rising over the village's small two-story inn. Fat raindrops splattered the deserted cobbled street. Lanterns hanging from iron shepherd's hooks were reflected in the inn's curtained windows.

The moment we stopped, Tadhg shrugged into his overcoat and collected his satchel from the floor. After his revelation about the kohl, he'd finished what was in his flask and promptly passed out.

"I'll meet you tomorrow afternoon," he said, reaching for the door's handle.

"Aren't you staying here?" It wasn't that I cared where he spent the night. But if he didn't show up tomorrow, I wouldn't know where to find him.

His teeth flashed in the shadows. "Is that an invitation, Maiden Death?" He clucked his tongue. "Think of the scandal."

"It wasn't— I didn't mean—" *Breathe. Don't let him rile you.* "How do I know you'll come back tomorrow?" I ground out.

"I suppose you're going to have to trust me, now aren't you?"

Tadhg threw open the door, slipped through the gap, and headed toward the village.

By the time I climbed out of the carriage, Padraig was at the door, offering a weathered hand. "Forgive me if this is out of turn, milady. But I don't trust that . . ." Padraig hesitated, watching Tadhg's retreating form disappear between two cottages. "That *young man*," he finished.

Tadhg was a creature.

A monster hiding beneath handsome human skin.

You're going to have to trust me.

Not bloody likely.

"Your concern is appreciated but unnecessary, Padraig," I said.

I knew better than to trust someone like Tadhg.

5

THREE DAYS.

That was how long we had been traveling in the wrong bloody direction. Every single time I had insisted we head north, Tadhg had threatened to abandon me if we didn't go south.

So what did we do?

We rode south.

Tadhg spent the hours in my carriage drinking or passed out on the trunk while I kept myself occupied with the handful of novels I had brought from home. It would've been bearable had we been making more headway.

On the fourth day, Tadhg arrived at the inn late in the afternoon, sporting the mussed hair of a man not long out of bed. He had changed into dark green breeches held in place by a pair of black braces and the same wrinkled shirt from yesterday.

There was no point asking where he had spent the night; he smelled like he'd bathed in women's perfumes. I'd have bet all my silver that he'd spent the night at the bawdy house we'd passed on the way in.

"I see you've been very busy with your *important business.*" I gestured toward the red mark shaped like a kiss peeking from beneath his open collar.

Tadhg's eyes narrowed into swirling black slits. "You think I like—" His mouth clamped shut and a pensive look crossed his face. "You know what? This isn't worth it." He turned on his heel and left.

I was too stunned to call after him. It wasn't as if I was out of line in pointing out the obvious. He was wasting my time, and this little tantrum of his wasn't earning him any goodwill.

I sank onto a low stone wall beside the carriage and stared down the alley where he had disappeared.

"Where's yer man going?" Padraig asked, easing himself onto the stones and stretching his legs in front of him. The soles of his old brown boots were unevenly worn, the left one almost down to the sole. I had offered to buy him a new pair, but he had refused.

"I haven't a clue," I confessed with a shrug.

When would Tadhg be back? Would he bother returning at all?

"Did ye have an argument?" Padraig glanced sidelong at me, disapproval evident in his flat tone.

Arguing with Tadhg would've been a waste of energy. "I simply pointed out that he has been wasting my time." And I was this close to leaving him behind and asking someone else for assistance.

Padraig pulled off his cap and crushed it between his hands. "It's the truth," he grumbled. The wrinkles around his mouth deepened when he frowned. "He's taking advantage of ye, milady. And I've half a mind to tell him what'll happen if it continues."

Like that would do any good. Still, I appreciated the sentiment and gave his knee a pat. He felt like skin and bones beneath his rough wool pants. Had he been eating enough? This journey was taking its toll on him already. The longer it lasted, the harder it would be for Padraig to endure.

I made a mental note to buy some brown rolls for him to snack on while driving. "Thank you, Padraig. But I will handle him myself."

Assuming Tadhg returned.

Padraig's brow furrowed, and he shook his head. It was obvious he wanted to say more but refrained.

"What would ye say to a game of piquet?" he asked, removing his faithful deck of cards from an overcoat pocket. Padraig's cards were as worn as he was.

I smiled and adjusted my seat on the flat stones. "I would say go on and deal, but only if you want to lose."

"That's it." I tossed my hand on the pile and folded my arms over my chest. "You're either cheating or using magic. There's no way you're that lucky." I hadn't won once.

"Luck's got nothin' to do with it," Padraig said with a gruff laugh. "Yer too preoccupied today."

"Perhaps you're right." I was still trying to figure out what to do about Tadhg.

If we kept on as we were, I would never reach my destination. Enough was enough. It was time to take back control. "Padraig?"

Curious blue eyes met mine. "Yes, milady?"

I handed him my cards and felt the tightness in my chest loosen. "Where's your map?"

Some time later, I saw Tadhg approaching from the road leading to the bawdy house. Having learned my lesson, I didn't mention the additional red marks on his neck and chest.

I smiled pleasantly and refrained from commenting when he demanded to be taken to another southern town. Padraig already knew he was to bring us north, to Buraos, no matter what. Without further delays, that would leave twelve more days of travel.

Tadhg settled himself on the trunk and withdrew his flask from his bag before balling up his overcoat to use as a pillow. It was the same routine he had followed every other day. If I was lucky, he'd be passed out before we got out of town.

"Let me know when you're ready to apologize," he said, the

liquid inside the flask sloshing when he knocked it against his knee.

"Why should I apologize to you?" If anyone deserved an apology, it was me.

Tadhg shifted and the trunk creaked as he stretched his long legs toward the door. His boots left muddy streaks all over the carriage floor. "You have been nothing but rude and condescending since the moment we met."

I had been rude and condescending? He thought *I* was the problem?

"I'm helping you, remember?" he added.

"Helping me?" I gripped the edge of the bench. Heat climbed up my neck, and I felt my face flush. Did he think me a fool? "You haven't been *helping*. You've been hijacking my carriage and using threats to keep us traveling in the wrong direction!"

"Did it ever occur to you that I have a reason for heading south?" Tadhg's eyes lifted heavenward and he muttered a curse to the low ceiling. "That I know more about my world than an ignorant human?"

"I am not ignorant!"

He twisted toward me faster than anyone should have been able to move. I pressed myself into the cushion at my back, desperate to put distance between us.

"You are if you believe that you can best an immortal who has been on this earth for centuries," he snarled, his lips curling back from his teeth. He threw the flask onto his abandoned bag and gripped his knees as though he was trying to hold himself back. The air in the carriage thickened. "I try to keep an open mind when it comes to humans, but you're making it exceedingly difficult. First you want to murder an innocent man and then——"

"The Gancanagh is *not* innocent." And he sure as hell wasn't a man. "He's a murderer who seduces maidens and kills them with his poisoned lips."

Tadhg blinked rapidly, his mouth hanging open. Then he barked a laugh so loud it made me jump. "Where did you hear

that load of bollocks? From your nursemaid? A crier?" He
gestured toward my book on the bench. "One of your *fairy tales*?"

"It's the truth," I countered, trying to keep the wobble from
my voice. "Otherwise, I wouldn't be able to say it."

"Let me explain how a truth curse works." Derision oozed
from every syllable. "You won't be able to tell an outright lie or
break your promises," Tadhg said, lifting a finger for each point,
"but if you are *ignorant* and truly believe the myths and lies
spouted by bigots, then you can say it without feeling like your
skull is being crushed. If Fiadh didn't use dark magic, this, like
most curses, will last a year and a day." He clasped his hands
together in his lap and propped his shoulder against the wall like
he hadn't a care in the world. "Now, let me give you a second
lesson."

Rage simmered in my chest, rising, rising, *rising* with each
drawled sentence.

"The Gancanagh is a shapeshifter. You know what that means,
yeah?"

It meant I was going to claw the smirk from his face.

Tadhg raised his eyebrows as if he expected me to respond to
the condescending question.

I crossed my arms and ground my teeth together so hard it
made my jaw ache. He didn't deserve my answer.

"I'll take that as a 'no.' Don't worry. We can circle back." He
rolled a hand toward the window. Outside, the sky was growing as
dark as my mood. "As I said, the Gancanagh is a shapeshifter who
determines his lover's deepest desires and seeks to fulfil them."

I tried to breathe through the rage, loosening my muscles one
by one. Exhale anger, inhale peace. But every time I looked at his
smug, smarmy face, it came back tenfold.

"His lips are *cursed*, not *poisoned*," Tadhg went on, his gaze
dropping to my mouth, "and he doesn't go around kissing women
unless they understand the consequences."

Lies.

Lies.

Lies.

Aveen wouldn't have jeopardized her life for a tryst with the Gancanagh. He must've put some sort of spell on her. Hidden his identity. Taken advantage of her innocence. Kissed her without revealing the consequences.

"You think you know everything, don't you?" I spat, a tornado of fury swirling inside of me.

His smirk widened. "I know more than you."

He thought he knew more than me?

I leaned forward, reveling in the confusion in his searching eyes when I smiled and said, "I *watched* your *innocent* Gancanagh murder my sister."

Tadhg's pupils blew out; blackness swallowed every last speck of green. He lunged, catching me by the shoulders, sending perfumed air crashing over me. "Tell me *exactly* what you saw." Heat radiated from him like a bloody bonfire, scorching my skin through my dress.

"I'm not telling you a thing." I knocked his hands away and scooted back to sitting, rubbing at my tingling arms. Why did it still feel like his hands were on me?

"If you don't, I will get out of this carriage and leave you to fend for yourself."

His hand fell to the latch on the door.

Would he do it?

One glance at his scowl answered that question.

I hated being powerless. I hated that Tadhg could walk all over me and demand whatever he wanted simply because I needed his help. But most of all, I hated *him*.

Seeing no other option, I told him what had happened, how she had kissed the monster and he had abandoned her like a bloody coward.

The pressure in my chest returned, more an ache than a sharp pain. I pressed a hand to my heart and massaged until it eased.

Tadhg swore; his heel cracked against the trunk. A powerful pulse vibrated through my body, tangible but invisible, making my heart race. I inched closer to the door, watching him wrestle his rage, waiting for him to lash out with writhing darkness.

Tadhg's ragged breathing eventually steadied and the blackness in his eyes faded. "I'm sorry," he said.

If I didn't know better, I would've thought he sounded embarrassed.

His gaze shifted to the window. "When I get angry, it's hard for me to—" His words trailed off and he flattened a hand against the glass. "This isn't the right road."

So much for this day going smoothly.

"There's been a change of plans." I straightened my shoulders, steeling myself for the inevitable argument. "We're traveling to Buraos."

His eyes snapped to mine. "We cannot stay in Buraos."

"We *will* stay in Buraos." Short of jumping from the moving carriage, there was nothing he could do about it.

Tadhg unfastened more buttons at his collar before retrieving his flask. He unscrewed the lid with jerking twists, mumbling the entire time. His throat bobbed as he drained what was left. I lifted my book and opened to a random page in the middle. Tadhg's fingers tapped against his knees, making it impossible to focus on the printed words.

The air thickened. Magic swelled, leaking out of him, smelling faintly of almonds. "We're not staying in Buraos," he insisted.

I'd had enough of his *help*. Of his damned *business*. Looking up from my book, I smiled and said, "You. Don't. Have. A. Choice."

Tadhg sneered and flicked his wrist.

The carriage bucked forward, sending me flying across the aisle and onto his lap. My face struck the hard wall of his chest and strong arms closed around my back. Something stirred inside of me, deep, primal. Yearning.

The horses neighed.

A litany of gruff curses echoed through the forest.

"Let go!" I wriggled from Tadhg's grasp and scrambled back

to the bench. My entire body was on fire. Something was seriously wrong with me. Had he put me under a spell? A curse?

Tadhg stared at me through wide eyes, his eyebrows knit in confusion. Then he blinked and a smirk replaced the confusion. "*You're* the one who climbed on top of *me*."

"Like I would ever want to be near something like *you* on purpose." I shoved stray hairs from my face and snagged my book from the floor. My hands trembled and I couldn't catch my breath. If only there were a river or lake or sea for me to jump into and douse these flames.

"Lady Keelynn?" Padraig called. "Could ye come out fer a moment? I need a word with ye in private."

I wrenched open the door and found my coachman standing next to the horses. The cool breeze swirling around us did little to staunch the flames. As much as I hated the delay, I was grateful for the interruption. There's no telling what Tadhg would've done to me in that carriage.

"Doesn't make a lick of sense." Padraig bent his flat cap between his hands as he scanned the area. His short white hair stuck out in every direction. "The wheel's just . . . disappeared. No sign of it anywhere."

Sure enough, the front left wheel was gone. No broken spokes. No apparent damage to the axle. The muddy cap on the end was still in place.

How had it come loose?

There was no sign of the blasted thing on the road or the dyke either.

"I don't mean to pry, milady," he said, glancing at me from beneath his thin lashes, "but did anything happen inside the carriage just now?"

What sort of question was that? "Besides our escort being an insufferable ass, you mean?"

Tadhg slipped out of the carriage, slung his bag across his chest, and started walking away.

"Where do you think you're going?" I shouted at his back.

"Away from you," he replied, not bothering to turn around.

He couldn't go away. We had a deal. He had promised to bring me to Tearmann. "But we need your help. We're missing a wheel."

"I know."

Padraig's eyes narrowed on Tadhg's retreating form. His knuckles turned white where he strangled his cap.

Understanding hit me like a hammer to the head.

The anger.

The indignation.

The twitchy fingers.

The flick of Tadhg's wrist right before the wheel vanished into thin air.

This was *his* fault.

I ran over the pitted road until I caught up and grabbed him by the arm. "*You* did this, didn't you?"

His body stiffened and his gaze dropped to my hand. My fingers stung like I'd grabbed a fist full of nettles. I let him go and scrubbed my palm against my cloak.

Using magic to harm a human or their property was illegal, punishable by death.

"Careful now. That's an awfully serious accusation." Tadhg's smirk returned.

It *was* him.

But there was no way to prove it.

"Well, Maiden Death," Tadhg said, his eyes sparkling like emeralds, "it appears I had a choice after all."

He turned and sauntered away.

Aveen had always said my temper would get me into trouble. I had never expected it to leave me stranded with darkness falling on a three-wheeled carriage, abandoned by my escort.

Something rattled the bushes across the road. The wind picked up, swirling my skirts and tearing at my pinned hair. Tree branches clawed the darkening sky.

The weight was back, threatening to crack my sternum.

Making it difficult to breathe. Making it nearly impossible to shout, "Stop! Don't leave us. Please don't go."

Tadhg's shoulders stiffened. When he paused his confident strides, the weight eased a fraction. When he turned and stalked back, it eased a bit more.

I opened my mouth to thank him, but he continued past without acknowledging my existence and did not stop until he reached Padraig. Their exchange consisted of low, serious tones from Tadhg and a lot of nodding from my coachman.

Then Tadhg pressed something into Padraig's palm.

"Go ahead with master Tadhg," Padraig said, tucking whatever Tadhg had given him into the pocket where he kept his playing cards. "He promised the wheel will return soon."

The wheel would return.

Like it was on a bloody holiday.

Tadhg swept past me, muttering, "Try to keep up."

My boots remained rooted in the mud like the many stones littering the road. "I cannot leave Padraig behind." His safety and wellbeing were my responsibility.

Tadhg stopped, and his head dropped as he exhaled a long sigh. "He will be fine."

"You expect me to take your word for it?" What good was the word of a creature who had deliberately sabotaged the carriage? "This is your doing. Just flick your wrist and give back the bloody wheel."

A muscle feathered in his jaw. "You have two choices: stay with him or come with me."

"Go with him, milady." Padraig patted one of the stomping horses. Its tack jingled when it shook its head. "All will be well."

How could he possibly know that? He'd said himself Tadhg couldn't be trusted and now Padraig wanted me to be on my own with him?

Padraig waved me away with his cap before rounding the back of the carriage. He truly didn't seem concerned.

After one final glance, I fell into step behind Tadhg. Puddles filled the deeper pits in the road. I skirted around them, careful to keep my boots from getting too wet and ruining the leather. "Do you swear he will be all right?"

Tadhg kicked a loose stone into one of the puddles. "I already told you that he will be fine."

How could he be so certain? "Nightfall is only an hour away."

Tadhg stomped right through a puddle, soaking his tall black boots and splattering my skirt. Glaring at him would've been a waste of energy. He obviously didn't give a damn about me or my clothes or my mission or my friend or anything but himself.

"You're a bit old to be afraid of the dark, aren't you?" he said with a laugh.

A veil of gray clouds obscured what remained of the waning sun. It wasn't the dark I feared but the beings who haunted it.

Tadhg was one of them.

Even knowing this, I drew closer to his stomping frame, hoping that if we were attacked, he wouldn't abandon me or use me as a human shield.

By the time we reached a village, my heels were blistered, my legs ached, and my face was sore from the wind whipping over the hillside.

"There's an inn just there," Tadhg said, pointing to a sign swinging above a red door down a side street. Behind the building was a substantial stable for my horses—*if* they arrived.

What if it was full? Where would I go?

"You must bring me to the door." It seemed like the safest option.

His heel ground the stones beneath his boots. "*Must I?*"

Instead of thumping his insufferable head, I pinned on a smile. Twelve more days. I could do this. "I would appreciate it if you accompanied me the rest of the way," I amended.

Twelve more days.

Twelve more days.

"What's this?" His eyebrows flew up, and he pressed a hand to his chest. "Are you asking me to be near you *on purpose?*"

Flickers of embarrassment burned my cheeks. I should have been able to control my irritation, but everything about him made me feel out of control. "I shouldn't have said that to you. It was awful, and I'm sorry."

Tadhg mumbled something under his breath but walked me past darkened shops and modest plaster homes to a door made to look like a red portcullis.

"Your door, milady." Tadhg gave a mocking bow. "Do you require additional assistance? I'm remarkably good at unlacing stays."

As if I would ever let him near my stays with his long, tanned —and likely very nimble—fingers.

Humming laces slipping through eyelets whispered in my ears.

I swore I could feel my bodice loosening, urging me to take a freeing breath.

Invisible hands caught my shift. Grazed down my shoulders.

My breathing hitched.

I could taste Tadhg's magic on my tongue, thick, like too-sweet icing with a hint of almonds.

"*Stop.*" I clutched my cloak closed over my heaving chest.

Tadhg's blank expression gave no indication that he knew what had happened. "Stop what?"

The air I drew into my lungs tasted of woodsmoke, not magic.

"N-nothing." I was exhausted. That's what it was. Exhaustion. My tired mind must've been playing tricks on me. I escaped through the door and slammed it behind me.

Twelve more days.

I could do this.

Twelve more days.

6

THE ROOM I HAD RENTED AT THE FRONT OF THE INN WAS MODEST but clean. The best part was the fire blazing in the hearth. If only its warmth could go deeper and return some of the fire to my soul.

I sipped my glass of wine slowly, needing to make it last. Why hadn't I ordered a bottle instead? Alcohol brought sleep and silence—and with the chaotic thoughts buzzing in my mind, I had a sinking feeling both would elude me tonight.

All of those thoughts could be summed up in one word: Tadhg.

The instant I saw two gray geldings trotting toward the inn, I slipped my blistered feet into my boots and readied myself to go back outside.

Downstairs, the woman who had checked me in was busy serving plates of bacon and smelly cabbage to patrons sitting at the tables. When she bustled past, I asked if it would be possible to have a bath sent to my room.

"All the tubs are spoken for, milady." She swiped a hand across her sweaty brow. Perspiration collected at the base of her throat like a necklace. "Although we should have a spare wash bucket around here somewhere." She nodded toward a boy, no older than six or seven, scurrying between the tables with a brush and pan. "I'll have one of the lads fetch it when we're finished."

"That will do. Thank you."

The chilly night air sent me deeper into my cloak. Each hurried step on the way to the stables rubbed at my already raw heels. The hum of low conversation lifted through the double doors propped open with bales of hay. The air smelled of sweaty horses, hay, and leather.

Oh, how I missed riding. Ever since my sixteenth birthday, my father had insisted we take the carriage to appear more civilized. The moment I returned from this journey, I was going to sell the bloody thing and use the proceeds to buy a new horse.

A foal with a diamond of white hair above its eyes knickered at me as I passed. Padraig looked up from where he and a young teen in mucky boots were feeding our horses.

"Milady?" Padraig offered a tight bob of his head. When the teen didn't acknowledge me, Padraig knocked him in the shoulder and glared. With his cheeks turning pink, the teen gave me an awkward bow.

"What brings ye here at such a god forsaken hour?" Padraig asked, a smile playing on his thin lips when the boy hurried on his way to the other side of the stable.

It was only half nine, but Padraig had always been more of a morning person, like myself. The night felt too restrictive. Darkness pressing in on all sides; monsters lurking in the shadows.

Daylight was safer.

Daylight was freedom.

"I couldn't sleep until I checked on you." I blinked away the tears welling in my eyes. If anything had happened to him, I would be lost. Padraig had always been there, a steady, solid presence when I'd needed one. His quiet strength had gotten me through the worst of the last four months.

Padraig was the only ally I had left.

"No trouble, I hope." I hid my wringing hands behind my back. He'd give out if he knew how much I'd worried about him.

Padraig stepped away from the horses, scratching the short white whiskers covering his chin. "None to speak of. Wheel showed up in the dyke not long after ye left. Took some time to get it back on"—his eyes darted to the teen plucking a coarse brush from a high shelf—"but I had help. Made it here not a bother."

"Someone helped you?" Who would've been out on the roads this late at night?

Padraig's white eyebrows knitted together. "Twasn't a man."

A lump formed in my throat. Padraig was safe. Padraig was here. There was no need to be frightened. "What was it?" I forced past the lump.

The stable hand brushed the gelding with long, smooth strokes but kept his head cocked toward us.

"He was short, not much taller than 'im." Padraig nodded toward the boy. "Arms covered in red hair. Voice of a man, strength of ten. Couldn't see his face on account of the hood, but he smelled like a pig sty."

The mysterious creature sounded like a grogoch. All I could recall of the half-faerie beings was that they despised members of the clergy and had fairly mild temperaments. As far as I knew, they didn't eat people. "Were you frightened?"

"I'd be lyin' if I said I wasn't a mite fearful. Then I showed 'im this like Master Tadhg told me to." He dug into his pocket and handed me an expensive gold cufflink embossed with a triskelion. I traced the triple spirals to where they interlocked in the middle.

"And then yer man offered to help with the wheel," Padraig finished.

I turned the cufflink over in my hand. Where had Tadhg gotten such a thing? That much gold could buy him a month's worth of new clothes. And he had given it to Padraig without batting an eye.

"I'll be sure to return it to him." A veil of unease settled over me as I tucked the gold into my pocket. "Will I organize dinner for you inside? They're serving your favorite. Bacon and cabbage."

"There's no need." Padraig rubbed his swollen stomach where it tested the buttons on his waistcoat. "Yer man left more food than I'm used to eatin' in a day."

"And you ate it?" What had he been thinking? If the food had been enchanted, it could have killed him.

Padraig nodded. "Hope he doesn't mind that I had every last bit of it. Told me to. Not sure he meant the wine." Shaking his head, he rocked back on his heels and tucked his thumbs into his belt loops. "Tasted awful expensive."

"That was kind of him." What did Tadhg stand to gain by helping Padraig? What game was he playing?

Nudging some hay with his boot, Padraig mumbled, "Seems I may have misjudged him."

Tadhg may have taken care of Padraig in this instance, but that didn't mean he was trustworthy. After all, he had been the one to break the carriage in the first place.

The food could've been his way of making amends.

Or it could have been an attempt to make me feel indebted to him. And in Tadhg's debt was not a place I wanted to stay.

I wished Padraig good night and made my way back to the inn.

Tadhg would probably be up until all hours drinking, or he'd find some other woman who needed help with her stay. How he spent his nights didn't matter. If he wanted to share beds with tarts or pass out on a drink-splattered table, that was his choice.

But tonight, I would give him another option.

Then we'd be even.

I hurried across the pavement to the pub I'd seen him enter not too long ago. My blistered heels made each step a challenge. The words "The Black Rabbit" had been embossed onto a bronze plaque attached to the wall.

Inside, one man with slicked back gray hair and a second with no hair at all hunkered over their pints at a low wooden table. A third, with a bushy black mustache concealing his upper lip, read behind the bar. The two lumps of coal burning in the fireplace barely warmed the candlelit room.

I could have sworn Tadhg had come in here. Had he left while I was speaking to Padraig? If so, where had he gone?

The bartender looked up from his book and clattered to his feet. "May I help you, milady?" he asked, smoothing a hand over his inky black hair.

Was this pub like the Green Serpent? Was there a haven for creatures in the back?

"This is going to sound strange, but is there another pub here?" I asked.

The bartender's mustache twitched with his frown. "The Starling would still be serving drinks at this hour. Or the inn across the way." He indicated the direction I had come from with the spine of his book.

"I meant in this building." I nodded toward the far wall. "At the back."

The two men drinking looked up from their pints. The bald one lifted his thick eyebrows.

"Only thing in the back is more storage," the bartender said, shaking his head.

"Yer not serving creatures again, are ye, Sean?" The gray-haired man rose to his feet and clutched his dagger's hilt. "Ye know folks won't be comin' in if ye are."

"Didn't ye hear what I told the lady? Those filthy monsters aren't welcome here."

The gray-haired man didn't look convinced, but he sat down. The bartender turned back to me, his eyebrows coming together in a silent plea. The last thing I wanted was to cause trouble, so I muttered an apology and retreated into the night.

Going back to the inn at this stage felt like failing, and I had already failed enough.

My fingertips brushed against the triskelion cufflink as I made my way past three houses to an alley. Flickering wall lanterns kept the narrow gap from being swallowed by darkness.

A dull pain started in my chest, spreading to my core.

How could I expect to defeat a monster if I couldn't even go down a bloody alley on my own?

I inhaled a deep breath and forced one foot in front of the other.

Glowing eyes stared at me from a pile of crushed crates. Something scurried across my path. The beast pounced.

A cat. It was only a cat.

My heart pummeled against the heel of my hand as I massaged the pain away.

The smell of magic grew harsher the closer I drew to the pub's green door.

All I needed to do was open it and find Tadhg.

Assuming he was in there.

It could be a room filled with unknown monsters waiting to murder me.

The door flew open with a blast of sweet air.

A bearded man stumbled out. When he saw me, his eyes widened. Was he . . . Was he *human*?

If he was leaving the place alive, perhaps I would be all right.

"Ye goin' in, milady?" he slurred, catching the handle and holding the door.

Barking laughter burst from inside the pub. Laughter was a good sign. I drew cool, magic-laced air into my lungs. "Yes, I am."

The pub was half the size of the Black Rabbit and twice as full. Two patrons seated next to the door had cloaks drawn over their faces. Their fur-covered hands were wrapped around steaming flagons, their fingers topped with claws.

Pooka.

A man no taller than a child sat next to the fire, a long pipe between his lips. Green smoke curled around his red-bearded chin. The gleaming gold buckles on his black shoes matched the buckle on his wide belt.

Another man—or monster—in a gold cloak crossed to a door that I assumed connected to the Black Rabbit.

Then I saw a familiar dark head buried in a busty barmaid's bosom.

One of the pooka shot to his feet, towering over me. Its wide yellow eyes glowed in the shadows of its hood.

"Are ye lost, milady?" it asked in a hoarse voice.

Am I lost? Did this monster just ask me if I needed *directions*? "No. I'm here for . . ." For what? Not a friend. "I'm here for someone."

If the beast knew I was planning to meet another person, perhaps he wouldn't bother eating me.

"*Keelynn!*" Hearing my name shouted in a high, happy tone was as unexpected as seeing Tadhg grinning. The barmaid remained on his lap, her chest painted with black streaks.

For some reason, I wanted to shove her to the floor.

Tadhg waved me over like I was a long-lost friend.

The barmaid pursed her lips before whispering something that made him chuckle. Whatever he whispered back left her face flushed.

"Have you come to join me for a drink?" Tadhg asked. The empty stool across from him rattled when he kicked it toward me.

When the barmaid huffed and sauntered back to the bar, I felt an unexplainable sense of relief.

Squinting, Tadhg reached an unsteady hand for a glass of clear liquid. Three more empty glasses littered the table.

He was drunk.

He swayed on the stool and had to catch himself on the table.

Very drunk.

"I've come to offer you a room," I said, sitting and spreading my skirts around my ankles to keep out the draft.

His grin turned wolfish. "Changed your mind about the laces?"

The reminder made my stomach flutter. "Don't be ridiculous. You're *not* unlacing my stay."

"You just missed me, then? Is that why you sought me out?" The liquid swirled as Tadhg rotated the glass.

"I sought you out to give you this." I pulled the cufflink from my pocket and slid it across the table. "You helped Padraig. In return, I would like to offer you proper lodgings."

"I'm perfectly capable of acquiring *proper lodgings* without your assistance." He shared a knowing smile with the barmaid. When he turned back to me, the smile faded. "Go back to your room before the *scary creatures* get you."

If only going back to my room would settle this debt between us.

"Are you staying with *her*?" I nodded toward the barmaid, and the woman's eyes narrowed into slits.

"Does it matter?"

It didn't matter. Not at all. Not one bloody bit. "If you want to debase yourself, be my guest. But if you'd like a clean, comfortable room at the inn, it's yours."

A bottle slammed against the bar and shattered. I almost smiled.

Tadhg took another sip of his drink. "You want *me* . . . to come with *you* . . . to *your* inn?"

"It's the least I can do after you helped Padraig."

"The least you can do," he muttered, the corner of his mouth lifting.

Was that a yes or a no? I didn't have all night to sit here and wait for an answer. "Well?"

Using the drink spilled on the table, Tadhg drew consecutive circles on the worn wood. Silence stretched, and I was about to give up when he suddenly said, "How can I resist such a magnanimous offer from a generous human such as yourself?"

His sarcasm was easy to ignore. I *was* being generous. "Wash the kohl from your eyes and fix"—I gestured to his clothes—"*this*, so we can be on our way." Tadhg wouldn't get in anywhere looking like a roguish pirate searching for maidens to plunder.

He flipped the cufflink into the air. It spun and landed in his waistcoat pocket. "Wait for me outside. I've some business to attend to first."

The barmaid was smiling again.

I didn't care. Not one bloody bit. But for some reason, my hands wanted to clench into fists. The only reason I stomped to the door was because of the time I had to waste coming here. It had nothing to do with Tadhg gesturing toward a closed door and the barmaid running after him. Fear quickly replaced my irritation when I saw the pooka holding the main door open.

What if it followed me into the alley? What if I became the beast's dinner before Tadhg finished his "business"? Waiting inside was always an option, except I couldn't stop staring at the door where they'd disappeared. I felt myself sinking lower, even as my irritation doubled and tripled, and suddenly the pooka at the door seemed the lesser of the two evils.

I nodded my thanks to the towering beast, not trusting my voice to hide my terror. When the door closed behind me, I turned to find myself completely alone. Why hadn't it attacked? Was it because there were witnesses? I filed away the information for a time when my brain wasn't addled and exhausted.

Waiting in the still night air, I kept one eye on the door as I marveled at the stars. Their lights were too weak to banish the darkness, but still they persisted, night after night. They gave me hope that if I, too, persisted, I really could resurrect my sister.

Tonight was a monumental step.

I had overcome my fear and entered a haven for creatures on my own. Tomorrow would bring me one step closer. All I had to do was keep Tadhg from sabotaging me again.

It felt like mortal ages had passed by the time Tadhg emerged from the pub wearing a clean shirt and loosely looped dark green cravat. The enchanted kohl was gone.

That nameless thing, whatever it was, stirred deep within the pit of my stomach.

How could one person look so bloody perfect?

Moonlight highlighted the tips of Tadhg's ears peeking through his hair.

Almost perfect.

"You'll need to cover those up," I said, indicating his ears.

He shook his head until his hair concealed them. "Am I human enough for you now, Maiden Death?"

Tadhg's face was too beautiful, his eyes too full of magic, his mouth far too sinful to ever pass for one of us. "I suppose you'll have to do."

Back at the inn, we found a woman filing her nails behind a small wooden desk. The smell of cabbage still permeated the air. When she saw us, her eyes widened.

"I need to purchase an additional room for the night," I told her, reaching for my purse.

"Fer yer friend 'ere?" The woman poked Tadhg with the file. He grinned back.

"Yes, please."

"Sure, ye dinna have to stand on pretense with me, milady." Her smile shifted to a smirk as she glanced between us. The file tapped slowly against the edge of the desk. "I'll turn a blind eye fer three coppers."

Turn a blind eye to what? "There is no pretense. I need a second room."

The tapping stopped. "Yer really not stayin' together?" she asked, her eyebrows lifting toward her thick fringe.

"Absolutely not." The very idea sent shivers of revulsion down my spine.

She dragged a nail along Tadhg's forearm, leaving a light pink line on his skin. "Then save yer coins. I've a cold bed he can warm if yer not usin' him."

The thing inside me surged, forcing a terrible shriek from my chest. "Don't *touch* him."

My hand flew to cover the vicious words lodged in my throat. What the hell was happening? I didn't care who touched Tadhg.

The woman's hand dropped.

Tadhg's head tilted as he watched me.

My purse fell to the desk with a *thunk*. "As I said, he will have his *own* room."

"Not a bit fun, is she?" the woman grumbled to Tadhg, accepting the money I handed her and sliding it into the desk's top drawer.

"Not a bit," Tadhg said with a wink.

The woman handed over a small silver key with the number six stamped into the metal.

I thanked her, collected my purse, and headed toward the staircase. Tadhg's light footsteps followed behind. When we reached the long hallway at the top, I indicated the blue number painted on a door to my right. "Your room for the night, as promised. Now we're even."

I turned, and my face met his chest.

"That's the second time you've tried to climb on top of me today," Tadhg murmured.

Cloying air glided over my skin like a whisper. I clamped my mouth shut and stepped back only to find myself pinned between the wall and Tadhg, struggling for breath.

His glowing eyes dropped to my mouth. My lungs ached and throat constricted and heart hummed as he eased forward, resting a forearm on the wall above my head.

"Keelynn?" His lips formed my name in a mesmerizing drawl. "Unless you need me to warm *your* cold bed . . ."

I gasped, forgetting his magic. It tasted sweet, like sugar on my tongue, spreading and tingling through my blood.

My bed *would* be cold.

So, *so* cold.

Tadhg's warm breath tickled my jaw as he whispered into my ear, "I'm going to need my key."

Key? What key? I didn't have a—

I did. I had a key.

A key in my hand that I shoved against his chest.

He took it from me, his fingers brushing mine, leaving my skin buzzing.

I ducked beneath his arm before his wicked magic consumed every rational thought in my traitorous mind. Tadhg's laughter echoed through the empty hallway as I raced to my door and escaped inside.

What had just happened, and how did I keep it from happening again?

7

THERE WAS A BLACK DRESS DRAPED OVER THE CHAIR, ONE ON THE
rug in front of the fire, two more on the bed, and still more in my
trunk. Three more months of black lay ahead of me.

If I had been the one to die, Edward would have only been
required to mourn for a month.

One bloody month.

I didn't want to pretend to mourn. I wanted to save my sister
and live.

Only twelve more days and we would reach Tearmann.

Twelve more days.

No amount of glaring could change the fabric's color, so I
chose the most flattering clean dress. It also happened to be the
only one with a neckline below my collarbone.

Tightening the laces on my stay, I wondered if Tadhg was
awake yet. Not that I had any desire to see him. I simply did not
want another late start.

The market below the window looked crowded. Assuming
Tadhg would be on time, I had an hour to stretch my legs before
the long day of travel ahead.

After twisting and pinning my hair into a knot at the nape of
my neck, I tucked away the emerald ring, strapped on the dagger,

and packed the rest of my things into the trunk. When I passed room number six, the door was still closed.

Good.

The broad smile felt foreign on my lips. And then I ran into Tadhg on the stairs, and it disappeared completely. Tadhg's hair was damp, his clothes free of stains and wrinkles, and he hadn't replaced the kohl.

I wanted to fill my lungs with his magical almondy scent, to inhale and keep it inside of me for all of eternity.

What was wrong with me? No I didn't. I didn't even *like* the way he smelled. I was losing my bloody mind.

"Good morning." He rested an elbow against the banister and gave me a smarmy smile. "Did you sleep well?"

"I did." Not that it was any of his business. It had taken an hour for my pulse to stop racing, but when sleep found me, it was blessedly deep and dreamless.

"Are you sure? Your face was awfully flushed when we parted."

If he hadn't been blocking my path, I would've gone around him. How much trouble would it cause if I shoved him down the staircase?

"I rather enjoyed seeing you flustered, Maiden Death," he crooned.

After hearing him use my given name last night, it was a relief to be back to this.

"I wasn't . . ." *Say it. One white lie.* I tried again but couldn't finish without my head feeling like a blacksmith's anvil.

Tadhg had the gall to laugh. *Bloody creature.* I didn't need this today. I pushed past him, clinging to the worn banister to keep from slipping and cracking my skull at the bottom.

"Where are you off to?" he called, clambering down the stairs after me. The tables were being cleared from breakfast. Unfortunately, I'd slept in too late to make the meal.

"That's none of your business."

"Would you like to accompany me to the market?"

"No."

"Then I'll have to go on my own."

"Brilliant." Only five more steps and I'd be out the door. Four more steps and I'd be free. Three more steps and—

"What time were you hoping to leave again?"

His words stopped me in my tracks. It wasn't so much the question as the *way* he'd said it. Far too snide. Far too *smirky*.

I whirled around.

Tadhg was indeed smirking at me. He'd probably be late out of spite.

Twelve days left.

Only twelve days.

"I'll go to the market with you on one condition," I ground out. "When I say it's time to leave, you must agree to come with me without delay."

"I'll come with you." Tadhg's grin flashed, sending a shudder through my bones. "All you have to do is say the word."

His eyes traveled down my body like an intimate caress, leaving my throat burning and heart pounding and core aching, and if I didn't escape, the spell he cast simply by existing would drag me to a place of sin and shadows.

I tripped over my own feet, and my shin collided with a wooden stool.

"Are you all right?" Tadhg asked, the tilt of his lips proving he already knew the answer.

"Don't do that." My words were a strangled plea.

The smirk disappeared. "Do what?"

He knew bloody well what he had done. "Use your magic on me."

He started shaking his head. "I wasn't—"

"You were! I could smell it." It clung to my tongue. Invaded my pores. Making me want this. Want *him*. Because there was no way I would feel this unbidden desire for a creature without it.

His head tilted, and he studied me until clinical coldness replaced the warmth in his glowing green gaze. "Sometimes it

74

slips free without my permission," he said quietly, looking down at his flexing hands. "I will try to control it better."

What was this? Tadhg was giving in? No lewd comment? No inappropriate suggestions?

I offered a cautious, "Thank you," straightened my skirts with clammy hands, and nodded toward the door. "Shall we go?"

Tadhg held the door and gestured for me to go first. My arm brushed against his chest as I passed, leaving me hurrying outside to put some distance between us.

Strips of sunshine fell between the clouds, bringing shoppers to the market in droves. I bought a currant-filled bun topped with sweet cream and a sack of rolls for Padraig. Feeling a new level of optimism after Tadhg's promise to control his magic, I offered to get one for Tadhg as well. He rolled his eyes, said he was perfectly capable of purchasing his own food, and bought two apple fritters smothered in icing.

He polished off one after the other, only pausing to lick the icing from his fingers. Again that thing stirred, but I smelled no magic, so it couldn't have been Tadhg.

He caught me watching and offered a slow, feline smile. I pretended to check out the vendor behind me, unable to focus on the pottery displayed around the wooden stall.

Tadhg moved through the crowded marketplace with his shoulders straight and head held high but stayed close to the vendors. His eyes darted to the least crowded sections, as if searching for an exit.

Two young women stopped beside him to giggle behind their gloved hands and titter like simpletons. Tadhg wiggled his fingers in a flirtatious wave, and I considered pushing the lot of them into the smelly fish stall.

Did they have no backbone? Weren't they taught to avoid creatures like him at all costs? I was beginning to think I was in the minority when it came to possessing any sense of propriety.

"Are you always this serious?" Tadhg asked.

I found him watching me, his head tilted and hair falling over his forehead. "Excuse me?"

He tapped the space between my eyebrows, and I smacked his hand away. "You've been scowling ever since we met."

Smiling used to feel as natural as breathing. Now it took too much effort. "I have a lot on my mind."

"Like death and murder?"

I rolled my eyes. If he wasn't careful, I was going to murder him. "Among other things."

"What do you like to do when you're not on a quest for vengeance?" he asked, running his fingers through the wildflowers tied into bouquets sitting on a wagon.

The colorful blooms made me think of joy and freedom—two things that had been lacking in my life since Aveen had passed.

"Why do you care?" I touched the silky, delicate petals on an arrangement of purple and white hydrangeas. I loved these pure, unblemished flowers. They reminded me of what I used to be.

Tadhg's eyes met mine over his shoulder. "Is it not considered polite conversation to ask after one's favorite pastimes? I could tell you a few of mine if you'd like." His gaze fell to my skirt, and instantly I became hyper-aware of the soft material swaying against my skin.

After seeing those rouge stains yesterday, I had a fairly good idea of what Tadhg's favorite pastime was.

Spools of delicate lace and bolts of fine fabric filled the next stall. Dressing up for parties used to be one of my favorite things to do. The bolder the dress, the better. I'd wanted to be seen and heard—and loved. All it took was one glance at my drab, boring gown to remember that death had made me a shadow.

"I suppose I enjoy reading," I said, moving on. As a child, I'd loved getting lost in a good fairy tale. Of course, that led to my obsession with finding my own dashing hero. Unfortunately, my social circle had been filled with cads more interested in lifting a girl's skirts than sweeping her off her feet.

Tadhg peered at me from beneath impossibly dark lashes. "I enjoy reading as well."

Damn it all—the confession made my stomach flutter.

We had one thing in common. So what? There were a lot of people in this world who liked to read.

"I used to enjoy riding," I told him. Growing up, Aveen and I had visited Padraig at the stables nearly every day. He always had horses saddled for us and waiting. We would race along the seashore, salty water spraying against our faces from the crashing waves. That was freedom. That was joy.

That was gone.

"So do I," Tadhg said with a wink before meandering toward a cluster of stalls selling fruit and veg.

The fluttering was getting out of control. "You know I meant horses."

His nose wrinkled and he made a face. "Too dangerous and not nearly as fun."

What was I doing? I shouldn't be engaging in such shameless banter with him. We had twelve days left. *Twelve.*

Then he would go his way and I would go mine and all would be right in the world because my sister would be back.

Someone like Tadhg didn't fit into my life.

Not that I wanted him to.

Talk about disasters.

Tadhg picked up a ripe red apple from a fruit stall and took a crunching bite. His tongue caught the juice spilling onto his lips.

"You didn't pay for that," I hissed, catching his sleeve and searching for the cart owner. Thankfully, the elderly gentleman was busy helping a woman load a bunch of carrots and potatoes into a basket.

"You really do think the worst of me, don't you?" Tadhg nodded to a copper coin on the plank beside the apples.

A coin he hadn't left with his hand.

"Have you lost your mind?" I tugged him closer so that my voice wouldn't carry. "You can't do that here. Someone may see you." Didn't he know how things worked on this island? The only thing worse than possessing magic was practicing it. If he was caught using his magic, he could be executed. And where would that leave me?

Tadhg rolled his eyes and took another bite. "How do you know it wasn't a simple sleight of hand? You were too busy looking at this"—he tossed the apple into the air—"to notice what was happening over here." There were now two coins on the plank, and a second apple had appeared in his hand.

He gave it to me.

Tadhg bit into his apple once more before offering the same challenging look he had when the wheel had disappeared. This had to be more than a parlor trick. He had used magic. It was bad enough being seen strolling through the market with him. But to be associated with magic? My reputation was already shot, but I didn't want to end up locked in a cell.

I twisted away in time to see a little boy in short pants and braces barrelling toward us, his head turned to look over his shoulder. Before I could shout a warning, the boy bounced off Tadhg's legs and landed on the ground.

Darkness flashed in Tadhg's eyes.

A bolt of lightning shot through my veins. Creatures had killed for less.

"Don't hurt him!" I grabbed Tadhg's arm and his muscles went taut beneath my fingers. "It was an accident."

Tadhg jerked free and knelt in the dirt.

The boy's wide eyes darted to me.

"When you're being chased, always keep your eyes forward," Tadhg said in a serious tone. "Checking what's behind you will only slow you down." He ruffled the boy's sand-colored hair and then stood and offered the boy a hand. The boy hesitated before accepting.

"My apologies, sir," a gray-haired woman wheezed, pink-cheeked and winded. She yanked the boy back by the collar. "This one has less manners than sense."

Tadhg pulled an apple from the cart and handed it to the boy. "I've always believed manners were overrated."

Three coins.

Tadhg smiled at them both. His eyes crinkled at the corners, making him look young and impish.

The woman's lined face paled and she shoved the boy behind her skirts. "We want nothing from yer sort," she spat, ripping the apple from the boy's hands and shoving it back at Tadhg.

Yer sort . . .

She must have noticed his ears.

I could understand her wariness, but Tadhg hadn't done anything wrong.

The boy peeked around the woman's skirts. Tadhg winked and patted his own pocket. Sure enough, there was an apple-sized bulge in the boy's pocket. He grinned, revealing a missing front tooth.

"Beware the creatures infesting this land—demons come to steal your children and feast on your souls!" A stooped man in bloodred robes climbed onto a set of stone stairs in front of the cathedral.

All traces of humor on Tadhg's face vanished. The woman ushered the boy away, against the crowd swelling toward the steps.

I turned the apple over in my hand.

Tadhg hadn't made any attempts to feast on my soul. And instead of kidnapping or killing that boy, he had given him advice.

"We've been charged by our Sovereign to eradicate the blight of magic plaguing this island," the crier bellowed to the growing crowd forming around him. "The creatures are not to be trusted. None of us are safe until they are wiped from Airren altogether!"

Don't trust the creatures.

It was a lesson we humans had been taught since birth.

But wiping them from the island?

That sounded wrong.

I dared another glance at Tadhg.

High cheekbones beneath tanned skin. Strong jaw flexing in irritation. Perfect lips made for sinful things.

I had kissed my fair share of boys—a consequence of growing up pretending to be a fairy tale princess. Most of them hadn't been worth remembering.

If Tadhg kissed me—

Don't trust the creatures.

I shoved the apple into my cloak pocket.

This was how they worked, burrowing into your head until you couldn't get rid of them.

I needed to be more vigilant.

"If you see one, be wary. If it tries to trick you into giving it refuge, send it away," the crier shouted, red-faced with passion. "If it tries to harm you . . . end its miserable life."

Murmurs from the crowd lifted in agreement.

"And you think *we're* the monsters," Tadhg muttered under his breath before turning on his heel and stalking toward the carriage.

Of course they were the monsters . . . weren't they?

8

PADRAIG GAVE ME A WORRIED LOOK FROM HIS BENCH BEHIND THE horses when I dropped off his rolls. "Is everything all right, milady? Yer man seems in an awful temper."

"It's nothing you need to concern yourself with." Yesterday, climbing into a carriage with an angry creature would've sounded like suicide. Today, I found myself drawn toward the vehicle, like I couldn't have stayed away if I tried.

Inside, I found Tadhg seated on the trunk, his head in his hands.

"My people were here centuries before you humans," he said quietly, raking his fingers through his hair, "and they'll be around long after fools like that crier turn to dust."

I eased onto the bench and smoothed a hand down my wrinkled skirts. "You cannot blame us for being fearful." The creatures wielded magic and hid in the shadows, waiting to pounce. Our fear kept us vigilant. Our fear kept us safe.

"Is that why you have such a problem with me?" His voice softened, and he sagged against the carriage wall. "Because you're afraid?"

"I'm not—" The lie left my head throbbing and tongue swelling. *Infernal bloody curse.* One lie. That's all I wanted.

He raised his eyebrows.

"All right. Part of me *is* afraid." I blew out a frustrated breath, instantly feeling better.

"Why? What have I done that's so terrifying?" he asked, shaking his head. "Yes, I took the carriage wheel, but that was because you insisted on traveling to a town crawling with mercenaries and bounty hunters, and I didn't fancy my head on a feckin' pike at sundown."

Padraig whistled and cracked the whip. The carriage lurched forward, and I braced myself against the drapes. Swearing, Tadhg gripped the handles on the trunk when his head slammed against the wall.

How was I to know the town wasn't welcoming toward creatures? "You could have explained instead of putting all of us in danger. The monsters—"

"Don't call us—" He dragged his fingers through his hair. "*Monsters*. Don't call us that."

"I'm sorry. I didn't mean to offend you." This truce—whatever it was—was proving difficult. "What should I call you?"

For some reason, my question made him chuckle. "You could always try calling us by our names. We have those, you know." His teeth scraped over his bottom lip, drawing my attention to his mouth. What was it about his lips that made my own mouth go dry?

"But collectively, I suppose you could refer to us as the Danú," he finished.

"The Danú?"

His brow furrowed. "The Tuatha Dé Danaan? Tuath Dé? Tribe of Danú?"

I shook my head. "I'm sorry. I don't know what any of those mean."

"What nonsense are they teaching you humans these days?" he muttered, resting his elbows on his knees and leaning toward me.

"You heard the crier. You creatures—you *Danú*—consume souls."

"*Souls*? Unless your soul is made of shortbread"—he flicked his wrist, conjuring a basket of biscuits from thin air—"we're not likely to consume it."

Bloody hell.

How did he do that? Could he summon anything he wanted? The heavenly aroma of vanilla wafting from the buttery golden treats made my stomach rumble. "Even if you don't consume souls, you could still kill us." With me dead, he could take my silver without bringing me to Tearmann. Come to think of it, why hadn't he done that already?

"That argument makes no sense. Technically, anyone can kill anyone. The little lad from the market could kill you if you gave him the right weapon."

"Yes, but you're all evil and you hate humans." And since they possessed magic, they'd be nearly impossible to stop.

Tadhg blinked at me. Slowly, he raised the shortbread biscuit and took a bite. Crumbs tumbled down his waistcoat, landing in his lap.

I shifted under the intensity of his stare, wishing he would find something else to look at. "Why are you staring at me like that?"

The shortbread crunched between his teeth when he took another bite. The muscles in his jaw flexed as he chewed.

"Stop *looking* at me."

Shaking his head, he brushed the crumbs from his lap. "I'm waiting for you to realize how ridiculous you sounded just then."

What was he on about? He'd asked what we'd been taught, and I'd answered.

"How can anyone with even an ounce of intelligence make such a blanket statement about an entire group of people? Humans murdered my father and my mother. Humans stole my family's land. Humans have taken more from us than you could ever imagine, and yet I am *still* willing to give you the benefit of the doubt. Why wouldn't you be willing to do the same for us?"

Humans had done all of those terrible things to him? And yet he was still sitting in this carriage.

Tadhg was right. That naïve statement sounded dreadfully ignorant. He was only the second Danú I had met, and he wasn't anything like I'd thought he'd be. I'd been taught that magic was evil and that those who possessed it were to be feared. But I didn't know these people. How could I judge them based on the murderous Gancanagh and vile Fiadh?

How could I assume all of them truly hated us as much as we were taught to hate them?

Tadhg stuffed the rest of the biscuit into his mouth. The carriage bucked forward, rattling the windows and jarring my teeth.

"It's like Padraig is aiming for the feckin' things," Tadhg grumbled, catching the basket of shortbread before it clattered to the floor.

"Aiming for what things?"

"Hmmm?" He glanced at me, startled. "Oh, nothing. It's just the rivets dig into my ass every time we hit a bump." Wincing, he shifted his weight on the trunk.

Desperate to make up for the terrible things I'd said and the horrible way I had been treating him, I offered Tadgh a smile and suggested he magic-up a pillow.

"One cannot simply 'magic-up' items," he said with a wave of his hand.

"Says the man with the basket of magical biscuits." If I had such magic, I'd fill this whole carriage with pillows and sleep the entire way to Tearmann.

He chewed on his lip as he stared inside basket. "I *shifted* the biscuits from someplace else. A sleight of hand—without my hands."

When my stomach let out a low growl, Tadhg tilted the basket toward me.

If it hadn't been enchanted, I would've eaten the whole lot.

My stomach howled again even as I turned it down. "Then why don't you *shift* a pillow to help with the trunk?"

"If I am comfortable, I will sleep," he said through a heavy exhale, brushing crumbs onto the floor. "And if you murder me in my sleep, then I won't be very happy, now will I?"

Tadhg thought I was going to murder him? That was ludicrous. I wouldn't murder anyone—

What was I thinking?

The reason we had met was because I needed to kill the Gancanagh. How did he know this wasn't a common occurrence? That I wasn't like the humans who had killed his parents?

"You've been sleeping all week, and I have yet to murder you," I pointed out.

His eyebrows flicked up beneath his hair. "Have I?"

Tadhg's breathing had been even and steady. His eyes closed for hours. He had certainly *looked* like he'd been sleeping.

The corner of his lips lifted a fraction and my stomach fluttered.

"Are you telling me that you've only been *pretending* to sleep?"

He shrugged. "It was better than engaging in conversation with you." The carriage jolted, sending us both careening into the wall. "*Dammit.* I've half a mind to take the wheel again just to give my arse a break."

If he did that, maybe I would kill him. "*Or* we could share the bench."

He frowned at the empty space beside me. "You've made it abundantly clear that you do not want me near you."

Was he saying that he stayed on the trunk for my sake? That didn't make any sense.

He retrieved his balled-up overcoat from where it had fallen and stuffed it under him.

Don't trust the creatures.

The warning rolled through my mind as if the crier had shouted it in my ear.

I was already in the carriage with Tadhg. What did it matter if he was on the trunk or the bench? "Don't be daft. There's more than enough room for the both of us." I scooted toward the window as a peace offering.

Instead of changing seats, Tadhg pulled out his flask and drained whatever was inside. His eyes met mine, and he said without a drop of humor, "Do you promise not to murder me?"

"I promise not to murder you *today*."

He gave a startled laugh. "Why, Maiden Death. Was that a *joke*?"

I bit my lip to keep from smiling. "Perhaps."

He returned the smile, and for a brief moment, I felt lighter, almost as if everything was as it should be.

Except it wasn't.

Aveen was still gone.

What right did I have to joke and laugh and smile? What right did I have to experience even a fleeting moment of happiness when my sister may never do any of those things again?

Tadhg stood but had to hunch so he didn't knock his head against the low ceiling. A whip cracked. I caught the drapes to steady myself for the inevitable jolt.

Tadhg's knee slammed against the bench and his shoulder banged the window. "I hate these damned boxes. Fancy feckin' cages on wheels is what they are." He collapsed beside me, rubbing his sore leg. Muscles flexed in his strong thigh where it pressed against mine, solid and warm.

I tore my gaze away and focused on counting the rivets in the trunk.

One. Two. Three—

If I shifted a fraction, our shoulders would touch.

Four. Five. Six—

His shirt smelled like it had been dried by the wind.

Dammit.

Seven. Eight. Nine—

It was no use. My mind kept drifting to him and the way the light played on his dark hair as he stared out the window. The slight pulse of his jaw as the muscles flexed beneath the layer of dark stubble.

I scrubbed a hand down my face, gritty from dried sweat. *Me.* I needed to focus on me.

My boots were in desperate need of a polish. The hems of my cloak and dress were caked in muck from the market, and my head was beginning to itch.

Did I smell as terrible as I looked?

What I wouldn't give for a bath.

"I'm keeping my magic to myself." Tadhg shoved himself further into the curtains.

Magic? What was he on about? "I didn't say anything."

"You didn't have to. I can tell from the look on your face that you find my scent unpleasant. Most women find it irresistible."

The way he said it was so matter-of-fact, the look on his face so bewildered, that I didn't respond with a snide remark. "I find my own scent unpleasant," I confessed, waving a dismissive hand. "You've had a bath, and I desperately need one." What I wouldn't give for a tub filled with steaming water, surrounded by flickering candles.

Tadhg angled his head toward my hair and inhaled. "You smell like sunshine and lavender."

"Liar." I smelled like sweat and muck and—Was that manure on my heel? Lovely.

He gave me a sidelong look. "I cannot lie."

I laughed.

Tadhg's expression didn't change.

"You expect me to believe a witch cursed you as well?" That wasn't happening. It would be too much of a coincidence. Too convenient. A ploy to make me trust him.

His chuckle sounded forced. "I don't expect you to believe anything I say."

I sat back and looked at him—*really* looked. If I didn't know better, I would have sworn sincerity touched the corners of his unnerving eyes as he returned my gaze.

"How do I know you're not lying?" I asked.

Tadhg's shoulders lifted in a shrug. "You don't."

Don't trust the creatures.

If he was lying, then nothing had changed. But if he was telling the truth and he was bound by his promises, I'd be a fool not to secure a vow of my own. "Do you swear you won't harm me or Padraig with your magic?"

The slight wrinkles at the corners of his eyes deepened. "I swear not to harm you *today*."

Touché.

A reluctant smile tugged at my lips. "Let's say I believe you. You can't lie. Why were you in the Green Serpent the night we met?"

With his shoulder propped against the window, Tadhg crossed his arms over his chest. This close, I could see a number of small silver scars marring the tanned skin at his wrist. "Someone I know bet that I wouldn't last an hour in the pub. I proved him wrong."

"What did you win?"

He withdrew the gold cufflink.

He'd bet his safety for a bloody cufflink?

Who was Tadhg, really? And why was he here? If he could shift biscuits, then he could presumably shift coins. Which meant he didn't need my silver. There had to be some other reason he had agreed to bring me to Tearmann.

"Why are you really helping me?"

Almond-scented air consumed my senses when he leaned forward to whisper against the shell of my ear, "Because you have something I want."

"What's that?" I breathed.

Tadhg traced a finger down my cheek, leaving my skin tingling when his finger looped beneath the chain and slid it free.

His eyes blazed with fierce need, but he wasn't looking at me. His full lips twisted into a derisive smile as he touched the emerald. "I want the ring."

The forest reflected in the lake turned the still water the same shade of dark green as the leaves fluttering on the trees. After traveling for three hours, I had been more than ready to escape the tension inside the carriage and stretch my legs.

Tadhg had refused to tell me why he wanted the ring or why he didn't just steal it from my neck. It wouldn't be that difficult. If he pulled hard enough, the chain would easily break. But Tadhg seemed content to keep his secrets, another reminder that he couldn't be trusted. Our conversation had waned, and I had spent the rest of the time trying not to be so aware of him.

The sun peeped through a break in the rolling clouds. I shoved my sleeves to my elbows and lifted my face to catch a few elusive rays. My cloak, purse, and dagger were safe in the carriage with Padraig. For a moment, I pretended it was just me, the sunshine, and the softly lapping water.

And then Tadhg coughed and ruined the illusion.

Every piece of the puzzle that was Tadhg left me more confused. The first few days, he had been irritable and downright rude, intent on sabotaging me at every turn. But since I'd offered him that room last night, he'd been almost congenial—until I started asking about the ring.

I dipped my fingertips beneath the lake's surface, sending ripples chasing one another away from the shore. The water was cold and clear, unlike my murky thoughts.

Why was the ring so important?

Wiping the drops on my cloak, I hugged my knees to my chest and studied the far bank.

I shouldn't be hurt that he'd refused to confide in me. We weren't enemies per se, but we weren't friends either. We were two people stuck together, trying to survive until we got what we wanted. And all Tadhg wanted was the ring.

To forget that would only lead to disaster.

Tadhg lounged in the soggy grass, legs propped on a boulder, lining breadcrumbs on his shins. "I wouldn't sit so close to the water if I were you," he said, breaking off a hunk of bread left over from lunch and scattering crumbs on his stomach.

"Oh, you're talking to me now, are you?"

"I was never *not* talking to you."

"Then tell me about the ring."

He went back to covering himself in crumbs.

"*I wouldn't sit so close to the water if I were you,*" I muttered. He thought he could order me around? The sooner he got that notion out of his head, the better. I removed my boots and stockings and crossed the pebbled shore to let the frigid water soothe the blisters on my feet.

"Is there something wrong with your hearing?" Tadhg clipped.

I snagged a pebble and launched it at his insufferable head. He was lucky I had terrible aim.

A pudgy black and white bird flitted from the briars and settled on his knee. Its tail feathers twitched as it picked up a crumb with its tiny black beak. A second bird, a red-breasted robin, landed on his other knee.

"My record is twenty-one," Tadhg whispered.

"I don't care." I lifted my skirts to keep them from getting soaked as I waded to my calves. The slick stones made it difficult to stay upright as I continued to my knees. Closing my eyes, I imagined I was going for a swim, letting the water support my weight as I glided through the lake, allowing it to wash away the sweat and grime and tension.

Tadhg's annoying voice cut through my fantasy. I ignored him. We would be leaving soon and there was no telling when I would get another opportunity to breathe and enjoy the peace and quiet.

Water splashed against my legs, and my eyes burst open.

In front of me stood a white horse, neck-deep in the lake. The beast shook its massive head, spraying my face and chest with droplets. The magnificent animal probably belonged to a wealthy lord living nearby. When I reached for its tarnished silver bridle, the horse backed into deeper water.

"*Shhhh*. I'm not going to hurt you." I dropped my skirt and followed it one step. Two. Three. I caught the dangling leather strap.

The horse whinnied. Its loose lips pulled back, revealing rows of razor-sharp silver teeth dripping with slimy green algae.

I screamed. Whirled. Bolted for the shore.

Birds scattered when Tadhg shot to his feet. He seemed miles away. How was that possible? I'd only taken a few steps.

The still lake came to life, churning into a whirlpool, sucking me beneath white-capped waves.

Water muted my thrashing. I spun out of control, legs and arms flailing. Murky liquid stung my eyes. The horse looked like it was running beneath the waves as it swam with powerful strides. Silver teeth flashed, seized my skirts, and jerked me toward the dark depths.

Which way was up?

Where was the shore?

Everything was dark and cold and heavy, and I kicked and flailed but I was no match for the sheer power of the white horse flying to the depths. My dress was an iron net, weighing me down down down.

Panic seized my chest in its vice like grip. My lungs burned in agony. The more I told myself not to breathe, the more I needed to breathe, and *oh god*, I was going to die in this lake, and my sister, my poor sister. No one would bring Aveen back. I was her only hope.

Something wrapped around my waist.

An arm.

Pain jolted the top of my spine. My dress and stay loosened; the swirling vortex swallowed the sliced fabric.

I could feel myself drifting. Fading gray light grew brighter and brighter until my head broke free from the water. I gasped, but there wasn't enough air to rid my lungs of the fire.

My savior hefted me to the shore.

It wasn't Padraig.

Tadhg swiped sticky hair from my cheeks, my forehead. Black kohl dripped into bloodshot eyes.

His palm flattened against my chest. "Deep breaths. That's it. In, in, in and out, out, out." Water tumbled down his face, falling onto mine. "Do it again."

I focused on expanding and contracting my lungs with his count of three. He had risked his life for me. I should be grateful. I *was* grateful. But part of me wondered if I deserved to be eaten by an underwater monster. At least then I'd be with Aveen.

Tadhg's shirt clung to his muscular chest, rising and falling in exaggerated movements as he dragged air into his lungs. His pointed ears refused to remain hidden.

He was too near and not near enough, kneeling between my thighs. A thin, sheer shift was the only barrier between his hand and my skin. Warmth collected in my belly. The thing living inside of me writhed, begging to be unleashed.

"Next time I tell you to avoid the water," Tadhg said, his voice huskier than I'd ever heard it, "I suggest you listen."

"I will." It was clear that I knew nothing of his world. There were dangers on this island that I'd never expected. Monsters that attacked in broad daylight. Nowhere was safe.

Tadhg nodded, then stiffened.

"Unhand my lady or I'll send ye straight to hell, ye rutting bastard," Padraig growled.

Where had he come from? Last I'd seen him, he'd been napping on the bench atop the carriage.

Tadhg removed his hand from my chest, taking his heat with him.

Padraig shifted. An emerald glowed in the hilt of the dagger pressed against Tadhg's ribs. "Stand up. *Now*."

Tadhg stumbled to his feet, hands raised in the air. "I understand how this looks, but I didn't hurt her. I swear." Wide green eyes begged for assistance, pleading silently.

"Is that true, milady?" Padraig adjusted his hold on the dagger. Tadhg winced and cursed.

"It's t-true," I forced through trembling lips. "He s-saved m-me from a . . . a . . ." What the hell had that thing been? A lake demon of some kind?

"Kelpie," Tadhg finished.

Padraig's white eyebrows came together. "Kelpie? I thought those cursed beasts were extinct." He removed the dagger and stepped back.

Tadhg's hands slowly lowered. "That's what they want you to think."

A blue heron flew across the lake's mirrored surface, landing in some reeds along the rocky shore. The scenery was so serene, so peaceful. How was anyone to know a ravenous beast lurked beneath the water?

"I suppose I owe ye an apology." Although Padraig still appeared wary, he held out a weathered hand.

Tadhg stared at it like he hadn't a clue what to do. Then he clasped Padraig's hand in his. "I . . . understand how it must've looked." He darted a glance at me. "And I appreciate that you didn't stab first and ask questions later."

"And I appreciate you saving Lady Keelynn."

Tadhg had risked his life for me.

Why had he bothered?

He wants the ring.

That was all. If the kelpie had eaten me, the ring would've been swallowed by the lake. Lost forever to the depths. Tadhg didn't care whether I lived or died.

All he wanted was the ring.

9

PEOPLE SANG IN THE STREETS AND HUNG OUT WINDOWS WITH drinks in their hands. Barrels had been set up outside the pubs to be used as extra tables for patrons spilling from within. Colorful banners zigzagged from one side of the street to the other, fluttering in the soft breeze.

The woman at the inn said we could have the two remaining rooms and that they'd be ready in another hour or two. Tadhg and Padraig were still in the stables when I returned. After the incident at the lake, I had changed into a dry dress and spent the next three hours trying to process what had happened.

If only I had listened when Tadhg said to avoid the water. The next time he told me something was dangerous, I would heed his warning.

The sight of Tadhg leaning against the wooden slatted wall, grinning, took me by surprise. He looked so carefree and was still by far the most handsome man I had ever encountered.

He muttered something low to Padraig that sent my coachman bowing over the horse trough in a fit of wheezing laughter.

"What's so funny?" I asked, closing the gap between us.

Padraig jerked upright and wiped a hand over his face.

"Nothing, milady." His words strained with pent up laughter.

I offered Tadhg a genuine smile, the one reserved for people I actually liked. Tadhg pushed away from the wall and stepped toward me. "All I said was that the horse"—he nodded toward a hulking black stallion tied behind him—"and I both have impressive—"

"I'm afraid Master Tadhg's humor isn't suited to a high-born lady's ears," Padraig blurted, his color rising beneath his whiskers.

Tadhg gestured beneath the horse, then held his hands in front of him and pretended to measure something. Heat crept from my neck to my ears when my gaze inadvertently dropped to Tadhg's breeches.

"The stall at the end's empty if you'd like a closer look," he drawled, reaching for the buckle on his belt.

My racing pulse left sweat collecting at the back of my neck. I could've ignored the challenge in his eyes but didn't want to. "Doesn't seem impressive enough to warrant my attention."

"Milady!" Padraig's gaping stare bounced between us.

Tadhg's grin turned wicked, leaving my knees trembling beneath my skirts. "You'd be surprised."

"Master Tadhg!" Padraig grabbed him by the collar and hauled him so that Tadhg was no longer facing me. "Ye will remember to whom ye are speaking and stop this sort of talk immediately."

Tadhg offered a conspiratorial wink over his shoulder.

Creature.

Dangerous.

Padraig let him go and stepped between us. "Did ye organize lodging fer tonight, milady?"

Lodging?

"Um . . . Oh, yes! I did." I explained about the delay, and we all agreed it would be best to find some sustenance before retiring for the night. It would have been a brilliant plan, except every pub and inn we tried was busier than the one before it.

"This one's full as well," Padraig said when he emerged from a blue-shuttered pub. "And that place doesn't look much better." He pointed a gnarled finger toward a red-and-white cottage at the end of the street with a line of patrons waiting to get inside.

"I know a place that shouldn't be crowded at this hour," Tadhg said from a few steps behind.

"Is it far?" I was so hungry I would've been willing to eat scraps.

"Not very. Come on." His arm brushed against mine when he passed.

Padraig kept glancing my way as Tadhg brought us to a narrow back alley behind one of the pubs. The cheers and laughter from the street became nothing more than a muffled buzz.

Tadhg told us to wait by a bunch of crates filled with empty green bottles. He strode to a green door and gave three swift knocks. A moment later, a plump woman with curly gray hair pinned to the top of her head answered. Her cheeks flushed when she saw Tadhg, and she swiped a hand down her grease-smeared apron.

She and Tadhg exchanged a few words before he handed her something and motioned for us to follow him.

With Padraig at my side, I wasn't nervous. And if I was being honest, I was glad Tadgh was there as well.

The scent of magic was as faint as the light filtering through the frosted lattice windows.

"We've only a bit of venison and some day-old vegetable soup left, I'm afraid," the woman said in a thick northern lilt. Her eyes landed on me and narrowed.

I offered a tentative smile. "Whatever you have would be wonderful. Thank you."

Her lips flattened. She nodded and suddenly disappeared.

"Did she just—" My eyes must be playing tricks. I rubbed them, but she was still gone.

"Evanesce?" Tadhg's head tilted as he stepped into the space where she had been a second ago.

Evanesce.

The woman wasn't human.

"Maeve's grandmother was a witch. Or was it great-grand-mother?" he muttered to himself, rubbing the back of his neck. "I can never keep it straight."

A *witch*?

Maeve didn't seem anything like Fiadh.

"Can"—I had to remind myself to breathe when his piercing eyes met mine—"can *you* do that?"

"I can do all sorts of things that would impress you," he purred, his smile cocky and confident.

My stomach fluttered.

Don't trust the creatures, that annoying voice whispered.

It was sage advice but Tadhg had proven himself trustworthy thus far.

Padraig's hand settled on my elbow. "Let's have a seat, shall we?" He escorted me to one of the benches at an empty trestle table.

Tadhg rolled up his sleeves, revealing forearms corded with muscles, and all I could think about was the way those strong arms had felt around me when he pulled me from the lake.

"What would you like to drink, *Lady* Keelynn?" There was no doubt in my mind that Tadhg had used my given name for Padraig's benefit. "A small glass of wine? A dram of something equally ladylike?"

He said it like a challenge. Like he didn't think I could handle my alcohol. I'd been handling my alcohol since I was thirteen years old.

"I'll have whatever you're having."

He chuckled and rubbed his hands together like he was plotting my demise. "A pint of stout it is. Padraig?"

Padraig only nodded, staring at me as though I had sprouted horns.

Tadhg withdrew three large glasses from beneath the bar, set one under the tap, and pulled the black lever. A few minutes later, he returned with three pints of black liquid topped with spongy white foam.

I sniffed tentatively. It didn't smell terrible. It didn't taste terrible either. Bitter with a hint of something sweet. Chocolate, perhaps? What I liked most was that the stout's heaviness soothed my ravenous stomach.

Maeve didn't return with our dinner until Tadhg and Padraig had started on their second pints. She set down three clay bowls of yellowish soup and a single plate of venison with three forks between. We all thanked her, and she told Tadhg to help himself to anything we needed so long as no one else was there.

With a flick of Tadhg's wrist, a basket of fresh bread rolls and a tray of pear tartlets appeared. Sugar glistened from the glaze, and I could almost feel the granules crunching between my teeth.

They were clearly enchanted.

Padraig reached for a roll. I knocked it out of his hand. "It could kill you," I reminded him under my breath.

Padraig's expression fell.

"Is our food not good enough for your refined human palate, *Lady* Keelynn?" Tadhg grabbed one of the rolls and shoved it into his mouth.

"No, no. It's nothing like that." I glanced at Padraig for assistance. He kept his gaze on the rolls. How did I say this without offending Tadhg and breaking the tentative balance between us?

"Humans cannot ingest enchanted food," I explained.

"Enchanted? *This?*" He gestured to the rolls and tartlets. I nodded. "My dear, ignorant human. There is no such thing as enchanted food. Poisoned, yes. But not enchanted."

Could it be true? My hand itched to reach for a tartlet.

"And before you ask," Tadhg said, nudging the tray toward me, "no, I did not poison it." He snagged a tartlet and popped it into his mouth. "See? Perfectly safe."

Padraig picked one up and took a small bite.

I took one. Sniffed. *Ripe pear and sugared pastry.* Not a hint of magic.

Death by dessert seemed a good way to die.

Oh. Oh my.

I closed my eyes to erase everything but the rich flavors bursting on my tongue. A moan escaped as I chewed. *If I died right now, I would die happy.*

I opened my eyes and found Tadhg staring, the tartlet in his hand frozen halfway to his gaping mouth. Padraig kicked him beneath the table, and Tadhg's mouth snapped shut.

I felt my face flush and quickly turned my attention to dinner. Warm, savory vegetable soup. Venison seasoned with cloves, so tender, it melted on my tongue. Every bite was better than the one before it.

Tadhg picked at the venison and slurped a few spoonfuls of soup. Then he polished off three more tartlets.

"Where did you steal—I mean, *shift* these from?" I asked, reaching for the final pastry.

He chewed thoughtfully, avoiding looking me directly in the eye. Eventually, he said, "They came from my own kitchen."

His cook must have been some sort of wizard. My stay felt so tight, the boning cut into my ribs with each inhale. "Why was I taught that your food would kill me?"

Tadhg flicked his wrist, sending the dishes back to wherever they belonged. "Probably because we don't want you humans eating all of our provisions," he said with a smirk, lifting his drink as if in toast.

Two pints led to three. Three led to four.

Knowing better than to try and keep up with the men, I sipped slowly, savoring the way the stout warmed me from the inside out.

A pooka came in at some point, nodded to us, and sat at the end of the table closest to the door. It had the ears of a rabbit, face of a wolf, and talons of a hawk, like it wasn't sure which animal to be, so it decided to be all of them.

It was so fascinating. How did it shift? Did it hurt? Could it only be an animal, or could it look like a human as well? Sharp yellow eyes landed on me. Panic seized my chest. The pooka nodded and went back to his pint. He didn't seem to care that Padraig and I were here. Did he feel the same way about humans as Tadhg?

Shortly after, a woman arrived. She would have been beautiful, with straight, strawberry-blond hair dusting her shoulders, but for her bulging blue eyes and elongated pupils. When she blinked, her lashless eyelids weren't in sync. Although she sidled up next to the pooka, she kept her unnerving eyes on Tadhg.

He saluted her with his drink.

Padraig didn't seem the least bit fazed by any of it, like he was used to consorting with creatures. On his fifth pint, with his eyes glazed, he removed his pipe to smile at Maeve. He had been trying to convince her to play cards with him since she had brought the last round.

Padraig sighed wistfully at Maeve as she cleared and cleaned tables. "Did you know my first love was a faerie?"

He'd loved a *faerie*? But Padraig's wife had been a human.

"What was her name?" Tadhg set his pint on the table and licked the foam from his lips.

His lips . . .

They were almost *too* perfect.

Like they'd be *too* soft.

Padraig's pipe tapped against the table, breaking whatever spell had come over me. I inhaled a tentative breath but smelled no magic. My fingers tightened on my pint, and I took a deep drink.

"She was called Binne."

Tadhg's smile was small and secretive. "Melodious Binne."

"Voice of an angel." Padraig blinked slowly, his face serene. "Legs for days."

Tadhg snorted but nodded in agreement. It made me wonder how well he knew this *Binne* person.

"Aren't faeries really small?" I asked, catching my frowning reflection in my glass.

"Not always," Tadhg said in a faintly amused tone. "I'm half-fae and no one's ever called me small."

Half-fae. That explained the ears and the magic.

I considered him as I drew a line in the condensation on my glass. So confident. So cocky. "I'm sure other faeries find you quite adequate."

Stout sprayed across the table. "*Milady!*" Padraig scrubbed the drips from his chin with his shirtsleeve.

Those perfect lips slowly lifted. "Oh, I like drunk Keelynn."

"Whatever's in yer head, boy, get it out." Padraig caught Tadhg's arm across the table. "She's had it hard enough since that wretch—"

"Thank you, Padraig." I squeezed his wrinkled hand. Defending my honor was pointless. I was on a mission to kill someone; I had no honor left. Still, that didn't mean I wanted Tadhg to learn about my past.

"You'll hear no argument here." Tadhg lifted his hands in mock surrender. "Any man with eyes in his head can see she's far too good for me."

Nodding, Padraig patted my hand before excusing himself and limping toward the privy.

Tadhg stared at me from across the table, an unreadable expression on his face.

Stout and dinner sloshed in my stomach as I shifted on the bench. "Why are you looking at me like that?" Surely there was somewhere else he could direct those unnerving eyes.

"You've confounded me." Tadhg's lips pressed into a disapproving line. Such a shame. They weren't nearly as kissable when he did that.

"Don't do that with your mouth." Where was my pint? *Oh!* There. I picked it up and had a sip. Stout was my new favorite drink.

Tadhg rested his elbows on the table and leaned until his chest met the wood. "Don't do *what* with my mouth?"

"When you get annoyed, you do this." I did my best impression—which lasted all of three seconds before a fit of giggling took over. Tadhg's eyes widened. "And it's a shame because you have a lovely mouth." My fingertips brushed against his lips.

Not too soft. Just perfect.

"No, *you* have a lovely mouth." His thumb grazed my bottom lip. "Whereas I have a wicked mouth that does terribly wicked things."

Heat pooled in my stomach. *Lower.*

I didn't want to know.

No, I didn't.

Didn't.

Did.

"Like what?" I whispered.

Coins slapped against the table, and Tadhg held a hand toward me. "Come with me and I'll show you."

This was a terrible idea.

Why were my fingers lacing with his, letting his callused palms press against mine?

"Not so fast, boy." Padraig was there. Where had he come from? Why was he tugging my hand free? "I'll take her away. Ye can stay here."

Tadhg's smile tightened and his hands flexed at his sides.

"I don't mean to overstep, milady." Padraig linked our arms and led me unsteadily toward the door. "But believe me when I say that nothing good will come from . . . *associating* with someone like him."

Maeve appeared, a tray of empty glasses balanced against her stomach. "Leaving so soon? I was hoping ye'd stay a bit longer. We could have that *card* game," she purred with a flirtatious wink.

Padraig tensed. "I need to see my lady safely to the inn."

"Allow me to escort her." This time, Tadhg offered his arm.

"I don't think—"

"Ye should stay——"

"What are you——"

My head swam on a sea of stout as the three of them argued. Accusations flew between Padraig and Tadhg. Maeve tugged on Padraig's sleeve, pleading with him to stay.

I couldn't keep up with the insults and snide remarks and——

"Enough!"

Three pairs of eyes locked on me.

"I am an adult," I reminded them, bracing my hands on my hips. "I will make my own decisions." I turned to Padraig and smoothed a hand down his lined cheek. "Stay with Maeve." After all he had done for me, he deserved a night with someone he obviously fancied—even if she was a witch. "Tadhg will escort me to the inn, won't you Tadhg?"

He grinned at Padraig. "I will, of course."

Padraig looked murderous, but then Maeve put a hand on his elbow. He offered her a tight smile before catching Tadhg by the collar and pulling him close.

After a moment of whispering, Tadhg frowned and nodded. "You have my word."

Padraig wished me good night, took the tray from Maeve, and hobbled toward the bar. She gave him the most adoring smile before trailing after him.

The heat from Tadhg's body warmed my entire left side as he took my arm and pulled me close. Fresh, crisp air hit my over-warm cheeks when he threw open the door.

"What did Padraig say to you?" I asked, stepping into the night.

Glancing at me from over his shoulder, he grinned and said, "He made me swear not to bed you tonight."

10

THE REVELERS WERE STILL OUT IN FORCE ON THE STREETS, dancing and singing. Musicians lifted the audience into a pulse-racing reel.

But it wasn't the music that made my heart feel like it would burst from my chest. It was the half-fae whose thigh rubbed against my skirts with each step, whose arm felt strong and defined.

He made me swear not to bed you tonight.

Tonight.

What about tomorrow?

The thought flitted through my mind, unbidden. I halted next to one of three fiddle players to catch my breath. The man's eyes closed as he violently sawed the strings with his bow.

I was supposed to hate Tadhg.

I *did* hate him.

The fact that he had saved me and made me laugh after a few pints and was the most handsome being I had ever encountered didn't change what he was. I wouldn't have been taught to fear the Danú if there wasn't *some* truth to the danger.

Fiadh had been malice incarnate.

And the Gancanagh had murdered my sister.

But . . .

A grogoch had helped Padraig with the wheel.

The pooka in the pub had seemed polite enough.

Maeve had magic, but she'd been kind.

And Padraig had loved a faerie.

I peered through my lashes at Tadhg. He watched the musicians, tapping his foot to the beat of the hand drum. There was darkness in him. I had seen it swirling in his eyes. Forgetting that could only end in disaster.

"What do you suppose they're celebrating?" I asked, disconnecting my arm from his.

I needed mundane small talk.

I needed something else to focus on besides *him*.

"It's Lughnasa."

The name sounded vaguely familiar. "Isn't that a pagan holiday?" It certainly wasn't celebrated in my village. But the east coast of the island had always been more refined because of its proximity to Vellana. The west coast was known to be wild and lawless because of its border with Tearmann.

Dancers weaved in and out, around and around. An entrancing pattern as old as the dance itself.

"It was centuries ago," Tadhg said, both boots tapping. "Now it's more of an excuse for a party than anything religious. I imagine there would've been some competitive games earlier in the week, and from the looks of it"—he inclined his head toward a couple caught in a passionate embrace against a darkened doorway—"a handfasting or two as well."

Handfasting. An ancient ceremony where vows were exchanged over a couple's bound hands, signifying the start of a trial marriage lasting a year and a day.

A year and a day.

The same as a curse.

It couldn't be a coincidence.

Music swelled into the night. Sweat dripped from the fiddler's brow onto his gleaming instrument.

"I think all marriages should start as handfastings," I confessed.

"Really?" Tadhg stepped forward, blocking the musicians and dancers from view as he crossed his arms over his chest. His shirt gaped at the neck, revealing a swath of smooth, tanned skin beneath. "And why is that?"

"Because sometimes people make mistakes," I said, thinking of my own miserable marriage. "And it's unfair for them to have to pay for those mistakes for the rest of their lives."

Shadows flared across the sharp planes of his face. His eyes. His lips.

A melodious hurricane spun around us, but we were in the eye of the storm, a place of peace and stillness. A place where everything else faded away until it was only the two of us.

Danú and human.

A man and a woman.

"You truly believe that?" he asked quietly, reaching to tuck a strand of hair behind my ear. His tongue darted between his perfect lips. The soft pink skin glistened in the lamplight.

"I wouldn't have been able to say it if I didn't."

He blinked, then shook his head as if snapping out of a trance. "Right. Yes. Of course."

I glanced around the street to where the dancers clapped, sweat shimmering on their faces. The music was replaced by quiet laughter and the colorful banners softly flapping in the breeze as the musicians packed up their instruments.

"It's late," he said, lacing our hands together. "We should go."

Something had changed between us.

We'd come to an understanding of sorts.

Tadhg wouldn't harm me, and I wouldn't harm him. He was only here for the ring, and I was only here for Aveen.

But what about the days and hours between this moment and when we got what we wanted?

Tadhg held open the inn's door and ushered me inside.

Chairs had been stacked atop the tables that had been packed with patrons earlier. The fire was down to ash and embers.

A portly man sat in a rocking chair, his swollen leg raised on a stool. One look at the two of us left him cursing. "Don't try asking me for lodging." His chins wobbled as he spewed spittle at Tadhg. "I will not rent that *thing* a room."

"Lucky for me, we've already organized rooms," Tadhg drawled, straightening his waistcoat. "Give us the keys so we can be on our way."

The man jabbed his meaty finger at a handwritten sign behind his bald head.

Do not ask for credit as refusal often offends.

"I'm not asking for *credit*." Tadhg withdrew a purse from beneath his overcoat and gave it a jingling shake.

The innkeeper harrumphed and pushed a load of nailed flyers out of the way.

No Dogs. No Creatures.

The man looked past Tadhg as though he were invisible. "Ye can stay, milady, but *that*"—he jerked his head toward Tadhg —"can sleep in the stable with the other filthy animals."

Tadhg's hands flexed at his sides. I could smell the magic leaking out of him as he struggled to keep his temper at bay. Tadhg turned to me and offered a sardonic smile. "I will meet you back here at noon tomorrow."

It was no different than what he'd done most nights. But the idea of Tadhg being forced to stay somewhere else—perhaps even *with* someone else—because of what he was felt wrong.

This was wrong.

"Nonsense." I had booked two rooms, and I was going to get them.

Green eyes narrowed. "Leave it."

I could have left it. But today, Tadhg had helped me in his world, and I was determined to help him in mine. Unfortunately for humans everywhere, this bald-headed buffoon was one of us.

I skirted around Tadhg to the innkeeper. "I want my keys." There was a basket of them beside the rocking chair. All he had to do was stick his hand inside, drag out two, and hand them over.

The innkeeper scrubbed a hand down his jowls. "Did ye *pay* fer the rooms?"

The woman had been so busy, she'd said I could give her the money in the morning. "Not yet, but—"

"Then I'm afraid yer outta luck. I have no tolerance for monsters," he ground out, eyes narrowing as they swept down my dress, "or their *whores*. Get the hell out of here—*both* of you."

He thought I was a— "How *dare* you! I am a *lady*. You will not treat me as though I am some common—"

A hand clamped around my elbow, and Tadhg hauled me toward the door. I tried to wrench free, but he didn't let go until we were back on the street. The unmistakable sound of a lock falling into place scraped from the other side of the door.

"What were you thinking?" Tadhg growled, dragging on the ends of his hair and scowling at the stars. "You could've had a feckin' room."

"*Me?*" He thought this was *my* fault? "I was defending myself! Defending *you*."

"And I told you to let it be."

The wind picked up, twisting my skirts about my ankles, whisking my anger and indignation into the night.

"Where am I going to sleep?" *Oh god. Oh no.* I steadied myself against the side of the building to keep from collapsing. I had nowhere to go. With the festival going on, the other inns would be full. With the rest of the humans returned to their safe havens, the empty streets were fit for things searching for a midnight meal. Tadhg had said not all of the Danú wanted to kill humans, but that didn't mean there weren't a few of them who did.

That damn pressure was back. All encompassing. Overwhelming. And I couldn't breathe.

"Come with me." Tadhg held out his hand.

The moment I focused on his eyes, the pressure vanished. "Come with you where?"

His head tilted, sending a lock of hair falling over his forehead. My fingers itched to brush it away. "I'm going to get you a room."

His hand was warm when I took it. Instead of going toward the street, he brought me to the back of the inn, across from the paddock and stables to where light filtered through the curtains in the ground-floor windows.

"Wait here," he said, giving my fingers a squeeze.

"You're *leaving*?"

Did that shadow move? It did. It definitely did.

What was that scraping sound? Was it a branch or claws? Claws. Definitely claws.

"Look at me." His commanding tone drew me back to his glowing eyes. "I will be right back." Slowly, he pried my fingers free, one by one, then nudged me toward the inn's chimney and vanished.

I pressed myself into the cold stone and prayed for survival as I listened to the sounds of the night. Footsteps crunched from the direction of the road, growing louder, louder, *louder* and then fading. Something howled. The beast sounded far away, but that didn't mean it was the only beast lurking in the woods behind the village. There could be more. They could be coming for me.

I squeezed my eyes shut and focused on breathing. How could something I'd done my entire life feel so difficult?

"There's one free room."

My eyes flashed open.

Tadhg stood in the same spot he'd vanished from. "It's on the third floor," he said, indicating a small circular window at the top of the inn.

There was no way he could've known that unless . . . "You got inside?"

His brow furrowed. "Of course I did."

"Weren't the doors locked? Can you just go wherever you want? Like, nothing can stop you?" If that was the case, then I had never known a day of safety in my life. Was it just him or all the Danú? The kelpie? The witch?

"There are rules about breaching locked doors, but as the room was unoccupied and I didn't steal anything, I'm fairly certain they do not apply," he explained. "Besides, these are extenuating circumstances, wouldn't you agree?"

I could only nod as another realization came over me. Tadhg could evanesce. But what did that mean exactly? Could he go anywhere he wanted at any time?

"Where have you been staying?" I asked, my suspicions growing.

Tadhg shoved his hands into his pockets and shifted his weight from one foot to the other. The mysterious howling beast wailed in the distance, but he didn't so much as flinch at the haunting sound.

"What do you mean?" he asked.

"I mean, where have you been sleeping at night?"

A shrug. "Here and there."

"That's not an answer."

Tadhg grimaced and kicked a stone with his toe. It bounced off the building and landed in the grass. "Most nights, I just go home."

No wonder he had been so indignant about staying at an inn. Tadhg had been going home to his own bed. His own pillow. His own bloody house.

"And where is home?" I asked, glancing up at the grimy third-story window, my hopes of the room inside being clean dwindling by the second.

"I live in Tearmann."

Here I'd thought I was being kind by paying for his rooms. At least now I knew I didn't have to waste any more money on him. He must think me an empty-headed dolt. "Well, then, I would appreciate it if you would help me get inside my inn before you pop off home."

"Ah, come now, Maiden Death." He knocked his hip against mine and gave me a playful smile. "There's no need to go back to being so formal. I appreciate what you tried to do tonight, it just wasn't necessary."

"Well, I would've appreciated if you would've told me instead of letting me make a fool of myself." The innkeeper really had thought I was Tadhg's whore. And the woman last night . . .

If yer not usin' him—

"I thought . . . What I mean is . . . I *assumed* you knew what inviting someone like me to your inn meant." Chuckling, he shook his head. "Although now that I think of it, you did the same thing last night and paid for a separate room."

He'd honestly thought I was going to sleep with him?

What was I thinking? Of course he bloody did. He didn't need an inn. The only reason for him to stay in one was to—

My stomach tightened and heat flooded my lower belly.

"Do you want to go inside or stay out here?" Tadhg swept a hand toward the building.

"Since I don't want to sleep in the stable and I can't go home, I don't have much of a choice, now do I?" I inhaled a shaky breath, but when I tried to exhale my anger, all it did was leave me more unsettled. "What do I need to do?"

Should I close my eyes or leave them open? Closed or opened? Closed or opened?

Opened.

I wanted to see what happened when one evanesced.

Tadhg pointed toward the slanted roof over the conservatory. "You need to climb."

"Are you mad? You expect *me* to climb up *there*?" Sober, it'd be difficult. But after all that stout, I'd probably end up breaking my neck.

"I'll help you."

"Can't you just"—I waved my fingers in his face—"make me disappear?"

"If only," he said with a small smile. "Unfortunately, it's not that simple. Evanescing is essentially shifting from one place to another. It doesn't work well with live humans—too draining."

He did not just say *live* humans. How many dead humans had he needed to transport to learn there was a difference? I didn't ask because I did *not* want to know.

"At this stage, the best I could do is get you to the first set of windows." His teeth scraped across his bottom lip. "But then I may not have anything left to get us inside."

"What will happen if the innkeeper catches us?" Being locked in a jail cell was less appealing than the stable. Not that Tadhg would be the one getting caught since he could vanish at will.

Tadhg blew out a breath. "At this stage, I'd kill him to get some feckin' sleep."

At this stage, I'd probably let him.

Climb or stable? Climb or stable?

Climb.

"All right. I'm in." I bent to hitch up my skirts and tie them between my knees, telling myself this was no different than all those times I used to sneak out of my bedroom to meet Robert.

Tadhg laced his fingers together and held his clasped hands toward my boot. Once I'd braced my hands on his shoulders, he hoisted me like I weighed no more than a child. I caught the edge of the drain and hauled myself onto the conservatory's slate tiles.

Tadhg appeared at my side a split second later. "Two more to go."

With only walls and windows between us and our destination, we had to rethink our strategy.

Tadhg's head tilted as he considered. "If you can get onto my shoulders, you should be able to reach the window ledge. I can boost you from there."

We had already come this far. "Only if you promise not to drop me."

"I'll do my best."

I punched him in the arm. His indignant yelp was worth the pain in my hand.

"All right, all right," he chuckled. "I promise."

He stooped so I could wrap my hands around his neck. The last thing I wanted to think about was the way it felt to have my chest pressed against his back. And then it was *all* I could think about. His dark hair tickling my cheek smelled like the soft strands had trapped the crisp autumn wind.

"I always knew you wanted to climb on top of me," he muttered with a gruff laugh.

I may have dug my nails into his back as I adjusted my grip and jammed my knee into his ribs on my way to his shoulders. He cursed and groaned as I steadied myself against the wall and rose to standing. Even with Tadhg's hands clamped around my ankles steadying me, my fingers barely reached the gritty windowsill. I didn't have the grip to get any higher. I tried and tried, but it was no use. "I can't do it."

"Just pull yourself up."

"What do you think I've been trying to do?" I braced one boot against the wall for leverage. The movement loosened the knot between my legs. If only I could get a little higher. "I may need to stand on your head."

"Are you mad? I'm not letting you stand on my head."

My fingers began to cramp. If I didn't get up there soon I may as well give up.

Tadhg adjusted his stance. I glanced down and caught him looking up. "I swear, if you so much as try to peek up my skirts, I'm going to kill you."

The last boy to do that had ended up with a black eye, courtesy of my sister.

"I'm too busy to peek up your skirts," Tadhg shot back. "Now, if you'd like to lift them for me as a reward when we get inside, that's another matter entirely."

If I hadn't needed him to hold me up, I would've kicked him in the face. Channeling my indignation, I tightened my grip, planted one foot against the wall, and launched myself upward with all my strength. My arms wobbled, but I managed to get my torso onto the ledge. Tadhg was too far below to be of any help now.

I should have chosen the bloody stable.

Something moved on the other side of the dark glass. A startled scream caught in my throat until I noticed a familiar face grinning at me from inside the room.

Tadhg pressed a finger to his lips before unlatching and opening the window. He caught me beneath the arms and dragged me until I was able to get a knee onto the windowsill.

The dark room's occupant snored quietly as we crept across the creaky floor to the door.

The turning key made a loud *click*, and the snoring stopped.

A gruff voice muttered something from behind me. I held my breath as Tadhg opened the door.

Despite the hallway being darker than the bedroom, we managed to find the stairs, and crept *up, up, up* until we reached the top. Once we were safely inside, I collapsed against the wall. The room smelled musty, like it hadn't been aired in a while.

At this point, I didn't care if it was covered in cobwebs and dust.

This had been the longest day of my entire life and sleep couldn't come fast enough.

Tadhg went to the far side of a small bed, near the only window, and sank onto the edge of the mattress.

Panic clawed at my stomach when he kicked off his boots, pulled one of the pillows beneath his head, and closed his eyes. There was room for two people, but there was no way in hell *that* was happening.

"Tadhg?"

One eye opened.

"I'm *not* sleeping with you." Not now. Not ever.

"Is it because you don't want to or are you afraid you won't be able to control yourself with no one watching?"

"I don't wa—" The alcohol was affecting my speech. I did *not* want to sleep with Tadhg. "I don't w-wa—"

"I believe the *lie* you're trying to tell," he drawled, propping himself on his elbow, "is that you *don't* want to sleep with me." The springs whined when he bounced on the mattress. "I doubt anyone would hear us unless I can make you squeal louder than the bed."

"Tadhg!"

His deep chuckle reverberated off the low ceiling. "Don't get your knickers in a bunch," he mumbled, rolling off the bed. His silhouette sauntered toward me. "I'm bound by my oath to Padraig, remember? Your maidenly virtue is safe . . . " Cold lips grazed my cheek as he whispered, "For tonight."

What would those lips feel like moving lower?

Teasing. Tasting. Touching.

Forbidden. Wicked.

"What's wrong, Maiden Death?" Tadhg exhaled against my ear. "Are you disappointed?"

No. No. *No* . . . "*Yes*."

His hand found my hip and squeezed. "Shall I make it up to you tomorrow?"

I bit my lip to keep from responding.

What if this was the real reason we'd been taught to stay away from the Danú? Because in darkness, inhibitions fell by the wayside. Weak, pathetic humans couldn't compete with what they were.

The magic they possessed.

The unnatural beauty.

The pull of darkness within them.

The promise of something so far beyond our limited imagination . . .

"I need to go to bed," I gasped.

Tadhg's hand dropped, and he stepped away. "Yes. You do." With a flick of his wrist, a small mattress appeared between the bed and the wall.

The fire in my blood turned to smoke. "I thought you were going home."

"That little swim with the kelpie wasted my supply of magic for the day." He collapsed onto the mattress he'd shifted from heaven-knows-where. "And I don't fancy a night in the stable."

It would be fine. He would be fine there, and I would be fine in the other bed, and everything was going to be fine.

My racing heart slowed as I made my way to the bed and unhooked my cloak. I untied my boots with stiff, trembling fingers, tucked the witch's dagger under the pillow, and slipped beneath the thin quilt.

"It's cold down here," Tadhg whined.

There was no way I would admit that I was cold as well. "Shift an extra blanket."

"I would rather use you as a blanket."

I screwed my eyes shut and focused on catching my breath. My traitorous mind kept saying I should let him. That it'd be worth it.

"Shall we talk about my mouth some more?" Tadhg crooned.

"All right." I left a healthy pause before saying, "Your mouth should stop talking. I'm exhausted."

A husky chuckle lifted into the darkness, wrapping around me like a warm pair of arms as I drifted off to sleep.

11

PAIN THROBBED THROUGH MY SKULL EVERY TIME I PEERED TOWARD the slash of muted sunlight cutting through a gap in the moth-eaten drapes. I tried sitting twice and ended up flat on the mattress, my stomach threatening to purge itself of the poison I had ingested last night. If I never saw another pint of stout, it would be too soon.

With my eyes screwed shut, I rolled onto my side and waited for the room to stop spinning before peering over at Tadhg. The space was empty save for a tall screen adorned with hand-painted daisies.

Please be a bath.

Please be a bath.

Please, please, please be a bath.

I steadied myself against the wall and managed to cross to the screen. Behind it sat a wide copper tub filled with steaming water.

For the second time in my life, I was grateful for the existence of magic.

Despite another bout of nausea, I shed my clothes and climbed in. A moan escaped as the water's heat closed over me. After so many days in hell, I had finally found a bit of heaven.

The lavender-scented soap left on the beveled ledge scrubbed away any lingering tension from yesterday. I even washed my hair. It would take hours to dry, but a late start would be worth it.

By the time I felt like moving, the air around me felt warmer than the water. Covered in goose flesh, I rose. The droplets cascading down my body made me shiver. If only Tadhg was around to conjure up a—

"Looking for this?" A fluffy length of linen appeared on the edge of the screen.

I dropped into the tub, sending a wave of soapy water surging over the edge and splattering onto the floor.

"Thank heavens you're having a bath," Tadhg said from the other side. "You were beginning to smell."

There didn't appear to be any gaps in the screen. I stood and snagged the towel. "Are you always this unpleasant in the morning?" I teased, wrapping the towel around my torso and tucking the end beneath my armpit.

"Only when I've had too much to drink."

We had that in common. If I didn't get some food in my stomach soon, I was liable to pass out.

"Do you need someone to scrub your back?" he asked. "I'm a remarkably good scrubber."

What would Tadhg do if I accepted his scandalous offer? Likely round the screen, brandishing a magical sponge in each hand. "You're too late."

"Next time, then." There was a smile in his voice.

I waited, knee-deep in tepid water, for him to say something else—for him to mention last night.

He didn't.

It wasn't until his boots clicked across the floorboards toward the door that I said, "Thank you, Tadhg."

The steps paused. "For what?"

"The bath."

"Are you accusing me of using magic, Maiden Death?"

The false horror in his tone made me chuckle. "Go away so I can dress."

Despite the lingering hangover, today had been a good day. I would even venture to say it had been pleasant. After not paying for the room, I had been hesitant about going downstairs. Tadhg had assured me the prejudiced innkeeper from last night was nowhere to be seen.

Besides a few scandalous comments, Tadhg had been a welcome companion. We even managed to make it all the way to Achad without biting each other's heads off.

It helped that I had slept a good part of the journey. I'd been in such a good mood when we arrived at the inn that, after I was able to organize a room without trouble, I agreed to join Tadhg for a drink before he went home. He must've won Padraig over with his "good behavior" last night, because my coachman said he would leave the pints to the young and left us in favor of his bed.

Two old men in flat caps, dark jackets, and mucky wellies hunched over pints at the bar, and a table of two other couples shared drinks and laughter near the fireplace. Flames from the turf fire lapped at the stones, and smoke twisted up the chimney.

The decorations in the small pub consisted of a few paper clippings tacked to the dark paneled walls and a crooked oil painting of the seaside. The place wasn't nice—or particularly clean—but it was cozy.

"Are you drinking stout?" Tadhg asked, a silent challenge in the mocking lift to his dark eyebrows.

"I can't stomach it tonight." The thought made my head pound as I took a seat near the door. "I'll have a glass of red wine, please."

Tadhg nodded and went to order our drinks.

A few moments later, he returned with a glass in each hand.

"One *ladylike* glass of wine." Tadhg set a long-stem glass in front of me. "And a *gentlemanly* glass of the same for myself."

"You? A gentleman? Hardly."

"I could be if I tried," he countered, slipping free of his over-coat and settling onto the carpeted stool across from me.

"Yeah, right." The idea of Tadhg being anything but an uncouth half-fae was ridiculous. He wouldn't know the first thing about being a gentleman.

"You don't believe me?"

I shook my head.

"All right, then. How about a wager?" He leaned his elbows on the table and clasped his hands beneath his stubbled chin. "For two hours of your choosing, I will be a perfect gentleman. If I don't meet your standards, you keep your coins when we reach Tearmann."

With his ability to shift, Tadhg clearly didn't need the funds. But I could use the money to start a new life for Aveen and myself, far, far away from Graystones. "And if you manage to pull it off?"

A grin. "You let me unlace your stay."

The fluttering in my stomach was almost unbearable. I should say no, but the odds were in my favor, and since I could choose the time and place . . . "All right." I held a hand across the table, and he gave it a firm shake.

The chatter from the couples suddenly quieted, and I found them staring toward our table and whispering.

Tadhg turned to see what had caught my attention, and his smile faltered. Instead of pretending not to notice, he saluted them with his glass of wine. They averted their gazes, but the whispers continued.

Surely they had better things to do than talk about us. "They're very rude."

"They're curious." Tadhg shrugged. "Most humans cannot see any reason for one of you to be associating with someone like me. Beyond the obvious." The last three words were mumbled into his glass.

"Which is?"

His eyebrows flicked up. "Do you really not know?"

Of course I knew. We had literally just made a bet that

included the possibility of him unlacing my stay. "They believe you and I are engaging in romantic relations."

A smile played on his lips, but he did not laugh. "Yes. *Romantic* relations."

Last night, the foolish part of me had been tempted.

What would happen tonight? More importantly: what did I *want* to happen?

I had only been with one man in my life. A man I had loved with my whole heart. A man who had made me feel like I was too much and not enough.

However, I wasn't naïve enough to believe love—or even fondness—was necessary in such an equation. I thought of Padraig and his faerie and last night's discussion about the inns. "Does it happen often?" I asked.

Tadhg's head tilted as he set his glass aside. A draft from the window at my back flickered the flames on the candles between us. "I'm not sure I understand your question."

"Humans and Danú. Being intimate. Together." Before last night, I had never heard of anything of the sort beyond the Gancanagh and a few other wicked faeries. Was that because it rarely occurred or because it was so taboo, no one talked about it?

He gaped at me as though I had spoken in tongues. "Only all the feckin' time."

The muscles in my stomach clenched. *Wine.* I needed more wine. After a large sip, I got up the nerve to ask, "Why?"

Why would a human risk such a relationship? The Danú would never be accepted in polite society or be allowed to obtain gainful employment. Why would one of us enter into an affair with one of them when it couldn't possibly end well? Was it the same for humans living in Tearmann?

Another question swirled in the back of my mind as Tadhg's eyes widened.

Would it be worth it?

"What do you mean, 'why?'" He gave me an incredulous look.

"For the same reason it happens between humans. Lust. A desire to procreate. Feckin' boredom. I don't know."

"Not love?"

"Not in my experience, no." A muscle in his jaw feathered. "This may come as a huge shock to you, but you're not that different from us." Tadhg's thumb tapped against the tabletop, vibrating the wine in my glass.

He couldn't be serious. All it took was one glance at the two of us to see how different we really were. "Then why haven't I been taught the 'truth' about the Danú?" If everything I had learned was a lie, why wasn't someone setting the record straight?

With his teeth scraping his bottom lip, he splayed his hands on top of the table. "Because it is easier to fear the unknown than to try and understand it. And unfortunately, the loudest voices often belong to the most fearful."

The deep red wine swayed as I twisted the stem of my glass.

Tadhg had called me ignorant.

Perhaps the next ten days with him were my chance to cure that ignorance.

"Do you truly believe the Gancanagh is innocent?" I had been too afraid to ask the question when he had first made the claim. Because if he was innocent—if he didn't murder Aveen—there was no way I could sacrifice him.

His hand stilled with the glass halfway to his waiting lips. "He's not innocent by any means," he said. "However, he and I are well acquainted. And as I told you in the carriage, I know for a fact that he would never kiss a woman unless she understood the consequences."

That would mean Aveen had *wanted* to die.

Tadhg may have known the Gancanagh, but I knew Aveen. She never would have willingly abandoned me.

Still . . . Tadhg seemed so sure of himself.

Don't trust the creatures. The voice grew fainter by the hour.

"Killing him is the only way to bring back Aveen," I told him.

Tracing a knot in the wood, Tadhg snorted. "Is that what Fiadh told you?"

I nodded.

He rolled his eyes. "Let me guess. She also said that if you used an enchanted dagger, then you could transfer his life force to Aveen, yeah?"

Again, I nodded.

Tadhg muttered under his breath before taking a gulp of wine. He used his sleeve to wipe his mouth, leaving a red stain on the wrinkled white cloth. "Did it ever cross your mind that perhaps she was *lying*?"

It had crossed my mind more times than I could count. The wine in my stomach bubbled with dread. "You're saying it won't work?"

"Oh, no. Immortal blood is powerful enough to raise the dead, so it'd work. But it's excessive." His hand moved back and forth as he rubbed the back of his neck. "And entirely unnecessary."

Excessive *and* unnecessary?

"What would you suggest I do?"

Tadhg braced his elbows on the table and leaned so close I could see his pupils dilate. "Nothing."

"You think I should accept my sister's fate even when I know I could change it?"

His brow furrowed like he was considering his next words very carefully. His teeth met his bottom lip over and over and over again. "The Gancanagh's lips are *cursed*. So, whoever he kisses is—"

His hand slammed on the tabletop, rattling the glasses, making me jump. Tadhg pinched the bridge of his nose, and his face contorted as if in pain.

The couples in the corner were staring at us again.

"Are you all right?" I reached across the table, but he jerked away.

"*Whoever he kisses is*—" He opened his mouth, but no words came out.

Wait a second.

Was he trying to *lie* to me?

Don't trust the creatures.

Did he think I was a fool? That I didn't understand the pain and frustration on his face?

"The ring," he rasped, motioning to where I had the emerald hidden. "Let me see the ring."

Don't trust the creatures.

Tadhg thought I would be stupid enough to hand over the ring after he'd admitted it was the only reason he'd helped me?

I clutched the emerald at my chest. "Absolutely not." The ring was mine.

His eyes narrowed into slits. "I cannot say what I need to say unless you give me the ring."

"Try."

"I. *Can't.*"

"And I'm *not* handing it over."

Tadhg blew out a breath before gulping his wine. He shoved the empty glass aside and raked his fingers through his hair. The green in his eyes glowed, forcing the blackness to the depths where it belonged. "Keelynn, please—"

The main door flew open, splintering when it collided with the plaster wall. The framed painting rattled, and candles flickered as an unforgiving wind whipped through the pub.

Two figures entered, hoods pulled over their heads and cloaks flaring wide over their skirts.

The door snicked shut of its own volition.

The women moved in tandem across the weathered floor, lifting their pale hands to remove their hoods and revealing identical pairs of glowing green eyes. I wasn't sure what they were, but they certainly weren't human.

Their faces were a reflection of one another. The only difference was that one's jet-black hair was straight and the other's had a slight wave.

The old men didn't bother looking up from their pints, but the table in the corner quieted. The women sitting there tucked themselves safely behind the men, who clutched the daggers at their waists.

The barman threw a towel over his broad shoulder and crossed his thick arms. Although he had served Tadhg without issue, it didn't look like it would be the same for these women.

Tadhg swore under his breath when the twins turned toward our table. With their feet hidden beneath their wide skirts, it appeared as though they floated toward us.

"We heard a rumor you were here," said the one with straight hair, her voice high, almost childlike.

There was no sign of the frustration and panic from only a moment ago as Tadhg offered them a slow smile. "You know better than to listen to rumors, Caer."

Tadhg knew these women.

I didn't want to know how well.

"Who is your friend?" The other one narrowed her eyes at me, her head tilting at an unnatural angle, reminding me of Fiadh.

Were they witches as well?

"No one you need to concern yourself with," Tadhg muttered.

The same woman jerked her pointed chin at me. "What's your name, girl?"

Tadhg rose to his feet and strolled toward them. "I said not to concern yourself with her. She's just someone I met at a pub."

Someone he met in a bloody *pub*?

Was he serious?

"If that's true"—the first woman dragged her long red nails up Tadhg's thigh—"then she wouldn't mind us stealing away her handsome companion for a little . . . fun."

There was no point telling them any different.

Tadhg was nothing to me—a means to an end.

Just someone I met in a pub.

"He's all yours." I gave a dismissive wave before drowning any lingering sense of betrayal with a large gulp of wine.

Although I kept my eyes on the knot in the wooden tabletop, I saw Tadhg's hands slip around their waists as he led them toward the exit. The women took turns whispering to him. He chuckled, a low, dark rumble from his chest. My stomach tightened as I watched him return their whispers with his own. Their peal of giggles was more cutting than the frigid wind that lanced through the inn when the door opened. Thankfully, both were cut off when it slammed shut.

I had barely set the glass back down before the door opened again. Tadhg rushed to the table and collected his overcoat. "Wait for me," he said breathlessly. "I'll be right back."

He didn't give me a chance to respond before he was gone.

The table in the corner went back to their whispers. I felt their eyes on me as I sipped my wine in silence. About ten minutes later, the door opened. A group of six men stumbled in, singing a bawdy song about a man named Willie. They ended up bringing their singsong to the table beside mine. As there were only five chairs at said table, one man remained standing.

Why was I still here, waiting like a besotted fool while Tadhg went off to do heaven-knows-what with those bloody women?

Tadhg wanted the ring.

That was it.

And all I wanted was safe passage to the Gancanagh's castle.

"That's an awfully serious face yer wearing." The man without a chair collapsed onto the one across from me. He was handsome enough, with brown hair and a short, well-groomed beard. "Yer too pretty to frown." He flashed a toothy grin before pushing Tadhg's wine glass to the side.

Too pretty. That was a new one.

"I could put a smile back on yer face if ye'd let me."

His friends sniggered.

"You think so?" I tapped my nail against the glass and offered him a practiced smile—the one I'd cultivated after being told one time too many that ladies should always look pleasant. "And how do you plan on doing that?"

"Come over here, and I'll show ye."

Another burst of laughter erupted from the table of drunken sods.

I stood and straightened my skirts. It was fulfilling to watch the man's eyes widen with something akin to panic when I sauntered over to him. But even more gratifying to hear his friends lose their minds when I dumped what remained of my wine into his lap.

12

THE NEXT MORNING, I FOUND PADRAIG AND TADHG ENGAGED IN quiet conversation beneath the stable's eaves, avoiding the deluge creating rivers in the street. I raced through the rain without stopping and climbed into the carriage, hoping to delay the inevitable confrontation for a little bit longer.

Ten days left. Only ten days.

Ignoring the opening door, I adjusted my soaked skirts around my boots. Tadhg pushed his damp hair out of his eyes and considered the bench. I made no effort to give him extra room. If he wanted to sit beside me, he was going to be squished into the drapes.

Tadhg ended up back on the trunk.

I secretly hoped the road would be riddled with potholes so his ass ended up as bruised as the trust I'd nearly placed in his cursed hands.

He smelled bloody awful, like perfume and stale booze.

My eyes remained trained on the window as Padraig maneuvered the carriage through the puddles and streams toward the edge of town.

"What's worse than one witch?" Tadhg grumbled.

I glanced up to find him watching me through red-rimmed,

bloodshot eyes. Angry red welts covered his forearms; bloody streaks marred his chest beneath his torn shirt.

What had happened to him?

"I said, what's worse than one witch?" he repeated, rolling his hand like he expected me to answer.

"I don't know."

He grinned. "*Two* witches."

I waited for him to say something more, for an explanation for the awful state he was in.

He was the first to look away. "I'm sorry for what happened last night. I was gone a lot longer than anticipated."

Gone away with two witches.

"What you do in your free time is no business of mine." He owed me nothing. The slight tug I'd felt wasn't worth remembering.

"That's all you have to say to me?"

How could I respond without giving myself away? Without telling him that I'd spent the entire night tossing and turning and wishing he hadn't left me in the bloody pub?

"*Dammit*, I said I was sorry. What do you want me to do?" Tadhg's eyes flashed, and the carriage came to a jolting halt.

"I want you to stop messing with my bloody carriage!" I didn't want another day added to this cursed journey because of his tantrums.

"That wasn't me!" He pulled the drapes aside and peered into the forest.

"You're so full of—"

Wait.

Tadhg couldn't lie.

"Padraig?" No answer. "Padraig? Is everything all right?" I unlatched the door and stepped down from the carriage. The rain had stopped, but the air was heavy, like it would begin again any moment.

My boots sank into the mud with a loud *squelch squelch.*

Padraig slumped in his seat, reins still in hand.

At first I thought he had fallen asleep.

Then I saw a dagger protruding from his chest.

"Padraig!" My cry echoed around the hollow. Who could have done such a thing? Was he breathing? He had to be breathing. Maybe the dagger had missed his heart. Maybe he was still clinging to life. I made to run to him, then froze when a man with silver hair rounded the skittish horses in a lazy stroll.

"What have you done?" I screeched.

Don't be dead.

Please don't be dead.

"Easiest way to make a man stop a carriage is to stop his heart," the man drawled, his grimy fingers drumming against a wicked looking knife hanging from his belt.

Crushing weight left me paralyzed. I darted a glance through the carriage door.

Tadhg was gone.

The selfish coward had abandoned me.

Had I really expected anything more from him?

The man stalked forward, withdrawing the dagger from its sheath. "Now, hand over yer coins or ye can join 'im." He gestured toward Padraig with the blade.

My staunch ally couldn't save me.

No one could.

The mud swallowing my boots felt like quicksand. I could feel myself sinking as I loosened the purse from my belt and set it in the man's dirt-crusted palm.

He leaned close, gagging me with the stench of sweat and rotting teeth. "And the ring."

The ring? "N-no." Not the ring. Anything but the ring.

He caught my wrist and yanked the wedding band from my finger. "There. That wasn't so hard, now, was it?"

When I tried to pull free, he dragged me against him and exhaled in my ear, "They're gonna 'ave fun with ye."

Three burly men emerged from some crumbling ruins beyond

the brambles. From the broken high cross and empty rosette window, it looked like the remains of an old abbey.

The tallest man wore more knives on bands around his thick biceps. An angry purple scar ran from his lip, across his too-square jaw, and down to his Adam's apple.

The man beside him wore thick leather armor that looked too heavy for his lanky frame. He gave a leering smile, revealing teeth as black as his greasy hair.

The third was stocky and made of muscles. His shirt had no sleeves, and his breeches had been cut off at the knee.

Bile rose in my throat, and the blood drained from my face, leaving me cold and shaking. "You have what you came for. Let me go."

The silver-haired man shoved me forward and backed toward the carriage. "I have what *I* came for," he cackled, climbing into the driver's seat and pushing Padraig's body to the ground with a sickening thud, "but my men need to claim their prize."

With a flick of the reins, the horses took off at a trot, and my carriage disappeared around the bend.

A twig snapped.

Three villains stalked toward me, knives drawn.

The witch's dagger was beneath my cloak, but my hands were dead at my sides. I would've run if I hadn't been waist-deep in terror. My breathing matched my racing pulse, my lungs and heart were about to explode . . . Until Tadhg appeared on the broken high cross with kohl over his eyes.

"Three against one isn't a fair fight, lads," he said, his feet swinging back and forth like he was on the edge of a dock, kicking the water.

I tried to call out to him, but the heavy air clogged my throat.

"We didn't know our prize had a *friend*." The biggest man cracked his knuckles; his lips twisted into a sneer.

"Look at its eyes." The man without sleeves tossed his dagger between his hands, shifting his weight from one foot to the other as he navigated the rubble. "Never seen anything like it."

Tadhg laced his fingers together and yawned as he flexed his hands over his head.

The lanky man stalked toward me.

My joints stiffened, refusing to yield. I wanted to run. I needed to run. Why couldn't I run?

"There's no need to be frightened," he crooned in a pleasant enough voice. "We're gonna treat ye like the lady ye are."

The other two sniggered.

Tadhg's head cocked to the side, reminding me of the twins last night. His movements were rigid, jerking. A puppet on a string being controlled by someone—or something—else.

A hand closed around my throat, stifling the cry in my strained windpipe.

Fight back. Fight back.

Dammit.

I couldn't bloody *move*.

A pulse of power, like a phantom wind, surged around me, sending my attacker flying headfirst into a tree. A sickening crack rattled the golden leaves, and the man's body crumpled onto the thick grass.

Tadhg vanished, reappearing behind the other two men. "I had a shitty night last night," he drawled, brushing some invisible specks from his waistcoat, "so consider yourselves lucky that I'm giving you a chance to run."

The largest one laughed. "Ye think ye can best the two of us?" He stopped in front of Tadhg. The stocky one continued circling, his expression growing more malicious with every step. "Ye think we 'aven't dealt with yer kind?" The man pulled something from beneath the neck of his shirt. Yellowed claws, a shriveled finger, and human teeth dangled from the leather strap. "We're gonna make ye watch us fuck yer one"—he winked at me—"then carve her up like the pretty bird she is. Then I'll cut out yer eyes and add 'em to this." The claws clacked together when he shook the necklace.

Tadhg's eyes were as black as the kohl around them, the light of magic swallowed by whatever darkness lived within him. "Turn around, Keelynn," he said in a quiet voice laced with rage.

How could I turn around when I couldn't move or speak or *breathe?*

The stocky man lunged, but Tadhg was quicker. Whirling, lifting his elbow, ramming it into the man's nose. The man howled. Blood gushed down his lips and dripped from his chin. The knife fell. Tadhg flicked his wrist. It was in his hand before it hit the ground. He caught the man by the chin, yanked his head back, and drew the blade across his throat.

Blood sprayed. A gurgling sound escaped.

Aveen.

She had made the same sound when the merciless Gancanagh had stolen her from this world.

I screwed my eyes shut against the horror. If only I could drown out the strained cries. Heavy grunts. Low groans. The unmistakable thud of a body connecting with the ground.

I clutched my chest, pulling and dragging at the lace and buttons, desperate to loosen them. To free myself.

"Look at me."

It was Tadhg.

I squeezed my eyes tighter.

Two hands settled on my shoulders. "*Look at me.*"

Tadhg's face was smeared with blood and kohl. Black eyes searched mine. There was a body to my right. And a second to my left. One man was missing his arms. *Where the hell are his arms?*

"*At me.*" His palm connected with my chest, steady against my raging heart. "Take a deep breath."

"I-I-I . . ."

"Deep."

I focused on the pressure of his hand and pushed it away with my expanding chest.

"Deeper. *Deeper.* Good. Hold it there. And release." Tadhg shifted his weight from one foot to the other. "Again."

Again and again, he reminded me how to breathe.

A shadow moved in my peripherals.

The lanky man hurtled toward us, dagger raised above his head.

"*Tadhg!*"

It was too late. The man buried the blade into Tadhg's side. Tadhg cursed and stumbled away, holding the wound with his hand.

The man glanced at the dripping steel, then back toward Tadhg's malicious grin.

Tadhg held out a blood-drenched hand and squeezed his fingers into a fist.

The knife disappeared. The man's eyes bulged, and he clawed at his throat, his face growing redder and redder. His body lifted off the ground, his feet kicking as he struggled and struggled to free himself from the invisible hold.

Tadhg's other hand drew circles at his side, as if stirring the air.

Then the earth began to shake. I stumbled away from the purple-faced man a second before the ground split open, swallowing the bodies of the other two villains. The final man opened his mouth, but before he could scream, Tadhg splayed his fingers, and the man dropped into the abyss.

Tadhg's spinning hand froze.

The ground stitched itself back together, leaving only a line of dirt-encrusted stones and blood-smeared grass where the fissure had been.

I caught the coppery bite of blood mixed with the lingering sweetness of Tadhg's magic. But the smell of fresh earth, the stench of a new grave, left my head spinning *spinning spinning* out of control. My knees cracked against sharp debris.

Tadhg called my name. Too far away.

Sharp stones sliced my palms when I fell forward, retching until my throat was on fire and my stomach was as empty as my soul.

Those villains had been human.

And I had stood by like a bloody coward and watched Tadhg take on all three of them—and nearly die in the process.

The same way I had watched Aveen die.

There was no way I could face the Gancanagh and hope to survive.

I pressed trembling hands to my sweaty forehead and tried to breathe. Something touched my shoulder, sending me skittering toward the broken bits of wall.

"It's only me." Tadhg's outstretched palms shook violently from where he crouched. "It's only me." Shadows still clouded his eyes, like the darkness didn't want to be contained. With a flick of his wrist, a silver flask appeared. "Here." He held it toward me.

I gulped a mouthful, swished, and spat into the grass. "It's just water." Had it been water the entire time?

Tadhg's eyebrows came together. "Would you rather something stronger?"

I shook my head and drank until it was gone. My attention drifted back to the bloodstains. "You killed them. *All* of them."

Tadhg's head tilted the same feral way it had before he'd attacked. "I told you to look away," he said, inching closer.

"I-I couldn't."

Tadhg swayed. Perspiration beaded on his forehead.

"Tadhg? Are you all right?"

His eyes met mine, dulled, and he collapsed.

I crawled toward his prone form and lifted his head onto my lap. Dark lashes dusted against the greasy kohl. Gaunt cheeks splattered with blood. The pulse at his neck barely fluttered. Too weak. Too fast.

His chest rose and fell, but it was shallow. Labored.

His face was as pale as his shirt beneath the bloodstains—

Bloodstains.

I dragged Tadhg's shirt from where it was tucked into his breeches, ignoring the tan, taut muscles stretching across his abdomen. Right above the deep cut of his hip was an open wound the length of my hand, oozing blood. If he lost much more, he wouldn't survive. He may have lost too much already.

There had to be something I could do. Some way to stop it. If only Aveen were here. She would know what to do. *Think, Keelynn. Think.*

I sliced off strips of my skirt with the witch's dagger and wrapped the fabric in a crude, makeshift bandage around his midsection. It would have to do until I could find a needle and thread.

What if it wasn't enough?

What if he died too?

Oh god. I really was Maiden Death. Not because of my plans to kill the Gancanagh but because those closest to me—those I cared about—ended up dead.

Tadhg couldn't die. He just couldn't.

My fingers trembled as I touched the dark stubble at his jaw. Rough, like sandpaper. I brushed the hair away from Tadhg's ear to study the delicate point at the top. The shape wasn't *that* different. Being this close, even with his ears, it was almost possible to forget that he wasn't human.

What was I thinking?

Only a short time ago, Tadhg had murdered three men and torn open the earth. His magic was the very thing I had been taught to fear and avoid at all costs.

But instead of killing me, he had saved me.

Twice.

In light of all that had happened, perhaps I could find it in myself to forgive him for trying to lie to get the ring last night. For leaving me in favor of two women from his own world.

I removed my cloak and used it to cover Tadhg where he slept. When the color eventually returned to his cheeks, I stood and inhaled a deep breath, praying for strength to do what needed to be done.

The air held a bitter nip, but I couldn't find it in myself to care as I crossed the ruins toward the road. Seeing my coachman's white hair sticking out amidst the grass made my legs falter. Flies swarmed around Padraig's vacant blue eyes and the jagged wound in his chest. His black flat cap had been mashed into the mud.

I fell to my knees and collected Padraig's cold hand. Calluses from a lifetime of holding reigns and training horses scratched against my fingertips for the last time.

"I'm so sorry, Padraig." My tears fell over his pale, weathered cheeks. "I'm so, so sorry."

How did I say goodbye to someone who had looked after me for so long? Who had been willing to bring me across the country to face a monster? Who had every faith that I could defeat him?

And whose death had been entirely my fault.

Thinning white hair, soft as a feather, slid through my fingers as I brushed it aside. My hand stilled.

Beneath the mud-covered strands, the tips of his ears weren't round.

They were pointed.

13

THE ABBEY'S CRUMBLING WALL CUT INTO MY SPINE. THE DAGGER clutched to my chest felt heavy and cold in my clenched fist. If Tadhg didn't wake up soon, it'd be dark. And I'd be alone. I had managed to drag Padraig's body off the road and cover him with stones and debris. The abbey's broken high cross now marked my friend's final resting place.

My friend wasn't human.

I'd never known. Never suspected. Padraig had always been a steady, protective presence in my world.

I'd trusted him with my secrets. My life.

The unmistakable sound of hooves and carriage wheels came and went. I had considered begging for help, then dismissed the notion. Even if the travelers took pity on me, the moment they saw Tadhg, they would likely refuse assistance. And I couldn't leave him behind.

Tingling numbness overtook my bent legs; I stretched them toward a patch of nettles, waiting for the feeling to return to my toes before crawling to where Tadhg slept. He had barely stirred since he'd collapsed.

His forehead was blessedly cool, his pulse steady.

I lifted my cloak from where it covered him and tugged up his shirt. The fabric from the makeshift bandage didn't appear damp, a good indication that the bleeding had stopped. The skin beneath was still smeared with blood, and the wound . . .

Where was it?

It had been there. I had *seen* it. Now, there only a faint silver scar.

"Anything else you want to check while you're down there?"

I shrieked and shoved away. Tadhg's head cracked against the ground.

"Why aren't you hurt?" A wound like that shouldn't have healed without stitches.

Cursing, he rubbed the top of his head and sat up. "I *am* hurt."

"Not your *head*, you fool. That man stabbed you."

"Did he?"

I crossed my arms and scowled, waiting for a proper explanation. We couldn't afford to play games any longer.

Tadhg watched me through eyes as clear and green as the grass he laid upon. "I should think the answer to your question would be obvious," he said finally, glancing toward the edge of the forest.

If he'd been human, the wound would've likely killed him. But he wasn't human. "Your magic did this?"

A nod.

Hope flickered inside of me. "Can it heal others as well?"

"Why? Did they hurt you?" Tadhg reached for me, his hands moving clinically from my neck to my arms.

I couldn't lie and say I wasn't hurt. Because I was. But magic couldn't fix a broken heart.

"Not me. Padraig." I grabbed Tadhg's hand and pushed to my feet. He swayed when he stood, giving me more of his weight than expected. A V formed between his bunched eyebrows as I towed him toward Padraig's grave.

"Keelynn . . . Stop."

I couldn't stop. I had to keep going.

Tadhg jerked out of my grasp.

"Padraig didn't deserve this," I cried, tears slipping free as fear and sorrow and regret raged inside me. "You have to heal him. You have to bring him back. I'm asking you to try. I'm *begging*."

"No."

"But he's one of you!"

Tadhg reached out a hand. "Keelynn . . . "

"Don't *touch* me."

His hand tightened into a fist that he smacked against his thigh. "I don't care if he's a human or a leprechaun or a feckin' dog. Life left Padraig the moment that dagger pierced his heart. This isn't a matter of healing, it's a matter of resurrection. I'm sorry, but he's gone."

I knew it was the truth, and yet it wasn't enough.

Tadhg was speaking, but his words didn't register. His hand clasped mine, tentative and slow, as if he was waiting for me to tell him to stop touching me again. I couldn't find it in myself to speak or protest as he pulled me away from the road, toward the ruins to collect my cloak, and into the forest.

Twigs and stones crunched under my boots. Birds chirped from their places high in the treetops. On and on we walked until pain lanced through my heels with each step forward.

"Where are we going?" If I didn't get these boots off soon, I wouldn't be able to walk tomorrow.

"It should be around this bend."

I stepped over a fallen log devoured by deep green moss. Ferns sprouting beneath the swaying trees shuddered in the soft evening breeze. "What should?"

Before he could answer, I heard it.

Water.

A small river cut through the hillside, falling toward the valley below. Tadhg dropped his bag, which had magically reappeared, next to a flat, moss-covered boulder. "Shelter or food?"

"Excuse me?"

Bracing his hands on his hips, he nodded toward the clearing.

"There was a time when I could manage both after a fight, but not anymore, so you're going to have to choose one."

"We're staying *here?*"

The pebble-strewn grass gave way to silty sand on the river-bank. Leaves swirled in an eddy below a massive boulder splitting the river in two. It was beautiful, but it was the middle of a bloody forest.

"We don't have much of a choice. We're too far from anyone I know, and the nearest village is hours away."

We couldn't stay *here*. It wasn't safe. "Why did you bring me through the forest? Why didn't we follow the road?"

"And risk encountering the man who murdered Padraig?" Tadhg removed his overcoat, balled it up, and stuffed it into his bag. "I don't fancy dying today, do you?"

I could only shake my head. I didn't deserve life, but for some reason, death didn't want me either.

The trees stirred in the wind, their branches creaked and leaves rustled.

Shelter or food?

There was no telling what manner of creature lurked in this forest. My aching stomach could wait until tomorrow. "Shelter."

Tadhg's lips flattened as he nodded. "We'll need firewood. Do you think you can handle that?"

Although my feet whimpered at the thought of traipsing around the forest, I steeled my shoulders and said, "I can handle it."

"Good." A nod. "Leave your cloak here and keep sight of the river so you don't get lost."

"My cloak? Why?"

He glanced toward the darkening sky. "Because the heavens are about to open, and you'll want something warm and dry to wear tonight."

Tonight. Alone. With Tadhg.

We'd shared a room two nights ago, but this felt different. More intimate. More dangerous.

I meandered upriver, collecting fallen sticks covered with lichens and slugs, bits of driftwood, and the largest log I could manage on top of it all. Everything on this cursed island was damp.

Once I dropped the load on the grass next to Tadhg's bag, I stretched my aching back.

In the distance I heard a splash followed by a litany of curses.

Downriver, a pair of willow trees draped over a pool of blue-green water. Tadhg's wet clothes had been spread over a rock, the bloodstains washed away in the river.

A dark head emerged from the pool, followed by broad, tanned shoulders. Heat unfurled in the pit of my stomach as I watched his toned arms stroke toward the shore.

I had no right to be attracted to him.

To feel anything when those I loved felt nothing.

We needed more wood.

On and on I walked, following the meandering river, collecting sticks and small logs until my arms were full again. On the way back, I stumbled upon a stretch of blackberry bushes, their thorny branches sagging with plump fruit. The wood rolled out of my arms and clattered to the ground. Tiny thorns scraped my hand as I freed a berry. Juice dribbled down my fingers, staining them a deep purple. Seeds crunched between my teeth, sweetness burst on my tongue, and some of the hollow ache in my belly subsided.

It began to rain, and heavy drops rattled the bush's leaves as I alternated between eating and filling my pockets with food for Tadhg. I didn't stop until my fingers were too cold to bend.

Shoving my dripping hair from my eyes, I retrieved the load of wood and made my way back to camp.

Woodsmoke carried on the breeze, promising fire and warmth, spurring me onward. Sopping skirts slapped against my frozen thighs. Icy raindrops glued the bodice and sleeves of my dress to my skin.

When I reached the bend in the river, my feet stilled at the sight of our "shelter." I had expected a tent or a shack, not a one-room cottage.

Tadhg could shift a whole bloody house?

My measly offering of blackberries and wood felt pathetic in comparison.

The hinges on the door whined when I let myself in. Heat prickled against my frozen fingers. There was no furniture and no decoration beyond a small stone fireplace. Tadhg's overcoat was stretched in front of the hearth with my cloak folded like a pillow at the top.

My stomach fluttered.

There would be no extra mattress shifted tonight.

Tadhg bent over the fire, wearing only his breeches. Silver scars covered his entire back. Some were small, like the one he'd received today. But others spanned from his shoulder down to the waistband. He glanced over, and when he saw me, he shot to his feet and came for the wood. "What took so long? I was afraid you'd gotten lost." He dropped the wood next to a massive pile of logs he must've collected himself.

"Don't worry, the ring and I are here safe and sound." There was no point fooling myself into pretending he cared about my well-being. I pulled a crushed berry from my pocket. "I brought you food."

"You brought me food?" His mouth gaped as though I'd said something scandalous.

"I'm hardly going to eat them all myself." My gaze landed on three fish roasting on a spit, and I deflated even more. "Although you obviously didn't need my help."

Tadhg plucked the berry from my fingers. "I'd take a bushel of blackberries over a trout any day," he said, popping the fruit into his mouth and cupping his hands together. "Give them here and get out of those wet clothes before you freeze to death."

There were enough half-crushed berries to fill both his hands. He brought them over to the fireplace and portioned them out on two small slabs of slate.

I unhooked the witch's dagger and set it next to Tadhg's bag and boots. When I tried to unfasten the front of my dress, my frozen fingers refused to cooperate.

Tadhg glanced sidelong at me; his gaze fell to my chest. Slowly, he rose and erased the distance between us. Hot, calloused hands closed over mine. "Allow me?"

This close, I could see his pupils dilate and feel the heat radiating off his bare chest. My mouth refused to work, so I nodded. Long, nimble fingers unfastened the hidden clasps and drew the black material down and down until it fell to the floorboards in a sodden heap.

The only sounds were my racing heart, our uneven breaths, and the soft patter of raindrops on the roof.

"Turn around," he said, his voice a gravelly whisper.

My body responded as though I was his to command.

With my back to him, Tadhg gathered my hair, settled the damp strands over my shoulder, and traced my spine down to where the laces on my stay waited. The garment loosened as the satin strings slipped through the eyelets with a soft hum until it fell to the ground on top of my dress.

Warm hands slid the top of my shift aside to make way for cold lips grazing over my bare shoulder. Heat surged in my core, pulsing with need.

And then Tadhg stepped away.

"Here." He shoved his shirt toward me. "Put this on."

Put this on? I didn't want to put anything *on*. I wanted to take everything off.

He went back to the fireplace and stooped to turn the fish like he wasn't affected. Like he didn't even feel a hint of desire. Like I'd imagined the entire bloody exchange.

I peeled my feet from my boots to find blood had fused the stockings to my heels. Removing them looked too painful, so I didn't bother. Tadhg's blessedly dry cotton shirt replaced my shift, and I hid the emerald beneath. My own clothes were so wet, they'd left a puddle. The only hope of drying them by morning was to spread them out on the dirty floor.

"Are you finished?" Tadhg asked, his back still to me.

"Yes."

He glanced over his shoulder, but quickly looked back to the fire. I sat on top of his overcoat and tucked my knees beneath his shirt. Tadhg passed me one of the shale "plates" with fish and a handful of berries on top.

"Thank you. And not just for this." I indicated the plate. "For everything."

Tadhg only nodded.

The piping hot meat burned my fingers, and I had to chew carefully to keep from choking on the tiny bones.

"I know it's not what you're used to," Tadhg said, picking at his fish before reaching for more berries.

"It's wonderful."

He gave me a skeptical look.

"It is. I didn't think I would get any food tonight, so this is a feast."

His brow furrowed, and he looked away, toward the hearth. "A feast. Right."

"Really. I've always wanted to go camping," I confessed. Although, my fantasies had been considerably more luxurious. "Aveen and I used to beg our mother and father to let us camp in the gardens. They never did." The night was the Danú's domain. "So we'd steal scraps from the kitchen and bring them to our bedroom and eat in a makeshift tent in front of the fire."

A small smile played on his lips. The memory of what those lips had felt like on my skin left heat creeping up my cheeks.

"Tell me about her."

He wanted to talk about Aveen? "Why?"

After wiping his hands on his breeches, Tadhg collected the remnants of our meal to throw in the fire. "I want to know about the woman who is worth all of this." He gestured around the cottage.

I found myself *wanting* to tell him so that he would believe this mission was for a worthy cause.

"After our mother died, our father threw himself into running our family's estate. She was only a year older, yet Aveen took it upon herself to look after me. Her childhood ended that day, but she ensured mine did not. She played every game I suggested, read every fairy tale, pretended to be witches and faeries and princesses with infinite patience, even though she had no interest in any of it." Aveen would've rather been in the gardens, pulling weeds, pruning bushes, and planting flowers.

Tadhg turned so his back was against the wall and drew one knee to his chest. "She sounds selfless."

"She was. Aveen was selfless so that I could be selfish. And I was. So, so selfish." I wrapped my arms tighter around myself, struggling to keep the tears at bay. Tadhg's gaze shifted to the flickering orange flames. "I told her everything. My hopes. My fears. My dreams. She bore it all—did her best to make them come true. I was so self-absorbed that I never asked about *her* life. What *she* wanted. The night she died . . ." I inhaled a shaky breath.

Tadhg was looking at me again, eyes wide, a V between his dark eyebrows.

"It was her betrothal ball, and I was so hateful and angry toward her for something that wasn't her fault. Our father had arranged for her to marry the man I loved." So much had happened, the ghost of that first love seemed a distant memory. "His name was Robert." Huffing a laugh, I scrubbed at my eyes with the back of my hand. "Aveen despised him." After what had happened, I couldn't blame her. He should have loved me enough to refuse the arrangement. "So did Padraig."

Padraig.

"He was one of you," I whispered.

The muscles in Tadhg's arms flexed as he leaned forward to add a few sticks to the fire. The light reflected off those scars. I wanted to hear their stories, trace them with my fingers, my lips.

"I know," he said quietly. "I could see his glamour on the day we met."

See his glamour?

Oh, right. The enchanted kohl. It was easy to forget when he wasn't wearing it. "Why don't you do that?"

"Do what?"

"Use a glamour to hide your ears."

Shrugging, he brushed his hair aside and touched a finger to the tips. "I used to hide them when I was young. But now it seems like a waste of magic."

How much magic must Padraig have possessed to be able to hold a consistent glamour day in and day out? He must've been incredibly powerful or constantly exhausted.

"I wish he would've confided me." I would've told him that I cared for him no matter what he was. That he didn't need to hide around me. A log in the fire popped, sending a shower of orange sparks onto the hearth. Smoke twisted up the chimney in a lazy dance. I'd trusted Padraig with my life. Had he not trusted me?

Tadhg snapped a twig and tossed it into the fire. "Living among humans is dangerous for us. The more people know, the higher the risk of discovery."

"Dangerous for *you*? But you have magic." With the sort of power Tadhg possessed, I didn't think he'd be afraid of anything.

"Magic isn't always enough to save us," he said with a sigh, resting his head against the wall. His eyes took on a faraway look, like he wasn't in this room but somewhere else. "All it takes is one human to make a false accusation. Airren law *always* rules in a human's favor. If Padraig had been caught using a glamour to conceal his identity, he would've been hanged."

The punishment for wielding magic was harsh, but I had never questioned it because in my mind, the magic being used was dark and destructive, not something as simple as a glamour for protection.

"If it was so dangerous, why did he stay?" He should've gone back to Tearmann where it was safe.

"Padraig said he and his human wife decided to live in her family's home in Graystones. When she passed"—green eyes met mine—"another human had stolen his heart."

Another human. "He stayed for me, didn't he?"

A nod.

Padraig had stayed to look out for me and keep me safe. And I had gotten him killed. His death was my fault. His blood was on my hands.

Padraig had been such a good and honorable man. Kind, loving, and loyal. He didn't deserve to have his life stolen like he was nothing. His fate should've been mine. It was no less than I deserved for being selfish and jealous and cruel and hateful.

I buried my face in my hands and let my tears flow free. Another piece of my shriveled heart turned to dust. "It hurts," I cried, clutching the material at my chest. "It hurts too much." If only someone would crush my hateful heart and end this pain.

The floorboards creaked, and Tadhg's arm came around my waist, holding me in the heat of his embrace until my sobs turned to soft sniffles.

"I can make it go away," he whispered against the shell of my ear. "Say the word, and I'll make the whole world go away."

I wanted to sink into his darkness. For the heat of forbidden desire to burn the pain and sadness until only ash remained. "Please." Anything had to be better than this. "I don't want to hurt anymore."

He dragged his mouth down my throat; unnaturally cold lips sent shivers down my spine. My head fell back; he could take what he wanted as long as he stopped the pain.

"Put on the ring." The rough command ignited my racing pulse.

"What?" Why would I put on the witch's ring?

"Put it on," he said again, almost desperately against my collarbone.

My hands shook as I lifted the chain from my neck and undid

the clasp. The ring slipped onto my finger, then tightened as if by magic.

His fingers tangled in my hair, holding me in place against his hungry mouth. "Tell me you love me."

"But . . . I don't." This wasn't about love. It was about forgetting.

"*Lie.*"

"I . . . I love you." The lie slipped through my lips without a sliver of pain.

Cold lips crashed against mine, stealing the breath from my lungs. Harsh stubble scratched my chin, so at odds with the sweet, sensual softness of his mouth. Tadhg drew his tongue across my lips. A silent request. When I opened for him, he swept inside and met my impatient tongue with a slow, deliberate caress.

"Say it again," he murmured, tracing my breast over the cotton shirt, his calluses scraping the sensitive tip.

"I love you." I'd lie to him every day for the rest of my life as long as he kept going.

Tadhg twisted the shirt's hem in his clenched fist and dragged it over my head.

Wind and rain battered the walls as Tadhg lowered his head and sampled my body with his tongue. I laced my fingers in his hair, clutching his head against me, relishing the way his throaty chuckle vibrated along my skin.

His hands were *everywhere*. My shoulders. My breasts. My stomach. My hips. My thighs.

It wasn't enough. Not nearly enough.

Between my knees.

Between my thighs—

Teasing. Flirting. Over and over and over and over.

Slipping beneath me. Wrapping around my hips. Dragging me toward where he knelt. "Do you want to know a secret?" he whispered against my knee, pressing a kiss to my inner thigh.

"Yes." I wanted to know all his secrets. All his truths. All his lies.

"I've fantasized about burying myself between your thighs since the night we met."

Another kiss. Higher. Harder.

And then he dragged his tongue north.

"Tadhg—"

His mouth. His lips. His *tongue.*

Stop. Don't stop.

Tadhg's shoulders pressed firmly against the underside of my thighs. His fingers dug into the bones at my hips. Vicelike. Insistent. As unforgiving as his tongue.

*Yes yes ye*s I wanted to shout.

But all I could manage was a breathless whimper, clutching his hair as if I would fall away and . . . *breathing* . . .

I was coming undone. It was all his fault. Whatever he was doing with his—

Oh god

I can't I can't I can't

Stop. Don't stop.

Firelight danced on his unruly mop of dark brown hair and the slightest point of his ears as he devoured every rational thought and reservation and bit of sense I possessed. No one had ever told me it could be like this.

Chaos building.

A thunderous wave.

Crashing and seizing. Forcing quivering breaths through my lips. I was splintering, breaking apart. I no longer existed.

And I'd never felt so free.

14

THERE WAS SOMETHING HOPEFUL ABOUT THE MOMENTS BEFORE one was fully awake, before reality caught you by the collar and dragged you into its dark abyss. Anything was possible at dawn's first light. By nightfall, you realized all the day had brought was failure. The small specks of hope that remained were like stars scattered across the vast night sky, reminding you that tomorrow could be different. Tomorrow could be the day you succeeded.

I had spent the last four months hopeful for tomorrows while tomorrows came and went, leaving me with the disappointment of yesterdays.

A vicious cycle. Over and over and over.

Tumbling down a never-ending spiral staircase leading nowhere.

Wake up. Fail. Go to sleep.

Repeat.

But not last night.

Last night, I had fallen asleep under a canopy of shimmering hope, wrapped in the strong arms of a devilishly handsome half-fae.

A smile played on my lips as my lashes fluttered open to find my cloak draped over me like a blanket. Sunlight drifted beneath the door. There was a new black dress, shift, stay, and stockings folded over a single chair sitting at a small table that hadn't been there when I'd fallen asleep.

Tadhg's magic must've returned.

The thought of seeing him again left my stomach tightening with sweet anticipation.

I'd never forget the way he'd made me feel—made me forget. I wanted that bliss again and again and again.

What would it be like if he'd had his magic?

The strange feeling in the pit of my stomach stretched, as if waking from an eternal slumber.

I examined the ring on my finger. The smiling reflection in the green stone caught me off guard. I shouldn't be smiling. I shouldn't be happy. Padraig had been brutally murdered.

I should be devastated.

I *was* devastated.

But the sharp pain had faded to a dull ache.

And for a few precious moments, Tadhg really had made the world go away. But the realities of today were returning with a vengeance, as unforgiving and ruthless as they'd been the day before.

By carriage, we would still have at least nine days of travel. By foot? I hadn't a clue. All my money was gone. How was I going to pay Tadhg for helping me? Would he accept the ring as payment when we reached Tearmann?

On the table, Tadhg had left a fresh scone and a pot of tea. I could get used to having him around. Not that he'd be around once we reached the castle. After I resurrected Aveen, Tadhg and his magic would be gone. For some reason, the idea made my stomach churn.

After breakfast, I found Tadhg on the riverbank, reading quietly from a green, leatherbound book. His clothes appeared fresh and clean, but his scuffed boots were caked in mud. He glanced at me, offering a hesitant smile. "Good morning."

My lips lifted of their own volition. "Good morning. How did you sleep?" I brought my boots to the edge of the river and eased onto the pebbled shore. Leaf-dappled sunlight sparkled on the burbling surface as I sank my feet into the clear, cold water. The blisters on my heels sighed.

"Quite well considering the woman beside me snored like a drunken pooka."

Aveen had used to claim I snored, but I'd never believed her. Edward had slept in his own chambers, so he wouldn't have known.

"Ladies don't snore," I told him, focusing on removing stray fluff from my skirt to hide my embarrassment. "And if they *did* snore, a gentleman wouldn't mention it." I wiggled my toes to keep the blood flowing. How had Tadhg bathed in this water last night?

"Ah, but I'm not a gentleman," he said, his piercing eyes dancing with mirth. With a flick of his wrist, the book vanished. "And after last night, I'm not entirely convinced you're a lady."

Dampness seeped into my skirts, and I shifted uncomfortably on the stones. I may not have acted like it, but I *was* a lady. "Last night was a moment of weakness," I said, heat creeping along my jaw. Why did I care what he thought? It wasn't as if his opinion mattered. "It won't happen again."

"Right. Of course." His lips lifted into a crooked grin. "Out of curiosity though, *why* can't it happen again?"

Wasn't it obvious? "For one, we don't even like each other. And we're from two different worlds." Worlds that had been segregated for a reason. He and I couldn't work, even if I wanted us to. Which I didn't. The emerald in the ring caught the sunlight when I smoothed a hand down my skirt. My fingers were still stained from the blackberry juice, so I reached into the water and did my best to scrub them clean. "Besides, you just want the ring so you can break your curse." To Tadhg, I wasn't a woman, just a means to an end.

He folded his arms over his unbuttoned waistcoat and studied me with an intensity that made my heart rate spike. "The ring doesn't break curses, it neutralizes them."

The fact that he finally trusted me enough to divulge information about the ring shouldn't have mattered. But it did.

I wanted Tadhg to trust me the way I trusted him. And despite every warning I'd heard against it, I did trust him.

No wonder he wanted the ring. Being able to lie in this world could mean the difference between life and death. "If you want it so badly, why haven't you tried to steal it?"

His gaze dropped to where his hands flexed between his knees. "Enchanted objects cannot be shifted or stolen. They must be freely gifted."

Would he have stolen the ring the very first day if he could've? I had a feeling I didn't want to know the answer. "I wish you would have told me about the ring."

He picked up a stone and launched it toward the river to land in the water with a *plop*. "I didn't want you to lie to me."

"Unless it's to tell you that I love you," I said with a laugh. What a strange request.

The smile slipped from his face.

"Yes. Well . . ." Tadhg's teeth scraped over his bottom lip. "Not all of us have the luxury of love. Sometimes we monsters like to pretend we're wanted for more than an escape or a distraction." He pushed to standing, dusted off his breeches, and started for the cottage.

Bloody hell. Why had I said that?

"Tadhg, wait." I clambered to my feet and raced after him. "I didn't mean that the way it came out. I genuinely—"

He whirled, eyes swirling with black. "Genuinely what? *Care?*" He huffed a humorless chuckle. "You're such a shit liar, it's a wonder Fiadh bothered cursing you at all."

"Tadhg—"

"Let's not pretend this is more than it is. Like you said, we don't even like each other. You needed a distraction, and I was more than happy to oblige. That's it. End of discussion." His gaze fell to my bare feet, covered in sand and bits of grass. "Get your boots on. We need to be on our way."

I watched him stalk to the door and rip it open.

You needed a distraction.

I could claim it wasn't true, but we both knew it was.

The forest ended in a valley, giving way to rolling hills separated by low stone fences and dotted with grazing sheep and cattle. Tadhg barely spoke to me other than to grumble "Hurry up" or "Could you walk any slower?" And he was back to referring to me as Maiden Death.

I hated it. I missed the teasing. I missed the closeness. I even missed the wildly inappropriate comments.

A few hours later, we found ourselves between two fields separated by a stretch of gnarled brambles. A tall hawthorn tree with wide branches grew in the center.

Hunger clawed at my stomach, and exhaustion weighed down my limbs. Tadhg had shifted some dried venison and smoky yellow cheese an hour ago, but it hadn't been enough to fill the void growing inside of me.

I had accepted, because if I hadn't, I would've collapsed. But I vowed to pay him back for everything he'd done, even if it meant returning to Graystones and giving him every coin in my coffers.

"Where are you going?" Tadhg called.

I glanced over my shoulder to find he had fallen behind. "I assume the village is that way," I said, gesturing at the puffs of smoke rising toward the low-lying gray clouds.

"My friends don't live in town." He nodded past the hawthorn. "They live over here."

There was no house or cottage or any manner of dwelling in view. When he'd mentioned his friends, for some reason I'd assumed they'd be human. What if they were terrifying beings living in a hovel or a cave or a crypt or somewhere far worse? Not that I could think of anything worse than living underground among skeletons.

"I need you to listen carefully." He waited for me to nod before continuing. "You cannot tell anyone the truth about why we are together. Do you understand?"

The Gancanagh was a prince in his world. To confess that I needed to kill him could only end in disaster. "What should I tell them instead?" I twisted the ring around my finger. I'd been telling the truth for so many days, it still felt strange to be able to lie.

"I don't care. Just say we met at a pub and I'm bringing you to Gaul."

It was partly true. We needed to go through Gaul to get to Tearmann, and technically, we had met at a pub.

Tadhg pressed an ear against a knot in the tree and knocked three times. Paused. And knocked twice more.

Black spots appeared on the trunk.

Not spots.

Doors.

The doors blew open and light burst forth, surrounding Tadhg and knocking him to the ground. Palm-sized women with iridescent wings tugged on his clothes and his hair, pressed kisses to his cheeks. One tucked herself into his waistcoat pocket; two more tried wiggling their way into his breeches.

All of them had hair that reached to their knees and tight-fitting dresses resembling feathers, leaves, or fish scales. Intricate knots and ancient symbols had been tattooed onto their golden skin.

"Enough, enough," Tadhg laughed, pulling the two at his waist out by their dainty feet. "Out of there, you two. We're in the presence of a *lady.*"

Every tiny head turned toward me. In a blink, I was surrounded by light, currents of air, and sharp, stinging pain. I cried out as they pinched and poked and prodded and—*dammit!* A blue faerie with a vicious gash of a mouth bit me, leaving a round red mark on my wrist.

"*Enough!*" Tadhg's command set their beautiful faces into looks of pinched irritation. They retreated to the tree's branches—all except a faerie with flowing white hair, who came to rest on Tadgh's shoulder.

Rubbing the sore spot on my wrist, I dared a step forward, too fascinated to let my wariness keep me from taking a closer look.

"I take it you've never met a faerie." Tadhg's voice was full of warmth. The faerie rubbed her head against his cheek, a serene smile on her glowing face. Her freckles sparkled like sunshine on water.

I shook my head. I'd dreamed of this moment when I was little, but I never believed it would really happen. "She's so beautiful." The most beautiful creature I'd ever seen. The faerie lifted her hand to her face and whispered something in Tadhg's ear that made him chuckle.

"What'd she say?"

"Áine thinks you look like a toad."

Wretched little mite. "Tell her I take it back."

"There's no need. She understands you perfectly well." The faerie whispered again. "She says you're the ignorant one."

Ignorant indeed. I had never met a bloody faerie, but I knew all about the ancient race of magical beings. They stole human babies from their Moses baskets and replaced them with hideous changelings and sent bad luck to anyone who disturbed their homes. They were vindictive, jealous, and despised humans.

It was close-minded to think it was true of all of them, but from the way they glared at me, I had a feeling it was more true than not.

Tadhg spoke in soft tones to the faerie. She listened intently, nodding every so often and darting looks of thinly veiled hatred toward me.

"It's settled." Tadhg stood and dusted grass and leaves from his breeches. "We'll stay here for the night and head off first thing in the morning."

The faerie clutching his neck snuggled closer.

I imagined how satisfying it'd be to crush her bones beneath the heel of my boot. There was no sane reason for me to be jealous of the tiny woman. Moving forward, my relationship with Tadhg was going to be strictly professional. Still, that didn't mean I wanted to watch some floozie faerie rubbing herself all over him.

Tadhg brought us across the field to an outcropping of tall trees with ivy climbing the trunks. Ferns and long grass fluttered on either side of a dirt path. The other faeries flew above us like iridescent starlings before disappearing into the treetops.

The path led to a collection of white stones set in a circle around a wide bonfire. Beyond the stones loomed the ruins of an old tower house with vines invading the empty arched windows.

"There are cots in the tower," Tadhg told me. Áine smirked from her perch. "You can sleep there tonight."

"Where are you sleeping?"

Áine flew and landed on the ground beside his boot. A sharp white light flashed, and when my sight cleared, Áine was still there, only she was no longer palm sized. Her white hair swayed in the breeze, and her legs seemed to go on forever beneath the scandalously short white *whatever* she was wearing. It was hardly enough cloth to be a dress.

Tadhg made no secret of his perusal from Áine's ethereal face to her high, firm breasts down to the curves of her waist and hips to her dainty, toeless feet. "I will be staying elsewhere."

My stomach twisted.

I didn't care.

I did *not* care.

"Come with me. I have a surprise for you," Áine said in a high, sing-song voice, holding out a hand toward him.

His gaze fell to her hand before returning to me. "I'll join you in a moment."

The way Tadhg emphasized the word "join" left a hole in my chest.

Perhaps I did care. But only a little. Not that it mattered. He wanted the ring, not me. Last night had been a mistake. A terrible, beautiful mistake.

Áine's smile broadened before she went to the crackling bonfire. Sparks flickered in the darkening sky. More lights flashed, revealing six more human-sized faeries.

"They can choose one day a month to walk the island as humans do," Tadhg explained, rubbing the back of his neck with a drawn-out sigh.

Some of the faeries sank onto the stones; others fell onto their stomachs in the grass.

"Isn't that *convenient*."

His lips flattened and he hummed. "As I was saying before, choose any room you want, but be sure to lock the door once you've gone in."

As if a locked door would keep me safe from any of these faeries. "Am I not allowed to stay out here?"

His eyebrows came together. "Do you *want* to stay out here?"

I shrugged. I didn't want to hide away for the night with only my dark thoughts for company.

Worrying his lower lip with his teeth, he darted a glance toward the gathering. "I'm not sure it would be safe. Things can get out of control, and there's no telling what you'd see."

"I will be fine."

Huffing a breath, he raked a hand through his hair. Again, he glanced over his shoulder to where more faeries had joined their friends. What was he so worried about? None of the women seemed to be paying me any attention.

"All right. You can stay, but only if you promise to avoid the wine," he said with a resigned sigh. "It's stronger than what you're used to, and I've seen the way you handle your stout."

Avoid the wine. I could do that.

A picnic had been laid on top of one of the stones. I filled a chipped porcelain plate with boiled potatoes dripping with butter, carrots, and a skewer of some type of charred meat that smelled savory and delicious.

Tadhg passed all of it to collect a bowl of blackberries topped with fresh cream. Instead of sitting next to me on a stone, he went to where Áine waited by the fire with a basket hanging from her elbow. When she handed it to him, he peeked beneath the cloth on top and kissed her cheek.

The crestfallen looks on the other faeries' faces would've been comical if I hadn't been wearing the same expression.

Perhaps I didn't want to stay after all. Especially if it meant watching the two of them together. Laughing. Whispering. Trading touches and secret looks.

I shoveled food into my mouth, barely tasting it. Tadgh removed the cloth with a flourish.

Cake.

That's what Áine had brought in the basket. Tadhg set his bowl of berries aside and ate the entire thing.

"Tell us a story, Tadhg," a human-sized faerie said from where she lounged. A few smaller faeries had wrapped themselves in the strands of her blue hair stretching across the grass.

"I'd rather he take off his shirt," another muttered.

"Take off your shirt *and* tell us a story!"

"Leave yer shirt on and take off yer breeches!"

Infectious giggling erupted.

Tadhg chuckled and set the basket at his feet. "Since I haven't the energy for much else, I suppose a story will have to satisfy you tonight."

He rubbed his hands together, then launched into a tale about the Tuatha Dé Danann—a magical race of supernatural beings, witches, and faeries who first settled in Airren centuries earlier.

The history was filled with war, mostly from invading human nations wanting to conquer the island. Those who fought, lost. But those who agreed to live in peace were allowed to stay. This went on for hundreds of years.

I had heard similar stories before, but from the human perspective, where the native Danú were depicted as wholly evil, plaguing the land with magic. Two hundred years ago, the human king from Vellana led his vast army to victory with weapons of iron and ash. When the remaining creatures yielded, they agreed to the terms of a treaty constructed by the king.

Tadhg's version spoke of how unfair it had been for the rightful inhabitants of this island to be given only a small swath of land and to be punished—even killed—for using their magic.

"Why are ye wasting the night listening to this old bollocks drone on about the past?" a deep male voice rumbled from the forest shadows. "I thought it was the fourth of the month." A massive beast emerged from between two wide trunks.

A riderless black horse with glowing yellow eyes

No, not a horse.

A pooka.

A moment later, a second horse-like creature joined him.

Tadhg cursed and dropped his head into his hands. Áine let out an ear-piercing squeal and launched herself at the newcomers. The other faeries followed, the larger ones giggling and the smaller ones chirping.

It may not be safe.

Why hadn't I listened to Tadhg? Faeries I could handle. But pooka? If the beasts hadn't been blocking the path to the tower house, I would've escaped inside.

Twin bursts of magic left me temporarily blinded. When my vision returned, two hulking men stood amidst the faeries. The tallest one had hair as black as a raven's wing falling to his shoulders. The white shirt he wore barely contained his broad chest and massive biceps. The only animal part of the pooka that remained were his eyes. The second pooka was shorter, his muscles less obvious, and his inky black hair cropped short.

The tall pooka smiled over the head of a faerie with her arms around him, flashing elongated canines made for ripping flesh from bone. Haunting yellow eyes landed on me and widened. "What do we have here?"

In a blink, he was in front of me, crouching so we were eye-to-eye. "A pretty little human has decided to join our soiree? Who invited you, pet?" He reached a hand toward my hair, then froze.

"Touch her and I'll send you to the underworld," Tadhg snarled, holding a blade against the pooka's neck.

"Ah . . . she's one of yours then." The pooka sighed. "Pity." His hand fell, but instead of leaving, he took the space beside me on the stone. "What's your name, human?"

Tadhg swore and re-sheathed his dagger. "Lady Keelynn, this is Ruairi."

"A *lady*. How fancy." Ruairi leaned forward and sniffed. His nose wrinkled. "She doesn't smell like a lady." Yellow eyes turned to Tadhg. "But she doesn't smell like you either."

Tadhg's hands clenched into fists. "Is anyone else coming that I should know about?"

Ruairi shook his head. "I couldn't convince Rían to leave his hovel."

I stiffened.

Rían.

The witch's dagger at my back gave an answering pulse.

The Gancanagh.

I smoothed an unsteady hand down my skirts. "Who is Rían?" I asked as casually as I could manage, brushing some crumbs from my lap.

The pooka nodded toward Tadhg and grinned. "Rían is Tadhg's younger brother."

15

My mind was playing tricks on me. There was no way Ruairi had said Rían was Tadhg's brother. No bloody way. That meant Tadhg was *related* to the monster who had murdered Aveen and had been lying to me this entire time.

I clutched the stone for support, trying to get my head around this.

The Gancanagh and I are well acquainted . . .

"Well acquainted" my foot.

"Keelynn? Are you feeling all right?" Tadhg asked. The pools of green I'd drowned in last night belonged to a stranger. A lying, manipulative being serving his own interests. He wasn't helping me. He was helping himself.

"I'm fine." *Thank heavens for this cursed ring.*

"Are you sure?" He knelt in the dirt and pressed a cool hand to my forehead. I could feel Ruairi's eyes on the two of us. Watching. Assessing.

I didn't want him to touch me. Didn't want him near me.

"I said I'm *fine*." I knocked his hand away and shot to my feet. Had he told Rían about me? Did the Gancanagh know I was coming to kill him? If I escaped to the tower house, the devastating revelations would only follow me. I didn't want to think. I didn't want to feel the all too familiar blade of betrayal slip between my ribs and cut out my heart.

Orange flames reflected off a deep green bottle abandoned a few stones over.

That's what I needed. I grabbed it, but before I could take a drink, the bottle disappeared.

"What did I tell you about the wine?" Tadhg clipped, the bottle now in his hands.

Ruairi snagged the drink and handed it back to me. "If the *lady* wants a drink, then I say let her drink."

Ignoring Tadhg's narrowed eyes, I took a deep swig of faerie wine. Liquid fire flooded my throat, burning all the way down to my belly. I coughed, sputtered, and nearly lost my dinner.

Ruairi laughed so hard he almost fell off the stone. The faeries giggled as they passed another bottle from one woman to the next.

The muscles in Tadhg's jaw pulsed. "That's enough."

He thought he could tell me what to do? He didn't give a whit about me or my mission. There was no way he'd let me murder his own brother. Was he bringing me to Tearmann at all?

And to think I had felt bad for making him feel used last night. He was using me too—for the ring. Once he got his hands on it, he'd be gone.

The second drink didn't go down any easier than the first and left my lips tingling and cheeks feeling too heavy to lift. The third brought about blessed numbness.

A hand clasped my elbow and dragged me toward the tower. "You're going to bed if I have to lock you in the feckin' room myself."

"No, I'm not." Tadhg's grip was too tight to tug free. "I'm going to stay and have a chat with the handsome pooka." How many times in my life would I be invited to a faerie party?

The pooka I had yet to meet watched us from the other side of the bonfire. Smoke twisted around his still form.

"Keelynn—"

"Let the human go." A dark hand settled on Tadhg's shoulder. The other pooka was glaring at Tadhg. "All it takes is one."

All it takes is one? One what?

Tadhg let me go so quickly, I toppled over. The pooka caught me beneath the arms and set me back on my feet. Tadhg scowled at the beast's back when he returned to the fire. The cloying scent of magic tangled with woodsmoke, but Tadhg's hands remained fisted at his sides.

A pale hand slid across Tadhg's chest. Áine appeared from behind him with a coy smile. "She's not worth it. Besides, you and I have some business to attend to."

His rigid shoulders seemed to curl in on themselves, making him look smaller. "You can wait until I'm finished here."

"I've waited long enough." Full lips pursed into a pout. "You promised, remember? I'm calling in our bargain."

The anger and betrayal churning inside me evaporated. There was no way of knowing what Tadhg had promised Áine, but it was clear from his narrowed black eyes that he didn't want to go with her.

"Go into the tower and lock the door." Tadhg's voice was quiet. Resigned. "Please."

Part of me wanted to give in as a kindness to him. The rest of me wanted to forget the entire exchange.

Áine's hand clamped around Tadhg's wrist, and she tugged him toward the forest. Tadhg glanced at me from over his shoulder as if he was waiting to see what I'd do.

I chose the fire and the wine.

My body swayed as I crossed the grass, vaguely aware of faeries dancing and drinking and climbing on top of the smaller pooka, removing his shirt. There was music coming from somewhere, fast and heavy, writhing with the flames licking the sky.

"Have a seat," Ruairi said, patting the stone next to him, "and tell me why my best mate threatened to kill me over ye."

I freed the wine from his grasp and decided to answer honestly. "I haven't a clue."

It really wasn't so bad, this faerie wine, once you got past the eye-watering sting and revolting taste of rotten fruit. Before I could take another swig, Ruairi plucked the bottle from my hand.

"What happened to, 'if the lady wants to drink, let her drink?'" I swiped for the bottle and missed.

"That was for Tadhg's benefit." Ruairi shook the bottle. "A few more drops of this and yer going to forget your own name."

"Maybe I want to forget." My name. My mission. The intoxicating taste of Tadhg's lips.

Rauiri's grin flashed, revealing those fangs. "It's not worth a day of retching, believe me."

I should've been running away. Instead, I edged closer. "I disagree." I'd take the threat of retching over the sting of betrayal any day. I gestured toward the bottle. Ruairi handed it over, albeit reluctantly. "Tell me about Tadhg's brother," I said, my words slurring together.

"Ask Tadhg tomorrow when he gets back."

Tomorrow? He was going to be gone all bloody night? The hollowness in my stomach got worse. "We've been traveling for over a week, and he has yet to tell me anything about himself or his family, so I'm *pretty sure* he's not going to tell me tomorrow." Or the next day. Or the next day. Or however long it was going to take us now that we had no carriage.

"Ye've been together for a feckin' week and ye haven't—" Ruairi's words trailed off. "Never mind." He took back the wine. "If he didn't tell you, then I'm sure he has his reasons."

Tadhg had his reasons, all right. He was obviously trying to protect his brother from death by the witch's blade.

The bottle stilled halfway to my mouth.

I was some fool.

Of course Tadhg was protecting his younger brother. Aveen would have done the same for me, no matter what atrocities I'd committed. How could I fault Tadhg for siding with family over a stranger wielding a weapon capable of killing immortals?

Which led to a bigger question: could I really kill Tadhg's brother?

There was far too much wine in my system to find an answer.

Speaking of wine . . . *Dammit*. The bottle was almost empty. The other pooka and his faerie companions were passing one between them.

Ruairi watched me through narrowed eyes, a slight smile tugging at his lips. "Tadhg won't be happy if ye drink yerself into a stupor."

"Tadhg can shove off," I said, standing and stumbling toward the faeries. By the time Tadhg returned, I wouldn't know his name.

"Dammit, Ruairi. What'd you do to her?"

"Me? I didn't do a feckin' thing."

"Why isn't she in the tower?"

"Because she insisted on waiting for ye."

Something warm scraped against my cheek. "How much did she drink?"

"Not as much as she wanted, but considerably more than she should've."

Arms slipped beneath my legs. Behind my back. Tadhg's neck smelled like candied almonds. Did his skin taste as sweet?

I decided to check.

Mmmm . . . it tasted better.

His grip on me tightened. "Did you just *lick* me?" he choked.

"You taste good."

"Feckin' hell, woman. You must've had a lot of wine."

Had I? I couldn't really remember. "What took you so long?" Was it morning already? He'd been gone ages. I vaguely recalled dancing around the bonfire with the faeries and the other pooka. And a river. Had we gone swimming?

"Shhh. Go back to sleep."

My body shifted against Tadhg's chest as he carried me through the darkness to the tower. Torches attached to the stone hallway fought to keep the shadows at bay. Tadhg stopped at the first door, checked the handle, cursed, and moved on to the next one. He did the same for a few more, until one opened.

The simple room had a small cot against the far wall highlighted by a silver of moonlight drifting through the lone window.

Tadhg set me onto my feet but left a hand around my waist, keeping me steady. The stones were cold on my toes. Where were my boots? *Hold on.* Where was my bloody dress?

Memories prickled in the back of my mind. A giggling, blue-haired faerie. Me laughing with her as we exchanged clothes. Her dancing around the fire in my mourning gown, spinning until she collapsed.

The faerie's dress I wore shimmered from the scooped neckline to where it ended midway down my thigh. Cool night air slipped beneath, making me shudder.

Tadhg squeezed my waist. "Can you stand on your own or do I need to bring you to the bed?"

"It would've been the second one if you hadn't gone off with *Áine.*" I stumbled forward and cracked my knee against stones. What fool thought to put a bloody wall there in the first place?

"Yes, well, I didn't have much of a choice." His boots scraped across the stones when he stepped toward me. "You need to get some sleep. Don't forget to lock the door." He tapped my shoulder. "Did you hear what I said? Lock the—"

"I heard you. Lock the bloody door." Where was the lock? I couldn't see—Oh, there it was. It looked complicated. "Why does it matter? It's not like a lock could keep one of you out."

"I've already told you that evanescing into a locked room breaks one of our most important laws. So, while a lock technically wouldn't keep us out, there'd be hell to pay if anyone came in."

I squinted at him, expecting green eyes but seeing only black.

The darkness was somehow linked to his magic. Magic I wanted to feel thrumming in my veins and sliding along my skin.

If I didn't stop thinking about it, my heart was going to explode. "Who's going to come in here?" I asked, licking my dry lips.

Tadhg smoothed his thumb along the ring's twisted gold band. His gaze dropped to my mouth. "A terrible monster who wants to take advantage of your inebriated state."

I lifted to my toes and kissed the pulse at his throat, lingering to taste his skin again. A featherlight sensation brushed my ankles, like a cat's tail.

"Do you think the monster would like my dress?" I whispered.

Tadhg's throat bobbed when he swallowed. His finger traced the neckline, then dipped below as his magic brushed against my trembling knees. "He would love your dress."

"He wouldn't think it was too short?"

A hand slipped along the outside of my thigh, up to and beneath the hem to knead my bare hip. "He'd think it was just right."

I was mad at him about something, but all I could focus on was his lips as he closed the gap between our mouths. Achingly slow. Testing. Teasing. Grazing in the faintest whisper.

"This can't happen again. You said that." His hips ground against mine, and I could feel him straining against his breeches. "We don't even like each other."

"I lied," I whimpered, my hips rolling, desperate for friction. He felt so damn good, but I knew what would feel even better.

Tadhg groaned, nipping my bottom lip, "Next time I tell you not to drink the wine, I suggest you listen."

I was about to catch his belt and then he vanished.

"Lock the damn door." His throaty command echoed through the hallway

I slammed the door and jammed the lock into place.

16

A DEAFENING RATTLE BROKE THROUGH THE HAZE OF MY DRUNKEN slumber. The hangover from the stout had been nothing compared to the unforgiving vice currently squeezing my head from all angles. Thankfully, someone had left a bucket and a glass of water beside the cot. So much for the laws about locked doors.

Where the hell was that noise coming from? A groan escaped as I shoved myself upright and reached for the glass. The water had a slightly sulfuric taste, but I drank like a woman too long in the desert. The rattling came and went, loud at first, then fading to a high-pitched whistle before rattling again.

My restless sleep had left the sparkling dress bunched around my waist. Trickles of memories returned through the fog.

Last night, I had been willing to give Tadhg all of me, and he'd *left*. He'd probably been up half the night laughing with his friends about the pathetic human. What had I been thinking, throwing myself at him like that? I was no better than a bloody hedge whore. No wonder he hadn't wanted anything to do with me. The sooner we parted ways, the better.

Which meant I needed to stop feeling sorry for myself, collect my things, and get to Tearmann. I slipped a hand beneath the pillow, searching for the witch's dagger. *Dammit.* It wasn't there. What had I done with it?

I remembered unfastening it when I'd traded clothes with that faerie. Had I left it by the river or brought it back to the fire?

I was such a disaster.

That dagger was one of only two things I needed, and I'd lost it.

My bare feet connected with the cold stones. Where had I left my boots? They weren't in the room or under the bed. Perhaps they were with the missing dagger. Before I could check, I had to figure out how to look respectable with half my arse hanging out of a faerie's dress.

Every time I tugged on the low neckline, the skirt got shorter.

If only I had my cloak.

Disaster.

Eventually, I gave up, hurried to the door, and slid the lock aside.

A hulking brute of a man was sprawled across the threshold, an overcoat tugged over his upper half, snoring loud enough to wake the dead.

Ruairi.

A pang of disappointment rang through my throbbing skull. Where was Tadhg? I nudged the pooka with my toe. He mumbled something and swatted at my foot like it was an annoying fly.

"Ruairi? Wake up." This time, I kicked him in the ribs.

He launched upright with a bellowed curse. When he saw me, his bloodshot eyes widened as his gaze raked down my bare legs. "Sorry. I must've fallen asleep."

"Why are you sleeping in front of my room?" Were there no rooms left?

Yawning, Ruairi stretched his large arms toward the ceiling. "I'm under orders to keep ye safe."

Safe from monsters.

"Here." Ruairi dug through a familiar leather satchel that he'd been using as a pillow and withdrew a stack of clothes, my gray cloak, boots, and the emerald dagger.

Oh, thank heavens.

"Tadhg said to give ye these. There'll be breakfast outside once yer finished."

"Where is Tadhg?" The hallway appeared empty on both sides. Had he stayed at home? Had he stayed alone?

Ruairi rubbed his eyes with the heels of his hands. "He's busy today."

"He's *busy*? Busy with what?"

Ruairi yawned again. "Important business."

Business with Áine or some other woman no doubt. Why was I destined to be attracted to men who were no good for me? "And what does he expect me to do while he's conducting this *important business*?"

The skin around Ruairi's eyes crinkled when he grinned. "Yer gonna travel with me to Kinnock. He'll meet us there."

Brilliant. Just bloody brilliant. Tadhg thought he could pawn me off on his friend. The nerve. I thanked Ruairi and retreated to my room. If Tadhg had been here, he could've shifted me a bath. But he was *busy*.

I wanted to throttle him. Instead, I took my frustration out on the cursed mourning gown. The boning in the stay jabbed my ribs, and the tight sleeves cut off my circulation, restricting my movements. Part of me wished I could just wear the faerie's dress.

When I finished, Ruairi wasn't in the hallway or outside the tower. In the clearing, the only signs of the bonfire were ashes, scorched earth, and a handful of broken green bottles. A small picnic had been spread atop one of the flat rocks.

My stomach protested at the idea of food, but I forced myself to eat a handful of strawberries and one of the buttery croissants. With no one around to distract me, last night's revelations slinked to the forefront of my mind.

Tadhg's brother was the Gancanagh.

What were the odds?

Fate had a terribly wicked sense of humor.

It was time to formulate a new plan. I'd started this journey relying on the word of one witch and very few facts. Now I had access to other sources. Access to the Danú. Perhaps Ruairi could shed some light on the Gancanagh and his motives for killing Aveen.

The other pooka emerged from the tower, shirtless and whistling a happy tune. His hair stuck up at all angles, and he didn't seem the least bit ashamed by his disheveled state when he saluted me and sauntered into the forest.

I snagged an apple, stuffed it into my cloak pocket, and started for the fields. Ruairi had a silver-haired faerie pinned against a tree at the edge of the forest. I wasn't sure whether to keep going and pretend I hadn't seen them or go back and wait at the stones.

"I'll be with ye in a moment, human," Ruairi threw over his shoulder. The faerie caught his jaw between her hands and brought his mouth to hers.

With my face burning, I continued into the sunlit field. A few moments later, a saddled black stallion emerged from the forest. The thought of riding again trumped any fear I had about traveling alone with a pooka. If he had wanted to hurt me, he would have done it already.

"I assumed we'd be walking," I told him, catching the leather bridle and giving Ruairi a pat on his powerful shoulder.

"Tadhg said yer feet were blistered." Ruairi shook his massive head, and his ears twitched. "He figured ye could use a break from trekking across the countryside."

And here I thought I'd concealed my limp yesterday.

I slipped my foot into the stirrup, gripped the horn, and launched myself into the saddle. The rich leather had been embossed with swirls and knots.

"Comfortable?" he asked.

"Very."

Ruairi started forward at a canter. It took my body a few minutes to adjust to the movement. He passed the hawthorn tree where the faeries lived and continued to a break in the crumbling stone wall separating the fields.

"Are we doing this fast or slow?"

When would I ever have another chance to do this? I grinned at the rolling countryside stretching before me and said, "Fast."

All plans for asking Ruairi about the Gancanagh evaporated the moment he rocketed forward, galloping like a host of sluagh nipped at his hooves. My hands gripped the reins so tightly they they fused to the leather. Hours slipped by like minutes as he ate up the distance between us and the city of Kinnock.

Kinnock was only seven days from Tearmann. I should've been excited about making up for lost time, but I wasn't. When we arrived at the castle, I would be forced to make some pretty big decisions.

My sister or Tadhg's brother? Who would live and who wouldn't? How was I supposed to choose?

My hair whipped, stinging my cheeks and neck. I drank the fresh air of freedom, letting it wash away the lingering effects of the faerie wine.

Eventually, my stomach could be heard growling over the sound of hooves on dirt. "Ruairi?" I gave the reins a slight tug.

He came to a sudden stop, jolting me forward. The horn rammed into my side.

"What is it? Do ye need to get sick?"

I pressed a shaking hand to my racing heart. "No, no. I'm just hungry."

"Can you wait a little longer? We're nearly at our rendezvous point."

I told him I could wait, and we continued for another ten minutes. Then Ruairi navigated off the road and squeezed his massive body between a gap in the hedge to where a familiar figure waited with a picnic spread across a plaid blanket.

Tadhg wore a black waistcoat missing all but the top button. The skin beneath his bloodshot eyes appeared bruised from exhaustion. "What took you so long?"

"Long?" Ruari snorted. "We made it in record time. Your little human is quite the horsewoman."

Hiding my smile, I climbed down. A day in the saddle left my legs weak and wobbly. Luckily, Tadhg caught me before I tumbled headfirst into the grass. "Sorry." I gave him a sheepish smile. "My legs are completely numb."

He brushed the hair from my face with the back of his hand, his eyes boring into mine. "Ruairi should've made you take a break."

"It's fine. Really." I tried to pull away, but he held firm.

"Are you well? Did you get sick?"

There had been some close calls on the way, but he didn't need to know about those. "I wasn't *that* drunk."

He rolled his eyes and chuckled. "You were dancing half-naked around a bonfire with a pooka. I'd say you were plenty drunk."

The reminder made my face burn. I *had* been dancing with Ruairi and the faeries, spinning and laughing and stumbling around. "You saw that?"

"I couldn't look away," he whispered against the shell of my ear. "Did you keep the dress?"

My breath caught in my throat when my skirts fluttered and his magic slipped around my ankles like it had last night. Words escaped me, so I shook my head.

"Pity."

"Are we going to eat, or do I need to evanesce and let the two of ye rut in the field like feckin' animals?" Ruairi muttered, his tail swishing in irritation.

Tadhg let me go and walked stiffly to our lunch. He'd brought a plate of beef brisket that smelled like it had been cooked in heaven, a bowl of crispy croquettes, and lemon cake wrapped in a tea towel. In a basket were clay plates, cups, and utensils.

Ruari collapsed onto his side in the grass and closed his eyes. The sunshine glinted off his onyx coat.

"Aren't you going to shift?" I asked, setting the dishes on the blanket in front of Tadhg and myself.

One yellow eye opened. "If any humans come by and see me, they'll know what I am. And I don't fancy getting run through today. I'm afraid I'm a horse until I get to go home."

What must it be like to need to hide your identity every day because you feared for your life? Padraig had used a glamour, and Ruairi could be a horse. Even Tadhg had his hair to cover his ears. Why did they need to hide in the first place? Really, what made them so fearsome though? Sure, some of them were evil, like Fiadh and the kelpie. But the majority of them were more like us than not.

You're not that different from us.

Tadhg had been right.

I cut off a bit of brisket and held it toward Ruairi.

He jerked his head away with a snort. "Pooka don't eat that shite. We're vegetarians."

Vegetarians? "All of you?"

He huffed a breath through his nose. I took that as a yes. Why were we taught that pooka ate humans when they didn't even eat meat? I traded the brisket for the apple from my pocket. I could've sworn Ruairi smiled when he delicately plucked it from my grasp with his teeth.

Tadhg pulled a croquette in half and popped it into his mouth, watching us as he chewed. I ate quietly, lost in my own thoughts as Tadhg and Ruairi traded good-natured insults. I liked seeing Tadhg like this, laughing and jovial. He was so different from the man who'd been cooped up with me in the carriage.

"How do you two know each other?" I asked between bites of brisket, using my sleeve to clean my mouth like a heathen.

Ruairi nudged Tadhg's shoulder with his muzzle. "I've known this bastard my entire life."

"Much to my eternal dismay," Tadhg sighed.

"I can imagine young Tadhg being quite a handful." An

unruly, dark-haired little boy who had grown into an unruly, dark-haired man.

Smirking, Tadhg wiped his hands on his breeches. "I prefer the term 'spirited.'"

"*Spirited? I* was spirited." Ruairi's ears twitched as he bobbed his head. "Ye were little devils. Always getting into trouble with Rían—and dragging me down with ye. We've had more than a few switches across our backsides. And Máire, Tadhg and Rían's governess, had a strong arm."

Tadhg had grown up with a governess? For some reason, I'd assumed he'd grown up in a small cottage somewhere in Tearmann. But if the Gancanagh was his brother, then Tadgh would be a prince as well. Although he didn't *look* like a prince. Did that mean he'd been raised in a castle?

If I asked, then he'd find out that I had learned his secret. Would he ever trust me enough to tell me himself?

Tadhg stretched his legs and crossed them at the ankles, brushing against my skirts. In the distance, sheep grazed in the rolling fields. "Do you remember how she insisted on serving liver and onions every Friday? The lying witch tried convincing me it was funny-tasting steak."

Liver and onions had been the bane of my existence growing up. Just the thought made my stomach lurch.

"When she wasn't looking," Tadhg went on, snagging another croquette, "I'd shift myself shortbread biscuits from the kitchens. And when my father dressed me in fancy clothes, I'd roll in mud puddles and stomp in muck and come home smelling worse than a grogoch."

"You did not." Although I hid my smile behind my hand, my laughter wasn't as easy to stifle. My mother would've lost her life if I'd tried anything like that when I was younger. Aveen and I had always been dressed to impress, like prized ponies at the fair.

"Tell her about the time ye found the man in a field," Ruairi urged, nudging Tadhg's shoulder.

"Once, I caught a drunkard going for a . . . ah . . . *relieving* himself near a faerie tree. I frightened him so badly that he ended up screaming through the field with his breeches around his ankles, tripping and getting stuck on a wall with his bare arse in the air."

Ruairi's laughter was a harsh wheeze. "And the wine. Tell her about the wine."

"What about the wine?" I leaned forward to brace my arms on my bent knees.

"I don't know why you find this story so amusing," Tadhg grumbled, rolling his eyes toward the gray sky. Crows circled overhead, no doubt waiting to see what we left behind. "All we did was drink some ceremonial wine."

"*Some*?" Ruairi snorted. "Ye drained every bottle in the feckin' church the night before Yule, and they had to use faerie wine instead. The parishioners were drunker than a clurichaun, stumbling down the chapel stairs after the service."

"I think I would've liked you when you were a boy," I confessed.

"He wouldn't have liked ye," Ruairi said. "Couldn't even talk to a lady without getting tongue-tied and sweaty. Nearly pissed himself when Shona tried to pull him into the forest for a snog."

Tadhg flicked his friend's ear. "I don't remember you seducing any of our playmates at eight years old."

"Most of the eight-year-old boys I knew were too busy fighting with wooden swords to pay Aveen and I any attention." She hadn't minded, preferring flowers to men. But I'd gone out of my way to try and draw their attention away from their pretend battles.

"That would've been myself and Rían—although he's useless with a sword."

I imagined a faceless little boy playing with a wooden sword. What had made him grow up to become a murderer?

Ruairi nuzzled the plate of croquettes. Tadhg grabbed one and tossed it at him.

"Tell her what ye did when ye were nine," Ruairi said when he'd finished chewing.

Tadhg's neck turned red beneath the collar. "I asked every female I met for a kiss for an entire year."

"It's true," Ruairi said with a laugh. "Old or young, pretty or plain, Tadhg would stroll up to them, bow, offer a gap-toothed grin, and then ask for a kiss."

Tadhg gave me a crooked smile and a wink. "How was I supposed to get any good at it if I didn't practice?"

My stomach fluttered when I thought of the way Tadhg had kissed me last night.

He must've had *a lot* of practice.

Kinnock was known for being a volatile city, with Danú often taking up arms against the human overlords. Chaotic energy swelled with the wide river cutting through the city's center, made more tense by the heavy Vellanian army presence.

Ruairi left us at the forest's edge, and we made our way toward the castle nestled at a bend in the river. The imposing gray fortress had four low turrets on each corner. Beyond it stretched an arched stone bridge lined with empty pikes, awaiting victims.

Women in fine dresses passed in swirls of perfume, looking down their noses at me as Tadhg and I strolled through the market.

Tadhg seemed oblivious to the looks he received—most filled with unveiled appreciation.

"I think the women of Kinnock are all besotted with you," I told him after yet another handkerchief had fallen at his feet. He hadn't bothered to pick up any of them.

"Do you think so?" He glanced around us as though he hadn't noticed the way women swooned when he passed. As if they knew who he really was, a Prince of Tearmann. That alone would make them look past his ears. And if he kissed them, they'd never recover.

"You're probably the most handsome man they've ever seen."

He knocked his hip against mine. "Am I the most handsome man *you've* ever seen?"

"No. I think you're atrocious."

A grin. "Liar."

I twisted toward a shop window to hide my answering smile. If he didn't stop being so damn charming, I was going to end up dragging him into an alley to finish what we'd started last night.

A lovely sapphire-blue gown encrusted with sparkling blue beads had been displayed on a dress form inside. It was wildly impractical, even for someone not in mourning and exactly what I would've worn a few months ago.

Tadhg watched me, his head cocked to the side. "If you like it so much, you should buy it."

"With what money?"

He raised his eyebrows. "Check your purse."

"I don't have a—" A purse that hadn't been there a moment ago dangled at my waist. It felt like there was more money inside than there had been when it was stolen. "You got it back?"

A smile. "Did I?"

Every part of me wanted to embrace him, but I refrained. Allowing my feelings for him to grow would be foolish considering the complicated situation with his brother. "Thank you, Tadhg. Sincerely."

Behind us, someone shouted. A crowd had gathered at the far end of the street, beside the castle wall, where soldiers led prisoners from the dark recesses beneath the structure. The people jeered; some spit, others threw stones.

The prisoners all wore hoods. Bare arms beneath ragged clothes, bound by iron chains, revealed them for what they were: *Danú*.

"What do you think they've done wrong?" I asked, careful to keep my voice down as we moved closer.

"Besides being born different, you mean?" Tadhg lifted to his toes to peer over another man's head. "Could be anything. That grogoch may have sneezed on a human; the pooka may have been caught shape-shifting." Pointing to the smallest figure in the line, he said, "The abcan may have written a poem that painted the king in a less-than-favorable light. And I'd imagine the far darrig at the end didn't pay taxes on the magic he wields but isn't allowed to use. They're notoriously tight bastards."

Soldiers led the prisoners to a large wooden dais where a giant man in a black cloak waited with a hulking axe.

"You really think they would execute someone for a poem?"

Tadhg's hand fell to the hilt of his dagger. "I've watched one of my friends be murdered because a human accused him of being rude."

All it takes is one.

One false accusation.

One lie.

And a life would be snuffed out.

I had heard the criers spreading messages of hate, seen the mercenaries collecting claws and teeth and eyes. I had been taught to avoid the Danú and fear the dark before I had learned the alphabet. But I had never connected the dots. Never allowed myself to see what was really happening to the native population of Airren, because it wasn't happening to me.

"It's not about a poem or taxes or even magic." Tadhg blew out a frustrated breath. "It's about being born different in a world that sees no value in diversity. It's about living under a regime that desires ultimate power over its citizens, one that is willing to murder anyone they believe could be a threat." He turned to me and touched a finger to my tangled hair. In a quiet voice laced with sadness, he said, "It's about people with fear so ingrained that they won't even sit in a field at dusk to look up at the stars because they believe the darkness is reserved for monsters."

Thwack

Thud

The crowd cheered.

More people pushed past us, including a man with a boy on his shoulders, eating sweets from a bag, watching the executions like he'd watch a puppet show.

Tadhg dropped his hand. "Most of the monsters I've met have lived in broad daylight."

Thwack

Thud

Cheer

In that moment, I realized I couldn't do it. I couldn't kill Tadhg's brother, even if he had killed Aveen. I needed to let my sister go. I needed to give Tadhg the ring and let him go too. "I'm so sorry, Tadhg."

"As am I." A sigh. "Come, let's get you to the inn." Tadhg gripped my elbow and turned me away from the cheering.

The inn was safe and warm and secure. Its thick plaster walls would drown out the horrifying cacophony echoing through the cobbled streets. I glanced over my shoulder to watch the smallest creature climb up onto the dais, her slim shoulders hunched over, like she could hide from her brutal fate by making herself smaller.

"This is wrong. We need to do something." I shook free of his hold.

When his gaze flicked toward the dais, his lips pressed into a thin line. "What do you suggest we do?"

Thwack

Thud

The cheering grew louder.

"I don't know. But it's so wrong that they should be killed for no reason at all." What if Ruairi had been the one caught shifting? What if Tadhg had been accused of being rude? What if Padraig had been caught using his glamour?

"Saving a handful of us won't change anything." Tadhg's flexed hands banged against his thighs. "This is all part of a systematic extermination that's been going on for centuries, and it won't stop until magic is wiped off the island."

Thwack

Thud

Cheer

Something rolled across the ground, landing against my foot. Sightless eyes stared up at me; a gruesome puddle of blood and fluid leaked from the neck of the abcan's tiny severed head.

Someone started screaming.

A hand clamped over my mouth. "*Be quiet.* You're drawing everyone's attention." Tadhg dragged me away from the executions. People saw us and stepped aside. In the distance, a cheerful yellow inn rose above the crowd.

Safe.

Warm.

From the corner of my eye, I saw two soldiers kicking something.

A child.

They were kicking a child in a cape.

The child fell forward, catching himself on the cobbled street with gnarled hands covered in red hair. An elongated nose peeked from beneath his hood. A heavy brow fell forward over dark, beady eyes.

Not a child. A grogoch.

The grogoch jerked when the soldiers' boots connected with his torso.

Thwack

Thud

Cheer

"He didn't do anything, did he," I said, unable to turn away.

"Most likely not." Swearing, Tadhg raked his hands over his face. "Keelynn, listen to me. I need you to . . ."

Tadhg's command faded into the background. One soldier stomped on the grogoch's arm. A sickening crack pierced the air, followed by a haggard scream. The other soldier reached for his sword.

They were going to kill him.

Those men were humans.

Monsters from my world.

"GET OFF HIM!"

The soldiers' heads jerked toward me.

I barreled into the one who had stomped, knocking him off the grogoch. My fists pummeled his black armor until the skin on my knuckles tore open.

He caught me by the hair, twisted, and kicked my legs from beneath me. My knees cracked against the cobblestones, shooting pain through my body. Something heavy and unyielding shoved against my back, pinning me to the ground.

"What the hell do you think yer doin', lady?" the soldier snarled.

My eyes met the grogoch's. "Thank you," he whispered, his lips and teeth stained red with blood.

There was a hard thud and a curse, and the second soldier fell to the ground. His helmet rolled away, revealing the face of a young man not much older than myself.

"What the—" The soldier on top of me collapsed beside his fallen comrade.

"Of all the feckin' days for you to want to commit treason." A pair of strong hands lifted me to my feet, and Tadhg's shadow-filled eyes met mine. "Get to the inn. *Now.*" Tadhg let me go, handed me his bag, and shoved his shirtsleeves over his forearms.

The people were no longer watching the executions. Now they were watching us.

Men in black helmets forced their way through, swords drawn, sending ice through my veins. "Tadhg! Come with me!" We could escape together.

When he looked at me again, his lips curved into a menacing smile. "You need to run."

I took one halting step backward, then another, watching Tadhg help the grogoch to his feet and force something into the creature's hairy hand.

People elbowed me in their haste to see what was happening.

Some shouted words of encouragement; others spewed curses and slurs. It took three soldiers to get Tadhg on the ground. Another two to shackle him with iron.

Tadhg's eyes met mine through the crowd, and he grinned. Blood dripped from a cut in his lip as they dragged him away. His heels left twin streaks in the muck on the street.

Thwack

Thud

Cheer

17

FOG DRIFTED ALONG THE RIVER IN THE EARLY MORNING LIGHT. The sun had yet to breach the horizon. My boots clicking on the cobblestones and squawking seabirds were the only sounds of life at this hour. Lack of sleep burned my eyes. I'd spent the entire night pacing in my room and praying for Tadhg to return.

He never did.

According to the innkeeper, the prison was in the bowels of the castle. A door of rusted iron bars blocked the entrance. I rattled them until a man appeared from the darkness, a heavy ring of keys jangling from his leather belt as he approached.

"Good morning." I offered him a full smile.

He ran a dirty hand down his dark leather vest, smelling of sweat and rotten fish. "Ye shouldna' be here. Tis no place fer a lady."

This was no place for anyone. "But I need your help. I'm seeking information on a man named Tadhg who was arrested yesterday."

He glanced over his shoulder, into the darkness. "I dinna think—"

"Please. There's no one else I can ask." I loosened the purse at my waist and withdrew four silver coins. "Here. For your trouble."

The guard's tongue flitted across his rotted teeth and then he held out his hand. "Tadhg, eh?" The coins *clinked* when they dropped into his vest pocket.

I nodded.

"I 'spose I could 'ave a look." He crossed to a concealed notch in the wall and withdrew a small leather-bound book. "What's yer man's surname?" He flipped through the pages, then stopped and slid a finger down the entries.

"I'm not sure." Did the Danú have surnames?

The guard lifted his eyebrows, no doubt thinking I was an empty-headed dolt.

"He's a bit taller than myself, with dark hair and green eyes." I didn't want to mention Tadhg's ears in case they hadn't noticed.

"We're not in the 'abit of keepin' records of hair 'n eyes." He adjusted the worn leather belt around his thick waist, rattling the keys. "Do ye know his crime?"

Groans echoed from the hallway. Did any of them belong to Tadhg? The pit forming in my stomach widened. "He saved a grogoch from being beaten."

"I hate the damned monsters as much as anyone," the guard muttered, tapping a blunt nail against the page, "but saving one's no more a crime than killin' one."

"He may have attacked some soldiers in the process."

The guard's face shifted into a tight grimace. "When did it 'appen?"

"Yesterday. In the afternoon."

"If he was arrested yesterday . . ." He closed the book. "What I'm trying to say is, there were no new prisoners brought in after the sentences were carried out."

He may have continued speaking.

He may have stopped with that damning statement.

All I could hear was my heart pounding in my ears as I stumbled from the stuffy enclave out onto the murky street.

Tadhg could have escaped. Evanesced before they had a chance to sentence him. Except I had seen the iron clamped around his wrists. His magic would've been useless. Had he been taken somewhere else? To another jail?

Or had he . . .

Oh god.

Had he been executed with the rest of them?

The bridge.

I had to check the pikes on the bridge. Had to know. To see for myself.

By the time I reached the stone bridge arching across the fog-drenched river, my heart and my stomach and my lungs were close to failing.

The first head belonged to a man with blood-smeared blond hair. A gaping mouth and sightless eyes watched the sea birds circling overhead. Gore and blood dripped down the iron.

Crows pecked at the yellow eyes of two furry black pooka.

The abcan, the far darrig . . .

And, at the very end, an empty pike stabbed the sky.

Not here.

Not here.

Where was he?

I weaved through men in dark overcoats and women strolling arm in arm beneath pastel parasols. Sweat dripped into my eyes and down my spine by the time I reached the cheerful yellow inn. The savory scent of bacon wafted from the tables full of patrons having breakfast, engaging in loud, boisterous conversation.

In my haste to reach the staircase, I collided with the back of a chair. Rubbing my sore hip, I muttered an apology and raced upstairs. How would I find him? Where did I begin? If I knew how to get in touch with Ruairi, I would've done that. Perhaps I could find a creature somewhere who'd be willing to talk to me.

I threw open the door to my rented room and froze.

Tadhg was sitting on the unmade bed, gripping the mattress with both hands. When he saw me, his lips curled into a slow smile. "Hello, Maiden Death."

His clothes appeared clean; there was a wine-colored cravat tied perfectly around his neck. I took a step forward. Then another. "You're alive."

A chuckle. "Disappointed?"

Disappointed? I shook my head. "Relieved." I didn't think I'd ever felt such relief.

He stood and straightened his breeches where they'd slipped down his hips. "Afraid I'd leave you to locate the Gancanagh on your—"

My mouth crashed against his with the force of a thousand fears. His lips were cold, but his tongue was fire and flame, darting and caressing. He lost his fingers in my hair and clutched my head to his as if this, this kiss, was life itself.

Perhaps it was. Perhaps it was enough to bring me back from the sorrows death had inflicted.

I tugged his cravat free. Struggled with the buttons on his waistcoat.

"You don't want this," he growled against my lips, his fingers fumbling with the fastenings on the front of my dress.

"Yes, I do." And this time, it wasn't about an escape. It wasn't about getting lost. It was about being found.

Insistent hands dragged my dress until it pooled around my ankles, freeing my body from its black shroud. "Turn around."

I twisted and flattened my hand against my pounding heart. The laces on my stay slipped through the eyelets. *Loosening. Loosening. Loosening.*

"Magic would be quicker," I said, not recognizing my own voice.

Tadhg let out a low, rumbling chuckle. "I'm giving you time to change your mind."

The stay met the same fate as my dress. "I'm not changing my mind." I turned to face him. "I want you."

"Wanting me and being with me are two very different things," he murmured against the hollow of my throat.

I freed the hem of his shirt from his breeches. With a flick of his wrist, his shirt and undershirt vanished. Our kisses grew frenzied, desperate. His solid, scarred chest slammed against me, urging me back and back and back until my legs collided with the mattress. And we were falling. Falling into the bed. Twisting. Twisting so that he was on top of me, holding his weight on his elbows, nudging my knees apart with his thigh. His mouth was on my throat, tasting my thrumming pulse with his tongue.

Tadhg's magic swirled around us like dancing shadows, tantalizing, stealing my sanity. I felt myself losing control, inhibitions slipping away with each exhale.

Every blessed inch of him rocked against me, slowly, ever so slowly. I wanted him to speed up but couldn't find the words, and then he . . .

Stopped.

Why did he stop?

"Keelynn?"

WHY. DID. HE. STOP?

"Look at me." His voice broke. Perspiration beaded on his furrowed brow. "Are you sure?"

He'd asked it as if my mind wasn't gone and could be changed.

"Yes." I wasn't sure about the future or anything beyond this moment. But this. I was sure about this.

He shuddered, and when he brought his lips to mine, he tasted of pure magic, sugar and sin. Powerful vibrations flooded my throat, pulsing with feral possession. His belt jingled as he slid the leather through the buckle with one hand and shoved down his breeches.

It was impossible to know where the magic ended and he began until he nudged against me, and a broken cry fell from my lips. *That* was all Tadhg.

My nails clawed down his back, digging into his tensed muscles. It wasn't close enough. I needed more, *more, more* of everything his breathless rocking promised. Over me. Under me.

Inside of me. Filling and plundering and plunging. Deeper and deeper, even as I climbed higher and higher. Fire and ice and wind, a chaotic storm building to a height. His teeth raked across my skin, feasting on flesh, dining on mutual desire.

And when the world shattered, I used my last breath to cry his name.

18

Tadhg collapsed onto the bed next to me, a thin sheen of perspiration glistening on his shoulders and chest. I loved his uneven, labored breathing. I loved the cocky tilt to his lips, like he knew he'd stolen my coherent thoughts and fractured my life and was proud of it. So bloody proud. He grinned like he was waiting for me to ask for them back, but I didn't want them. Thinking would lead to reality, and reality would lead to goodbye.

Instead, I rested my head on my hand and traced a finger down the strong shape of his sculpted jaw, over the pulse at his neck, to a silver line across his throat that hadn't been there when we were in the shifted cottage.

"Tadhg?"

The dark lashes on his closed eyes dusted his cheeks. "Hmmm?"

I tapped the scar. "Where'd you get this?"

He caught my fingers and brought them to his cold lips to kiss the pulse at my wrist. "Let's just say that it wasn't a very pleasant stay with the soldiers of Kinnock and leave it at that."

Oh god. They'd tortured him because of me. If his magic hadn't healed him, he could've been killed. It was a good thing this was over. He didn't belong in my world, just as I didn't belong in his. When I let him go, he could return to Tearmann where he'd be safe. "I'm so sorry." It wasn't enough for the pain I'd caused. "If I'd have stayed silent, they wouldn't have taken you."

His lips slid to my palm. "What you did was reckless and foolish."

Too reckless. Too foolish.

"But I'm so feckin' proud of you."

"You . . . you are?"

A nod. "You took a stand against your own. You stood up for one of us. You *did* something."

I *had* done something.

And it felt *good*. It felt *right*.

His fingers brushed the emerald ring, reminding me our time together was almost through. Saying goodbye was going to be harder than I'd ever imagined. "Is this ring the only way to break your curse?" I asked.

"*Curses,*" he whispered.

"There's more than one?"

"At this point, I'm more cursed than not," he said with a humorless laugh, drawing idle circles on my bare shoulder. "And no. There is one other way."

"What is it?"

His finger stilled, and he drew back to look at me. For the first time in my life, I felt seen. "You're the one who reads fairy tales. You tell me."

I thought of all the stories I'd loved as a child. Tales of evil witches and the unsuspecting princesses who fell victim to their wicked curses. And the dashing heroes who saved them despite dire circumstances. All of them had one thing in common. "True love's kiss."

"Now you have it."

Tell me you love me . . .

Had no one ever loved him? How was that possible? He was beautiful and kind. Rude and uncouth as well, but also funny and fiercely protective. "That shouldn't be hard for you. You're not hideous."

He snorted. "High praise, indeed, Maiden Death. Every man wishes a woman would refer to him as 'not hideous.'"

"You know what I mean." I smacked his chest and snuggled closer, nestling my head into the crook of his shoulder. His heart beat strong and steady beneath my cheek. "You're handsome, and you bloody well know it. Surely you could find a woman to fall in love with you to break your curses."

"If only love was that simple," he said through a heavy exhale.

He had a point.

Love was complicated.

I'd loved Robert and look where I'd ended up.

"There's something I need to tell you," he said at the same time I said, "We need to talk."

We both laughed.

"You first." I wanted to delay the inevitable for as long as possible.

"*Ladies* first. I insist."

Leave it to Tadhg to start acting like a gentleman when it was inconvenient. "All right." I extricated myself from his hold and propped myself up with my elbow. Tadhg had a hand tucked beneath his head. His body stretched across the mattress like there was no place he'd rather be than here with me. Silver scars dotted his sculpted chest. Muscled ridges in his abdomen led to the deep cuts of his hips peeking from beneath the white sheet. I wanted to map every scar and hear the stories behind each one. But it wasn't meant to be.

"I've decided to return to Graystones."

His smile vanished. "But we're only a few days out from Tearmann." He sat upright and shoved himself against the bed's wooden headboard.

"I'm not going to Tearmann. Not anymore." I slipped the ring from my finger and held it toward him. "Take it. It's yours."

He hesitated before accepting the ring. "I don't understand. Aveen—"

"Is gone." Somehow I managed to keep the tears at bay. Once he left, I could cry. For my sister. For Padraig. And now, for Tadhg. "And I cannot sacrifice another person's life to bring her back."

He glanced at me from beneath his lashes. "So you're giving up."

"I'm going to do what you said. I'm going to do nothing." *I'm going to spare your brother.*

His eyebrows came together, disbelief clear in his searching gaze.

"You've opened my eyes to a whole new world, where monsters aren't monsters at all," I explained, my voice catching. "If I killed the Gancanagh, even after what he took from me, I'd be no better than he is."

Tadhg stared at the ring as though he couldn't believe it was in his possession.

"I want you to take the ring and go home." I leaned in to press a kiss to the corner of his mouth. He jerked away as though I'd been about to slap him.

"Sorry," he muttered, slipping the ring on his littlest finger. "Force of habit." The kiss he gave me was nothing more than a polite peck.

I turned away and focused on drawing the sheet to cover myself instead of on the disappointment blooming in my chest. I had given him the key to breaking his curses and all I got was "sorry"?

Tadhg flicked his wrist, and his clothes were back on, like he'd never removed them in the first place. He shoved out of the bed and bent to retrieve his boots.

He still hadn't said anything.

Surely he had *something* to say.

Once he'd slipped his arms into his overcoat and settled it over his shoulders, he finally looked at me. But it was as if he were staring through me. As if I wasn't even there.

"Thank you, Lady Keelynn." Gone was the teasing tone from a few moments earlier. The voice that'd replaced it sounded cold and formal. The voice of a prince. "I appreciate this gesture of goodwill more than you will ever know."

He *appreciated* it?

What was I supposed to say to that? Somehow "you're welcome" didn't feel quite right since I was lying naked in a bed we had just shared. Tears burned the backs of my eyes, but I refused to let him see me cry.

In the end, I only nodded.

Tadhg opened his mouth as if to say something more. He must've thought better of it because he shook his head and left via the door. I fell back onto the pillow and pressed the heels of my hands to my eyes. This didn't feel right anymore. It felt wrong.

Nearly two weeks together, and he'd left as if I meant nothing. As if the experiences we'd shared, the journey we'd been on, hadn't happened.

"You *fool*."

I jerked upright and clutched the sheet where it had slipped down my chest. In the corner beneath the cobwebs stood Fiadh in a dress the shade of shadows and with eyes the color of hell.

This couldn't be happening. This couldn't be real. I was dreaming. Fiadh was *not* in my bedroom.

"What have you done?" Fiadh hissed, her hair dragging behind her as she floated toward the bed.

How had she found me? Did she know I had given Tadhg the ring? "What are you doing here?"

My gaze flicked to the rumpled dress on the floor and the glowing emerald dagger discarded on top. There was no way I could make it to the dagger before the witch.

"We had a bargain, you and I." Darkness leaked from beneath her skirt, flowing toward me like fog on water. Magic crawled over the edge of the bed, creeping like a thousand shadowy spiders. I clamped my lips shut, refusing to breathe as it slithered beneath the sheet. Over my chest. Around my throat.

Fiadh's pointed black nail dragged down my cheek. The breath trapped in my lungs screamed to be let go.

I inhaled quickly.

Magic pounced.

"There you go." Nails dug into my skin when she clasped my jaw. "Drink it in. *That's* it."

A dull haze clouded my senses, like I'd had too much faerie wine.

"You were to lure the Gancanagh close enough to kill him. Do you remember?" The witch's grip tightened as she nodded my head for me. "And you remember me telling you to guard the ring with your life?"

Again, she forced me to nod. "Did you do *any* of those things?"

She shook my head.

Her lips grazed my ear as she whispered, "I want to hear you say it."

"N-no. I d-didn't. But it wasn't my fault," I cried, tears welling in my eyes. "We never made it to Tearmann."

The dagger appeared in Fiadh's hand, the glowing emerald casting her face in green light. "*Tearmann?*" Her eyes widened. "Why the hell would ye go all the way to Tearmann? Ye could've killed the bastard when ye met him in the Green Serpent."

The Green Serpent? What was she talking about?

Dread filled my belly even as I said, "I've never met the Gancanagh."

"Never met him?" she cackled. "You just shared his bed."

It couldn't be true. Tadhg couldn't be the Gancanagh. "Then who is Rían?"

The witch adjusted her grip on the hilt of the blade.

And buried it into my stomach

Pain ripped the air from my lungs. Burning, burning, *burning* my innards.

"Rían," the witch whispered, twisting the blade in my gut, "is the Gancanagh's brother."

19

THE THICK, DAMP GRASS WAS COLD BUT SOOTHING ON MY BARE FEET. *My body craved the chill as fire engulfed my torso. The silver silk gown I wore swayed in the breeze, and the ribbons on the bouquet of hydrangeas tickled my thigh. Tadhg stood across from me, swearing.*

I wanted to shout at him, but my lips refused to move.

He took my hands in his, right to right and left to left, crossed like an infinity knot.

Ruairi and the other pooka waited in the dense shadows, yellow eyes glowing like lanterns.

A man in a dark hooded cloak stood before us, holding a length of green lace, the ends undulating and twisting. He spoke a jumble of meaningless words as he wove the ribbon over and around and between our hands. I peered into his hood but saw only darkness.

Tadhg drew my attention back to him when he started whispering. The words came so fast, I couldn't understand them. I opened my mouth to ask him to speak up, but something else entirely sprang from within me, like the words were forced from my throat.

Tadhg pressed his lips to my cheek, leaving a searing mark.

I stared at our bound hands, fairly certain I should protest.

Then I saw a bloody red stain spread across my abdomen, drip down my knees, and fall onto my bare toes.

20

SOMEONE SIGHED AND TURNED A PAGE IN A BOOK. IN THE distance, a bird chirped. A door slammed—not close by, but far away. I kept still, allowing myself to wake slowly, terrified of what I would find when I finally opened my eyes.

A mound of quilts covered me on an unfamiliar sofa in someone's sitting room. The room had been painted red, and a floor-to-ceiling bookshelf ran the length of the far wall. Very little light came through the latticed window framed by heavy black drapes. Was it late at night or early in the morning?

The scent of lingering magic tickled my nostrils, and a bitter metallic taste coated my tongue. My stiff limbs felt as if they were made of wood.

Another page rustled, and I turned to find a figure lounging on a chaise beside a brick fireplace, reading.

Was I dreaming? "*Tadhg?*"

Kohl-blackened eyes lifted from the book.

"What are you doing here?" My voice cracked with dryness. I had sent him away with the ring. Hadn't I? "Why aren't you in Tearmann?"

He didn't say anything. He just kept staring.

I nudged the stifling blankets to the whitewashed wooden

floor. Someone had put me in a gown of silver silk that clung to my body like liquid moonlight. "What am I wearing?"

The chaise creaked when Tadhg shifted. "It's a dress."

Red stains marred the material at my waist. They looked an awful lot like blood.

Blood drenched sheets.

A blood drenched blade.

This was *my* blood.

I shoved off the sofa. Waves of dizziness knocked me back, forcing me to steady myself against the rolled velvet arm to keep from falling over. My hand slid down my stomach, searching for stitches. There should've been stitches. There should've been pain. There should have been some sign of the trauma from the witch's dagger.

"*Fiadh* stabbed me." My gaze connected with Tadhg's, and I stilled. "She stabbed me and said . . ."

Slowly he rose and abandoned the book on the chaise.

"It can't be true," I whispered, taking a halting step toward him. The witch had been lying. That was the only explanation that made any sense. "Tell me you're not the Gancanagh."

Silence stretched between us and then Tadhg grimaced. "I can't."

It was true.

Oh god.

I had slept with my sister's murderer.

"You *bastard*!" I launched forward, beating his chest with my fists, hating him for lying to me. Hating myself for not seeing through him. "I *trusted* you!"

I was such a fool. A bloody fool.

Cool fingers locked around my wrists. "Calm down, Keelynn." Tadhg's grip tightened, and he dragged me against him. "Stop fighting me, *dammit*. I know you're angry, but I had no choice." The strong arms that had held me so gently were like a steel cage.

"You could've told me the truth!"

"And have you run me through with that cursed dagger?" he

growled against my ear. "From the moment we met, all you've done is claim you need to kill the Gancanagh. Did you honestly believe I would raise my feckin' hand and say, 'here I am,' and let you steal my life? It may not be worth much, but it's still *mine*." He let me go and straightened his pristine black waistcoat. For the first time since we'd met, his clothes weren't missing any buttons.

It may not be worth much . . .

Tadhg's life was worth *nothing* after what he'd done. To me. To Aveen. If I still had the dagger, I would've stabbed him in his cursed heart. "I *slept* with you!"

The corner of his mouth lifted. "I remember."

The memory of those sinful lips on my body was too raw. Too painful. And to think I had started to *care* about the deceitful lout. "All this time you acted like you didn't know who Aveen was, but you knew. You *knew* she was good and kind and selfless, and you murdered her anyway."

"I *didn't* murder her."

"I saw you kill her with your poisoned lips." He'd stolen her last breath. He'd taken my sister away from me.

"For the last time: my lips are *cursed*, not *poisoned*," Tadhg groaned, lifting his eyes toward the ceiling.

"Like it makes any bloody difference! Aveen is dead because of you!"

"She's not dead!" he roared. A pulse of magic threw me onto the sofa, knocking the wind from my lungs.

Not dead.

Not dead.

Not dead.

"She had no pulse." The room spun like the dancers the night of the ball. Around and around, becoming nothing more than blurs of color and light. *Aveen was dead.* "I picked out her dress for the casket." *Aveen was dead.* "I gave the eulogy at her funeral." *Aveen was dead.*

A pair of scuffed black boots stepped in front of me, and the spinning stopped. I looked up to find Tadhg watching me. "You're right. Technically, she *is* dead. But she won't be forever. My lips are *cursed*," he repeated slowly, as if speaking to a child.

"I heard you the first time," I snapped.

"You may have heard, but it's obvious you don't understand. If my lips are cursed, then whoever kisses me is—" He opened his mouth, but no words emerged. His features contorted in a pained wince. The same thing had happened the night he'd asked for the ring.

He tugged at the dark cravat tied loosely around his throat and unbuttoned his collar. His hands fisted at his sides, and he took a deep breath. "Whoever. Kisses. Me. Is—"

Beads of perspiration broke across his brow; a vein in his forehead pulsed. Whatever he was trying to say remained on his tongue.

Tadhg was a cursed monster with a cursed kiss.

Cursed kiss.

If Tadhg was cursed, then anyone he kissed would be . . . "Cursed."

Aveen was cursed.

Cursed, *not* dead.

Cursed, but not forever.

For how long?

"A year and a day." It couldn't be that simple, could it?

Tadhg blew out a relieved breath and raked a hand through his dark hair. Firelight reflected off the exposed tips of his ears. "It's about feckin' time you figured it out."

"She's coming back." The words didn't register. *Aveen is coming back.* That night in the pub, when I'd asked Tadhg what I should do, he'd said that killing the Gancanagh was excessive and unnecessary. It had been true. All of it.

There was still one piece of the puzzle that didn't fit. "Why did you do it?" What had possessed him to prey on my sister in the first place?

Tadhg dragged a hand down his face, smearing kohl across his cheekbone. "I promised Aveen I wouldn't tell, but I think you already know the answer."

I will fix it, Aveen had said the night she'd died.

You have to trust me.

I love you, Keelynn. No matter what happens, please remember that.

Had Aveen sacrificed herself for me?

What was I thinking? This was *exactly* the type of thing my selfless sister would do. Give up a year of her life so that I could marry the man I loved. If she had called off the engagement, Robert's father would've been shamed and never considered a union with my family. But with Aveen presumed dead, *my* husband would have inherited my father's estates and fortune. And with the bargain already struck between our families, I would have been the obvious choice for Robert's wife.

It was brilliant. Absolutely brilliant.

And there was no doubt in my mind that it would've worked—if I hadn't been a selfish fool and gone into that hallway with Edward.

I dropped my head into my hands to keep from spinning out of control. All this time, I'd believed I had a role to play in this story, that I could save my sister.

My mission, my purpose. All pointless.

A warm hand settled on my shoulder. I shrugged it off. Tadhg could keep his false comfort and pity. I didn't want either.

"You could have found a way to tell me." If I had known the truth, Padraig would still be alive. I wouldn't have let Tadhg share my bed, and I wouldn't have gotten stabbed.

"Not while you possessed one of the only weapons capable of killing me." He crouched so we were eye level but did not try to touch me again. "I've spent the last two centuries drowning under the weight of these curses. I thought that ring was my only chance at freedom, and I wasn't letting it out of my sight."

A ring enchanted to neutralize curses.

A ring that he had asked me to wear so he didn't kill me when we kissed.

Now that I knew the truth, I understood why he'd lied. It didn't make things better, but I understood.

The person I'd been when we first began this journey wasn't the woman I was now. That Keelynn would have killed the Ganganagh without a second thought. As painful as it was to admit, Tadhg had been right to keep his secret.

"You may not believe me, but I am deeply sorry for deceiving you," he said, his shoulders falling. "I never meant for any of this to happen. I just wanted the ring. You weren't supposed to get caught up in this disaster."

I believed him. How could he have known I was going to go off with Edward? How could he have known I was going to track down the witch? The answer was simple: he couldn't. Everything that had happened in the wake of Aveen's death had been my fault.

"Where's my sister now?"

His mouth pressed into a tight line. "She's in the underworld, but her body is being held at my castle. My brother and I retrieved it after the funeral."

At least that was something. It would do no good to have her wake up in a few months and find herself six feet underground.

"I want to see her." I needed to know that she would be all right when she awoke.

Tadhg nodded. "That's why I was bringing you to Tearmann."

He had been trying to show me the truth all along, and I had been too stubborn to see it.

Flames winked in the emerald ring on my left hand. A ring that shouldn't be there. "You gave it back." If all of this had been about the ring, why would he give it away so easily?

Tadhg stood and averted his eyes. "The emerald is cursed to draw out a being's life force and keep an immortal's body from healing. If you had been wearing the ring when Fiadh stabbed you, there's a chance you would've survived. But without it . . ." He cleared thickness from his throat and grimaced. "You were dying, Keelynn, and my magic was powerless to save you. I had to convince my *friend* Brigid to help."

The hairs at the nape of my neck prickled. "I take it your *friend* isn't human."

His hair fell over his brow when he shook his head. "She's a witch. And she hates your kind more than anyone I know. She refused to help, so I had to do something drastic."

"What did you do?" I clutched the edge of the sofa. Surely it couldn't be as bad as what he'd already done.

His gaze darted to me, then fell to his flexing fingers. "She said she wouldn't help unless I could make you one of us, you see. So I . . . Um . . . I did."

Made me one of them? That wasn't possible, was it? "How?" I didn't feel any different. My ears were still rounded, and I didn't have wings or magic or anything else that separated the Danú from humans.

Tadhg's eyes lifted, boring into me like he could see all the way to my tattered soul. "I married you."

I married you.

"You married me?" Three simple words on their own. But when strung together in that order, they didn't make sense. Tadhg and I weren't *married*.

When I pulled the emerald from my finger, a tattooed band branded the skin beneath.

I married you.

"No . . . No . . . ." This couldn't be happening. I couldn't be married to the Gancanagh. This had to be a mistake. A misunderstanding. A twisted joke.

"There's no need to panic. It's only a handfasting," he said with a dismissive wave. There was a black tattoo on his left ring finger as well. "After a year and a day, you'll be free."

A year and a day.

Did everything in his cursed world last a year and a bloody day?

It didn't matter if we were handfasted for an hour a week or a lifetime. We were still legally bound to one another, a marriage the same as any other according to the law.

Another marriage I hadn't consented to.

Another man making my decisions.

"Why would you do this to me?" I whispered, my voice and body trembling. Hadn't he taken enough?

Tadhg reached for my fingers to smooth his thumb over the tattoo. "Haven't you been listening? It was either marry you or let you die."

I don't know if it was the revelation or the brush with Fiadh or the exhaustion or whatever strange medicine Tadhg's friend had given me, but at the moment, the idea of being married to another man who didn't love me felt like a fate worse than death.

I knocked his hand from mine, looked him in the eye, and said, "You should have let me die."

Tadhg's mouth opened. Then closed. His brow furrowed and shoulders slumped and—

Shit.

Why had I said that to him? I hadn't meant it. "I'm so—"

"Do you think I wanted this?" he snarled, eyes flooding with black. "Do you think my people will accept you as my bride? To dally with humans is one thing, but to *marry* one? Not a feckin' hope." Magic leaked from his pores, flooding toward me like writhing shadows. His hands flexed as his sides over and over and over. The glass in the windows began to rattle. The books on the shelves vibrated toward the edge, some tumbling onto the floor. "I owed you for giving me the ring, so I saved your pathetic life. But don't think for a *second* that it didn't cost me dearly."

My life may have seemed pathetic to a powerful immortal, but it was *mine.* "At least you had a choice." Tadhg had taken away the only thing I had left that was truly mine: my free will.

His lips curled back from his teeth. "And I can see that I made the wrong one."

This was my punishment for putting my faith in someone like him. "I suppose now you expect a wedding night." There was no way he had married me out of the goodness of his heart. He didn't have one.

Tadhg leaned so close the heat of his breath burned my cheek. "Why would I want something I've already had?"

Numbness settled into my bones as I watched Tadhg stomp to the chaise and drag his overcoat from the back of it. With a flick of his wrist, my boots and cloak appeared beside me. "Get dressed. We're leaving."

"I'm not going anywhere with you."

His posture went rigid, but instead of looking at me, he kept his gaze on the floorboards. "As my wife, you are my responsibility."

"I am *not* your wife." If people found out, my reputation would never recover. "I want . . ." I wanted a bloody time machine so I could go back to the day Aveen had constructed this foolish plan and beg her to stop. But since that couldn't happen . . . "I want an annulment."

"Brilliant idea. We'll get one in Gaul," Tadhg muttered, stalking to the door.

On the other side, a man with flowing black hair and glowing yellow eyes waited with a broad shoulder propped against the doorframe. "How's the happy couple?" Ruairi asked with a grin.

"Feck off and shift. We're going to Gaul." Tadhg shoved past him and into the night.

"That good, huh?" Ruairi said with a chuckle, giving me a wink. "Told ye she'd rather marry me," he shouted over his shoulder.

I slipped on my boots and stood to fasten my cloak.

"Don't ye want to ask your husband for a new dress, princess?"

"Don't call me that."

Ruairi shrugged. "Suit yerself, human."

I lifted the hood of my cloak and settled it over my matted hair. Hell would freeze over before I asked Tadhg for anything.

Ruairi pushed away from the doorframe and followed me to

where Tadhg waited at the start of a dark, barren road drenched in fog.

With a flash of light, Ruairi shifted into the black stallion and stamped his hoof in the mud. I ignored the hand Tadhg offered and mounted on my own. The saddle was as fine as the one Ruairi had worn the last time, but it was meant for a man. Tadhg gripped the horn and slipped his foot into the stirrup. Before I could protest, he slid in behind me. Strong thighs held me in place, shifting and rubbing as he settled himself into the saddle. His chest molded to my back, unyielding and strong when he reached around me to grab the reins.

"I thought you didn't ride horses," I choked, trying and failing to put distance between us.

"Ruairi isn't a horse," he grumbled, giving Ruairi a kick.

Ruairi galloped into the fog.

Cool, damp air slid past my cheeks. Tadhg kept silent, leaving only my dismal thoughts to distract me.

Married.

To the Gancanagh.

What were the odds? Of all the people in all the world, how had I stumbled upon the one I needed to kill on the very first day of this cursed mission? And now we were wed.

The longer we rode, the more guilty I felt for my outburst. This wasn't Tadhg's fault, it was mine. I had been the one to bargain with a witch. All he'd done from the very first day was try to save me.

Tadhg tugged the reins, slowing Ruairi to a canter. "When we reach Gaul, we can stay with one of my friends in the city. We should be safe there until I can find a magistrate willing to grant us an annulment."

Safe? What was he on about? "Why can't I just stay at an inn?" Gaul was the third largest city in Airren; surely we could find a place to stay.

He shifted on the saddle, his chest rubbing against my back. "The inns are the first places Fiadh will check."

"Fiadh is coming back?"

"Fiadh never forgives or forgets. What do you think she'll do to you if she finds you again?"

So I was supposed to stay with Tadhg at his friend's house and hope Fiadh didn't find me? It sounded like the safest place to be was as far from his world as possible. "You can do what you want, but I'm not staying with your *friend*." I had taken enough from Tadhg.

"Have you been listening to a word I've said?" His hand fell to my shoulder, but I shrugged him off. "The inns *aren't safe*," he ground out.

"I have friends too, you know. And it just so happens, one of them lives in Gaul."

What was I saying? This was a terrible idea.

The only person I knew in Gaul was Robert.

21

ARCHED STREETLAMPS CAST GOLDEN LIGHT ALONG THE FOOTPATH leading to Robert's townhouse. Tadhg's footsteps were almost silent behind me. When I had suggested he go with Ruairi and meet me in the morning, he had claimed it would be safer for us to stay together. But I knew the truth. He didn't want to lose sight of his precious ring. I had offered to give it back, but he insisted I needed it for my own protection. Why did he continue pretending to care? If I was dead, he wouldn't be tied to me anymore.

Arriving in a blood-stained gown with a man in tow wasn't ideal, but I refused to ask Tadhg for a new dress. When I told him to remove the kohl and tie his cravat properly so he made a good first impression, Tadhg had agreed to do one or the other, not both. I had chosen the kohl.

The line of brick townhouses continued on and on, each home a carbon copy of the one before it. The only differences were the brass numbers and the color of the doors.

When we reached number thirty-six, I stopped outside the small iron gate. "You should wait out here. I'd like a chance to explain our situation without an audience."

He leaned his hip against the low brick wall and said, "You have three minutes."

Three minutes was better than nothing. I opened the gate and made my way along the tiled path, through a manicured garden, to a set of stairs in front of a cheerful red door. My heart clattered against my ribs as I climbed. Perhaps I should have taken my chances with the Danú.

I filled my lungs with crisp autumn air, lifted the brass knocker, and let it fall.

A moment later, the knob turned. The door opened, and—

"*Keelynn?*" Robert grabbed me in a bone-crushing hug so unexpected, so unlike him, that it took me a moment before I wrapped my arms around his waist and returned the embrace. "I don't believe this. What are you doing here?" He pressed kisses to my hair. My forehead. My cheeks. "I thought you never wanted to see me again."

His thumbs stroked my jaw, and when he smiled, the weight of everything that had happened felt no heavier than my own shadow. This was the power of love.

He smelled the same, like leather and a sea breeze, comforting and familiar.

"I never should've said that to you." My voice trembled with unshed tears for what could've been. "I was just so angry."

"It's all right, my darling. It's all right. You're here now. That's all that matters."

A throat cleared behind us.

Robert glanced over my shoulder and went rigid. "Get inside. *Quickly.*" He shoved me behind him and backed toward the door. "Leave us alone, you filthy monster. We want nothing to do with you."

I peered around his broad frame to find Tadhg smiling at us from the bottom of the stairs, his eyes faintly glowing.

"He's not going to hurt us. He's here with me." I skirted around him and motioned Tadhg closer. "Robert, this is Tadhg. He's helping me get Aveen back."

Tadhg didn't move.

"What do you mean get Aveen back?" Robert stepped forward

and tucked me beneath his arm. My hand slipped around his waist like it belonged there.

"I have so much to tell you. Do you mind if we come inside?"

Robert nudged the door wider with his free hand. "Of course. We can speak in the parlor."

He ushered me into a dimly lit hallway with black and white starburst tiles. When Tadhg started climbing the steps, Robert blocked the entrance with an arm across the threshold. "*You* will wait out here."

Tadhg's hands stretched and flexed at his sides. Then he grinned. "I think that's for the best."

Robert shut the door in his face.

"That was terribly rude." Tadhg and I weren't on the best of terms, but he didn't deserve to be treated like a nuisance.

Grumbling under his breath, Robert stalked past and led me into a small parlor on the left side of the hall. There were no curtains on the rails above the wide bay windows. A thick silver nail protruded from the wood paneling over the fireplace. The marble mantlepiece and two bookshelves flanking it were empty as well.

Robert yanked a poker from the coal bucket and stabbed at the burning red coals in the grate. "What are you doing walking around in public with that *thing*?"

"That *man*—"

"*That* was not a man. Did you see its ears and eyes?"

"Are you quite finished?" I clipped, bracing my hands on my hips and reminding myself that I had treated Tadhg with the same contempt when we'd first met.

Wincing, Robert knocked the poker against his boot. "My apologies. Continue."

"Thank you." *Now, where was I?* I brushed my hair over my shoulders and took a deep breath. "I've hired Tadhg to bring me to Tearmann."

Robert jammed the poker into the bucket and closed the gap

between us. "Have you lost your damn mind? Why are you going to Tearmann?"

"Because the Gancanagh killed Aveen, and—"

"Not this again," he muttered, pinching the bridge of his nose and sinking onto the settee. "Darling, I know you're still grieving over your sister, but this is *nonsense*. The physician said Aveen died of a failed heart."

A failed heart, my foot.

I sat beside him and adjusted my cloak so he couldn't see the bloodstains beneath. "No, *that's* nonsense. Who ever heard of a failed heart turning someone's lips black?" I had tried telling everyone what had happened that night, but no one believed me. The imbecile doctor had claimed the stress of losing Aveen had caused me to hallucinate.

"And you think her black lips mean she kissed an immortal prince from Tearmann?"

"I saw them together, Robert. He kissed her, and she fell under a terrible curse."

"Do you hear yourself right now?" Robert laughed. "That sounds like a bloomin' fairy tale. Who told you this fantasy? Was it the creature outside?"

"It's the truth."

"Keelynn—"

I narrowed my eyes. "*Robert.*"

He groaned and threw himself back against the cushions. "Fine. Let's say I believe this fantastical yarn." He waved a hand in the air. "Aveen is under a *terrible curse*. I still fail to see why you're traipsing across the country in search of the monster's haven."

"The Gancanagh is keeping her body in his castle."

"So you're just going to, what? Waltz in and ask for her back?"

That was a good question. Was I going to ask for Aveen's body? Where would I bring her? We couldn't return to Gray-stones. What if someone found her and accused me of digging up her body? No one would believe Aveen was coming back from the dead until she actually did. I really needed to think this through.

"I know it sounds mad, but Tadhg said—"

"Whatever Tadhg said was obviously a lie. He's probably only telling you what you want to hear so he can take advantage of you."

"He's not lying."

Robert glanced over his shoulder to peer out the dark window. Whatever he saw made him frown. "How can you be so sure?"

"I just know, all right?"

"You just know," Robert repeated, shaking his head. "Well then. I suppose I should thank you for taking time out of your journey to stop by and see me." He threw a hand toward the entrance. "Best be going though, wouldn't want to waste time on your way to visit a murderer."

I understood this sounded far-fetched, and if I hadn't lived through the last few weeks, I wouldn't have believed it either. "Before you kick me out, I need to ask for a favor."

Robert's eyebrows arched when I stood and removed my cloak.

"Bloody hell," he gasped, shooting to his feet when he saw the bloodstains. "What happened? If that bastard hurt you, I'll kill him."

Tadhg had hurt me, but those wounds hadn't drawn blood. "I was stabbed by a witch and would've died if Tadhg hadn't saved me."

The truth of those words rocked me to my core. Tadhg didn't want to be married to me any more than I wanted to be married to him, and yet he had done it to save my life.

Robert's arms came around me. I buried my head in his chest and allowed my tears to fall. Tadhg hadn't done anything wrong, and I had been treating him like a villain. Fiadh was the villain in this story, not Tadhg. If anything, Tadhg was the hero for saving me over and over and over and over again.

"My darling, my darling." The tender kiss he pressed to my hair made my heart swell. "What do you need from me? Just name it and it's yours."

"It's no longer safe for us at the inns. If the witch finds out I survived, she will come looking for me."

"And you want to stay here." Again, he glanced toward the window. "*Both* of you."

"I can see it's too much to ask."

"It's not." He sighed. "It's not too much."

Hope warmed my chest. "You'll let us stay?"

A nod.

I threw my arms around his neck, holding tight when he stumbled back. "Thank you, Robert. You have no idea how much this means to me."

"I would do anything for you, Keelynn." He kissed my temple and slid his hands around my waist. "*Anything.*"

❦

Tadhg sat on the stairs with his back to the door, facing the night-shrouded front garden. A heavy breeze tousled his hair, carrying the salty smell of the sea.

"Well? What did he say?" Tadhg asked without turning around.

I rubbed my arms to stave off the chill. "We can stay for as long as we need."

He nodded.

"Robert's organizing dinner for us inside."

"I'm allowed in, am I?"

"Tadhg, you must understand—"

He waved a hand. "Save the excuses for someone who cares. Go inside so you don't freeze. I'll join you shortly."

Robert and I were halfway through our meal when Tadhg strode in, settled a leather satchel beside the empty chair to my left, then loaded a plate with turkey, mashed potatoes, and far too many candied carrots. I had just finished explaining the story of what had transpired for the second time.

Robert watched Tadhg shovel a bite of turkey into his mouth

like a hawk tracking its prey. "So, let me make sure I understand all of this," he said slowly, taking a sip of wine. "A witch thought you had stolen something from her and stabbed you."

Tadhg glanced at me, then looked quickly back to his dinner.

"That's right." I lifted my glass of wine to my nose and inhaled. Dry, with a hint of elderberries. Sweetness exploded on my tongue when I took a sip. "It was simply a matter of being in the wrong place at the wrong time."

Robert dabbed at his pinched mouth with the corner of his serviette. "And then *Tadhg* miraculously healed you."

"Yes."

"Unbelievable," Robert muttered, shaking his head and drinking more wine. "Learning you've been forced to endure such hardships because of these creatures breaks my heart." He placed his hand atop mine where it rested on the corner of the table. "I hope you'll let me take care of you while you're here. Tomorrow, we can go into the city and replenish some of the items that were stolen from you."

"That would be wonderful. Thank you."

"There's no need to thank me. No lady should be forced to wear blood-soiled rags to dinner." He glared at Tadhg. "Any gentleman worth his salt would feel the same. I'm only sorry I don't have garments here for you to change into."

Tadhg's fork screeched over the china when he stabbed a pile of carrots. "Don't forget, Keelynn, you and I have some business to attend to before we leave the city."

I could have thrown my plate at him for bringing up our annulment.

"What business is that?" Robert asked, his eyebrows raised as he picked up the wine bottle and tipped it into my glass.

"It's nothing." I kicked Tadhg beneath the table. He swore and shot me a warning glare.

Pain lanced up my shin. The bastard had kicked me back. "I think *Robert* deserves to know," he said far too sweetly.

The less Robert knew, the better.

"It's only a tiny misunderstanding that hardly warrants any attention at all." Tadhg's eyebrows flicked up, and I twisted away from him to smile at our host. "It was so good of Robert to offer us rooms, wasn't it, Tadhg?"

Robert brushed my hair back from my face and smiled. "My home is your home."

Tadhg slammed down his fork, rattling the plates. "It was very kind of your *friend* to make such a generous offer."

"It's better than being murdered in our sleep."

"Is it?"

"Robert, would you excuse us for a moment?" I shot to my feet and tugged on Tadhg's sleeve until he stood as well. Once I was sure he'd follow, I escaped into the hallway.

The front door creaked from the wind outside, and the flames in the wall sconces shuddered.

I whirled to find Tadhg leaning against the paneled walls, grinning. "What the hell was that?" I demanded, struggling to keep my voice level. "Robert has offered us a place to stay so we don't get *murdered*, and you're acting like a petulant child!"

"Me?" He pressed a hand to his chest in mock horror. "You think *I'm* the problem here? He's the one keeping his feckin' knife on his lap like he expects me to attack him. As if a knife would do anything to hold me off if I decided to break every bone in his worthless—"

"Tadhg!"

His mouth clamped shut, but I could tell from the wicked gleam in his eyes that he was picturing all of the horrible things he wanted to do to Robert. How was I supposed to survive this dinner? All I needed was for him to pretend to be a gentleman, then Robert wouldn't be so on edge.

"I'm calling in our wager," I said, planting my hands on my hips. I had no idea if this was going to work, but I had to do something.

Tadhg's eyebrows came together, and he shook his head. "Excuse me?"

"You promised to act like a gentleman for two hours. I'm calling it in."

Tadhg's hands flexed at his sides, and his expression turned stormy. Then his eyes widened imperceptibly, and his frown twisted into a smirk. "Are you sure?"

The way he asked was far too calm. "Yes."

A silver pocket watch appeared in his hand, and he showed me the time. It was a quarter till eight. "Two hours, starting now. And you remember what I get if I win?" he drawled, tucking the watch into his waistcoat pocket.

Shit.

If Tadhg won, he got to unlace my stay.

22

Back in the dining room, I saw the silver gleam of a knife on Robert's lap when I passed. The idea of a butter knife being able to stop Tadhg was laughable. I apologized again for the interruption and reached for my wine glass before taking my seat. Robert had been good enough to refill it. Tadhg sat next to me, his back ramrod straight as he pinned the turkey with his fork and sliced off a tiny bite.

We continued our meal in silence but for the sound of cutlery on china and an occasional *clink* whenever someone would set down their wine glass. Every few minutes, Tadhg would take out that bloody pocket watch, flip it open, smile, then close it and return it to his pocket.

The longer the silence stretched, the more tension collected in my stomach.

Suddenly, Robert leaned forward and squeezed my knee beneath the table. "Do you remember our picnic on the beach before I left for university?"

The memory left my stomach fluttering. "How could I forget?" The weather had turned unseasonably cold, and we had ended up bundled together in his overcoat, watching ships sail into the harbor.

It seemed an odd memory to bring up after everything had gone so terribly wrong.

"I know how much you loved the scones that day and asked the cook to bake a fresh batch for breakfast tomorrow." Robert's eyes crinkled when he smiled.

Scones had always been my favorite treat.

And Robert had remembered.

"That was very thoughtful of you."

When his engagement to Aveen had been announced, Robert had acted like I no longer existed. Like our time together had been forgettable. To find out that he recalled such insignificant details—and seemed to hold them close—meant the world to me.

Tadhg ripped the watch from his pocket and scowled. I almost smiled.

"Where did you get such a fine piece?" Robert asked, nodding toward the watch.

"This?" Tadhg held it aloft and grinned. "It belonged to my wife's close friend."

His wife's friend? What was he up to?

"You're *married*?" Robert scoffed, his mouth gaping open.

Tadhg dabbed at his lips with the corner of his serviette, then picked up his wine glass for a tiny sip. "I am."

Robert shook his head, and the tension in his shoulders seemed to ease a fraction. "Well, it's a lovely watch. I have one just like it from my father. Very expensive."

"Oh, really? What a coincidence."

It belonged to my wife's close friend.

Bloody hell. Tadhg had stolen Robert's watch. When I got him alone, I was going to kill him myself.

Tadhg set the watch on the table between us so that I could see the face. It was already nine o'clock. There were only forty-five minutes left for Tadhg to feign manners.

My stomach filled with dread.

"So, Tadhg," Robert drawled, drizzling gravy over his second helping of turkey, "I'm still a little confused as to your role in all of this."

When Tadhg looked at me, his lips curled into a slow smile. I pleaded silently, praying he wouldn't ruin everything by telling Robert about us. "Didn't Keelynn tell you?" he said, drawing out the torture. Tadhg caught my hand and lifted it to his mouth. "I've been hired to bring this stunning woman to the Gancanagh's castle." Cold lips grazed my knuckles.

The world faded away, leaving only my hand and Tadhg's lips.

"Are you still confused," Tadhg said quietly, looking pointedly at Robert, "or would you like me to draw you a picture?"

Robert's face flushed. I jerked free and wiped my clammy hand against my skirt before going for more wine. How was my glass empty again? Robert was good enough to refill it.

"You must excuse Tadhg," I said. "He doesn't understand how a *gentleman* should act at the dinner table." And if he didn't get it together, I was going to win the wager.

The muscles in Robert's square jaw flexed, and his eyes narrowed. "Does he understand how a gentleman acts elsewhere?"

Tadhg smirked. "Ask Keelynn."

Robert's fists slammed against the table, knocking over the saltshaker and rattling the dishes. "You bloody bastard! If you touched her, I'll kill you." He jabbed his butter knife across the table at Tadhg.

Tadhg shook his head and clucked his tongue, checking the time and closing the watch with a *click*. "Now, now, Robert. Surely a gentleman shouldn't make such threats."

I balled up my serviette and threw it onto the table. "Stop it. Both of you." I twisted to glare at Tadhg. "I know what you're doing, and it ends now." They were grown men. They could tolerate one another for one meal. "You will be civil to one another."

Robert ripped his glass off the table and slumped back into his seat. "You expect me to be civil to a monster who is clearly taking advantage of you? I've half a mind to call the guards and have him arrested."

Tadhg glared at Robert, his fingers tapping rapidly against his knee. The pewter gravy dish slid toward the end of the table, precariously close to Robert's lap.

I caught the dish right before it fell over the edge.

Tadhg's glare shifted toward me. And then he smirked.

Robert's knife clattered to the floor, and he made a terrible gagging sound. His eyes bulged as he clawed at his throat.

"Robert? Are you all right?"

His face turned redder and redder—

Choking.

He was choking.

I shoved away from the table, knocking the chair to the ground, and pummeled between his shoulder blades hard enough to dislodge whatever was cutting off his airway. But it wasn't working. Why wasn't it working?

"Tadhg! Do something!"

Robert's face had gone purple.

Tadhg pulled the watch out by the chain and tossed it onto the table next to the gravy boat.

"Please!"

Robert fell forward, gasping for breath. After a few moments, his color returned to normal. Cursing, Robert wiped his sweaty brow with his sleeve and loosened his cravat.

He must've had such a fright. Thank heavens he was breathing again.

"What do you need, my love? Tell me how to help." I wrapped my arms around his shoulders. My heart beat so frantically, I was sure everyone could hear it.

Robert shrugged me off. "Stop fussing. I'm fine."

"Are you certain? I could get you more—"

Robert knocked my hand away. "I said, I'm fine."

He was embarrassed. That was all. And I wasn't helping matters by trying to coddle him.

I righted my chair and grabbed my own drink with an unsteady hand. Had Tadhg lost his mind? Robert was helping us, and Tadhg had choked him. From the blackness in his eyes, it looked like he was going to try again. I had to do something to distract him.

"Tadhg?"

Tadhg blinked, and at once, the blackness disappeared.

"How long will it take us to reach Tearmann?" The sooner I got to my sister, the better. *Wine.* I needed more wine.

"Four days."

"I believe you mean *three* days," Robert countered, piling cutlery atop his plate and setting it aside for collection.

Tadhg picked up his wine glass, leaned back in the chair, and took a long, slow sip. "I believe I meant what I said. It will take us four."

"The creatures' haven is only three days north of here. You could make it in two if you went on horseback and the weather was fine."

Groaning, I dropped my head into my hands. If they didn't stop this nonsense, I was going to leave the room and let them kill each other.

"That's if you cross through the thickest part of the Black Forest." Tadhg swirled the liquid in his glass. Around and around. "Which isn't safe—especially for a human."

"You're referring to the Phantom Queen?" At Tadhg's nod, Robert snorted. "Utter nonsense."

"Have you met the Queen?" Tadhg asked, picking up one of the rolls and turning it over in his hand.

Robert fiddled with his sapphire cufflinks, his face pinched in irritation, like holding a conversation with Tadhg took every ounce of patience he possessed. "I've heard the stories about her. Everyone has."

"Did you know that if you enter the Black Forest without her permission or a sacrifice, you *will* die?" Tadhg sawed the roll in half with his knife. "She has a son who could turn you into ash with an errant thought." He dropped the knife and tore the roll into tiny pieces, the crumbs falling all over the white tablecloth. "And Tearmann is filled with people desperate to see the humans pay for what they've taken from us." Tadhg picked up his serviette and used it to clean the crumbs from his fingers. "So, when I say it will take *four days*, that is how long it will take."

That's what awaited us in Tearmann? I thought Tadhg had said the Danú didn't hate humans.

Staring at those bits of roll, obliterated by Tadhg's hands, turned the wine and food in my stomach sour. Why hadn't he warned me about the terror we would face? I had thought that, with Tadhg at my side, we would be able to slip into their territory unnoticed and make it to the castle unscathed.

"Oh, *I see*." Robert huffed a laugh. "You don't want to take a shortcut because you're concerned with Lady Keelynn's *safety*." Sarcasm dripped from every word. "Perhaps you should've thought of that *before* you promised to bring her to a monster's castle."

Tadhg sat back and sipped his wine, eyes never leaving Robert.

"It seems to me you care about one thing," Robert went on, baring his teeth, "and that's getting paid."

Tadhg flicked his wrist. The wine glass in Robert's hand vanished and reappeared in Tadhg's. "If I wanted Keelynn's money, I could just take it." Grinning, he dumped Robert's wine into his own glass.

Robert swore and retrieved his empty glass from across the table.

I scowled at Tadhg.

Wide green eyes met mine, full of false innocence.

"That's it. I'm done." I pushed back from the table and stood. Both men stared at me as though I had gone mad. Perhaps I had. "The two of you can sit here and argue all night, but I am going to bed."

Tadhg and Robert clambered to their feet. They glared at one another, but Robert was the first to speak. "Don't go. Please. Join me for a nightcap in the parlor."

"Am I the only one invited?"

Robert's gaze flicked to Tadhg before returning to me. "I would *love* it if your *guest* would join us as well."

Tadhg gave him a vicious smile and said, "I'd rather be hung, drawn, and quartered."

✦

The candelabras on the parlor walls had been lit, and a fire still blazed in the hearth, giving the room a lovely, amber glow.

"That was interesting," Robert muttered, continuing to a drink cart in the far corner while I dropped onto the edge of the settee.

Interesting? It had been a disaster. "You could have at least tried being nice."

"That *was* me trying. I don't know how you can stand being near that *thing*." He joined me on the settee a moment later, carrying two crystal glasses filled with deep red liquid.

"He's not so bad after you get to know him."

Robert offered a non-committal hum.

A log crackled in the fire, sending a shower of orange sparks bursting onto the hearth.

All that wine made my head feel fuzzy, and the sweet port wasn't going to help. But the more I drank, the less worried I'd be about surviving in Tearmann.

Robert's nail tapped against the glass in his hand. "I'm just going to come right out and say it. I don't want you going with Tadhg."

When I glanced over at him, his lips were pressed into a thin line. "Robert—"

"Before you respond, hear me out." He gulped his drink before setting the glass on the coffee table. "It's dangerous,

Keelynn," he said, lacing our fingers together. "Far too dangerous for a fool's errand. Who's to say Aveen is really there?"

"I appreciate your concern." If I was being honest, I was more than a little concerned myself. "But this is something I have to do." The rest of the port slid down my throat like water.

"Why?" His thumbs brushed against my knuckles. "What guarantee do you have that the Gancanagh won't kill you on sight?"

"Tadhg said—"

"*Bloody Tadhg.*" Robert dropped his head and swore. "Why do you keep insisting on trusting the wrong man?"

"You mean the way I trusted you?" There it was. I had said it. Drudging up the past wasn't what I had planned for tonight, but if Robert wanted to talk about trust and betrayal, then we were going to start with him.

"Don't you think I know how badly I screwed up? That I haven't regretted letting you go every minute of every day since? You were always the one for me, and I was too much of a fool to see it."

My heart stuttered. Was I dreaming? This had to be a dream. "Do you truly mean that?"

He nodded and pulled me close enough to see the varying shades in his hazel eyes. "Yes. And I don't want you to go with him. I want you to stay with me."

The firelight caught a few stray hairs in the cleft of his chin that he had missed while shaving. Robert was still as handsome as he had been the first time I saw him outside our estate. It had been around Yule, and he'd come with his father, bearing brightly wrapped packages and baskets of minced pies and puddings.

And he wanted me to stay with him.

"I made so many mistakes with you." Robert's thumb brushed across my lips. "You believed once that I could make you happy. All I'm asking for is a chance to prove I still can."

The man I had loved for so long was finally ready to be with me. I should have been ecstatic. I should have been jumping up and down celebrating. But staying with Robert meant leaving my sister in Tearmann. "What about Aveen?"

"She's gone, Keelynn." Robert tilted my chin so our mouths were only a breath apart. "But I'm not. I'm right here." He leaned forward and pressed his lips to mine.

The empty glass slipped from my grasp, shattering on the tiles. I laced my fingers through his short hair and dragged him closer.

Heat. Passion. Desire. The months hadn't dulled my need for him, only intensified it.

Robert shifted and slipped a hand beneath my skirt, up my calf, to my knee and—My thigh. His hand was on my thigh. A few inches higher and—

Tadhg.

I was married to Tadhg.

"Robert," I whispered between his insistent kisses, cupping his square jaw. "Today has been overwhelming."

Groaning, Robert adjusted his weight on top of me and rested his forehead against mine. "Don't go yet." The husky timbre of his voice left heat pooling in my stomach. "Please." His hand inched higher.

I wanted him, but not like this.

"I'll still be here tomorrow."

I needed time to figure out whether or not to accept his proposal. If I stayed with Robert, I would need to secure a vow from Tadhg that he would ensure Aveen's safe return once the curse was broken.

And I needed to get that annulment.

"Yes. Yes, of course." Robert's hand emerged from my skirts. "Give me a moment to"—he blew out a shaky breath and adjusted his breeches—"*compose* myself." He didn't speak again until his breathing returned to normal. "Come. I'll bring you to your room."

I smoothed a hand over my disastrous hair and adjusted the front of my dress. Robert tucked his shirt back into his breeches and chuckled when he saw the glittering shards of glass. "My maid will not be impressed when she finds this mess in the morning."

I stifled a giggle with my fingers. If I'd been sober, I would've tried to clean it myself, but at this point, I'd only make more of a mess.

He stood and, instead of offering a hand, swept me into his arms. I laughed the entire way up the stairs, relishing how it felt to be in his arms again. If we could do this every day for the rest of our lives, I would die happy.

Moonlight drifted through the arched window at the end of the upstairs hall. Robert didn't put me down until he'd opened the bedroom door. My body slid down his, and I could feel him harden beneath his breeches. His gaze dropped to my lips, sending my pulse racing out of control. My resolve cracked and—

"I hope I'm not interrupting." Tadhg propped a shoulder against the door to my right; his lips lifted into a smirk.

Robert stumbled back, his face a mixture of fury and desire. "Goodnight, Lady Keelynn," he ground out, turning on his heel and stalking toward the room to my left.

Tadhg shouted, "Goodnight," at his back.

The slamming of his door echoed through the corridor.

Tadhg shoved away from the wall and meandered toward me. "You and I need to talk."

The last thing I wanted was to speak to him. I escaped to my room and flung the door shut.

When I turned around, Tadhg was sitting on the edge of the window, gripping the sill with both hands. "Slamming a door in a man's face when he's speaking is terribly rude."

"So is trying to kill our host."

"Kill our host? Such a terrible accusation."

"You promised to be a gentleman."

He shrugged, not bothering to look the least bit repentant. "Turns out seeing another man fondling my wife brings out the monster in me."

I opened the armoire, searching for something to wear to bed.

Inside was a stack of clean white shirts. "My relationship with Robert is none of your business," I reminded him, pulling one from the top.

"None of my business?" he muttered, scratching his ear. "Have you forgotten that you and I are married? And if I hadn't been at dinner tonight, you would've let your precious *Robert* bend you over the table and have his way with you right on top of the feckin' turkey."

White hot rage exploded inside of me. I whirled around and slapped him across the face. "How dare you speak to me like that." The cold silk of my dress did nothing to relieve the vicious stinging in my palm.

Tadhg raised a hand to his reddened cheek, his eyes blown wide.

"I am *nothing* to you," I hissed, struggling to keep my voice down, "and you are nothing to me. A means to an end. An escape from reality. A handsome distraction."

"Keelynn—" He stepped forward.

I backed away. "No. You don't get to talk to me. I want you out of this house. And don't think about coming back until you've organized a magistrate."

"I'm sorry. I don't know what came over me." He inhaled a shaking breath and combed his fingers through his hair. "I shouldn't have said that, and I shouldn't have acted so childish at dinner. I'm sorry."

Sorry.

Sorry.

Sorry.

"Save your worthless apologies for someone who cares and get the hell out of my room."

23

The following morning, soft knocking left me rolling out of bed and hurrying toward the door.

"Mornin', milady," said a pretty young maid with springy red hair peeking from beneath a white mop cap. "Master Robert asked me to bring a tub to yer room."

It was like he could read my mind. A bath was just what I needed to start this day off right. "A bath sounds heavenly. Thank you . . . ?"

"Daisy."

"Thank you, Daisy."

Ten minutes later, a small porcelain tub had been dragged in front of the barren fireplace and filled. When the last kettle arrived, Daisy had a white box tucked beneath her other arm. "This is from Master Robert." She handed me the box and dumped the kettle into the tub. Steam curled from the water. "Is there anything else ye need?"

"No. This is wonderful."

A fine black mourning dress was folded inside the box. More black. More darkness. Why couldn't Robert have bought me a nice green dress?

Green like Tadhg's eyes.

No. Not green. Blue maybe. Or red. Anything but green.

I abandoned the box and dress on the unmade bed and stripped out of the cotton shirt I'd worn to sleep. Dried blood stained my stomach, smeared around a jagged black scar from my belly button to the base of my ribs. Last night, I had been too exhausted and tipsy to get a good look at it. The scar was smooth but unsightly. What would Robert say when he saw it? Would it disgust him?

I stepped into the tub and sank into the cocoon of liquid silence, dulling the world and its decisions

Stay with Robert or go to Aveen.

If it had to be one or the other, my sister would win hands down every time. But why couldn't I do both?

If I secured a promise from Tadhg to bring me to Tearmann a day or two before she returned, then I could have everything I had ever wanted.

Daisy had left lavender scented soap and a coarse sponge on top of a stool beside the tub. I scrubbed away the dirt and grime lingering from my encounter with Fiadh until only the black scar remained. The emerald ring slipped down my finger, revealing a sliver of tattoo.

The fight with Tadgh replayed in my mind.

You are my wife.

As if I needed the reminder with a brand around my finger. It wasn't as if ours was a real marriage. The memory of his lewd comment made my face burn.

Tadhg had ruined my night, but I refused to let him ruin my day.

My hair was still damp when I left the bedroom and made my way down the hall, past the room Tadhg had been given. The door was ajar, and the bed inside was still made. There was no sign of Tadhg.

Good. I didn't want to see him anyway.

Robert met me at the bottom of the stairs, looking resplendent in a tailored blue waistcoat and dark breeches. "You're as beautiful as ever this morning, Lady Keelynn," he said, bowing over my hand and brushing his lips across my knuckles. "I trust you slept well?"

"I did. And thank you for the dress." I smoothed a hand down the lace at my skirts. "A woman could get used to this sort of treatment."

Chuckling, he offered his elbow. "I could hardly expect you to ride into town looking like anything but the lady you are."

We shared a quiet breakfast of rich, buttery scones and tea in the dining room. When Robert asked if Tadhg would be joining us, I lied and said he had business to attend to. Robert didn't bother hiding his elation.

Afterwards, we took the carriage into Gaul and strolled through the bustling city arm-in-arm, from one fine shop to the next. Robert insisted on buying me three new dresses, and I used some of my own money on two new shifts, some impractical, lacy underthings, and splurged on a soft pink stay with delicate lace made on the continent.

Robert had a meeting with his solicitor at lunch, so I waited for him at a lovely blue-and-white tea house beside the river. In the distance, ships sailed into port. After growing up on the east coast of the island, being back at the seaside felt like coming home.

It was easy to imagine what life would be like if I lived here, with Robert. Visiting the city while he worked. Sharing dinner and drinks at night before retiring. Entertaining our friends and guests. The townhouse was small but not uncomfortable. Simple, not pretentious.

"I see someone's away with the faeries."

I turned to find Tadhg standing beside the table, watching me through bloodshot eyes. He slumped into the open seat and gestured toward my half-eaten cherry tart. I pushed the plate toward him as a peace offering. I didn't have it in me to fight today.

"Where's Prince Charming?" he asked, taking a massive bite and spilling crumbs onto the white tablecloth.

"*Robert* should be here any minute." My tea had gone cold ages ago, but I sipped it anyway to keep my hands busy.

Tadhg's fingers tapped against the edge of the table as he chewed. "Then I suppose I'll make this brief." His ears peeked out of his hair when his head tilted. "We have a meeting with a magistrate on Friday at four."

Two elderly women at another table twisted in their chairs to stare at us and whisper behind gloved hands. They needed to mind their own bloody business.

"I cannot believe you actually organized it." After the way he'd acted last night, I'd been afraid he'd hold me to our vows out of spite. I set the teacup aside and scowled at the old biddies until they turned away.

Tadhg didn't seem to notice our audience as he looped a finger through the teacup's handle and took a sip. He made a face, dumped in three more lumps of sugar, stirred, and then took another drink. "Even *handsome distractions* such as myself have been known to keep the odd promise."

Handsome distraction.

After a good deal of reflection over my tea, I'd realized I was as much to blame for our fight last night as Tadhg. We were married for the time being, and out of respect for him, I should've acted with more decorum around Robert—at least while Tadhg was around.

"I'm sorry for saying such awful things to you last night. They were spoken out of anger."

His face remained expressionless as he finished my tea and set the cup on the saucer with a delicate *tink*. "'Save your worthless apologies for someone who cares. You are nothing to me, and I am nothing to you.'"

Hearing him repeat the hateful things I'd said last night stung more than I'd admit. "Tadhg . . ."

"No, no. It's all right. I like knowing where I stand with

233

people. Makes life easier." Tadhg tossed a sugar cube into his mouth and stood. "I'll meet you on Friday at half three in the Arches pub." A grin. "Wear something nice." With that, he turned and strode up the street.

Someone came up behind me and settled a hand on my elbow. "Where's Tadhg off to?" Robert scowled at Tadhg as he made his way between pedestrians and disappeared around the back side of a jewellery shop.

"He's staying elsewhere for the next few nights," I assumed. He'd probably evanesce to his castle and spend the rest of the week doing whatever princes did. Count gold, read missives, seduce women.

Robert caught me by the waist and spun around. The old women were watching again, but this time they wore approving smiles.

"That's bloody brilliant," he laughed. "I cannot wait to have you all to myself."

Alone with Robert. The only place I'd rather be was with Aveen. But since that wasn't possible for a few more months, I figured I may as well enjoy my time with him.

The fish and seaweed breeze blowing in off the coast tugged at my pinned hair as we made our way to the carriage. A swarm of seagulls cawed for their next meal, circling the gray clouds above. Children wove between us in a rowdy game of tag, giggling and shouting. We stopped to let them pass, but one ended up caught in my skirts.

The little girl's face was dirty, her hands stained purple. "S-sorry milady," she said in a mousy voice, offering an awkward curtsy.

"It's all right—"

Robert shoved her away. "Watch where you're going, filthy mite."

The girl skittered off after her friends, nearly ramming into another couple ahead of us.

"Filthy mite? Really, Robert?" I glowered at his pinched expression. "It was clearly an accident."

"Accident or not, those heathens will never learn manners if no one teaches them what is—and is *not*—socially acceptable," he clipped, gesturing toward where the children had disappeared.

"That *child* couldn't have been more than seven or eight. She still has plenty of time to learn social graces."

Robert's hand felt too heavy where it rested on my own. I offered a tight smile before pulling free and pretending to adjust the pins in my hair. "When I was that age, I was still making magic potions in the forest behind my house." And kissing boys, hoping to find a charming prince.

"Yes, I know," Robert said with a humorless chuckle. "I do hope you'll raise our children with a bit more decorum."

"*Our* children?" My stomach tightened at the prospect.

The carriage was parked up ahead, in front of a crumbling stone wall next to a flower stall.

"You do want children, don't you?" he asked, his eyebrows pulling together when he glanced sidelong at me.

"Oh, yes. Of course, I do. I just . . . I don't know. I suppose we've never spoken about children, so I wasn't sure how you felt about them." Our drawing room conversations centered around the weather, our families, and his mates from university. The handful of times we were alone, we were too busy to discuss our future together.

"I want to give you everything you've ever wanted." He tucked a stray hair behind my ear and smiled. "A family. A home. If it is within my power, it's yours."

I turned my head to kiss his palm and said, "All I want is you."

❧

The only sound in the silent townhouse was the crackling fire in the parlor's narrow fireplace. Daisy and the rest of the servants

235

had disappeared after the dinner dishes had been cleared, leaving Robert and I alone.

Flames reflected off the two empty bottles of wine and glasses abandoned on the coffee table. Robert's waistcoat sat bunched up on the floor next to our discarded boots.

"I hate that you still wear your wedding ring," Robert said, smoothing a thumb over the enchanted emerald.

I tucked my hand under my thigh before he could see what was concealed beneath, praying the brand would disappear once the annulment was finalized. "Why does it matter? It's not like I'm still married," I said with a tight laugh, nestling deeper into his embrace. His heart beat steady and strong beneath his partially unbuttoned shirt.

He squeezed me closer, like he never wanted me to leave. "I don't like being reminded that you belonged to someone else."

I didn't like it either.

Three more days—or was it only two? I couldn't quite remember. Either way, I'd have my annulment soon.

And then—

And then what?

Would Tadhg take back the ring? If he did, I'd be powerless against Fiadh, and I'd be forced to tell the truth for the rest of the year.

I wasn't sure which would be more disastrous.

Dying a slow painful death would be bad.

But being forced to tell Robert the truth about what had really happened these past few weeks would be worse. Could he find it in his heart to forgive me, or would he cast me aside?

Perhaps I could convince Tadhg to leave the ring with me until my curse had expired. But then how would I explain wanting to wear the ring after I finished mourning?

If only there were a way to break the curse entirely.

Hold on. There *was* a way to break it.

True love's kiss.

The answer to the most pressing problem had been in front of me all along.

"I love you, Robert." I loved the way his eyes crinkled at the corners when he smiled. I loved the way he looked at me like I was the only woman in the world. I loved everything about him.

He smiled down at me, then pressed a kiss to my temple. "I love you too."

Our kiss tasted like wine and love, heady and sweet.

"I love kissing you," I told him, slipping the ring from my finger but keeping my hand hidden beneath my skirts. If only this night could last forever, and we never had to leave this settee.

"I should hope so," he murmured against my mouth, "since I'm the only man you'll be kissing for the rest of your life."

Hearing Robert talk about forever made me giddy. Life with Robert would be perfect. We could travel to Graystones in the summer and visit our families at Yule. We could pick a favorite restaurant in the city and visit every Friday when he finished work. We could have two children—no, three. No, four. Four children with golden hair and hazel eyes and—

"What did Tadhg want today?"

Tadhg? I didn't want to talk about *him*. "What do you mean?"

"When he met you at the tea house. The two of you looked like you were engaged in serious conversation."

"I didn't realize you saw us." Had he been close enough to overhear us? No, that was crazy. He wouldn't be asking if he already knew. "We were talking about—" *Aveen*. Sharp pain rattled through my brain. "We were talking about—" *Aveen*.

I couldn't lie.

The curse.

It should've been broken.

Why wasn't it broken?

"Talking about what?" Robert prompted, gesturing for me to continue.

The ring. I had to put on the ring. I felt beneath my leg but

237

couldn't find it. *Dammit*. It must've slipped. I scooted out of Robert's embrace and shot to my feet.

"What's wrong?" Robert's eyebrows came together. "Are you all right?"

"I lost my ring."

He frowned at the settee. "It's not a big deal, is it? We can find it in the morning."

"No. I need it now." Hiding my left hand behind my back, I searched between the cushions. "Help me find it. Please."

Robert swore under his breath and moved the cushions aside. Something *pinged* off the floor and rolled next to my boot. I snatched the ring before Robert could and shoved it back onto my finger.

"What the hell was that about?" he growled, folding his arms over his chest and scowling at my clasped hands.

"Nothing. I just . . ." *Think, Keelynn. Think.* "This ring isn't the one Edward gave me. It belonged to Aveen," I explained, the lie sliding free without a spark of pain.

"Why didn't you just tell me that when I asked about it?"

"I . . . um . . . didn't want to upset you. I know the two of you were engaged and thought the reminder might be painful." That sounded convincing, right?

"I never loved your sister," Robert said, stepping closer and brushing my hair back from my face. "I've never loved anyone but you."

His words made my legs weak, and his kiss took my breath and—

Wait.

I loved Robert.

And yet my curse hadn't been broken.

Robert's hands slid from my hips to my backside, pulling me hard against him. He groaned against my lips and urged me toward the settee.

Why hadn't the curse been broken?

I loved Robert, but did he not really love me?

No. That was insane. Of course he loved me.

The backs of my legs collided with the settee, and I fell to the cushions. Robert dropped to his knees and nudged my thighs apart with his hip. The buckle on his belt jingled when he slipped the leather strap free.

"We can't do this," I gasped when cold hands slipped beneath my skirt.

Hooded hazel eyes met mine, clouded with desire. "Yes, we can."

He loves me.

He loves me.

He loves me.

If that was true, why was I still cursed?

He dotted hot, open-mouth kisses down my chest. My head fell back against the crooked cushion.

He loves me.

He loves me.

One hand found my breast, the other slipped higher . . .

He loves me.

What if he didn't?

The emerald ring shifted when I threaded my fingers through his short hair; the tattoo beneath was a mocking sliver of black.

You are my wife.

"No," I whispered. We couldn't do this. Not yet. Not until I was free from my marriage. And not until I knew for sure that Robert loved me.

Robert stilled. Chest heaving. Eyes burning. "Do you need more wine? I have more bottles in the cellar."

Wine? I didn't need more bloody wine. I needed to know he wasn't lying. I needed to know that this was real and not some fantasy inside my muddled mind. "No. I just want to wait."

He sat back on his haunches and raked a hand down his face. "Wait for what?"

"For a time when my mind isn't clouded with drink."

"This is about Aveen, isn't it? I knew you hadn't forgiven me."

He shoved to his feet and fastened his belt. "How long do you plan on torturing me for one bloody mistake?"

Torture? How could he think I was trying to torture him?

"Robert, this has nothing to do with your engagement to my sister. I've spent the last few weeks traveling across this cursed island, and nearly died." *Multiple times.* "I just need a little space to breathe before I jump into anything."

The last four months had been riddled with mistakes. What if this was another one?

24

SHADOWS SHUDDERED IN MY PERIPHERALS. HELLISH BLACK EYES peered from between trees with bone-white bark. Magic writhed like smoke over the fresh dirt piled next to an empty grave, creeping closer and closer until its cloying stench wrapped around my tongue. Footsteps thundered through the forest, louder and louder and louder until—

Crash

I shot upright and slammed a hand against my racing heart. A thin layer of sweat coated my face and neck, like I had been the one running through that cursed forest. But I wasn't in a forest. I was in a bedroom. In Robert's townhouse.

Thankfully, my head felt clearer than it had when I'd stumbled into bed. With a few more hours of sleep, I thought I might avoid a hangover altogether.

The vase of roses Robert had bought before we left the city wasn't on the bedside table where Daisy had put it. Shards of glass glistened in the puddle of water and roses spreading across the wooden floor. Had I knocked it over in my sleep?

A shadowy figure emerged from the nook between the wall and the fireplace.

I opened my mouth to scream—

The figure flicked its wrist, and the mess on the floor vanished.

"*Tadhg?*"

"Shhhh . . . Go back to sleep," he slurred, stumbling toward the door. Where was he going? He couldn't be here. If Robert found out, he'd never forgive me.

I threw the quilt aside and jumped out of bed. The floor-boards were dry underfoot. "What are you doing?"

He caught himself on the wall with two hands and gave the patterned wallpaper a kiss. "Nothing. I'm not here."

"Yes, you are. I can see you."

"No, you can't." Bracing a shoulder against the wall, Tadhg slid into a heap on the ground.

The smell of stale alcohol gagged me when I knelt beside him. "Are you drunk?" Just what I needed to deal with tonight. At least I had sobered up. The two of us drunk would only lead to another fight or something worse.

Tadhg hiccuped and rubbed his eyes with the heels of his hands, smearing kohl to his cheekbones. "Yup."

"You're drunk and you came here?" He could've evanesced anywhere in the world. I tugged the hem of my shift to cover my ankles and clutched my knees to my chest.

"If Fiadh wants to kill my wife, she's going to have to"—*hiccup*— "go through me first."

"And you thought you could defeat her in this state?" Even with all his faculties, Fiadh and her dark magic would be a formidable opponent. Tadhg was powerful, but he had been fighting humans, not an evil witch with a score to settle.

"It's not about defeating her." His heavy exhale rustled the hair falling over my shoulders. "It's about giving her a more enticing target."

Fiadh's hatred of the Gancanagh, of Tadhg, was the reason I had been sent on this pointless quest. As angry as I was with him for the decisions he'd made, I didn't wish him dead. At least not at the moment. "Tadhg—"

"I like the way you say my name." He booped me on the nose with his finger and giggled. *Giggled.* This man, a Prince of Tearmann, giggled like a schoolgirl when he was drunk.

I don't know why I found the fact so endearing. "You like the way I say your name?" I repeated. Why was my stomach fluttering? It should *not* be fluttering. Those flutters belonged to Robert now.

The wind outside howled. A draft made its way down the chimney, leaving me shivering against the cold. Not adding coal to the fire when I'd come to bed had been a mistake.

Tadhg nodded, and the corners of his lips lifted in a slow, sleepy smile. "I like a lot of things about you."

I snorted. "Like what?"

He pressed his finger to his lips and shushed himself. "Don't think I should tell you. Don't want to get slapped again."

I shouldn't want to know. I should leave it, kick him out, and go back to bed. For some reason, I couldn't. For some reason, hearing his answer had become my sole purpose in life. "I promise not to slap you."

"Ah, but you can lie."

The house creaked from the battering storm. There was something eerie about the storms that struck at night and left with the dawn. Legend claimed the coastal winds were only this frenzied when the banshee culled the seas of the dead.

I removed the ring and set it on the floor between us. "There. I promise I won't slap you."

Tadhg's fingers tapped against his knees, and his teeth scraped his bottom lip as he considered. "All right. Why not?" Slowly, he leaned forward and inhaled against my hair. "I like the way you smell." Candied almonds replaced stale alcohol as his magic brushed against my bare ankles.

"That's it?" Could he not think of anything else? That certainly didn't warrant a slap.

"No." Tadhg's exhale tickled my neck. "I like the dreadfully high collars you wear that conceal this lavender-scented patch of skin right here." Cold lips trailed along my collar bone. "I like the way you taste." His tongue nipped out, leaving wetness glistening on my skin.

The world stopped.

The wind. The rain.

All of it stopped.

"But most of all," he said, placing a final kiss over my pulse, "I like the way you hate me."

I like the way you hate me, the silence echoed.

I like the way you hate me.

A flash of lightning illuminated the room. Tadhg's wide, kohl-smeared eyes. His sinful lips.

And then the night returned with a single clap of thunder.

"I don't hate you," I said, edging closer to his warmth. It wasn't a lie. I felt *something* toward him. Gratitude, mostly. Perhaps there was some fondness there as well. But not hate. Not anymore.

He caught a loose curl and wrapped it around his finger. "Loathe? Or detest? Ohhh, *despise*. That's a good one. You *despise* me."

"And you think that's a good thing?"

A nod. "If you didn't hate me so much, I would've seduced you that very first night and never gotten the chance to know you."

"You don't know me." A lifetime wasn't long enough to truly know someone. How could he think he knew me in only a handful of days?

"I know you love your sister and would do anything to get her back. I know you didn't care for your husband. I know you hate mourning dresses and like hydrangeas." He slid a finger along my foot, to the healing blisters at my heel. "I know you don't complain, even when you're in pain. I know you whimper when you find release and sigh just before you fall asleep."

Heat bloomed across my cheeks.

On and on he went, telling me small details about myself that were more accurate than any description I had ever heard.

We had only known one another for a few weeks, but in that time, we had experienced both adventure and heartache. We had gone from enemies to partners in crime to lovers to whatever we were now. Friends didn't feel like a strong enough word.

Tadhg smiled down at my hand and laced our fingers together. "Most importantly, I know that you are the type of woman others are willing to die for—myself included."

Aveen may have willingly died for me, but I hadn't deserved her sacrifice. And I couldn't let Tadhg do the same if Fiadh came.

The pelting rain became a soft, humming drizzle.

Tadhg let go of my hand to stretch his arms toward the ceiling with a yawn. "Right. Wake me if the murderous witch shows up."

He curled up on the hard floor and closed his eyes.

Tadhg knew so many things about me, I felt guilty knowing next to nothing about him. I wanted to learn about his life, his joys, his heartaches. And his curses.

"Tadhg?" I poked his shoulder. He looked dreadfully uncomfortable on the floorboards, using his hands as a pillow.

He hummed softly.

"Why did Fiadh curse you?"

He was silent for so long, I thought he'd fallen asleep.

"I told women I loved them so they'd come to bed with me," he said quietly, his eyes still closed as he confessed to the night. "And one of them happened to be a hateful witch who doesn't know the meaning of forgiveness. She ripped away my magic, leaving only a pittance, and cursed me to be used by women the way I had used her. And then she took my lies and cursed my lips so that I could never escape."

I couldn't move, couldn't breathe, as he raised onto his elbow and looked at me as though he saw me. As though he felt not only the weight of his own sins but the weight of mine as well.

"I deserved all of it," he said. "I have done terrible things,

things that would make you hate me more than you already do. But I am not the man I was.

"I don't want to be a catalyst for death. I don't want to be used and cast aside like I am nothing. I have served my time, and now I want to be free."

No one deserved eternal torment for a mistake made long ago. And it had taken me far too long to realize that everyone, even cursed monsters, deserved forgiveness.

"Here." I collected the ring from the floor and placed it in his palm. "You deserve to be free."

I would find a way to deal with my truth curse. It was nothing compared to Tadhg's suffering. And if my truth cost me Robert, then he didn't deserve me in the first place.

Tadhg shook his head. Tears spilled from his eyes, trailing streaks of kohl down his cheeks and landing on the collar of his wrinkled white shirt.

"It doesn't work." He took my hand and slipped it back on my finger. "I tried but couldn't lie. Or say no."

Cursed to be used and cast aside.

"It was my mother's, you know." Tadhg's expression took on a strange, faraway look. "She enchanted it to keep me safe from curses."

"Was your mother a witch?"

He nodded. "She was called Bronah. She married my father Midir when they found out she was pregnant. My father was never the same after she passed and didn't know what to do with me. He had more interest in women than raising a child. Luckily, I had this ring to keep me out of harm's way."

According to legend, Bronah was one of the fiercest witches to have ever walked this island. She was burned centuries ago. And Midir, the infamous fae ruler, slaughtered thousands of humans in the war. What had it been like for Tadhg growing up with such terrifying parents?

"Fiadh knew about the ring and must've tailored the curses to bypass the spell. She asked for it that day, said she wanted to see how it looked on her finger. I hadn't cared . . . about the ring. About Fiadh. About anyone but myself, really."

My heart ached for this cursed prince. If only I loved him. and he loved me, so I could break his curse.

We could pretend, couldn't we? It wouldn't affect the curse, but perhaps it would help him forget, if only for tonight.

"I love you," I whispered, pressing kisses to the hair at his temple. The delicate points of his ears.

"You don't have to say that."

"I want to." I kissed his cheekbone. His jaw. "Let me help you."

Tadhg sat up but kept me at arm's length with two hands on my shoulders. "I don't . . ." A wince. "I'm too drunk to be of any use to you."

"I don't want to use you." No matter how attracted I was to Tadhg, I couldn't do that to Robert. I was willing to toe the line but not cross it.

A V formed between his eyebrows. He looked so confused, I almost laughed.

"Come here." I helped him off the floor and escorted him to the bed. He sank onto the edge of the mattress and sat as still as a statue, watching me remove his waistcoat, belt, dagger, and boots.

"Take off your shirt."

With a flick of his wrist, it disappeared. Broad shoulders. Sculpted chest. Lean waist. The indentations at his hips leading to—

Swallowing over and over was the only way to clear the thickness from my throat. *Damn* he was beautiful. "Scoot over and lay down."

Tadhg followed my instructions but remained rigid when I climbed in beside him and drew the quilt over us. "Head here." I patted my left breast.

Tadhg gave me a skeptical glance before resting his head at my heart. After a moment, he reached across my stomach and hugged me against him.

Any time I was sad or struggling, Aveen would sneak into my room to comfort me, not with words and promises but with the strength of silence. She'd held me like this the night our mother had passed; the time Padraig had fallen gravely ill; the night I had given myself to Robert in the garden.

No matter the situation, my sister had been there to cradle my head and play with my hair until my tears subsided and I fell asleep.

Tadhg's soft, silky hair slid through my fingers. When I traced the point of his ear, his breathing hitched.

"That tickles."

"Sorry." I went back to his hair.

"You don't have to stop. It's nice."

I held him in silence, wishing there were something more I could do to help.

The light in the room grew brighter as we edged toward dawn. When my eyelashes became too heavy to lift, I let them fall closed. "What are you going to do about your curse?" I asked, fighting a yawn.

"I can either wait for Fiadh," he said, the words fading to a whisper. His hair tickled my chin when he nestled closer. "Or beg you to stay married to me."

Beg you to stay married to me.

Wait. What?

My eyes flew open.

"What do you mean *stay married?*" I poked his tanned shoulder. "Tadhg? Wake up. *Tadhg.*"

The only response was a soft snore followed by a murmured, "I love you too."

25

THE BED WAS EMPTY.

Tadhg was gone.

I would've believed last night had just been a strange, beautiful dream if it wasn't for the purple hydrangea on the pillow next to me.

My stomach tightened at the memory of Tadhg's whispered confessions.

I love you too.

Tadhg didn't love me.

Tadhg couldn't lie.

He couldn't lie, but he could've been speaking to someone in his dreams. His mother, perhaps. Or some former lover.

Tadhg did *not* love me.

I chose the mourning dress with the lowest collar. Having no desire to pin my hair, I asked Daisy to leave it unbound. The strands swayed when I walked, reminding me of my night with the faeries. She told me Robert wasn't awake yet and asked if I wanted breakfast now or preferred to wait. If my stomach hadn't been howling with hunger, I would've waited.

It was such a fine morning, I asked to have breakfast in the back garden, and Daisy promised to arrange it.

The air smelled crisp and salty. The hedges and grass still glistened from last night's storm. Although the faint breeze had a wintry bite, the sun rising in the cloudless sky seeped into my black dress, warming me straight to my core.

A servant came out with an armful of tea towels to wipe down the ornate iron table on the sandstone patio. Daisy followed him, carrying a tray of tea, toast, butter, and homemade blackberry jam.

Robert joined me a short time later, a rolled-up newspaper beneath his arm. His clothes, as always, were impeccable. When he saw me, he stopped and frowned. "You're wearing your hair down."

What an odd greeting. "Yes, I am."

"I prefer it up." He continued to the free chair and tossed the paper next to the teapot. "Down makes you look too young."

I was too young now? That was a new one. "I wasn't aware my hair was any of your concern." I smeared another spoonful of jam onto my toast. The seeds stuck between my teeth when I took a bite.

Robert poured himself a cup of tea from the porcelain kettle, his mouth pinched. "It's just that you always seem so put together and proper." No sugar, only a drop of milk. "And down is too unruly."

"When you've been sticking pins in your scalp for nineteen years, you can weigh in on my hairstyle choices. Until then, I will wear my hair how I like."

"Someone's in a mood this morning," he muttered.

"I'm not the one in a mood." I grabbed another slice of cold toast and slathered on a thick layer of butter and jam.

"Then why are you rage-spreading the butter?"

"Because I *like* butter."

Robert's eyebrows lifted as he selected a slice of toast from the bottom of the basket. For some reason, the thin layer of butter he scraped on top annoyed me.

Perhaps I *was* in a mood.

I inhaled a deep breath and exhaled my irritation. If Robert and I were going to be together, we would have to get used to each other's quirks and habits. He didn't like my hair down, and I didn't like the way he nibbled his toast like a mouse. Small irritations in the grand scheme of forever.

"What's your plan for the day?" I asked, cleaning my fingers on the serviette spread across my lap. "Do you need to go into the office?"

"Yes, but only for a few hours." He slurped his tea when he sipped. Had he always done that? Surely I would've noticed. "Would you like to come with me? We could visit the pier afterwards since we couldn't fit it in yesterday."

"That sounds lovely."

Robert smiled. He didn't know the main reason I agreed was because I wanted to find Tadhg. I needed to know what he meant by those final words uttered before he passed out.

I could beg you to stay married.

He didn't *want* to be married to me. There had to be some other explanation, something that had to do with his curses.

I love you too.

That had been a drunken mistake.

"You'll be pleased to hear that I've been invited to a party Friday night for Lady Alva Lynch."

Why would that news please me? Lady Alva was a year younger than me, and her family was obscenely rich, with houses and estates across the country. The handful of times I'd met her at their seaside mansion in Graystones, she'd come off as an entitled brat.

"I wasn't aware that you and Lady Alva were close." I poured myself another cup of tea and added an extra lump of sugar when I caught Robert's judgemental stare.

"We aren't. Her youngest brother Gary and I went to university together. It's her eighteenth birthday this weekend, and her parents invited the local gentry to their manor to celebrate."

"That sounds like fun," I lied. It sounded awful.

"I was hoping you'd say that, because I want you to accompany me."

A late night Friday would lead to a late start on Saturday when Tadhg and I left for Tearmann. Unless Tadhg came with us, and we left straight from the estate.

"Can Tadhg come?"

Robert choked on the bite of toast he'd taken and swiped for his teacup. After a gulp, he set it down and popped the top button on his collar. "You want *Tadhg* to come to one of *our* parties?"

"Why not?" At least he'd be sure to liven it up a bit.

"Why would you want him there? I thought that your dealings with one another were through," he said pointedly, drumming his fingers on the tabletop and narrowing his eyes.

"I need him to bring me to Tearmann, remember?"

"If you are to be my wife, you cannot go off gallivanting with monsters like him."

"*If* I am to be your wife, then I will gallivant with whomever I like." I balled up the serviette and tossed it onto the table. "Need I remind you that this"—I gestured between us—"is not set in stone. You haven't asked me to marry you, and I have not agreed."

"Bloody hell, Keelynn, calm down. If it will make you happy, I will speak to Lord Lynch on Tadhg's behalf," he said, "but I cannot guarantee a positive outcome."

"Thank you." I picked up my teacup and took a sip.

"'Not in a mood' my arse," Robert mumbled under his breath.

The Arches pub was a grandiose establishment with a dry stacked-stone exterior and a bold red sign that read *Everyone Welcome.*

It was strange—and refreshing—to see a business take such an inclusive stance toward Airren's native population.

Humans and Danú packed the tables inside, separated, not

mixing. Instead of being one big room, the pub had been chopped into multiple, more intimate spaces. I made my way through each one, but there was no sign of Tadhg. Was it any wonder? This was one of an infinite number of places he could be.

A bartender with short black hair and yellow eyes approached me from behind the bar. He looked like a pooka, but when he smiled, there were no fangs. "You look lost," he said, his accent lilting like Tadhg's. He must've been from Tearmann as well.

"Not lost. Just looking for someone." I searched the sea of faces being served by two pretty barmaids with iridescent scales.

Shelves on the back wall displayed bottles of all colors and row after row of different types of glasses.

"Perhaps I can help." The barman dragged a cloth from over his shoulder and started wiping the drink-splattered bar. "What's her name?"

"*His* name is Tadhg."

The bartender's hand stilled. "Another pretty human looking for Tadhg," he chuckled, shaking his head as he rinsed the cloth in a bucket behind the bar. "He's one lucky bastard, I'll tell ya that." He nodded his chin toward a green door between two paintings of ships at sea. "He came in an hour ago. If he's still here, he'd be in there."

"Thank you."

"Would you like a drink before you go in? We're famous for our witch's brews."

The thought of drinking before lunch made my stomach ache. I hadn't been sick this morning and I wanted to keep it that way. "Maybe next time."

He nodded, wrung out the rag, and went back to cleaning the bar.

People nodded as I passed. No one tried to speak to me, but I felt their eyes burning into my back as I approached the green door. The room on the other side smelled of pipe smoke and perfume.

The windowless space had been painted black, making it

impossible to know if it was night or day. Perhaps that was the point. This looked like the type of room where people came to forget the world and time existed.

The only light came from the candles stuck into the tops of wine bottles, dripping colourful wax down the glass.

Tadhg was playing a round of draughts with Ruairi in his human form. A blue-skinned faerie balanced on Ruairi's knee, and a woman slept on the floor, curled around Tadhg's boots.

There were other people scattered around the carpet-covered booths, most of them guzzling pints or passed out on the tables.

Tadhg didn't bother acknowledging me when I stopped next to him.

Ruairi shoved the faerie off his lap and stumbled to his feet. The faerie glared at Ruairi, then at me.

"Lady Keelynn. What a pleasant surprise," he rushed, scrubbing his hands down his thighs to straighten his breeches. "We weren't expecting ye."

"I can see that."

So much for Tadhg loving me. And he'd had the gall to give me hell about Robert.

"Who the hell is *she?*" the faerie hissed in a grating, nasally voice.

"She's um . . ." Ruairi glanced at Tadhg for assistance. Tadhg kept staring at the board. "She's no one."

No one? I wasn't no one.

When I stepped forward, I accidentally kicked the sleeping woman's tatty slipper. "Pardon me," I muttered.

Tadhg moved one of the black pawns to a different green square. "She can't hear you. She's dead."

"She's *what?*" I stumbled, my feet caught in my skirts, and I fell on my backside next to the woman's body. Sightless blue eyes stared at the specks of dirt covering the floor. Short red curls framed the gray skin of her face. Blackness devoured her lips, spreading like onyx veins down her chin and across her cheeks.

Just like Aveen.

254

The woman would be alive in a year and a day. But right now, she was dead.

Dead.

Dead.

Dead.

The reality of Tadhg's curse left me heaving. "Why'd you kiss her?" I gasped.

"I didn't kiss her," he said without a hint of remorse. "She kissed me. I told her not to, but she didn't listen. And now she's dead, and her children will starve because her husband is a worthless drunk who spends more time drinking in the pub than working at the mill."

Ruairi offered me a hand up, his expression grave as he scowled at Tadhg. The top of his shirt was unbuttoned, revealing what appeared to be rouge stains beneath. "Ye must excuse Tadhg this morning. He's in a foul humor."

"Oh, she's one of *his*," the faerie said with a knowing smirk. When she shifted her weight, her sparkling blue dress flickered in the candlelight.

"Do us all a favor, Giselle," Tadhg drawled, tapping one of the pawns against the edge of the table, "and slither back to the hole you crawled out of."

The faerie reached for Ruairi's hand; he shrugged her off and told her to go away. With her hands fisted at her sides, she stomped out of the room.

My gaze dropped again to the poor woman on the floor. "You can't let her children starve. This is your fault. You have to fix it."

Ruairi slumped onto his chair and nudged one of the green pieces forward.

Tadhg snorted, keeping his focus on the black and green board. "What would you have me do?"

I would have him not have kissed the woman in the first place. But since that wasn't an option, "Give them money."

"So their father can use it to buy drink? Not a feckin' hope.

There are too many of you humans on this island anyway. You procreate like feckin' rabbits."

Ruairi kicked him in the shin. Tadhg swore and glared at his friend as he massaged his sore leg.

I understood why he could be so callous toward humans. We treated the Danú with the same disregard. But we were discussing innocent children. "Where do they live?"

Tadhg finally looked at me, but there was no sign of the sweet, giggling man who had stumbled into my room last night. "In a cottage by the sea."

"Take me there."

"No." He went back to the board and moved another pawn. "Now, tell me why you're here or leave me alone."

From the stiffness in his shoulders and the muscles pulsing in his jaw, it was clear I wouldn't be able to sway him. Perhaps Robert knew this woman and where she lived. If I could find the cottage, I could at least give the children something to get them by for a little while until their mother returned.

But all of that would have to wait until I was back with Robert.

"You said something before you passed out last night, and I wanted clarification."

Ruairi's dark eyebrows flicked up; a smile tugged at the corner of his lips.

Tadhg's hand stilled halfway to his pint. "What did I say?"

"You don't remember?"

Tadhg grimaced.

"You said that you wanted to stay married to me."

Tadhg flicked his wrist. Ruairi's mouth moved like he was speaking, and a barman knocked over one of the open stools, but there was no noise.

"Have you lost your damn mind?" Tadhg scowled at me through black eyes. His voice echoed like we were in an invisible closet. "I don't need everyone in the feckin' pub knowing my business."

None of this was my fault. It was his. Every part of this bloody nightmare was *his* fault.

"I never said I *wanted* to stay married," he went on. "This isn't a matter of *wanting* anything. It's a matter of accidentally discovering a loophole in my curse."

I really must be losing my mind. I knew he didn't want to be married to me. And I didn't want to be married to him either. I wanted to marry Robert. I loved Robert.

"What loophole?" I asked.

He glanced at me, then looked away. "Have you listened to wedding vows?"

Wedding vows? What sort of question was that?

"Of course I have. I was married, remember?"

Tadhg grabbed both my hands and yanked me forward. "To you, I pledge my body and soul," he said, staring me dead in the eye. "All that I am and all that I have is yours."

Body and soul.

Yours.

"What are you doing?" I tried to pull away. He held firm. Ruairi stood and stalked toward us.

"I bind myself to you and you alone, forsaking all others."

"Stop talking. Let me go."

"In giving you my hands, I give you my life, to have and to cherish until death do us part."

Give you my life.

Until death do us part.

Ruairi pounded on the barrier, his face a mask of fury.

Tadhg let go, and I fell back against the invisible wall. "What the hell has gotten into you? What was that?"

"*That's* what I promised when I saved your life." He shoved his sleeves to his elbows and dropped his head into his hands. "That ring cannot save me from this curse, but you can."

The jumbled mess of vows pounded through my skull. None of this made any sense.

"How does being married help you lie?"

"I don't give a shit about lying." He raked his hands through his hair, leaving the dark strands standing on end. "And I no longer care that death lives on my lips. Anyone foolish enough to kiss me despite the consequences deserves to die."

My eyes flashed to the body on the floor. A year of life wasted for a kiss.

"But I am done being used. I am the crown prince of Tearmann and I cannot even turn down an ancient feckin' scullery maid looking for a ride. All a woman has to do is say she wants me, and my body, my magic, responds. I am powerless to stop it. Or at least I was powerless"—his eyes met mine—"until I married you."

"I still don't understand."

"I bind myself to you and you alone," Tadhg repeated, emphasizing each word, "forsaking *all others*."

Vows were promises—sacred covenants.

And for Tadhg to say the words aloud, he had to mean them.

Holy hell.

"Because you made that vow to me, you're free to make your own choices," I whispered.

"I will never be free. But at least I don't have to go off with anyone else for as long as we are wed."

He was right. Being tied to me wasn't the same as being free. And it wasn't going to last forever. "We're getting an annulment in two days."

Tadhg winced and scratched his ear. "And this is where the begging comes in."

Ruairi watched us, his arms folded across his broad chest. The other people in the room were watching as well.

"You know who I am," Tadhg said, opening his hands and letting them fall into his lap. "You know what I'm capable of." He nodded toward the dead woman at his feet. "And yet you seem to hold me in some regard. Last night, you said you didn't hate me. But you used to. You hated me so much I could taste it. And if you can go from hating me to caring enough to give me that ring in only a matter of days, imagine what could happen in a month —in a year. All I'm asking for is a chance, for a respite from the burdens I've carried for so long."

Giving Tadhg a year meant letting go of the man I loved. Robert wouldn't wait for me—and I wouldn't expect him to. Tadhg wasn't only asking for a year. He was asking for my future.

"It doesn't have to be me," I told him, closing the gap between us. "You could marry anyone."

He was the Gancanagh, the bloody Prince of Seduction. Surely he could convince *someone* to be his bride.

He shook his head, his face twisting with a look of horror. "And give someone else power over me? Not a feckin' hope. There are very few people in this world I trust, and you are one of them."

After all I'd done, after he'd seen the hate in my heart, he trusted me.

How was that possible?

"Tadhg . . ." He looked so hopeful, I almost gave him what he wanted.

No. Not what he wanted.

If Tadhg had *wanted* to stay married to me, if I was more than a means to an end, perhaps my choice would have been different. He knew how awful it felt to be used and cast aside. And yet he was trying to do the same thing to me.

I wanted more. Needed more. *Deserved* more.

I inhaled a shaky breath and smoothed a hand down my stomach to the sash at my waist. "I'm sorry, but I cannot stay married to you."

The spark of hope in his eyes vanished, replaced by vacant black. Tadhg withdrew the dagger at his waist and flipped it so the hilt was facing me. "Then I want you to kill me."

I skirted back, trying to escape the barrier. "Are you mad? I'm not killing you."

Tadhg gestured with the dagger toward where Ruairi waited, fists braced on his hips, looking murderous. "I'd let him do it," he said, his mouth twisting into a mocking smile, "but I think you'd enjoy it more."

"No one is killing you."

"*Until death do us part,* Keelynn. If you want out of this marriage, one of us needs to die. And unless you're immortal and haven't told me, I'm the only one who can come back from the underworld."

Until death do us part.

I took the dagger and wrapped my fingers around the cold hilt. "What about our annulment?"

Until death do us part.

"Apparently, my eejit brother doesn't know the difference between a handfasting and proper wedding vows. And as we were in a bit of a rush, I didn't take too much notice of the words at the time," he said, massaging the black band on his finger. "Even if we went ahead with the annulment, it wouldn't break the promises I made to you or the ones you made to me. We would still be married."

My palms began to sweat and shake, forcing me to adjust my grip. "Won't it hurt?"

"Does it matter?" He caught my wrist and forced the blade to the base of his ribs. "Go on, Keelynn. This is what you wanted, isn't it? To kill the Gancanagh. Now's your chance."

This was my chance.

One thrust, and he'd be dead.

Not forever. Just long enough to break this connection before coming back.

This was my chance.

I could do this.

I could release myself.

I could—

I *couldn't.*

"What's wrong? Don't you want to screw Robert-the-bland with a clear conscience? Don't you want to rid yourself of our marriage bond?" Tadhg spat, eyes no longer vacant but narrowed and vicious. Magic swelled, stealing the air from inside the tiny bubble. "Although, going back to a human after you've been with one of us will be disappointing. Just ask Marina." Tadhg nudged the dead woman's torso with his boot. "Oh, wait. You can't. She's dead."

"I know what you're doing." I tried and failed to pull away. "But it won't work." Tadhg said mean, awful things to hide the fact that he was hurting. "Hearing you spew hate doesn't make me hate you, Tadhg. It makes me *pity* you."

He released his hold, and the dagger clattered to the ground.

Sound exploded, and Ruairi was there, clutching my elbow, asking if I was all right and apologizing for Tadhg. I didn't have it in me to respond as I turned and ran for home.

26

CANDLELIGHT WINKED IN MY PLATE'S GILDED EDGES. THE PASTEL roses printed on the china peeked from between leftover pieces of ham and sweet potatoes. Robert's knife screeched across his plate as he tucked into his third helping of ham. I'd forced myself to eat a few bites, but mostly I drank. Thankfully, Robert kept my wine glass filled to the brim.

"You are particularly melancholy this evening, my darling," he said between bites. "Are you sure nothing is bothering you?"

"I'm not feeling very well." Because I was hollow and growing more numb with every glass.

Robert frowned and dabbed at his lips with a serviette. He'd changed into a coat and tails for dinner. It's what most households did when dining, but I'd never understood the tradition, especially when it was just the two of us. Due to my limited wardrobe—and lack of caring—I hadn't bothered changing.

"Perhaps you should retire early," he said, taking a sip of red wine.

"Perhaps you're right."

He went back to eating, and I went back to my liquid anaesthetic. Discreetly, I checked for the marriage bond beneath the ring. The black band was still there. Instead of disappointment, I felt relief. There had to be some other way around this curse. Something that would give us both what we wanted without tying ourselves to one another.

You know who I am.

I love you too.

This wine was muddling my brain. Tadhg was a master at manipulating the truth. He was a terrible, terrible person who told women he loved them so he could convince them to sleep with him.

He was a murderer.

I knew all of these things, and yet the idea of being the one who could save him stirred something in my heart. If only my heart didn't belong to someone else.

Robert looked up from his plate and smiled a contented smile. And why wouldn't he be content? He had been born into privilege, never wanted for anything a day in his entire life. A human man, one of the lucky ones in charge of his own destiny.

"Robert? What do you like about me?" I had waited years for him to notice me. And when he did notice, his attention was all I craved. What had been the turning point for him? What was it about me that made him so sure I was the one?

"What do you mean?" he asked, a wrinkle forming between his eyebrows.

"It's a fairly simple question. I want to know what you like about me."

He picked up his wine glass and settled himself against the back of the chair, twisting the stem between his fingers. The deep red liquid sloshed inside. "I like your hair when it's up and that you do not paint your face with rouge."

"Is that all?"

"Don't be absurd. Of course that's not all." He took a drink and then went back to swirling. "I like that I've known you for almost my entire life, and that our families get on. I like that you come from a respectable home and that you are well read."

None of those qualities set me apart from any other woman of my station. Surely, there had to be more driving his feelings for me than my upbringing.

"What about something personal?"

He pursed his lips, and the wrinkle between his eyebrows deepened. "Such as?"

I gulped some wine. By the time I set the glass back onto the table, Robert was ready and waiting with the bottle in his hand. Red drops spilled into the glass. Filling. Filling. Filling. Once it was full, he set the bottle aside.

What did I like about Robert? There were so many things, it was hard to think of just a few. Or it could've been the wine. "Let's see. I like that you remembered how much I love scones. And I like that you always smell like leather and the ocean. And I like the way it feels when you hold my hand."

"Well, good. Because I like holding your hand," he said with that contented smile. It didn't turn into a mischievous grin or lift higher on one side. It remained plastered on his face like a mask. Robert's smile was bland.

"I like the way you smell like roses," he said, bland smile never wavering.

Roses? I didn't smell like roses. "You mean lavender." Aveen had been the one to smell like roses. Not because she loved the flowers but because she tended them so often.

"Yes, yes, of course. I meant lavender. I always get those two mixed up."

I picked up my wine glass, then set it back down. "Do you know my favorite flower?"

"Of course I do. You've always loved fuschia."

"Fuschia were Aveen's favorite flowers. Not mine."

He shook his head slowly, brow furrowed in confusion. "That's strange. I could've sworn you told me fuschia were your favorite."

"No. I love hydrangeas."

It wasn't a big deal. In the grand scheme of life, my favorite flower didn't matter. None of this mattered because we loved each other, and love conquered all.

"Now I know," he said. "Thank you for telling me."

That smile. That *bloody* smile.

Pounding echoed from the dark hallway.

"Who's calling at this hour?" he muttered, balling up the serviette on his lap and tossing it onto the table. The chair scraped the tiles when he stood.

Shouts and boisterous laughter echoed down the hallway. Two men around my own age bounded in, a heavy sack thrown over the taller one's shoulder.

Robert rushed toward them. "What are you two doing here?"

"You missed a good night, mate," the taller one said, dropping the sack onto the floor with a heavy *thud*. The knees of his breeches and his black boots were caked with mud. The shorter one didn't look much better, with clumps of grass springing from the top of his high hessians.

Robert's gaze flicked to mine.

The two men turned and startled when they saw me. I offered a small wave and a false smile because my real one seemed to be missing.

"My apologies, milady. We didn't know Robert had company." The taller one grabbed the bag and hefted it back over his shoulder. "We can call another time."

"That would be best," Robert said tightly, ushering them toward the hallway.

"There's no need to dismiss them on my account. I don't mind if they stay." If we were going to get married, I would need to meet his friends. Now was as good a time as any.

Robert adjusted the cuffs at his wrists and tugged down his waistcoat. "William, Gary, I'd like to introduce you to Lady Keelynn Bannon. My father's estate in Graystones shares a border with Lord Bannon's land. He's Lady Keelynn's father."

"*Bannon*," the taller one, William, repeated, rubbing a hand across his bearded chin. "Weren't you engaged to someone by that name?"

Robert's shoulders stiffened.

"Robert was engaged to my sister, Aveen," I explained. Aveen, who smelled like roses and loved fuschia.

"Very sorry to hear of her passing. Such a tragedy." William bowed his head. "Robert was beside himself for months."

Beside himself? Over my sister? All he'd ever felt for her was disdain.

"Thank you. I appreciate it." I waited for Robert to offer his friends some refreshments. This wasn't my home, so it wasn't my place. But when he didn't ask them to sit down, the manners instilled in me since childhood kicked in. "Why don't you both have a seat? We can ask the footman to bring two extra plates. There's plenty of food."

"There's no need," Robert clipped, narrowing his eyes at his friends. "We will see one another at the ball on Friday night."

"Robert's right," Gary said, backing toward the door. "We've outstayed our welcome. It was lovely to meet you, Lady Keelynn. I hope we will see each other again soon."

They were almost through the door when I remembered the bag.

"What did you bring?" I asked, my curiosity getting out of hand.

All three of them froze and exchanged panicked glances.

"Bring? Oh, you mean *this*." William gestured toward the bag. "This is nothing."

"It looks a little heavy to be nothing," I said, tapping a nail against my wine glass.

"You're right. It's not nothing," William amended. "It is, however, not something a woman with such delicate sensibilities should see."

"Now I'm more curious."

"I'm afraid you'll have to remain curious." Robert threw a hand toward the entrance. "They need to get on their way."

There was something in that bag that these men didn't want me to see. And from the worried looks they shared, it was something bad. The hairs on the back of my neck prickled as I stood and dropped my serviette onto the chair. "Show me what is in that bag."

Robert's face paled. "It's not for a lady——"

With my hands on my hips, I stalked forward until I was within arm's reach of the bag. "Show me *now*." If he refused, then I'd look for myself.

Robert swore and nodded to William. Gary rubbed the back of his neck and shifted his weight from one foot to the other as William set the bag onto the ground and untied the string cinching the top together.

The metallic stench of blood invaded my nostrils. At the bottom of the bag was the head of a black horse with one of its yellow eyes gouged out.

Not a horse.

A pooka.

Bile burned the back of my throat. I pressed a hand to my mouth to keep my dinner from splattering all over the gleaming tiles.

These men had killed a pooka.

Robert caught me by the elbow. "I warned you, didn't I? But you just had to keep pushing." He settled me onto a chair and pushed the wine glass into my hand.

The other men looked appropriately concerned.

"Why did you kill him?"

"Life on this side of the island isn't as peaceful as it is on the east coast," William said, words tumbling out of him as he wrung his hands together. "Creatures run rampant around these parts, milady."

"Run rampant? They're not wild animals."

"This one tried to eat poor Tommy O'Brien," Gary said, gesturing toward the bag.

Pooka didn't eat people. "They're vegetarians."

"Excuse me?" Gary glanced at his friends, then back to me.

"Pooka. They're vegetarians. It means they don't eat meat."

"I know what it means." He rubbed his neck and kept looking

to his silent friends for support, his face growing redder and redder. "But how do you know that?"

"Because I've met one."

They backed up a step, whispering to each other and taking turns casting furtive glances my way.

I took a drink of wine to try and settle my stomach. Then my gaze landed on that burlap sack and my stomach roiled all over again.

If I stayed in this room another minute, I was going to get sick.

I stood and wobbled unsteadily past Robert and his friends. When I reached the base of the stairs, I gripped the railing to keep from collapsing. By the time I made it to the hallway at the top, Robert had caught up to me.

"What was that down there?" he hissed, hands fisted at his side. "Were you trying to make me look a fool in front of my friends?"

Hold on. He thought I was the problem?

"You think this is *my* fault? They murdered someone, and you're condoning their lawless behavior."

"Lawless behavior?" he scoffed, looking at me as though I'd sprouted a third eye. "You of all people should be happy there's one less monster lurking on this island. That pooka has been seen prowling around our neighborhood the last few nights. None of us were safe until it was dead."

My stomach sank to my toes, and I grabbed for the railing. "He was caught in *this* neighborhood?"

Robert nodded.

Oh god.

What if the pooka they'd killed had been Ruairi?

The fire crackling in the hearth may as well have been a match in a bloody snowstorm for all the warmth it gave. I'd added two lumps of coal when I'd escaped into my bedroom three hours earlier, but it hadn't helped. Robert had come to check on me, but I hadn't bothered answering when he knocked. I didn't want to talk to Robert. I wanted to talk to Tadhg.

I sank onto the coarse rug in front of the fire and held my hands toward the flames. I could've been sitting in the middle of the thing and still been cold.

What if Ruairi was dead?

He'd been so kind to me. And he was Tadhg's best friend.

What would Tadhg do when he found out?

"*Tadhg?*" My voice carried through the silent bedchamber. I tugged my shift down to cover my frozen toes and wrapped my arms around my knees, attempting to hold myself together. "*Tadhg?* Are you there?"

What was I doing? He couldn't hear me. And even if he could, he wouldn't come to my aid after I'd turned him down. We'd left things so badly, I wasn't sure what was supposed to happen now. The annulment was a pointless formality at this stage so we could start for Tearmann tomorrow. No, no. We couldn't even do that. I had the bloody party to go to tomorrow night.

We could still leave Saturday, assuming Tadhg bothered to show up.

Assuming he didn't abandon me out of spite.

I pulled the cursed emerald from my finger to ensure the black band was still there. "Where are you, Tadhg?"

There was a soft thump from behind me. I looked over my shoulder to find a prince in scuffed black boots standing in the shadows. "What is it?" Tadhg blurted, spinning as if searching for an invisible threat. "What's wrong?"

I jumped to my feet and threw my arms around his neck. He stumbled backward with a muttered curse. Strong hands fell to my waist, holding me against him.

"It's awful." Tears seeped into his soft white shirt. "I'm so sorry. So sorry."

"What's awful?" The question rumbled through his chest. "Tell me what happened."

"Robert's friends showed up. I think they killed Ruairi," I sniffed, rubbing my nose with my sleeve. "I mean, I don't know if it was him, but I'm afraid it was. And if it wasn't, then they killed some other poor pooka, and I'm so sorry, Tadhg. I didn't know. I swear I didn't know."

Tadhg pulled away, cupped my face in his hands, and bent so we were eye-to-eye. There should've been rage in his eyes. They should have been narrowed and black, not clear and green. Where was the anger and hatred of my people—of me? Did he not hear what I'd said?

"First," he said, "Ruairi is fine. There's no fear for him, all right? Second, there is no need to apologize because you did nothing wrong."

"I'm one of them. Isn't that wrong enough?" It felt wrong. It felt shameful.

"You're human, but you're *not* one of them."

It was the same thing, wasn't it?

"I know better than to judge an entire population based on the actions of a few." His thumbs stroked my cheeks, wiping away the tumbling tears. "This isn't a rare occurrence. My people have been persecuted for centuries. There is risk involved for those of us who choose to live outside of Tearmann. Everyone knows that, including the pooka they killed."

Knowing didn't make it any better. Didn't solve the problem.

I scrubbed at my eyes until the skin beneath was sore. I was such a bloody disaster. My heart and head were wrecked from being pulled and dragged in so many different directions. Between humans and Danú. Between Tadhg and Robert.

"You're sure it wasn't Ruairi?" I asked.

"Positive." Tadhg's hands fell away from my face. "Ruairi spent the evening with me. We had to get Marina's body to the castle," he said quietly, his gaze dropping to the floor.

Marina. The woman he'd killed. No, the woman who had kissed him against his will.

I had begged Robert to bring me up the coast when we left the city, but he'd refused. I'd explained that a woman had passed away, leaving behind helpless children, and that I wanted to help. Robert said I was too caring and that there were too many ruffians on the coast. He'd refused to jeopardize my safety.

"I couldn't stop thinking about what you said about her children," Tadhg said with a wince. "So, we went to her cottage and . . . It was bad. So much worse than I'd imagined."

My chest began to ache. "Tell me."

He raised his head slightly, glancing at me from beneath his dark lashes. "It'll upset you."

I was already upset. I should've fought harder to find them. Stood my ground. Threatened to go on my own without Robert. But I had given in to avoid an argument because it had been easier. Because to be with the man I thought I loved, I needed to be a placid, obedient wife.

"Tell me anyway."

He bit his lip, leaving an indentation in the center. "They'd been locked in the shed with the pigs," he said. "The eldest one had a black eye. They were nothing more than skin and bones, freezing and covered in filth. I couldn't just leave them there to be beaten again when their father came home. So . . ." Tadhg grimaced. "We may have stolen them."

I stepped away to get a better look at his face. "You *stole* children."

Tadhg refused to meet my eyes, instead looking past me, into the dying fire. "Technically, Ruairi did. I just took a pig."

"A pig?" Was that what he'd said? I mustn't have been as sober as I thought.

Tadhg nodded. "The little boy seemed overly fond of a runt and wouldn't come with us unless the pig came too. Now they're with some friends who live on the edge of the Black Forest. They don't have much, but they are good, kind people."

I had been sitting on my ass in Robert's warm, comfortable townhome, filling my belly with dinner that had been prepared for me while the Crown Prince of Tearmann was out kidnapping children and pigs.

He'd been helping humans while Robert's friends had been slaughtering a pooka.

Tadhg sighed, looking worn and weary from the weight of his burdens. "Look," he said, "I am dreadfully sorry for the way I treated you earlier. You'd think at this stage I'd be used to not getting what I want, but for a moment, I saw a light at the end of this long, miserable tunnel and thought it was within my grasp. I never should have suggested we stay married. No one deserves that kind of punishment. And I shouldn't have asked you to kill me when Rían will be more than happy to do it when I get home."

I couldn't say it was all right, because it wasn't. No one deserved to have such hateful words spat at them. But I understood his desperation. "I forgive you. For everything."

His eyebrows drew together, and his lips turned down as he searched my face. "You do?"

I nodded.

"You *forgive* me," he repeated, his tone rife with disbelief. "That's it? You have no requests or bargains? You don't desire reparation?"

"Padraig always said true forgiveness is freely given."

Forgiveness wasn't a commodity to be bought and paid for. Forgiveness was a matter of the heart. A matter of choosing love over hate. Forgiveness was a release. Forgiveness was freedom.

Tadhg's shoulders rose and fell when he sighed. "Padraig was a good man."

"Yes, he was." Padraig had been the best kind of man.

Silence fell between us. The longer it stretched, the more uncomfortable it became. I wanted to fill it, but what should I say?

"I'm . . . um . . . I'm going to go." Tadhg backed toward the window, like he wasn't quite ready to turn his back. Wasn't quite ready to leave.

I wasn't quite ready to let him go. "How did you know I needed you?"

The corner of his lips crooked into a guilty half-smile. "I may or may not have been sitting in the back garden."

My gaze flicked to the firelight reflecting in the dark window-pane. "You were sitting in the garden?"

The smile widened to a grin. "I said may or may not."

He truly was incorrigible. "If you *happened* to be sitting in the garden, what would you have been doing there?"

He shrugged again, this time tucking his thumbs into the belt loops on his breeches. "I would've been making sure a vengeful witch didn't murder my wife in her sleep."

Always looking out for me. Even when he was angry. Even when I didn't deserve it.

"Careful, now. I may start believing you actually care about me."

"That would be disastrous," he said with a chuckle, slowly backing toward the window. "Could you imagine the scandal? I have a terrible reputation to uphold."

He didn't deny it.

I love you too.

My stomach fluttered at the thought. I stepped forward, having the sudden urge to erase the distance between us. "It would only be worse if I believed you loved me."

His backward steps faltered. "You're right. That would be far worse."

I moved closer, wishing his face wasn't veiled by shadows. "Because you don't," I said, needing to hear his outright denial so the fluttering in my stomach would stop. So the heat blooming in my chest would cease.

Tadhg's back collided with the window, rattling the glass. "Don't what?"

"Love me."

His eyes widened. "Don't be absurd. I've only known you for a few weeks."

Still not an answer.

I stopped a breath away. His ragged exhales tangled with mine. Heat from his body burned hotter than the fire crackling behind me. "I want to hear you say it. Say you don't love me."

He opened his mouth, then closed it again.

I couldn't hear anything over my pounding heart. "Go on. It's easy. Four little words: *I don't love you.*"

"I—*Shit.*" He licked his lips and winced. "I don't—" He swore again and dashed his hands through his hair, tugging on the ends. Then his hands dropped. Green eyes met mine. Tadhg took a deep breath and said, "I do. I love you."

He loved me. How? When? *Why?*

When I reached for Tadhg, my fingertips met frigid glass.

Tadhg was gone.

27

LOVE.

Four letters capable of changing your life.

One solitary syllable powerful enough to alter the world.

I braced my hands on the windowsill, trying to process what had just happened.

I do. I love you.

What did this mean?

Nothing.

Tadhg's love meant nothing because it wasn't *true* love. True love happened over the course of years, not a handful of days. True love couldn't grow from seeds of hate.

Tadhg was obviously confused about what was between us. All he had to do was believe something was true and he could say it aloud. He simply believed he loved me. That's all this was.

A misunderstanding.

I dragged the ring from my finger to make sure the tattoo was still there, and that Tadhg hadn't gone straight to Rían and asked him to end his life. To end our marriage and set me free.

I didn't love Tadhg. How could I? "I love Ro—" An invisible mallet drove an invisible spike into my skull. "*I love Ro—*" I stumbled away from the window and caught myself on the bedpost to keep from falling face-first onto the floorboards.

I loved Robert. It wasn't a lie. *I loved Robert.*

Robert, with his kind hazel eyes.

Robert, with his bland smile.

Robert, with his comfort and familiarity and . . .

Dammit! I loved Robert.

Robert.

Robert.

Robert.

His name became my lifeline as I sprinted for the door. The drafty air in the dark hallway left gooseflesh on my bare ankles. I stopped outside Robert's door, needing to talk to him. To see him. To figure out what the hell was going on with my brain. It had to be some sort of mistake. Or a spell! That's what it was. Tadhg had put me under a spell.

Before my hand connected with the wood, I heard a sound.

Whispering.

The hallway was empty. Who was whispering?

Wait.

The sounds were coming from *inside* Robert's bedroom.

There was another noise.

A feminine giggle.

My heart hammered against my ribs, and my head spun with possibilities. There was no reason for a woman to be in Robert's room at this hour. Unless . . .

A moan.

My hand fell to the cold brass handle, and I threw the door aside.

Springy red curls fell down a woman's bare back where she straddled Robert on the bed. Robert's eyes were closed, his head thrown back against the black tufted headboard. The door crashed against the wall.

His eyes flew open and landed on me. "*Shit.*"

He shoved the woman off him and onto the rumpled sheets.

She let out an indignant squeak and dragged the quilt to cover herself, but nothing could hide what they'd been doing.

"This isn't what it looks like," he blurted, turning away to hike up and fasten his breeches. The girl covered her face with her hands, but it was too late. I'd already recognized Daisy. Robert was screwing his bloody maid.

Numbness slowed my heart until it barely beat, spreading through my chest and into my limbs, leaving me with nothing. No heat as I turned woodenly back toward my bedroom. No emotion as I walked forward. *Nothing.*

"*Dammit,* Keelynn," Robert shouted. I didn't bother turning toward his thumping footsteps. "Stop and listen to me for one bloody minute, will you?"

My feet stilled the moment I crossed the threshold into my room. "You said you loved me." The words held no inflection. No feeling. "And yet you're sleeping with her."

No wonder my curse hadn't been broken. Robert didn't love me. Had he ever?

"This isn't about love." He caught me by the elbow, forcing me to face him. His hair was mussed by someone else's fingers. His lips swollen from someone else's kisses. His bare chest marked by someone else's nails. "Once we marry, I will send her away."

There was a gasp from the hallway. Tears filled Daisy's wide eyes and her hand flew to her gaping mouth.

"Oh, please. Don't look so shocked." Robert waved a dismissive hand at Daisy's wrinkled dress and disheveled hair. "You're a bloody maid. What did you think I was going to do? Marry you?"

Daisy stumbled for the staircase, her sobs growing louder and louder until the front door slammed and silence descended on the townhouse. I wrenched my arm free of Robert's grasp. Nothing he said would heal this wound. This was the end of us.

"Look, I'm sorry you found out," he said, folding his arms across his bare chest.

Sparks of indignation flared against the numbness. He wasn't sorry for sleeping with her, only that I had caught him. And if I hadn't, he probably would've kept on with the affair even after we'd exchanged vows.

Exhaling a frustrated breath, Robert pinched the bridge of his nose and started speaking like I was an imbecile. Like I didn't know the way the world worked. "Keelynn, you must understand that a man has needs—"

"And a woman doesn't?" My voice shook. To hell with men and their bloody *needs*. He was perfectly capable of saying no if he wanted to. The problem was that he felt entitled to take and take without a second thought. "What if that had been me? What if you'd walked in on me in bed with someone else? What then?"

His eyes narrowed. "It's not the same thing."

"You're right. It's not. I got caught kissing someone at a ball and was forced to *marry* him. You can screw whoever you want and have absolutely no consequences!"

"That's right." His mouth twisted into a sneer. "I can."

Who was this monster and what had he done with the man I had loved for so long? Had that Robert ever existed? Or had this one been living inside him the entire time, pulling his strings like a bloody marionette?

I wanted him *out*. Out of my room, my life, my head, and my heart.

When I shoved against his chest, he didn't budge. "Get out of my room."

He stalked forward, sending me back and back until my legs connected with the solid footboard. "This is *my* house, and I will go wherever I damn well please." His gaze dropped to my heaving chest and a strange smile twisted his lips.

Panic squeezed my lungs, making it nearly impossible to say, "*Get. Out.*"

He twisted my hair in his fist. Stinging pain exploded from my scalp when he dragged me against him, rattling my teeth. "*Make me.*"

He tried to force his mouth against mine, but I fought against the pain of his grip and turned my face away so that his lips landed on my jaw.

Make me.

I was too weak.

Make me.

Robert was too strong.

Make me.

But I knew someone stronger.

"Tadhg!"

All of a sudden, the pain disappeared. Robert let go and stumbled back. "What the hell are you doing?"

I shouted his name again, praying that he was close enough to hear, trying not to think of what would happen if he wasn't.

"Stop it. Stop it this instant—" Robert's head whipped toward the window, and his face paled.

"I believe the lady asked you to get out of her room," said a dark voice from the shadows. Sweet, almond-scented magic filled my nostrils, tickling my skin.

Robert backed toward the door. His face contorted with rage when his gaze met mine. "You have the nerve to give me shit over Daisy when you've been rutting with this monster behind my back?"

Tadhg's chuckle sent ice through my blood.

I moved closer to where he stood, shrouded by darkness, green eyes narrowed and glowing.

"You know what? I don't give a shit. She's a bloody prude anyway. I hope you enjoy her. I know I certainly did."

Fire engulfed my neck and cheeks. Tears stung the backs of my eyes. Did his cruelty know no bounds?

Tadhg evanesced and caught Robert by the throat, slamming him against the wall. Robert's eyes bulged; his face turned red as he spluttered and scraped at Tadhg's hand.

This time, I didn't stop him.

"You've always said that I was too much for you," I said. *Too naïve. Too reckless. Too young. Too kind.* I stepped forward so I could see the panic in his wild eyes. "I'm not too much, Robert. You were never enough."

I deserved someone who would fight for me. Someone who loved me enough to remain faithful. Someone willing to put my needs above his own.

I put a hand on Tadhg's shoulder and squeezed. "Let him go. He's not worth it."

Tadhg released his hold, and Robert collapsed into a wheezing, pathetic heap on the floor. If I'd had my boots on, I would've kicked him in the ribs.

"I want you out of my bloody house," he rasped, holding his throat as he dragged in choked gasps. "*Both of you.*"

Like I wanted to stay in this place for another second anyway. I crossed to the armoire and pulled the first dress from the hanger. As soon as I got dressed—

"Oh no you don't," Robert ground out. "*I* bought those dresses. They belong to me, and if you take them, I'll report you for theft and demand you be thrown into jail."

Tadhg flicked his wrist, and I was no longer in my shift but in a gorgeous mauve day gown with lace cuffs and a pair of matching slippers. Robert's expression turned murderous, but he didn't try to stand or say anything more when Tadhg took my hand and led me into the hallway. My heavy footsteps *click click clicked* as we descended, and I collected my cloak from the coat hook at the entrance. The night was crisp and cold, moisture clinging to the air like it could rain at any moment.

Tadhg threw open the garden gate and turned toward the faint amber glow of the city.

"Where are we going?" I asked, sounding empty and hollow. Although I clutched my cloak closed, it did little to stave off the chill. The coldness came from inside me

"Tonight, we'll stay in the city," Tadhg said quietly, scanning the path ahead. "And in the morning, we'll leave for Tearmann."

There was no longer any point in delaying the final leg of our journey. I should've been elated, but the joy of seeing my sister again was eclipsed by all that had just happened.

Iron streetlamps illuminated intervals of the footpath. Darkness. Light. Darkness. Light. Darkness.

The closer we got to Gaul, the heavier my heart became. Robert had been my future, my goal, for so long, I wasn't sure what I was meant to do now. Once Aveen returned, we couldn't go back to Graystones. There was no guarantee our father would take her back after what had happened. What if he tried to marry her off? What if he expected her to marry Robert since they had been betrothed? I couldn't let that happen. No one deserved that fate.

Perhaps we could find a cottage somewhere and live out the rest of our lives together. But how would we support ourselves? I had no skills to speak of, and the funds I had from Edward wouldn't last forever. I had won the wager with Tadhg, so I didn't owe him any of that money, but it still wouldn't be enough.

I glanced at Tadhg from beneath my lashes. He conquered the distance with long, confident strides, like he was the master of his own fate, even though it wasn't true. If anyone was the master of Tadhg's fate, it was me.

Staying married to him would solve so many problems. I felt something for Tadhg, and those feelings grew stronger every day. Could they eventually blossom into love? I'd thought I knew what love was, but now I wasn't so sure.

The rows of houses on either side of the cobblestone road grew narrower and taller as we descended into Gaul. We passed the blue-and-white teahouse where I sat and dreamed only a few days ago, a naïve fool who believed herself in love. The river rushed toward the sea, and we followed it until we reached a large building decorated with dry-stacked stone.

The ground floor windows in the Arches pub were dark; light leaked from between cracks in the curtains on the first floor.

"We're staying here?" I asked.

Tadhg pounded on the front door, rattling the brass knob. "The owner has a few spare rooms, and I know he won't mind."

A few moments later, footsteps sounded from within. Locks scraped from the other side, and the door opened. The black-haired bartender I'd met earlier peered through the gap. When he saw us, his yellow eyes widened.

"I apologize for calling this late, Lorcan, but would it be possible for us to sleep here tonight?" Tadhg asked, looking pointedly at me.

"Of course." The man opened the door wider and waved us inside. "Come in, come in. Hello again, pretty human. I see you found your Tadhg."

My Tadhg. "Please, call me Keelynn."

The foyer had a set of massive double doors that would lead into the pub. There was a second smaller door to the right.

"Lovely to meet you *officially*, Princess Keelynn." The man opened the smaller door, which led to a curved wrought iron staircase that creaked as we climbed.

"I'm not a princess." I was no one.

Lorcan glanced at me from over his shoulder, his brow furrowed. "I thought the two of you were married." He stopped when we reached a small landing.

I darted a look at Tadhg. He waited and watched, giving no indication of whether or not I should answer honestly. He was the one who had said he didn't want others knowing his business. Did this man count? He'd called me a princess, so he must know something.

"Yes," I said. "We are."

If Tadhg got upset, it was his own fault for not speaking up.

Lorcan's eyes bounced between the two of us. Then he shrugged and opened the door to a candlelit living room with mustard-colored walls and a welcoming fire blazing in the fireplace. Piles of colorful cushions spread over a thick Aubusson carpet in front of the hearth, looking plush and inviting.

A familiar figure sat on the arm of one of the sofas. His yellow eyes widened, and his fangs appeared when he grinned. "Hello, human."

"Ruairi!" I ran toward him and threw my arms around his broad shoulders. His long hair tickled my cheek, and his shirt smelled faintly of pine sap and alcohol. *He was alive.* Not that I hadn't believed Tadhg, but there was a rush of relief in seeing him for myself.

"And ye thought I was messin' when I said she'd rather marry me." His laugh rumbled as he gave me an awkward pat on the back.

Remembering my manners, I promptly let go and pressed a hand to my quivering stomach. "I'm sorry. I don't know what came over me."

"I have that effect on most women. Don't worry. I won't tell Tadhg ye secretly fancy me," Ruairi said with a wink.

Tadhg snorted and dropped onto the floor, propping himself up with two of the wide cushions. He undid the buckles at the top of his boots and tossed them in front of the fire.

A woman came into the room from the hallway, wearing a simple blue dress with a black corset and apron. When she saw me, she froze. "Is this who I think it is?"

Tadhg nodded, and the woman dropped into an awkward curtsy. "It's such a pleasure to finally meet you, Princess Keelynn. Tadhg has told us such wonderful things."

"Has he?" I glanced over to find Tadhg staring intently at the fire.

"Don't listen to Deirdre," he muttered. "She lies."

"Never mind him." The woman, Deirdre, waved a hand in his direction. "He's been in a foul mood all day. Would you like some food, princess? Or a drink, perhaps?"

After everything that had happened, I should want a drink. I should want to drown my sorrows into tomorrow. Instead, I wanted to remember this night and the way it felt to be betrayed by Robert so that it didn't happen a third time.

"A bit to eat would be lovely, thank you. And please, just call me Keelynn." I was no more a princess than the cushion I sat on beside Tadhg. I removed my slippers and set them beside Tadhg's boots. Ruairi fell backward onto the turquoise sofa, and Lorcan went with Deirdre into what I assumed was the kitchen.

"Is Deirdre a witch?" I whispered to Tadhg.

He shook his head. "She's human."

"Oh. Right." A human who was friendly with the Danú. "And she and Lorcan are . . . ?"

"Married," he said with a soft chuckle. He flexed the fingers on his left hand, and I couldn't help but stare at the black band around his ring finger.

"And Lorcan is a . . . ?"

"A thieving bastard who stole my feckin' woman," Ruairi grumbled from the sofa, bouncing his heels off the arm.

"I was never *your* woman," Deirdre said on her way out of the kitchen, pushing a cart laden with tea cakes and a porcelain tea set. "And to answer your question, Keelynn, my husband is a pooka."

"Like hell he is," Ruairi said. "He's a rutting half-breed who wishes he was one of us."

Lorcan came out laughing, two wine bottles in hand. "You're just jealous because I'm prettier than you."

Ruari shot upright and glared at Lorcan's grinning face. "Ye are not."

"Am too. Ask Keelynn." Lorcan gestured toward me with a bottle. "She can't lie."

Four sets of eyes locked on me.

If Tadhg had let that little detail slip as well, he must trust these people. And if Tadhg trusted them, then I was determined to do the same. "Sorry, Ruairi. Lorcan is prettier because he doesn't have scary fangs."

Lorcan gave a victorious bow. "Thank you, milady." He pulled a wine key from his breast pocket and started removing the cork from one of the bottles.

"Ah, come on. These little things?" Ruairi flicked his tongue over the tips of his canines. "They wouldn't hurt ye—unless yer into a bit of pain with your pleasure." He wiggled his eyebrows.

"Has that line ever worked for you?" Deirdre asked with a laugh, offering me the tray of cakes. I chose a sticky cherry tart dusted with icing sugar.

"Ye'd be surprised what some humans like. Just last month, I met a woman who wanted me to—"

Tadhg cleared his throat, and Ruairi stopped. He looked confused at first, then his gaze found mine. "Let's just say she didn't mind my fangs one bit," he finished with a wink.

The exchange brought me back to another conversation I'd had with Tadhg, back when I'd asked about humans and creatures together. No wonder he'd called me ignorant. It was obvious now that they mixed all the time. And they intermarried—at least, they did this close to Tearmann.

But he had also said that his people wouldn't accept me as his bride. Was that because he was a prince?

Tadhg snagged a pear tart and took a massive bite. Crumbs and icing sugar fell to his lap.

"Must you eat like you were raised in a feckin' field?" Deirdre snatched a serviette from the cart and tossed it at Tadhg. "Use that or you'll get crumbs all over my new cushions."

Tadhg mumbled an apology and slipped the serviette beneath the tart. His next bite was more civilized.

Deirdre nodded and asked what I wanted to drink. "We have faerie wine, witch's brew, puitín, and stout."

"I'll just have tea, please."

"Tadhg?"

He glanced at me, then back to the tart. "I'll have the same."

"Wine for me, Lorcan." Ruairi threw an arm over the back of the sofa and propped his ankle on his knee, watching Lorcan retrieve wine glasses from a hutch behind the dining table.

Deirdre set out three cups and filled them with dark, fragrant tea. To the first, she added one cube of sugar and a dash of milk, then offered it to me. I thanked her and set the tart on my lap to let the hot cup thaw my frigid fingers. For the next cup, she dropped in five sugar cubes. There was no need to ask whose it was.

"You eat far too much sugar," I said, watching Tadhg sip and settle deeper into the cushions.

"Sickening, isn't it?" Deirdre brought her cup to the other sofa. "These bastards could live on custard and cakes and not put on a feckin' pound. And if I so much as look at sweets, my stay feels too tight."

"I see nothing wrong with your stays, love," Lorcan said, pouring greenish yellow liquid into the wine glasses. He handed one glass to Ruairi and brought the other to the sofa beside his wife.

"That's because you get distracted by what they're holding in." She gave him a saucy smile. His grin turned sheepish, and a slight blush painted his cheeks.

"Someone stab me, please," Ruairi groaned. "I refuse to watch the couples in the room make moon eyes at each other all feckin' night."

"You're just jealous." Deirdre grabbed a cushion and launched it at Ruairi's head.

Ruairi spilled some of his drink dodging it. "You mean relieved. What's love ever done but make folks miserable?"

I had to agree with him there.

Ruairi knocked my foot with his boot. "Take this human here. She's in love, and she looks proper miserable."

"I'm not in love. I'm not sure I ever was."

His dark eyebrows came together. Deirdre and Lorcan exchanged confused looks. Tadhg just sat and fiddled with the buttons at his wrists.

"So you're not marrying your childhood sweetheart?" Deirdre asked carefully, casting a furtive glance at Tadhg.

Had he given them every detail of my entire life? "I'd rather not marry a man who's been screwing the maid."

"Oh, you poor dear." Deirdre leaned forward to pat my shoulder, her ample chest testing the strength of the laces on her stay. "Did you kill him? I would've stabbed the bastard straight in the heart. Isn't that right, Lorcan?"

He rolled his eyes heavenward. "That's right, love."

"I've him well warned," she whispered with a conspiratorial nudge.

"No, I didn't stab him. But I should have."

Everyone nodded in agreement, especially Tadhg.

I sat and listened to the friendly banter go back and forth between everyone. Lorcan's mother was human—hence the lack of fangs—and he and Deirdre had been married for two years.

The conversation ebbed and flowed, and the brief moments of silence were comfortable, with no one hurrying to fill them. Eventually, Ruairi brought up the events from earlier in the evening, when he and Tadhg had gone to Marina's house on the coast.

"Ye should've seen him," Ruairi said through his laughter, clutching his stomach and wiping tears from his eyes. "Fell on his arse in the middle of a pile of shite chasing a feckin' pig around a sty."

Tadhg's grin was infectious. "Like you could've done any better. You had the easy part."

"*Easy*? The little one *bit* me." Ruairi shoved up his sleeves and pointed to a non-existent mark on his forearm.

"Says the pooka with big, scary fangs," Lorcan teased.

I could only imagine the chaos of the two of them trying to convince three scared children and a squealing pig to leave their home. "I would've loved to have seen it."

"Tell you what." Tadhg's hand fell to my knee. "Next time we decide to go kidnapping, I'll be sure to let you know."

The heat from his palm scorched through the layers of fabric to the skin beneath, leaving the muscles in my stomach clenching.

His gaze dropped to his hand, and his smile faltered. When he went to move, I covered his hand with mine. Now that I felt his touch, I didn't want to be without it.

"Oh, would you look at the time? We're off to bed." Deirdre shot to her feet and dragged her husband to his. She kicked Ruairi's boot on the way past and nodded toward the hallway.

"Oh. Right." He groaned as he sat upright. "I suppose I should retire as well. Night, Tadhg. Night, human."

The three of them disappeared down the hallway. There was a distinctive *click* from one door closing, then a second.

Tadhg's gaze shifted between my eyes and my mouth. "Sorry they kept you up so late. You must be wrecked."

"I should be." But at the moment, sleep was the last thing on my mind, as his callused thumb scraped idle circles over my knuckles.

His eyes met mine, and I could feel my stomach tighten and my breath catch. Leaning forward, I brushed my lips over Tadhg's, inhaling his sigh. This was what I wanted. This was what I needed. This was what I had been searching for.

When I went to deepen the kiss, his hands came around my hips and pulled me on top of him.

"This is a terrible idea," he groaned, adjusting his grip on my hips, urging me to move against him.

He felt so good beneath me, and I rolled my hips forward, craving more of him. *This. Us.* What if we stayed married? What if we tried to make this work? *Bloody hell.* This was *definitely* working for me.

"It would seem your body disagrees," I said with a smile.

His hips bucked, grinding into mine. "Yes, well, my body and I are rarely in agreement."

Realization set in, and I stopped moving.

The curse. How could I forget that he couldn't say no to me? I'd been so consumed by what I wanted, I hadn't made sure this was what he wanted as well.

"I'm sorry. I thought you wanted to—"

"I did. I do." He lifted his hips and groaned.

"*Shit.* I *really* do . . ." His eyes fell closed, and he inhaled a ragged breath. "I just . . . I don't think . . ." He winced. "After everything that's happened today, I'm not sure it's what either of us need."

My body screamed when I rolled off of him and collapsed onto the cushions. I didn't want him to be right, but he was. Until a few hours ago, I had believed myself in love with another man. It wasn't fair to toy with Tadhg's emotions like this. He loved me and wanted to stay married to me, and I honestly didn't know what I wanted.

Tadhg adjusted his breeches and scrubbed a hand down his face.

That wasn't entirely true. I knew I wanted him. Staying married was the easiest choice, but was it the right one?

Tadhg watched me through clear eyes, a wrinkle forming as his eyebrows slowly drew together. "You look troubled," he said, his voice husky and thick.

"I don't know what to do," I confessed, feeling like a fool.

"About what?"

"Anything."

Tadhg chuckled and shook his head. "I know what you need."

"Do you now? What's that?"

He settled himself onto the pillows and patted his chest. "Head here."

My heart swelled as I laid my head over his heart and snuggled into his warm embrace. When he started playing with my hair, tears welled in my eyes. Instead of wiping them away, I let them seep into the soft linen of his shirt as I cried.

For my sister.

For the future I had lost.

And for the future that could still be.

28

A FADED GREEN DOME CROWNED THE GREAT CATHEDRAL IN GAUL. I half expected Tadhg to burst into flames the moment we passed the vat of holy water at the threshold.

Two people knelt in front of the pews, facing the grandiose altar below a rosette window. I had expected him to ask Ruairi to bring us to Tearmann, but Tadhg had said he had some business to attend to in the city. Instead of leaving me behind, he asked if I wanted to join him. I wasn't sure what sort of business took place in a cathedral, but I supposed I was about to find out.

Sunlight streamed through panel after panel of stained glass, casting rainbows across the floor. The only noise in the breath-taking space was the sound of our boots clicking on the marble tiles. Tadhg stopped when he reached the purple curtains of the confessional and told me to wait for him.

He hadn't said much since we'd woken in each other's arms. Lorcan and Deirdre had been bustling around the apartments getting ready to open the pub downstairs, so we hadn't had time to talk. After he finished whatever business he had here, we would be on our way to Tearmann. In a few days, I would get to see my sister.

If only there were a way to bring her back without having to wait for the curse to end. I could really use her advice about the tangled mess that had become my life.

There were low murmurs from within the confessional, but I couldn't see the person with whom Tadhg spoke. Was it a priest or someone else? A few minutes later, Tadhg emerged clutching a golden key.

Instead of going to the exit, Tadhg brought me to an arched doorway at the back, concealing two sets of stairs: one curving upward toward the belltower, the other twisting down to the crypts.

"Do I want to know what sort of business happens down here?" I asked when Tadhg took the second. The smell of mold and mildew grew stronger as we descended.

"It's a surprise." There was mischief in his voice.

Three doors waited at the base of the stairs, two black and one green. Tadhg used the key to unlock the green one, then left it on the ledge at the top of the doorframe. From inside the dark room, I could hear water dripping.

My hand automatically found his. We stepped inside, and the door snicked shut, enveloping us in darkness.

"What are we doing?" My whisper echoed like a shout.

"*Shhhh.* I need to concentrate." It sounded like something was sliding along the wall in front of us. Tadhg muttered in a language I'd never heard before, and a triskelion carved into the stone began to glow.

"Close your eyes," he said.

I did. The glowing symbol still scorched through my lids.

"Are they closed?"

"Yes."

"Good. Now, hold on tight and don't let me go," he said, adjusting his grip on my fingers.

Don't let me go.

It felt like he meant more than here and now. The thought of letting him go was becoming harder and harder to imagine.

A cyclone of mildew-drenched air lifted around us, whipping at my hair, tearing at my skirts.

Thump

The shaking ground made my legs wobble but then it stopped. Vanilla and lavender replaced the damp smells, and muffled laughter replaced the sound of whipping wind. My free hand brushed against something soft. Tadhg opened the door, and light burst into the space. We were no longer in a musty cellar but in someone's linen closet, full of floral sheets and fluffy towels.

"Was that a portal?" There were myths surrounding hidden portals on the island, but I had never believed they really existed. After all that I'd seen on this journey, I should've known better.

Tadhg chuckled and kept my hand in his as he brought me out of the closet and into a sun-speckled hallway. The furniture in the three tidy bedrooms we passed was solid but worn. "It was."

"How far are we from Tearmann?"

"All going well, we'll be there in two hours."

Two hours? "I thought you said it'd take four days."

"It would take four days, if you took the human route. Not that I'd say that in front of your *friend*."

At the bottom of some creaky wooden stairs, a man with thinning red hair sat at the head of an uneven table, eating a bowl of stew. A red-haired woman sat next to him, holding a small child, asleep in her arms.

When they saw us, they didn't look the least bit concerned that we had appeared in their house without warning.

"Morning, Tadhg," the man said with a nod.

Tadhg returned the nod. "Ronan. Sive. How're the little ones settling in?"

The top half of the split front door was open; children's shouts filled the yard beyond.

The woman smiled, revealing a mouthful of crooked yellow teeth. "This one's a dote. Other two have been runnin' like mad all mornin', but it's great to have a bit of life 'round the place."

Chuckling, Tadhg flattened the corner of a wrinkled runner

with the toe of his boot. "You'll send word if you have any trouble, yeah?"

"Won't be no trouble at all," the man said with another nod, his mouth full of stew.

"Even so."

The woman put a hand on the man's arm and gave him a smile. "We'll let ye know."

Tadhg said goodbye, waved, and pushed the half-door aside. The exterior of the house was painted white with green sills. The thatched roof had gone black from mold, but a stack of fresh golden thatch sat at the corner beside a massive woodpile.

Two children screamed and threw mud at one another while a tiny pink piglet squealed and raced between them. At the edge of the fenced yard, a cow with ribs protruding beneath its tan hide munched on the few remaining clumps of grass.

"Tadhg!" The taller of the two children bounced over and hugged his legs, leaving his breeches smeared with small, muddy handprints. Her short red hair made it impossible to hide the deep purple bruise around her left eye.

Tadhg bent at the waist and gave the back of her dirty hand a chaste peck. "Are you feeling better today, Mila?"

My heart clenched in my chest. Were these the children Tadhg had kidnapped? What kind of monster would inflict that kind of wound onto a child?

"Yup." A grin. "Our new mammy gave us sweets."

"Did she now?"

"Yup. And they was the best sweets I ever had."

I shifted uncomfortably, wishing I had actually done something to help these poor children.

The little girl's eyes landed on me . . . and narrowed. "Who're you?" she asked, poking my thigh with a bony finger.

"My name is Lady Keelynn."

The girl's eyes widened, and she brought a self-conscious hand to her shorn hair. "Are ye a *real* lady?"

"I am."

"What're ye doin' with Tadhg?"

I glanced at Tadhg. He smiled and waved for me to proceed. How did I even begin to explain our relationship? "Tadhg and I are friends."

We were friends, I realized.

Being married to an insanely attractive friend who loved me sounded like a blessing, not a curse. I knew plenty of women who didn't even like their husbands. What if this was my one chance at happiness? Was I being crazy to even consider a real relationship with someone I barely knew?

The other child, a boy in short pants and shoes that were far too big for his small feet, caught the piglet and hauled it into his too-thin arms. The pig squealed and grunted, trying to wriggle free. He ran over and hid behind his sister's skirts, looking up at Tadhg with a mixture of awe and fear on his grubby face.

"And how's Cian this morning?" Tadhg asked, kneeling down to ruffle the boy's hair. "And Jordie?" The pig received a pat as well.

"I got my own bed," the little boy said with a shy grin. He was missing two of his bottom teeth.

"Isn't that brilliant?"

"Would be if my new mammy let Jordie sleep in it with me." He rubbed his cheek against the pig's wiry head. "But she says pigs isn't allowed in the house."

The little girl groaned. "I already told ye, Cian. Pigs isn't allowed in the house 'cause they make everything smell like shite."

"Not Jordie." He pressed his nose against the pig's snout. "She's a clean pig."

Mila planted her fists on her bony hips. "She's the dirtiest pig we got."

"Is not."

"Is too."

"Is not."

"Is too."

The little boy glared at her, then turned to Tadhg and grinned. "Mila told me she's gonna *maaaarry* ye."

The girl elbowed her brother, her cheeks pink. "Shut yer gob, Cian."

"Mila deserves to marry someone far better than me," Tadhg said with the sweetest smile.

From the starry-eyed look Mila gave him, it seemed like she didn't agree.

"I'm in a bit of a hurry today," Tadhg went on, "but I'll be back to check that you're minding your new mammy and daddy."

Mila's lips puckered. "Yer leavin' already? But ye promised to bring me something from Gaul."

"Did I?"

Her head dropped as she twisted her toe in the mud. "Ye forgot, huh?"

"I never break a promise—especially not one made to such a pretty girl." Tadhg winked and nodded toward her skirt. "Perhaps you should check your pockets."

Mila's eyes widened when she reached into her dress and withdrew a small present wrapped in cheesecloth. "Thank you! Thank you!" She hugged Tadhg again and ran into the house, carrying the bundle as though it were the most precious gift in the world. Her brother raced behind her, the poor pig swinging and squealing the whole way.

"What did you give her?"

"More sweets," he said with a wink before turning and starting down the muddy lane.

"Those were Marina's children, weren't they?"

Tadhg's shoulders seemed to cave in on themselves when he dropped his head and sighed. "Yes."

Marina's life must've truly been terrible for her to beg Tadhg for a kiss. And to have left her children behind with a man who used his fists on them. She must've believed there was no other way out.

Marina had been married to a monster, whereas I was

currently married to a prince. Tadhg was kind and thoughtful and seemed to genuinely care about others, human or Danú. I may not have known him for very long, but I knew he would never hurt a child the way Marina's husband had.

I could've been stuck with someone far worse. Someone like Robert.

The lane ended at an unpaved road pitted with carriage and hoof tracks. We followed the road for a short while, then turned off on a grassy path between two large redwood trees where birds chirped and flitted from branch to branch.

My mind was as tangled as the brambles on either side of the path. I needed something to focus on besides this predicament. Otherwise, I'd end up going mad before we reached Tearmann.

"Tell me about the portal."

Tadhg held back a low-hanging branch, allowing me to pass before releasing it. "There's not much to tell. Technically, we're not supposed to bring humans through, but since I'm the one in charge . . ." He shrugged.

The one in charge. I knew he was a prince but I hadn't realized that put him in charge.

"Are there more?"

"Yes."

"Where?"

"There's one in Port Fear."

My footsteps stilled, and I glared at Tadhg's back until he turned around. "If we'd taken a portal, we could've been here ages ago."

"I know." A small smile played on his lips. "But *someone* insisted the fastest way to Tearmann was to travel north by carriage."

If we had continued on his route, we would've reached Port Fear within six days of leaving. Instead, I had insisted on bringing us north, to Buraos.

I know my world better than you do.

That's what Tadhg had said.

He'd been truly trying to help me all along.

The forest grew thicker, and the path grew narrower until it stopped abruptly at a line of polished black stones, as if all the travelers before us had reached this point, thought better of continuing, and turned back. In the distance loomed a wall of black trees, their sharp, barren branches like gigantic pikes stabbing the gray sky.

Tadhg flicked his wrist, and a leather satchel appeared across his chest. He dug through and withdrew a silver container of kohl. "I want you to listen carefully," he said, dipping two fingers into the pot and smearing kohl across his eyes. "You need to follow in my footsteps and remain completely silent. All right?"

Follow him and stay quiet. "I think I can handle that."

Everyone on this island had heard of the Phantom Queen. The tales were even more awful than her name implied. During the war, she'd slaughtered humans on the battlefield without mercy and consumed the souls of those who perished. When the battle ended, her bloodlust remained. If you met her, you were as good as dead.

The Queen's castle was somewhere in the Black Forest. No one knew exactly where because no one dared to trespass on her land.

Yet here we were, about to trespass.

The black earth shifted like it was alive, waiting to swallow us whole. Piles of bones floated along the rolling, tar-like surface, then disappeared beneath the ground. Twisted trees with bark as black as ink oozed bloody red sap into puddles that soaked into the blackness.

Every step Tadhg made seemed to take careful consideration. He'd walk forward a short distance, stop, take a step to the right or left, then continue a few more steps like he was following a narrow trail only he could see.

The place reeked of rot and death; no plants grew, only soulless black trees.

My heart thundered in my chest, and air escaped my lungs,

but neither made a sound. What sort of horrible beings would choose to call this desolate place home?

The sky darkened, and it began to rain. Only the drops weren't clear and refreshing but red, like the clouds were crying tears of blood.

Tadhg swore and rubbed at his red-rimmed eyes, smearing kohl onto his shirtsleeve. With his hair matted to his head, the points of his ears stuck out even more.

We'd only been in the forest for twenty minutes when Tadhg stopped so suddenly, I rammed into his back.

He dragged a hand through his drenched hair. "Why can't things go right for once in my cursed life?"

From over his shoulder, I could see an endless lake of black crows spread across a gap in the trees ahead.

He dug into the bag and retrieved the kohl. When he looked back at me, a V formed between his eyebrows. "You need to put this on in case we get separated."

Separated? I wasn't letting him out of my sight. Still, if he wanted me to put it on as a precaution, I would. I reached for the tin, but he didn't let it go.

"Do you want me to put it on or not?" I asked, tugging harder.

Tadhg grimaced but released it with a sigh. The kohl was sticky and warm on my fingertips, and it stung when I smeared it over my eyes. I blinked against the pain, wishing I could rub it right off.

And then everything around me changed.

The trees weren't black, they were bone white. A broken black path twisted along the ground in the odd way Tadhg had been walking. The ring on my finger gave off a faint glow, covering me in green light.

No wonder Tadhg had known about the ring when we first met.

Tadhg.

I looked over at him and felt the smile slip from my face.

Tadhg's features morphed into different faces, all of them handsome and all of them wearing the same resigned expression. His nose, eyes, and cheekbones changed fluidly, like his face wasn't sure what it wanted to look like. The only thing that didn't change was the color of his eyes, green swirling with black.

The most disturbing thing was his mouth.

Like the ground of the Black Forest, black lingering death slithered along his lips, awaiting its next victim.

"Don't look at me," he whispered, turning his face toward the crows.

He took back the kohl and stuffed it into his bag. With a flick of his wrist, the bag disappeared. "We cannot linger any longer," he said. "Do you think you can run along the path?"

I tore my gaze from his cursed face and tried to focus on the broken path cutting through the hundreds of birds pecking at the rolling ground.

"My land borders the Queen's." He pointed to a faint green light, barely visible between the white trunks on the other side of the birds.

My land.

"If we can reach it in time," he said, adjusting the belt and dagger at his waist, "she won't dare cross it."

"Is she near?" I glanced around but saw only trees and crows.

"She's always near."

I had never been very athletic, but I would do my best to keep from slowing him down. "I can run."

He nodded and faced forward. "On the count of three. One. Two. *Three.*"

We sprinted for the crows. I willed my legs to move faster, weaving along the broken path. A skull rose from the ground, and I stumbled. Tadhg caught me before I fell. When the birds saw us, they lifted into the sky, a tidal wave of black feathers and talons.

He would have been so much faster without me.

What was I thinking? Without me, he could have evanesced and avoided the forest altogether.

My lungs screamed, aching for oxygen they couldn't find; the muscles in my legs burned and throbbed. Beyond the gap flowed a wide black river with glowing green trees on the far bank.

Thump thump thump

At first I thought the noise was my heart.

Then it got louder. Closer.

Hooves pounding on earth.

I glanced over my shoulder, sure that something was chasing us, but there was nothing—

"*Going somewhere?*"

Tadhg skidded to a halt. I slammed into his back.

The voice, haunting in its sweetness, belonged to a gaunt older woman wearing a cape of black feathers and sitting astride a white horse. On top of her thinning mahogany hair sat a black crown that came to a point in the center of her wrinkled forehead like the beak of one of her crows.

A shudder ran through my body.

The Phantom Queen had found us.

29

Two broad-shouldered guards in black masks and black leather uniforms flanked the Queen on onyx steeds. Battle axes stuck out from leather straps on their backs. The tips of the broadswords in their hands reached the ground.

Tadhg's kohl had all but disappeared in the rain. He wiped his eyes with his shirtsleeve, smearing it off completely. "Hello, Auntie."

Auntie?

The Queen was Tadhg's *aunt?*

"I take it you don't plan on staying for tea?" The Queen's light, pleasant voice contrasted with the wicked gleam in her depthless black eyes.

Tadhg tucked his hands into his pockets and rocked back on his heels, a picture of nonchalance. "Must you always ask the most inane questions?"

Shouldn't he be bowing or trying to placate instead of antagonizing her?

Clucking her tongue, the Queen drummed her pointed black nails against her horse's saddle. "After all these years, I'm shocked you haven't found any manners."

Tadhg stepped closer, positioning himself in front of me. I

couldn't find enough air to sigh in relief. Perhaps she hadn't noticed me. Perhaps she would let us go since I was with her nephew.

"If I had manners, I wouldn't waste them on you."

Dammit, Tadhg. She was going to kill us both if he didn't at least pretend to be nice. I peeked around him to see how the rude comment was received. She didn't *look* angry. If anything she appeared indifferent.

"You and Rían missed my birthday last month," she sniffed, brushing a careless hand down the feathers on her cape. Black eyes met mine, and a slow smile spread across her lips. "But I suppose the pretty present you brought me makes up for it. Come out here, girl. Let me get a look at you."

Tadhg's shoulders stiffened.

I had no plan to comply, but something cold slithered up my legs. Black roots wrapped around my ankles, my calves, my knees, pulling me forward.

"I'll pay twice next time," Tadhg snapped, his hands flexing at his sides. Magic leaked out of him like glittering shadows.

"That's not the way this works, Tadhg," the Queen crooned, urging her mount forward to meet me. "Such a pretty little thing you are. My dear nephew knows better than to try and smuggle humans into Tearmann."

Tadhg's magic swirled around his legs, fluttering his overcoat.

The Queen's cold hand caught my chin, forcing me to look at her. Webs of black veins spread beneath her paper-thin, wrinkled skin. "Do you know the penalty for being caught crossing the Black Forest without my permission, *girl?*"

My voice was gone, so I shook my head.

"One life." The Queen's eyes flashed as she withdrew a dagger from beneath her feathered cloak. Bloodred raindrops rolled down the gleaming silver blade.

Tadhg appeared beside me, knocking the Queen's dagger to the ground.

Her eyes narrowed into slits. "You arrogant little—"

"Oh, be quiet, you old crow." Tadhg turned his back on her, took my hand, and brought my knuckles to his cursed mouth.

The blackness had been there all along, yet seeing it crawling along his lips made me want to pull away.

As if he'd heard my thoughts, Tadhg winced. Instead of kissing them, he gave my fingers a squeeze and let go. "It's been a pleasure being your husband," he whispered, face still shifting and lips lifting into a sad smile.

Before I could respond, he let me go and turned toward the Queen. "Make it quick. She's in a bit of a hurry."

The Queen's mouth twisted into a deranged smile. She shifted the dagger back into her hand, bent forward to whisper something into Tadhg's ear . . . and plunged the dagger into his heart.

"No!" I lunged, catching Tadhg's body before he fell; his dead weight pulled us both down into the writhing dirt. The shifting stopped, and all that was left was Tadhg. The life in his green eyes faded to black. Hot, sticky blood gushed from the wound in his chest, staining my hands. My dress. My soul.

The Queen inhaled a hissing breath through her teeth. The wrinkles on her forehead smoothed, and the hard lines around her mouth softened.

Tadhg was immortal.

He would be back.

But would it be in time to save me?

"*Again*," the Queen cackled, motioning toward me.

One of the soldiers jabbed his sword into the ground, summoning a well of black tar from beneath the surface. He climbed off his horse and strode toward me with purpose.

"No." A whisper. A plea. One life. That was the penalty. She'd said one life. "*No* . . . Please . . ."

The soldier leaned forward, dagger in hand.

I closed my eyes and prayed for a quick death. The weight of Tadhg against me vanished. The guard had him by the ankle, tugging him toward the river. He stopped, knelt, raised the dagger over his head, and let it fall. Over and over and over.

A terrible cackle shuddered through the bare black branches. "That bastard's harder to kill than I am," the Queen said between harsh inhales.

Tears tumbled down my cheeks as the guard replaced his bloody dagger in its sheath and resumed dragging Tadhg to the river. Tadhg's head bounced across the black ground, arms akimbo, flailing over the roots and stones and bones.

When the guard reached the river, he kicked Tadhg's body into the water.

The Queen smiled at me, the face of a young, beautiful woman where the old crone had been only moments ago, and said, "Welcome to Tearmann."

30

*T*ADHG IS COMING BACK.

Tadhg is coming back.

Those four words clanged through my mind over and over and over as the icy water from the black river slapped my torso. I floated Tadhg's body to the opposite shore. The rain stopped the moment I reached the silty sand.

I didn't know how long it would take, but I knew he'd come back, because there was no way he'd sacrifice himself for me if he couldn't. I slipped my arms beneath Tadhg's and managed to drag him through the sand to a patch of glowing grass before collapsing.

He is coming back.

No matter how many times I said it, the tears kept falling, burning my eyes. Although his face no longer shifted, the black curse on his mouth remained. I touched a finger to his lips. The blackness tried to climb onto my skin, but the green aura of the ring fought to keep it at bay.

My stomach lurched at the thought of where his mouth had touched my body. I grabbed the sopping hem of my dress and scrubbed the last of the kohl from my eyes. It was Tadhg lying beside me. Just Tadhg. My husband—

Wait.

I twisted the emerald from my finger. The black band was gone. Not my husband. Not anymore.

What was left of my heart turned to dust. I should have been happy to have my freedom back, but I was bloody miserable. It wasn't until this moment, with him lying dead in my arms and our vows broken, that I realized how much I wanted to stay married to Tadhg.

"What the hell have you done to my brother?"

I whirled to find a man with short-cropped mahogany hair looming above me, bracing his hands on his slim hips. His dark eyebrows slashed angrily above stunning blue eyes. The cravat at his throat was perfectly tied, and his black waistcoat threaded with silver stood out in contrast to his pristine white shirt.

Brother.

This must be Rían.

And he thought I'd killed Tadhg.

Stumbling to my feet, I shoved my hair back from my sticky cheeks. Rían's gaze dropped to the bloodstains across my chest, then returned to my face.

"I didn't kill him," I said, my voice trembling and stomach twisting. "I swear, it wasn't me."

Rían's eyebrows flicked up, and his eyes narrowed. "I'm not talking about killing him," he grumbled. "What I meant was you turning the poor man into a simpering eejit who's forgotten his duty is to *his people* and not some foolish human *girl* with chronic bad luck."

Chronic bad luck.

My life was plagued by more than bad luck. Ever since Aveen had kissed the Gancanagh, death and danger had become my shadows, refusing to let me have one day of peace.

"I didn't turn Tadhg into anything."

Rían's mouth twisted into a sneer. "Yes, you did. And since he's been neglecting his duties to play the doting courtier, they've all fallen on my shoulders. And I do not appreciate it one bit."

"That sounds like something you need to discuss with Tadhg," I clipped, glancing down at his body. His face still held no color; his eyes were still black.

Rían's teeth flashed when he grinned. The hairs on the back of my neck prickled. There was something about him that set me on edge.

"When is Tadhg coming back?" I rushed.

Rían squatted next to his brother to check the wounds littered across his chest. They were still red and angry but beginning to close at the edges. "Feckin' hell. How many times did she stab you?" he muttered to Tadhg's body.

Rían withdrew a handkerchief from his pocket to clean the dirt from his hand. His nose wrinkled at the blood and dirt stains on the previously white fabric. Instead of returning it to his pocket, he tucked it into Tadhg's. "He should be back in an hour or so, depending on how much of his magic was left."

What was it about him that made me want to run in the opposite direction?

Using a twig he found on the ground, he opened Tadhg's shirt to check the wounds again. Some of the redness had subsided, and his skin was almost fully closed. "You'd think he'd know better than to antagonize her. But he just can't keep his gob shut." He tossed the stick over his shoulder. "Can you grab his arm there?" Rían gestured toward Tadhg's twisted limb. "I don't really feel like getting blood and grime all over my new shirt."

I took Tadhg's cold hand, and together, we hauled him farther into the grass, to the forest of healthy trees. Rían's boot caught on a stone, and he fell onto his backside in the dirt. A torrent of profanity flew from his mouth as he scrubbed at the stains on his fine black breeches. When he kicked Tadhg's slumped body, I shoved him into a tree. "Don't touch him!"

"Look what he did!" Rían swore again as he twisted to show me his backside. "These are from the feckin' continent."

"This isn't Tadhg's fault. He's *dead*, remember?"

"Oh, my dear Keelynn, you'll soon come to find that *everything* is Tadhg's fault." Rían tugged on the ends of his waistcoat and smoothed a hand to fix his perfect hair. "If you'll excuse me for a moment, I need to get this irritating bastard to the castle." Rían's nose wrinkled when he laced their fingers together, and then they both vanished.

I scrubbed a hand down my sodden skirts in a useless attempt to rid myself of sand and grime, then squeezed out the excess moisture making them cling to my freezing legs. I didn't know what I had expected from Tadhg's brother, but it certainly hadn't been *that*.

"Here." Rían was back with an armful of women's clothes. "Put these on. The last thing I need is to be seen with a human in such a horrendous state." He said it like I didn't already know how terrible I looked.

"Turn around and give me some privacy," I snapped, wishing he weren't Tadhg's brother and my only guide so I could slap the smug smile off his face.

Rían snorted and sauntered toward a big tree. Once he was hidden from view, I peeled myself out of the dress, stay, and shift, and changed into the soft gray gown. Instead of putting my cloak back on, I balled up the rest of my garments inside.

"Are you finished yet?" Rían whined.

"Yes."

"Good." He appeared from around the trunk, took the bundle from me, and flicked his wrist, sending it heaven-knows-where. "Let's get a move on. I don't have all feckin' day."

I followed Rían through a forest that looked like it was in the height of spring instead of the start of autumn, with colorful buds and bees buzzing to and fro. Plump, vibrant birds flew overhead, singing happy tunes. The forest ended at the edge of a green field dotted with tiny cottages. Each cottage had a wooden fence, a small garden, and at least one fruit tree growing in the yard.

A wrinkled grogoch knelt in one of the gardens, his hairy hands covered in dark soil as he pulled carrots from the ground.

When he noticed us, his beady eyes widened. He continued watching until we passed.

A few cottages down the road, a gorgeous woman with flowing orange hair balanced a baby on her hip while hanging laundry on a clothesline. She gave us the same odd look. Rían grumbled and kept walking.

The fields gave way to steep cliffs, with waves battering against the high stone walls in a never-ending battle. In the distance rose a magnificent castle, the same shade of gray as the craggy boulders at its base, like it had grown from the rock itself.

Never in my life had I seen a place as breathtaking or as imposing. *This* was where Tadhg had grown up? This beautiful place full of sunlight and serenity? Why would anyone ever want to venture into Airren when they could live *here*?

I had only ever been in one castle, and it had been damp and dank, and smelled of mildew and age and decay from disuse. But the Gancanagh's castle was a timeless testament to its architect and its owner, a towering fortress with slits for windows and guard-topped turrets.

The barbican jutted out on either side of the gates, creating a narrow passageway to the keep's main entrance. An aged black portcullis had been left open, lulling unsuspecting visitors into a sense of ease. Ease that quickly dissipated with one glance at the five murder holes carved into the ceiling. Sunlight, not boiling oil, fell through, crowning Rían's mahogany hair when he passed beneath them, a reminder that he was also a prince here.

A strange sensation came over me, like I was walking through cobwebs.

I scrubbed at my face and arms, but there was nothing there.

"It's the wards," Rían explained in an exasperated voice.

Wards to keep out unwanted intruders. If I had tried to enter without an escort, would I have been able to? I'd have to ask Tadhg later, because I sure as hell wasn't asking Rían.

The area between the outer wall and main castle bustled with Danú. Two grogoch pushed wheelbarrows of unnaturally large red apples. A pooka lounging on a bench had one arm wrapped around the barrel at his side and the other around a human-sized faerie.

A sharp-toothed merrow sunned herself on the edge of a wide fountain, her beautiful sea-colored face upturned toward the sun. The green scales starting below her navel glistened. I could have stood there all day studying her ethereal beauty.

Rían didn't bother acknowledging any of the Danú we passed on our way to the castle's arched green door. The moment his foot hit the first step, the door swung open, and a hairy red head popped out.

"Good to see yer back, Prince Rían," the grogoch said, his voice little more than a wheeze. "There's quite a line today."

Rían groaned and turned to glare at me over his shoulder. "This is your fault, you know."

"My fault?" How could anything be my fault? I had only just arrived.

Instead of explaining, Rían thanked the grogoch and waved me inside. The grogoch bowed his head as we passed.

The ancient scent inside the castle reminded me of the cathedral in Gaul. Instead of echoing, our footsteps soaked into the stones, becoming forever etched into the unforgiving gray. We passed a wide, round oak table decorated with a crystal vase of stunning blue flowers. Tapestries hung on the walls, depicting scenes from the stories Tadhg had told to the faeries.

The one with banshees circling the gray sky above a corpse-strewn battlefield was by far the most gruesome. I recognized the Phantom Queen, wearing black armor and her beak-like crown, eyes closed, and beautifully terrifying face upturned as if in the throes of passion. Her chin dripped with blood as she cradled two severed heads.

"I've told him to burn these rags time and again, but Tadhg always refuses," Rían said, stopping outside a set of wide double doors. It sounded like a large group of people waited on the other side. Rían raked a hand through his short hair and swore. "I don't want you snooping around the place, so I'm going to let you come inside. But don't say a word." Unnerving blue eyes bore into mine. Again, that prickle of unease tickled against my stomach. Rían quickly looked away.

Go in. Keep silent. I could do that.

Rían shoved open the doors, and I held my breath. Danú of all kinds milled about a great hall with thick wooden beams across the vaulted ceiling. When they heard the doors open, they all turned to face us.

I kept my head down and followed Rían to a raised dais with a large wooden throne and a smaller chair to its right. "Stand over there," he said, gesturing to a spot next to the smaller chair. I waited and watched as the crowd formed an orderly line. At the front stood a plump woman with pointed ears and a bulbous nose.

"Where's Prince Tadhg?" she asked, her deep-set brown eyes narrowing on Rían.

"He's indisposed at the moment," Rían said, stretching his legs out in front of him. "Is there something I can help you with?"

"Ye promised Tadhg would be here." The woman planted her fists on her wide hips and stomped up a step. "I've been tryin' to meet with 'im fer two feckin' weeks."

"And it looks as though you'll have to wait a little while longer, now doesn't it?" Rían said through his teeth. "Unless there is something *I* can do for you."

"I wouldn't trust ye with my feckin' laundry, let alone my land."

"So you've a border dispute?"

She lifted her chin and turned for the door. A handful of other people glared toward the dais before following her out.

"If anyone else takes issue with speaking to me in my brother's stead, you may as well leave now and save us all some time." Rían's announcement cut the crowd in half. The ones who left grumbled on their way out the door.

No wonder Rían didn't like me.

Tadhg was the rightful ruler of Tearmann, and if it weren't

for me, he would be here doing his job instead of being held up in the underworld.

The next person in line had a chicken beneath his skinny brown arm. "Was hopin' to see yer brother, but since I came all this way, I may as well give it to ye." He held the chicken toward Rían. "Nettie here is my best hen. She's worth twice as much as I owe in taxes this year."

Rían's nose wrinkled, and he shirked away from the offering. "Oscar!" he shouted. The grogoch from the door hurried in, collected the chicken, thanked the man, and brought the offering out into the hallway.

Next in line were three small faeries, all of them with varying shades of blue hair. They flew forward, landing on the bottom step of the dais.

"You're going to have to come closer than that," Rían said, rolling his eyes. "I cannot hear you from down there."

"Apologies for being late," a familiar voice echoed through the hall. My breath caught in my throat when Tadhg strolled in, looking resplendent in a black waistcoat and breeches with a dark green cravat draped around his open collar like a scarf. "I was unfortunately detained for longer than expected."

"Oh, thank heavens," Rían muttered under his breath, flicking his wrist and appearing in the smaller chair.

Tadhg's long legs made short work of the distance, and he took the steps two at a time. He gave me a wink and a crooked grin that left my stomach fluttering, then twisted and sank onto the throne. "Now, let's get down to business, shall we? Muire, Lena, Sorcha, what seems to be the problem?"

Business.

All this time, I had assumed Tadhg's business had been conducted in the bedroom. He had been trying to rule a bloody kingdom, and I had expected him to escort me across the country so I could sacrifice him for my sister. I had never felt as foolish as I did standing there, watching Tadhg solve disputes between neighbors, collect taxes and rent, and give his blessing for upcoming nuptials.

Once upon a time, I had actually thought his business couldn't possibly be as important as my mission to resurrect Aveen. A mission that had ended up being entirely and utterly pointless.

Rían glanced over his shoulder at me, and the fluttering in my stomach turned to dread.

"This is going to take ages," he whispered. "You're welcome to stay and watch the crowd fawn over my brother, or you can escape with me." He nodded toward a door behind the dais.

I glanced at the door, then back at Tadhg, who was settling an argument over who owned a fruit tree that had sprouted between two cottages. As much as I didn't want to go with Rían, my stomach was starting to ache from hunger.

"I'll go with you."

Tadhg's shoulders seemed to stiffen, but it could've been my imagination.

Rían shoved himself from his chair and jogged down the stairs to the door. I followed him through a dark passageway into an office with floor-to-ceiling bookshelves and a wide mahogany desk in front of the biggest fireplace I'd ever seen.

"I *hate* Fridays," Rían grumbled on his way out of the office and back into the tapestry-lined hallway. "They're so exceedingly dull. Did you see that man try to hand me a feckin' chicken?" He shuddered. "Livestock belongs in a field, not a castle." He flicked his wrist, and a red apple appeared in his hand. "Do you want one?"

My stomach responded with a loud growl. Rían shoved the apple at me and shifted another. When my teeth pierced the crisp flesh, the juice tasted extra sweet, like it had been laced with sugar.

Rían stopped at the base of a staircase that curved along the wall to pull a knife from a sheath at his waist. He sliced off a thick chunk and popped it into his mouth. "Come on," he said, gesturing toward the stairs with the dagger. Juice dripped down the blade and onto the stone floor. "Tadhg said you want to see Aveen. Although, I'm not sure why. She's still dead."

Rían strolled up the stairs, slicing and eating the apple like he hadn't a care in the world.

On and on we climbed. By the time we reached the top floor, my legs ached, and the apple was nothing more than a core. Rían flicked his wrist and it disappeared, along with his own.

Colorful tapestries brightened the dark, narrow hallway leading to one of the castle's turrets. Rían twisted the golden handle on a small, unassuming door, revealing a chamber with rounded walls. A crystal vase overflowing with pink and purple bell-shaped blossoms sat under a thin window. Sunlight streamed through the leaded glass pane, landing on a large wooden box with no lid.

The memory of Aveen's body the night she'd died kept me rooted to the stones. Why had I insisted on coming to Tearmann to see her? I didn't want to remember her like this. I didn't want to be reminded that my sister was dead.

Rían walked over to the box and peered inside, a small smile lifting his lips. "She's so beautiful when she's not giving out," he said with a soft chuckle.

The unease returned ten-fold. "Excuse me?" I took a halting step forward.

Blue eyes met mine. "Your sister is beautiful when she's not giving out or ranting or ordering me around the place."

"Ordering *you* around?"

His eyebrows came together. "Did Tadhg not tell you?"

"Tell me what?"

Rían's head tilted as he tapped a nail against the edge of the box. "Your sister and I are engaged."

"What do you mean you're *engaged*?" My legs unlocked, and I rushed forward to catch Rían by the shoulders. "Aveen was betrothed to Robert."

Rían's nose scrunched as he slowly pried himself free. "She didn't want to marry him. She wanted to marry me."

How could Aveen have known Rían—loved him enough to want to marry him—and never tell me that he existed?

My eyes inadvertently fell to the box, and the air evaporated from my lungs.

My perfect sister's golden hair cascaded down her slim shoulders, falling in soft curls around her icy blue gown. Her skin was as pale as the clouds in the sky. The only color in her face was the black stain on her lips. She'd been gone almost five months, and yet there were no signs of decay.

I sank onto the stool beside her coffin, my mind racing with questions.

"When did the two of you meet?" I asked, my voice barely a whisper. Dust motes spun in the sunlight falling through the window.

"Ages ago, at the market in Graystones. We had planned on eloping, but then your father announced her betrothal to Robert."

They were going to elope? Aveen had been planning on leaving me all along? Was she going to tell me or just disappear?

"She outright refused to call off the engagement for fear of how it would impact you," Rían went on, eyes narrowed as his gaze raked from my disheveled hair, down my borrowed dress, to my muddy slippers. "If it weren't for you, she would've left that very night. As the betrothal ball approached, it became clear that we needed to take drastic measures. I suggested my brother's unique way of dealing with problems, and she agreed."

This whole debacle was Rían's fault. "So she's dead because of you." A year of her life snuffed out because this man suggested she kiss the Gancanagh.

Rían folded his arms over his chest and glared down at me. "No, she's dead because of *you*. If you weren't so head over heels in love with that wretched human, she would've told him to shove off, consequences be damned."

I touched a lock of Aveen's silky hair and let it slip through my fingers. A weaker woman would have given in and married Robert. A more obstinate woman would have refused outright.

But my sister, my brilliant, strong sister, had sacrificed a year of her life so that I could get everything I had ever wanted.

And in the end, I hadn't wanted it at all.

I braced my hands on either side of Aveen's gilded coffin and pressed a kiss to her cold cheek. "When I see you again, you have *a lot* of explaining to do." And I wouldn't let her out of my sight until she answered every single question. I stood and smoothed an unsteady hand down my skirts. I missed her so much, it felt like someone had stabbed me in the chest and cut out my heart. Tears collected behind my lashes, but I refused to let them fall. This wasn't a sad day. It was a happy one.

The soles of Rían's polished boots scuffed against the stones when he shifted his weight. "We should get going. This place is depressing." He pulled a pristine handkerchief from his breast pocket and held it awkwardly toward me.

"Thank you." I dabbed at the corners of my eyes and offered Rían a watery smile, determined to give him a chance now that I knew Aveen cared for him. The light from the window highlighted the rich, reddish tones in his hair. The blue of his eyes was so unusual, the color of a crystal-clear sky. There was something so familiar, and yet I couldn't place—

A chill shuddered through me. Rían started for the door, but I caught him by the sleeve. "Look at me," I said, my voice faltering.

"What're you doing? Let me go." Rían tried brushing me off, but I held firm.

"I said, *look at me.*"

Blue eyes bore into mine. The sunlight made his pupil shrink, revealing a thin golden ring around the center.

No. It couldn't be.

He was dead.

He.

Was.

Dead.

"*Edward?*"

31

THERE WAS A MUFFLED CHOKE FROM THE DOORWAY. I TURNED IN time to catch the smile fading from Tadhg's face. "What do you mean, *Edward*?"

Rían's eyes widened, and he started shaking his head. "I don't know what she's on about. You know humans and their fanciful notions."

Tadhg stalked forward, his face a mask of lethal calm as an almond-scented breeze tickled my cheek. "Keelynn?" He stopped at my side. "Why did you call my brother by your husband's name?"

I couldn't tear my attention from Rían's panicked gaze. This wasn't some fanciful notion. It was him. I'd know those eyes anywhere. "I recognize his eyes from the night we . . . from the ball." The only explanation was that he was a shifter like Tadhg and had concealed his identity. Why? For what purpose? Had he been hiding from Aveen? Had he been Edward all along, or was there another Edward out there, serving as an ambassador between Airren and Vellana?

Perspiration beaded on Rían's brow; a vein in his forehead pulsed. "It's not what you think," he wheezed, arms hanging limp at his sides, face growing redder and redder. "I swear. We weren't supposed to get caught, but her dress ripped, and her father found us, and it all went to shit."

Tadhg's hands squeezed into white-knuckled fists, and he slowly turned to me, hurt and rage swirling in his narrowed black eyes. "Is that true?"

I could only nod, unable to find my voice. It was true. All of it had gone to shit.

Rían swore and kicked frantically, his feet hovering above the ground. Tadhg ripped the dagger from his waist and drew it across Rían's throat. Blood sprayed from the wound, showering us both. Rían's head lolled forward, and when he fell, Tadhg let his body collapse to the stones in a growing pool of red.

"What have you done?" I cried, pressing a trembling hand to my chest. Rían was also immortal, but that didn't change the fact that Tadhg had murdered his brother.

Tadhg cleaned the blade against his thigh and jammed the dagger back into its sheath. "Till death do us part."

Till death do us part . . .

If Edward . . . Rían had never actually died, he would've been my husband this whole time. My stomach roiled, and I backed away from the body and the blood. But if we'd been married, I would've had a brand, like with Tadhg. I checked my finger beneath the emerald even though I knew there was nothing there. None of this made any sense.

"I am sorry my brother deceived you." Tadhg's frosty tone left me shivering. "He's not known for his honesty."

How far did Rían's lies extend? "He told me he and Aveen were engaged." Was that true or another lie?

Tadhg stepped over his brother's legs, took my hand in his, and towed me toward the door. "I wouldn't believe a word out of that lying bastard's mouth."

He brought me two floors down, to a beautiful bedroom overlooking the castle's central courtyard.

A large four-poster bed with a flowing white canopy took up most of one wall, and a bench built beneath a wide window took up the wall next to it. Across from the bed was a fireplace, a rich mahogany armoire, and a matching dressing table.

"Stay here until someone comes to get you for dinner," Tadhg clipped, letting me go and scrubbing his hand down his thigh like he wanted to rid himself of my touch. His gaze stayed on the stones beneath his scuffed boots. "There are a few matters I need to take care of, and I cannot leave you to wander about the castle on your own."

He didn't try to touch me again or leave me with a kiss or even a smile as he turned and closed the door with a quiet click.

I sank onto the downy mattress and tried to process the last twenty-four hours, starting with Rían. *Err . . .* Edward. My first husband. My second husband's brother.

Why had he been at the betrothal ball?

Why had he asked me to meet him in the hall?

Why had he been sleeping with our maid if he loved Aveen?

Was it all a lie?

I laid there, staring at the fluttering curtains until the sunlight faded into shadows and someone knocked softly on the door. I expected a servant, not Rían wearing a dark blue shirt and black braces. His hair was damp at the temples like he'd recently bathed.

"May I come in for a moment?" he asked, keeping his eyes fixed on his polished boots and his hands shoved into his pockets.

"I don't think that's the best idea." The little goodwill I'd been willing to spare him for being my sister's fiancée was gone.

"Please? I owe you an explanation."

The only person who truly knew the answers to all of my questions was standing right in front of me. It would be foolish not to hear him out, as long as I kept in mind that he was likely lying.

I opened the door wider and let him inside. He walked straight to the window and sank onto the bench. With a flick of his wrist, a fire appeared in the barren grate, instantly heating the room.

"First, I must apologize," he said, leaning forward to brace his elbows on his knees. "You were never meant to be part of this mess."

Tadhg had said the same thing, so I chose to believe him. I sank onto the end of the bed and hugged my knees to my chest, waiting for more.

"I had everything planned out that night. Aveen was to meet Tadhg in the garden, and I was in charge of distracting you, so you didn't notice her leaving and try to follow. I thought we could share a glass of champagne, chat for a short while, then return to the ballroom unnoticed. Aveen said you were enamored with Robert, so the last thing I expected was for you to throw yourself at me and—"

"I didn't *throw* myself at you." At least, that's not how the events had played out in my mind. I'd had a good deal to drink, sure. And I remembered going into the hallway and being so enraged at Robert that I couldn't think straight.

Rían crossed his arms and leaned back against the wall. Moonlight highlighted his dark silhouette. "What would you call shoving me into an alcove and pinning me against the window?"

Had I shoved him?

Had I been the one to take advantage of him and not the other way around?

My face flushed with embarrassment. "I'm sorry. I didn't mean—"

"Oh, please." Rían waved away the broken apology with a tanned hand. "You're hardly the first woman to lose her head over me."

Lose my head? That was a little dramatic considering I had only been using him to make Robert jealous. "Someone's awfully full of himself."

Rían's dark chuckle made me shudder. "For good reason."

Rían was handsome, but not nearly as handsome as Tadhg. He was too refined, too clean. I loved Tadhg's ruggedness, the way he constantly looked like he'd just returned from a tumble in a field. The way his stubble scratched my cheeks, my chin, my thighs—

No. Bad idea. Very bad idea. The last thing I needed was to let my mind go down that road. Tadhg didn't seem to want anything to do with me now that he knew I'd accidentally married Rían.

"Anyway," Rían said, drawing me back to the present, "you insisted on punching me while I was trying to extricate myself and then . . ." A shrug.

And then my father found us.

It could've been a lie, but I was fairly certain it wasn't. "Why did you agree to marry me when you could've evanesced and disappeared forever?"

"What would've happened to you then?" he asked, massaging his throat and wincing as though he was in pain. Did wounds bother immortals even after they'd healed?

"Aveen was dead, and you were all but ruined," he went on. "I figured being married to me for a short while would be the lesser of many evils, and as a widow, you'd have the freedom to do as you pleased." He shook his head and gave a mirthless chuckle. "I never thought you'd use that freedom to track down my brother."

I could've used my freedom for anything, and yet fate had led me here. To Tearmann. To Rían. To Tadhg.

Rían drew in a deep breath and sighed, rubbing a mark at the top of his boot. "I don't suppose there's any way I could convince you to keep this debacle between the three of us?"

"I'm not going to lie to my sister, if that's what you're asking." Secrets were what had caused these problems in the first place. If Aveen had told me her plan, none of this would've happened. Rían nodded and stood, smoothing his hands down his thighs to straighten his breeches. "However, I will give you the opportunity to explain yourself first."

Nodding again, he offered me a sad smile. "That is most kind. Far kinder than I deserve. I can see why my brother is smitten with you."

Perhaps before. But after this recent revelation, it was obvious Tadhg didn't want anything to do with me.

Before he reached the door, Rían asked if I was coming to dinner.

"Tadhg said he'd send an escort." Although part of me wished I could simply have a tray brought to the bedroom. Even my bones were weary.

Rían flicked his wrist, and a fabulous blue gown appeared on the bed. "Wear that. It'll suit you." With another flick, a hot tub of water appeared by the fireplace.

When was the last time I'd had a proper bath? It felt like forever.

"Where do you two get these tubs?" I asked, dipping my fingers into the hot water. I couldn't wait to get in and scrub away the day.

Rían glanced toward the rising steam, a small smile playing on his lips. "Mostly from each other. It's quite irritating to be looking forward to a bath only to have it evanesce right before your eyes."

I could only imagine. If someone tried to take this bath from me, I think I'd cry.

"It's a good thing no one was in it."

"You can tell if it's occupied—it gets too heavy to shift." His lips lifted into a crooked grin. "The trick is snagging it at just the right time for maximum annoyance."

As if on cue, Tadhg began roaring from somewhere down the hall.

"Better hurry and hop in before he steals it back," Rían said with a wink, opening the door and letting it fall behind him.

I stripped quickly and jumped into the tub to clean the river sand from between my toes and the blood from beneath my nails. I scrubbed until my skin was pink and sore and my scalp ached. Inside the armoire, I found a pile of linen towels and a small hand mirror and brush. The tangles in my hair took forever to work out, but eventually the long, dark strands were tamed into soft waves. Instead of tying it up, I left it free.

The blue gown slipped like liquid against my overwarm skin. I had just finished tying the sash at my waist when there was a knock at the door.

"Are you decent?"

It was Rían again.

I opened the door to find my former husband waiting outside. "What do you think? I was feeling nostalgic," he said with a wicked grin.

I knew it was Rían, but he now looked exactly like Edward, down to the slight curl in his brown hair. "That's not funny," I gasped, my throat suddenly dry. It was like coming face to face with a bloody ghost.

"Oh, fine." Rían flicked his wrist, and his face shifted back into the man I had met in the forest. "Shall we?" He offered his elbow, but I hesitated.

I didn't want to go to dinner with Rían, I wanted to go with Tadhg. "I think I should wait for your brother." There was no sign of him in the hallway. Was he already downstairs?

"Oh, he's not coming."

My stomach sank. "Why not?"

Rían shrugged. "I heard him mention something about a special guest for dinner."

A special guest? Who could that be?

Instead of waiting around to see if Rían was lying, I laced my arm through his. Together we descended the stairs and walked through the hallway, past the great room where Tadhg had held court, and into a large dining room set with six place settings. A moment later, Tadhg and two short men with wiry red beards, dressed head to toe in tweed, entered through an adjoining door, deep in discussion. When Tadhg's eyes met mine, his footsteps faltered.

A heated blush crept up my neck as his gaze slowly moved from my unbound hair to the low sweetheart neckline on the dress, down the curves of my hips, all the way to the silver slippers on my feet. Fire collected in my belly, and my legs began to tremble.

Then his gaze landed on Rían's hand at my elbow and his expression darkened. "If you'll excuse me for just a moment," he said to the men, who continued on to their chairs. Tadhg walked stiffly toward us, his hands flexing at his sides.

Rían grinned when Tadhg unhooked his hand from my arm and laced our fingers together. Instead of bringing me to the table, he tugged me to a secluded corner beside a pair of glass doors overlooking the garden.

I could smell his magic, like he couldn't contain it, and inhaled through my nose and mouth. I wanted to kiss him so badly, I thought I'd die from wanting—

Tadhg dropped my hand and stepped away like I'd been about to slap him.

"Where did you get that dress?" he snapped in a harsh whisper, pupils blown wide.

My dress? I couldn't even remember what I was wearing. Oh, right. Blue silk. "Rían gave it to me."

He blanched, but quickly schooled his features into a blank mask. "You are free to do as you please, of course. But I would appreciate it if you did not flaunt your relationship with my brother so blatantly in my face."

He thought I was flaunting my relationship? Rían and I didn't have a relationship. I barely knew the man—and what I did know, I certainly didn't like. "I wasn't—I didn't mean—"

Tadhg turned on his heel and went to greet a stunning woman with short black hair and a beautiful, dark complexion waiting in the entrance.

A special guest.

The woman wore a dress made of tanned fur that hugged her shapely figure like a second skin. My stomach sank as she collected Tadhg in an enthusiastic embrace.

A grogoch rang the dinner bell, and Tadhg settled into the chair at the head of the table, the two old men to his right, and the woman to his left. Rían sat beside her, leaving me at the end. No one bothered to introduce me, and apart from a few curious glances from the old men, everyone pretended I wasn't there.

Tadhg flicked his wrist, and our food magically appeared, cooked to perfection. A steaming turkey, skin crispy and brown, stuffed with fragrant sprigs of rosemary and sage, accompanied by roast potatoes and honey glazed carrots and parsnips.

I waited until everyone had served themselves to get my own. I ate and drank without joining in their conversation, spiraling deeper and deeper into my own mind.

Aveen had Rían.

When she awoke, she wouldn't need me.

What reason had I to stay?

Whatever misplaced love Tadhg may have felt for me had evaporated the moment he found out about Rían. Could I really remain in his castle and watch him fawn over women and pretend it didn't crush my heart?

What other choice did I have?

With the Black Forest cutting Tearmann off from the rest of Airren, there was no way to return to my world without having Tadgh or another immortal accompany me and offer his life as a sacrifice for my own.

I was trapped.

I stole a look at Tadhg where he smiled and laughed with the woman in the fur.

I do. I love you.

Rían wasn't the only liar in this dining room.

The moment my stomach felt full, I excused myself from the table. Rían tossed his serviette beside his empty plate and followed me out the door like a lost puppy. Tadhg was too busy fawning over his *special guest* to notice.

"Go back in," I told Rían when we reached the stairs. "I can find my own way back." My room was two stories up, the third door on the left.

"I'd rather not," he said, taking the steps two at a time. When we reached my door, he left me with a bow and returned to the staircase. Instead of going down, he continued upward. Was his own room upstairs, or was he going to visit Aveen?

Too tired to change but too agitated to sleep, I curled onto the window seat and stared into the dark garden. A sliver of moon highlighted the high boxwood hedges and manicured laurels creating a maze around a central fountain.

A tall figure emerged from the castle and made his way toward the maze's entrance. I held my breath, waiting for the woman from dinner to follow Tadhg, but there was no one else. From this vantage point, I watched him navigate to the center and drop onto the edge of the fountain.

I thought back to what he'd said before dinner, about flaunting my relationship with his brother in front of him. I'd spent more time with Tadhg in the last few weeks than I had with Rían for the entire four months we were married.

But how was Tadhg supposed to know any of that?

He didn't know I hadn't loved Edward. Could he possibly think I would want to be with Rían instead? That sounded as appealing as a hole in the head.

I could be wrong, but if I was right . . .

I ran to the door, wrenched it aside, and hurtled down the stairs. No one was in the entry hall, and the dining room was blessedly empty. A cool breeze twisted through the open glass doors as I escaped into the garden.

The hedges were too high to see over and too thick to see through. I followed the gravel path, not knowing which way to go when it split into two. Right or left? I tried to picture it in my mind, but my view from the bedroom had been from a different angle. *Right.* I could feel the small stones crunching beneath my thin slippers as I rounded the corner and came to another split.

Whoever had invented the maze deserved to be run through. I took another right, but it led to a dead end, and when I got back to the break, I couldn't remember which way I'd come and which way I wanted to go and I was exhausted and my heart hurt and I just wanted, "*Tadhg!*"

There was a crunch behind me. "What is it? Is something wrong?" Warm hands settled on my upper arms and spun me to face him.

"Yes, something is terribly wrong," I said, tugging on his black waistcoat, drawing his warmth to me.

"Tell me. Was it Rían? I swear, if he did *anything* to harm you, I'll run him through and lock his corpse in an iron casket for all of eternity."

Tadhg *was* jealous. I almost smiled but managed to keep a straight face when I told him, "I haven't seen Rían since dinner. In all honesty, I'd be happy never seeing him again."

He pulled away to look down at me, searching my face, his brow becoming more furrowed.

"Nothing *happened*, Tadhg. Between your brother and me, I mean." I could almost feel his relief as some of the tension in his body uncoiled. "Yes, I kissed him to make Robert jealous, but we didn't have a *real* marriage. He was barely around, and when he *was* around, we didn't see each other. And he insisted on sleeping in his own chambers."

"The two of you didn't . . . ?"

My hair tickled my back when I shook my head. "No. Absolutely not."

The smile on his face was short-lived. He let me go and stepped back, like he wanted to sink into the night and hide. "You may not care for him, but that doesn't mean you care for me."

"That's just it. I *do* care for you." Even now, knowing he was here and safe, the memory of that dagger stealing his life still haunted me. "When the Queen killed you, I couldn't stop crying. It was like she'd stabbed me in the heart as well."

"You *cried*? Over *me*?" He looked so confused, I wanted to kiss away the wrinkles on his brow. "But you knew I'd be back."

I collected his hand and touched the spot where our marriage bond had been. "But you wouldn't be my husband."

Clutching my fingers in his, he lifted my chin with his free hand. "Are you saying you *wanted* to stay married?" Starlight reflected in his hopeful green eyes.

"Yes."

He toyed with the emerald ring, and his face fell. "I know you're lying. You saw the curse and now you pity me. That's what this is, right?" He began pacing back and forth, boots crunching in the gravel. "You think I'm some sort of charity case? Well, I'm not, you know. I may want to be free, but I'll not accept your life as payment for my sins. It was wrong to have asked you to keep our vows in the first place."

How could I make him see that I was telling the truth? That it wasn't pity I felt but respect. That in saving him, I was also saving myself.

I dragged the ring from my finger and dropped it into the gravel between us. Tadhg stopped his pacing, his gaze falling to the green stone, then rising to meet mine.

"I want to be bound to you," I said.

"Why?"

"Why do you mean, why?"

"Why would someone like you want to be with something like me?" he asked, his voice desperate as he raked his fingers through his hair, dragging on the ends. "Is it all of this?" He waved toward the castle. "Is this what you're after? Because it sure as hell isn't my winning personality or impeccable style or flawless manners."

Why did I want to be with Tadhg?

I thought of the night I'd listed what I liked about Robert and had struggled to find more than two things. For Tadhg, I had the opposite problem. There were so many reasons, I didn't know where to start.

"I want to be with you because you make me laugh."

His mouth opened, then closed. "I make you *laugh?*"

"Yes. Even when I know I shouldn't," I added, stepping closer. "You left food for Padraig and gave an apple to the boy in the market. And you saved that grogoch in Kinnock. You stole a pig and kidnapped those children." *Another step.* "You have taken care of me and kept me safe even when I was rude and condescending and horrible." *Another step.*

I was close enough to feel the heat from his skin. To touch his stubbled cheek. Tadhg's throat bobbed when he swallowed, and his tongue darted out to wet his lips. Depthless green eyes swirled with shadows.

I slid my hands up his torso, and he made a strangled sound when I pressed a kiss to his pounding heart. "Today, you died for me."

His hands slipped around my waist, drawing me closer, molding our bodies together.

"So the real question isn't why someone like me would want to be with someone like you," I whispered against his jaw, the taste of candied almonds tickling my tongue. "It's whether or not someone like you would want to be with someone like me."

Tadhg's chest rose and fell as he took ragged breaths. His forehead came to rest against mine, and he said, "There will never be a time or place when I won't want to be with you."

It meant the world knowing he could only say those words because they were true.

I leaned forward and—

Tadhg vanished.

Then he was kneeling beside me, collecting something from the stones. *The ring.* How could I have forgotten the ring? If I'd kissed him without it, I'd be dead.

"Since I'm already down here," he said, smiling up at me with the emerald pinched between his fingers, "I may as well ask you to marry me."

32

MARRY ME.

"Don't feel like you have to say yes," Tadhg rushed, shooting to his feet and taking my hand. "It's just that it'll be impossible to make you fall madly in love with me if I'm forced to go off with every woman who invites me to her bed."

Marry me.

He was leaving it up to me. This was my choice.

And I wanted to marry the enemy who had become my friend. My friend who had become my lover. My lover who could be so much more.

Still, he'd had so many women falling at his feet, I couldn't make it too easy on him.

"Is that the best you can do? 'I may as well ask you to marry me,'" I teased, bracing my hand against my hip. I'd been married twice now and had yet to receive a proper proposal.

Frowning down at the ring, he chuckled and said, "No. I can do better." His grip on my hand tightened, and he dragged me deeper into the maze. The sound of trickling water grew louder as we ran hand-in-hand toward the central fountain. And then he stopped.

"Wait here," he said with a cheeky grin that made my stomach drop.

It was impossible not to smile back at him as he backed toward the corner, keeping his eyes on me like I was the one who could vanish. When he ducked around the hedge, I waited in the still night air, a bundle of fluttering nerves and excitement.

A few moments later, he returned, laced our fingers together, and brought me into the center of the maze. White light twinkled from the hedges like Tadhg had stolen the stars from the sky and brought them here for me.

He flicked his wrist, and a bouquet of colorful hydrangeas appeared in my hands, wrapped with lace.

"Lady Keelynn Bannon," he said, going down on one knee, "I'd given up hope of ever finding someone I loved. And then you waltzed into a pub and threatened to kill me."

The flowers in my hand began to tremble. Was this really happening? This was really happening.

"I am wrecked by you," he said, "completely undone. I would trade my soul for a smile. My kingdom for a kiss. My world to call you my wife. Will you give me the honor of a second chance to be your husband?"

He extended his hand. In his palm was a length of silver ribbon.

The wisp of a memory from when we'd first wed came flying back. "You want to get married *now*?"

A wrinkle formed between his eyebrows. "What's wrong with now?"

When I was small and imagined myself marrying a prince, I had wanted fanfare and white dresses and loads of people gathered to watch me walk down an aisle laden with flowers and candles to exchange vows with the man I loved.

But for some reason, the idea of marrying Tadhg in his silent castle gardens with only the stars for witnesses sounded like a dream come true.

"Nothing is wrong with now. Now is perfect." With my heart

battering my breastbone, I stretched my hand toward him. He stood and clasped my fingers, wrapping the ribbon over and around until only the ends dangled between us.

"To you I pledge my body and soul." Tadhg's lilting accent caressed the night as he slipped the emerald ring onto my finger. "All that I am and all that I have is yours. I bind myself to you and you alone, forsaking all others. In giving you my hands, I give you my life, to have and to cherish until death do us part."

I repeated the vows in a steady voice, pledging myself to this cursed prince. Before the final word left my lips, Tadhg's cold mouth crashed against mine. His unbound hand slipped into my hair, drawing me closer and closer as his tongue devastated my senses, tasting of magic and madness.

The bouquet tumbled to the ground, and I caught his neck with my free hand, pulling until our bodies melted together. Shaking free of our binding, he swept me into his arms and carried me to the biggest bed I had ever seen, with a heavy green canopy and white silk sheets, planted right in the middle of the garden.

Tadhg kissed me again, more insistent, every flick of his tongue a silent promise of what was to come. "What would you say to a wedding night, Maiden Death?" he whispered.

I caught his lower lip between my teeth, and he moaned into my mouth.

"I'm taking that as a yes."

My back met the mattress, and my husband dropped forward, bracing his weight on one elbow, his hard chest pressing me into the soft sheets.

My husband.

This felt different than before. Special. Sacred.

I could feel him swelling, straining against his breeches, grinding against my center in a tantalizing rhythm, leaving me clawing at his shirt, desperate for release.

His hips shifted to just the right angle, and I cried, *"Hurry."* I needed him more than I needed air in my lungs.

And then he stilled, drew away, and stared down at me as if I'd told him to stop. Didn't he know the meaning of *hurry*?

"My dear mortal wife," he said, his face a mix of shadows and moonlight, "if you think I am going to rush this, you must be mad. Although, you did marry me of your own free will, so perhaps you are."

I was mad.

Mad with desire and need and wanting *him*.

I reached for the buckle on his belt, and he smacked my hand away.

"Don't make me stab you," I hissed, sounding like a broken woman.

The wicked glint in Tadhg's eye grew with his mischievous smile, and he held up one finger. He slipped that one finger along the side of my foot to my heel and proceeded to drag it up my calf, over the back of my knee, to the underside of my thigh, hooking it into the top of my stocking and dragging it *down down down*.

I was losing my bloody mind, and I didn't even care as he removed the second one the exact same infuriating way. Fire pooled in my belly, delicious heat that moved lower until I thought I'd burst into flames.

When Tadhg reached for my skirt, I shook my head.

He thought he could torture me and suffer no consequences?

I was going to make him beg.

"My turn." I sat up and pushed him onto his back. The pointed tips of his ears stood out against the white sheets. My skirt rode to my waist when I straddled him and rolled my hips once . . . twice . . . pulling a strained curse from Tadhg while I unfastened . . . each . . . individual . . . button . . . on his waistcoat and shirt, exposing the finely sculpted muscles of his chest and abdomen.

His insistent fingers dug into my upper thighs. He lifted his hips, urging me to move harder and faster, climbing higher and higher. I raised to my knees, breaking the connection. My body screamed, and Tadhg growled, but somehow, I managed to say in a clear voice, "My dear immortal husband, if you think I'm going to rush this—"

The low noise in Tadhg's throat sounded like a strangled plea. He squeezed my waist, flipped me onto my back, and suddenly, our clothes were gone. Magic slipped down my throat, heightening my senses, intensifying every touch, every sound, every color.

"Wicked, wicked woman," Tadhg purred, swallowing my victorious smile with a punishing kiss. When he parted my thighs with his knee, I sighed. When he tore his mouth away, my whimper of protest became a moan of ecstasy as his cold, cursed mouth sampled my body, eventually reaching the place where he knelt.

Now he could take his time.

And *bloody hell* did he take his time, coaxing me to the top of a cliff and pushing me over the edge. Before my shuddering subsided, Tadgh stretched and filled my body with his. We became the waves, crashing, slipping, rolling, colliding

over

and over

and over . . .

"Lie to me," he breathed against the shell of my ear.

"I love you." It wasn't true yet, but I desperately wanted it to be.

"Again," he begged, thrusting harder, faster, almost to the breaking point.

My nails raked down his shoulders, his back, his waist, and when I said I loved him, his sweat-slickened body collapsed on top of mine with a shudder and the sweetest curse.

"I was told you'd be the death of me," he murmured, withdrawing slowly and falling onto his back, arms splayed wide and chest heaving. The closed curtains swayed in the breeze, letting in a draft that prickled my overheated skin.

Struggling to catch my breath, I pressed a hand to my leaping heart. Tadgh pulled me against him. The soft hair on his thighs tickled mine when he draped my leg over his.

"Who said that? Ruairi or Rían?"

Tadhg pinched my backside. "We're *not* talking about my brother."

Didn't he know there was no reason to be jealous? "You know nothing happened."

"Doesn't matter. Just imagining the two of you together nearly destroyed me," he confessed, pressing a tender kiss to my hair.

How would I feel if I thought Tadhg's interaction with Aveen had gone further than a kiss? The twisting in my stomach was decidedly green.

I took his hand and brushed a kiss to his knuckles. Even if Rían had touched me, the memory of anyone else's hands would've been eclipsed by *these* hands. The one time Rían and I had kissed was nothing more than a fading memory. "What would you have done if I did care for him?"

Tadhg pulled me closer. "Killed him every time he came into the room."

A laugh escaped before I could catch it. "That's not funny."

"It wasn't meant to be. I would've killed Robert too, except it would've upset you."

Even after everything he'd done, I didn't wish Robert dead. Perhaps thrown in jail for a good long while, but not dead.

"I think we need to discuss your penchant for murder." I didn't want my husband going around killing people simply because they made him angry.

"What's there to discuss? Some people deserve to die."

Some people did deserve to die. Like those villains who had killed Padraig. But the majority deserved a chance to redeem themselves. Tadhg, of all people, should have understood the concept of redemption.

I kissed a particularly nasty scar across his right pectoral muscle. A wound that horrific would've killed him. "Does it hurt to die?" Or had he done it so often that the pain barely registered?

He shifted his hold so he could trace the hideous black mark on my stomach. If only there was a way to hide the unsightly reminder of how close I came to becoming a permanent resident in the underworld. "You've been stabbed. You tell me."

The memory of the blade meeting my belly, of scalding fire and searing ice, left me trembling. Being stabbed was horrific, and by the looks of it, Tadhg had been stabbed a lot.

The scar at his throat from Kinnock was faded but still visible. Had they cut his throat the way he'd cut Rían's? Had they actually killed him?

"Tadhg?"

"Hmmmm?"

"What did they do to you in Kinnock?"

He pulled my fingers from his neck and pressed a kiss to my palm. "I'm fairly certain you already know the answer to that question."

They'd been executing Danú that day—with an axe. Did that mean . . . "They cut off your *head*?"

"Don't look so appalled." His low, rumbling chuckle vibrated his chest. He pulled me on top of him, and my legs automatically fell on either side of his hips. "It always finds its way back."

I sat up straighter so I could memorize the way his dark hair splayed across the pillow. The slight glow of his emerald eyes. The way his lips curled into a wolfish smile as his gaze roved down my body. A delicious thrill zinged through my blood.

What had we been talking about?

Oh, yes. Beheading.

"How—"

"This isn't what I want to discuss on our wedding night." He caught me by the waist and flipped me onto my back.

As interested as I was in the way he trailed kisses down my chest, I wanted to finish this *conversaaaaation*. "Tadhg?"

He hummed against my breast.

"What does it feel like? Coming back."

His hair tickled my chest when he dropped his forehead

against me and groaned. "It hurts almost as bad as being stabbed. Like you're trapped inside your body and can't move. Taking in air for the first time burns like the fires of hell, and you can't escape it. You just have to push through the pain and pray you come out on the other side with"—he shifted his hips, nudging his hard length against my thigh—"*all* your parts intact."

The yearning deep in my belly returned with a vengeance. I took him in my hand and guided him into me. "I'm certainly glad you still have all your parts."

Tadhg's breathing hitched as he eased his hips forward. "You and me both."

33

Birds chirped and waves crashed. The heavy drapes around me fluttered with an errant breeze. I stretched my arms over my head and relished every delicious ache in my body. When I rolled over, my bouquet of hydrangeas and a note sat next to Tadhg's empty pillow.

Don't go anywhere.
I won't be long.
-T

Part of me was relieved that I didn't have to see him first thing. His absence gave me a chance to compose myself and finger-comb my tangled hair without an audience. But a larger part was disappointed.

I wanted to know how his hair looked in the mornings. Did it stick up at the sides where his head met the pillow, or was it as delightfully windswept as it always seemed to be? Did he lounge abed when he first woke, or did he spring from the mattress, ready to greet the day? I had a feeling it was the former.

What would it be like to lie around in bed all morning with my husband?

The wicked thoughts flitting through my mind made my face burn.

I drew the sheet over my shoulders and pushed through the break in the heavy velvet canopy, only to escape back to the mattress when I realized the bed was still in the garden. Tadhg expected me to sit in the middle of the garden naked, waiting for him to return? What if someone else came?

I searched the tangle of sheets and found my blue dress from last night. Kneeling on the mattress, I wiggled back into the dress and did my best to make it look like I hadn't spent the whole night rolling around in bed with Tearmann's prince.

My stomach ached from hunger. When I peered through the curtains again, there was no sign of anyone. Sunlight glistened off the water flowing over the fountain, and suddenly I was in desperate need of the privy. The maze left me turned around for far longer than I'd wanted, but eventually I made it out.

Back in my room, I used the privy, then sponged off with the cold water left over from last night. Someone had left a handful of gowns in soft jewel tones hanging inside the armoire. I changed into one the color of Tadhg's emerald ring, then found my way back downstairs.

Where was Tadhg?

Bloody hell, I was hungry enough to eat an entire loaf of bread. Perhaps Tadhg was in the dining room. My fingers slid along the rough stone wall as I descended to the entrance hall. Brilliant pink and purple fuchsia blooms had replaced the blue flowers from yesterday. The dining room was empty, but the savory smell of bacon lingered. Forget Tadhg. I needed to find the kitchens.

The first room beyond the dining hall was a parlor with overly ornate furniture and golden drapes. The second room was a closet of some sort, piled with crates and dusty books.

The third room was dark, with the curtains pulled so that only a sliver of light fell through the gap. It took my eyes a moment to adjust, but when they did, I was paralyzed.

The room was filled with coffins—twenty, at least. Lined up side by side with only enough space to walk sideways between them. Most were empty. But not all.

Six of the coffins held bodies.

All of them were women.

The first was beautiful, with a round, cherub-like face caked in makeup and short blond hair in tight, springy curls. The second was a dark-haired beauty with a deep scar across her sunken left eye. She reminded me of a younger version of the barmaid I'd met in the Green Serpent.

The third woman, I recognized. She was the innkeeper who had assumed Tadhg and I were sharing a room. Around her were the barmaid from the Black Rabbit, Áine the faerie, and the woman from the Arches, Marina.

All of their lips were black.

Tadhg had killed all of them.

Why?

He had said Marina kissed him, which had to be true. But what about the other women?

There were footsteps outside, in the hallway. I dropped to the ground and held my breath, listening to boots click on the stones.

My heart ached as I crawled to the door and peered through the crack, catching a glimpse of Tadhg as he passed. His hair was damp, as though he'd bathed. And he carried a tray with a silver lid. As hungry and heartbroken as I was, I couldn't let him know I'd found this place. I needed time to think before confronting him.

The air in this cursed room was too stifling. I needed to get out of here and find someplace where I could breathe and process.

The moment Tadhg rounded the corner, I pushed open the door, closed it behind me, and started for the main entrance.

My boots slipped against the stones and my hair flew behind me as I escaped from that horrific room and the growing realization of what Tadhg had done.

All those women.

Murdered.

He'd said that he didn't kiss anyone unless they understood the consequences, but how could all of those women have been willing to give up their lives for a kiss?

I caught the heavy handle on the front door, lifted, and threw it open.

People milled about the courtyard between the castle and the main gates. The black-haired woman from last night lounged on the edge of the fountain, her smiling face upturned to the sun as a blue-skinned merrow played with her short hair.

The air was overly warm, damp and close like the inside of a greenhouse. The long grass swaying outside the castle gates called to me like a siren's song.

Tadhg shouted my name as I passed a hulking black stallion with yellow eyes and two clurichauns pushing wheelbarrows of dirt-crusted root vegetables. The wards brushed my face, and then the coolness of the breeze kissed my cheeks. Bending in half, I braced my hands on my knees and tried to catch my breath.

There had to be a good explanation.

Tadhg was good. Tadhg was kind. He wouldn't kill anyone who didn't deserve to die—

A pair of scuffed boots appeared in my peripherals. When I raised my head, I met Tadhg's concerned gaze.

"Keelynn?" He reached for my shoulder, but I skirted away.

When he touched me, I wasn't able to think straight, and my mind was already muddled enough. "Why did you kill them?"

His eyebrows drew together in confusion. How could he be confused? Surely he knew what I was talking about.

"You have an entire room full of dead bodies!"

His posture fell. "You know who I am," he said, opening his empty hands and letting them fall. "You know what I've done. I've already told you—"

All that was true, but there was something heavy and sobering about seeing the reality in the flesh. "Did all of those women force you to kiss them?"

Tadhg's hands flexed and jaw pulsed. "No. They didn't." His voice was as dead as those poor women.

"Clara McNulty was a whore," he said, looking me straight in the eye. "Her life was shit, and she still had three years left in her contract. I kissed her so that she could be free. Orla Crowley was a fool and fancied herself in love with me. You see how that turned out. The barmaid from the Black Rabbit thought it'd be worth it. It wasn't. The innkeeper from Newtown refused to let me leave the room. And you already know about Marina."

"What about Áine?"

Tadhg winced. "Áine and I had an arrangement. I kept my end of the bargain, but she wanted more. And then she said that if I didn't agree to the new terms, she'd slip poison into your wine."

He'd killed Áine to protect me? Of course he'd been protecting me.

This was Tadhg. He was good. He was kind.

Some people deserve to die.

"In two hundred and fifty years, there have been seven hundred and eighty-eight bodies in those coffins," he confessed. "I've tasted their last breaths. Held them in my arms as their souls left their bodies. Watched the light of life vanish from their eyes. And I remember every single one."

So many women. So many years lost. And for what?

"Do you remember me?" a high, sing-song voice asked.

My heart stopped beating. Tadhg's head jerked up, and his eyes widened. I didn't need to turn around to know who was behind me.

It was Fiadh.

34

The black-haired witch stood in the center of the path leading to the castle, tapping her sharpened black nail against her pale cheek. Bloodred lips curled into a malicious smile as her soulless black eyes fixed on Tadhg. "It's been too long, my love."

It felt like the castle walls had caved in on my chest. What had I done? We were outside the wards. Tadhg could evanesce to escape. But I was trapped.

Tadhg swore and caught my hand, pulling me behind him.

Fiadh's head jerked to the side. "I see you met my human friend. She's a dote, isn't she? So young. So *naïve*." A silver dagger appeared in her clenched fist. The green fields looked dull compared to the unearthly glow from the emerald in the hilt. "I'd thought her dead," she said, the deranged smile overtaking her ethereal face, "but this is far more delicious."

Why wasn't she angry? She should've been raging that I'd survived her attack.

Tadhg's shoulders stiffened. "Your fight is with me, not with her."

Fiadh's head snapped to the other side. "Look who finally found someone he loves more than himself." Pressing a hand to her chest, she sighed wistfully toward the darkening clouds. "If only our young friend's weak human heart could love a murderous monster." Her hair captured bits of grass along the ground as she sauntered toward us. Bare feet peeked from beneath her heavy green skirts.

"Evanesce," I whispered, clutching the back of Tadhg's shirt. He was a prince, responsible for ruling all of Tearmann. I was nothing and no one. My life didn't matter. Fiadh wouldn't even be here if it weren't for me.

Tadhg pulled from my hold and stepped toward Fiadh. The wind kicked up, fluttering his hair, uncovering the tips of his ears. "I am sorry for what happened all those years ago. I was young and foolish and too in love with myself to care about those I hurt. But this has gone on long enough."

Fiadh's steps halted, and that crazed smile returned. "You're *sorry*?" She adjusted her hold on the cursed dagger. "You think an apology can absolve you of all your sins?" Her shrill laugh made my legs go weak. "You took my life from me," she hissed. "*You* made me what I am. This is all *your* fault." The blade *tap tap tapped* against her thigh, the emerald growing brighter and brighter.

Tadhg had lied and broken her heart, and he had spent the last two hundred and fifty years being punished for it. He was responsible for what he had done to her, but Fiadh was responsible for what she had done to others. She had let bitterness and rage consume her. Instead of rejecting the darkness, she had let it live inside her heart.

I wanted to speak up, but someone had sewn my lips closed and stolen my air, and the pain in my chest was all consuming, and all I could do was watch as Fiadh's black eyes left Tadhg and landed on me.

"I'm calling in our bargain, *girl*," she spat, motioning me forward.

A bargain made when I thought I had nothing left to lose.

Everyone has something to lose.

Tadhg's panicked gaze bounced between me and the

witch. The bargain for the dagger and the ring hadn't been the only one struck that fateful day.

My legs moved of their own volition. I was a puppet on her string, unable to stop or fight. "Evanesce, Tadhg." The plea wrenched from my dry throat. "Please. I'm begging you. *Go.*"

Why wasn't he listening? Didn't he realize what was about to happen?

When I reached Fiadh, she forced the hilt into my hand. I told my fingers not to close, to let the cursed dagger fall, but they refused to listen.

"You said you'd kill the Gancanagh." Fiadh's white teeth gleamed between her red lips; her black eyes reflected my pale face. "Now, *do it.*"

She forced me to turn, and I watched helplessly as Tadhg's confusion shifted to understanding. He offered me a sad smile.

"It's all right, Keelynn." He dropped his hands to his sides like he wasn't going to fight. Like he was giving up.

He couldn't give up. He needed to fight. Why wasn't he fighting?

"You don't understand. I can't stop myself. Please go. Please." My legs moved forward. One step. Another. I wanted them to stop. *Why won't they stop? Please stop. I don't want to do this. It isn't fair. Stop. Stop. Stop.* "I'm so sorry, Tadhg. I just wanted my sister back. I was foolish and naïve, and I thought I had nothing left to lose." Tears clouded my vision, making it difficult to see his beautiful face crumpling in defeat.

"This isn't your fault," he said, blinking back tears of his own as his shoulders bowed forward. "It's mine."

A crowd had formed inside the gates. Rían stood at the front, holding his head in his hands, frozen, watching from behind the safety of the wards. Why was no one helping us? There had to be at least fifty of them and only one of Fiadh. Why were they hiding like cowards?

Rían had magic. He had power. Why wasn't he coming to our aid?

The sounds of waves crashing against the cliffs were drowned out by Fiadh's delighted cackle. She clasped her hands beneath her pointed chin and rocked back and forth on her toes, her skirts swaying.

Tadhg was within arm's reach. If only I could hold him one last time. If only I could tell him how much I cared. But the words would only make what I was about to do even more painful.

"This will be a mercy," he said. "You'll be ending a cursed life with a cursed blade."

Cursed blade.

The clouds broke, and a solitary ray of sunlight fell on the glowing emerald in the dagger and the emerald in the ring.

Cursed blade.

If you had been wearing the ring when she stabbed you—

The ring doesn't break curses, it neutralizes them—

Perhaps I could save him. Perhaps it didn't have to end like this. I brought my other hand to the hilt and tried to pull the ring free without making it obvious. Tadhg's eyes never left mine.

"Thank you for giving me hope," he said, brushing the hair back from my face and wiping my tears with his thumb. "Thank you for letting me love you."

I took his hand and pressed the ring between our palms. His eyes widened slightly. When I pulled back, the ring was no longer in my grasp. I tried with all my might to fight my own body as I slipped the point of the dagger to the soft flesh below his sternum.

He dropped his forehead against mine and whispered, "Thank you for setting me free."

And I thrust the blade into his heart.

The crowd hiding behind the wards let out a collective wail.

Rían's hands dropped from his head, his mouth gaping open.

The green in Tadhg's eyes faded to black, and his body slumped to the ground. Blood spread down his white shirt, painting the grass red. The marriage bond was no longer on my finger, and Tadhg's was gone as well. He was truly dead, but he would come back because he was wearing the—

Tadhg's clenched fist opened, and the emerald ring tumbled into the grass.

"*No . . .*" No. No. No. No.

Why hadn't he put it on? Why hadn't he saved himself from this terrible fate?

Thunder cracked above us like the sky was being cleaved in two. The dagger began to vibrate, and a shimmering white light emerged from Tadgh's prone form, swirling and twisting until it reached the emerald and vanished inside. Green light burst from the gem, so bright it burned my eyes.

Fiadh's delighted laughter rekindled the hate in my heart. How could she do this to someone she'd once loved? How could she still want vengeance after all this time? Why hadn't she forgiven Tadgh? Moved on with her life? Found the light in the world instead of sinking into the darkness?

"Give me the dagger." Fiadh's hair lifted in the breeze, her black eyes wild as she motioned toward the weapon dripping blood on my green skirt.

My legs shook as I turned and told her, "No," with a strength I didn't think I possessed.

"Give it to me!"

I clutched the dagger to my aching chest. "I said *no*."

Magic leaked from beneath her skirts, twisting and stretching its spindly black fingers toward me. "Have you learned *nothing*, you foolish girl? You can hide inside this warded castle for the rest of your pathetic life, but I will get back what is mine. I will curse your family, your children, everyone you love. I will never stop haunting you unless you *give me that dagger.*"

Fiadh never forgives.

Fiadh never forgets.

Tadhg knew. That's why he didn't put on the ring. If he had come back, he would've been a prisoner in this castle. No one he loved or cared about would've been safe from her wrath. He never would have been free. And now that I had defied her, there was no way she would let me leave this hillside alive.

"Our bargain isn't through," I said. Fiadh's magic halted, waiting for her command. "I killed the Gancanagh, and now I get to resurrect my sister."

Some good had to come of this. Aveen would be alive, and she would have Rían to take care of her. I wouldn't be there to see it, but at least I could die knowing Tadhg's life hadn't been sacrificed in vain.

"Go on then." Fiadh waved a hand toward the castle. "Resurrect your precious sister."

My legs moved woodenly toward where Rían waited with a dagger of his own. The creatures flanking him held pitchforks and hoes, swords and axes. None of them were looking at Fiadh. They were all glaring at me.

"Not so fast, girl." Fiadh appeared at my side, keeping an arm's length away. "I'm not letting you or that dagger out of my sight."

"You can't get past the wards."

"Then ask your *friend* to let me inside," she sneered.

When I reached the castle and went to step inside the barbican, my foot struck an invisible wall. I pressed against it, but the ward refused to budge.

"Rían, please." My voice cracked as I stared into his hardened blue gaze. "I need to see Aveen." It was the only way to end this bargain. The only way I would be free of Fiadh's control.

"Have you lost your feckin' mind?" Rían growled, gesturing toward Tadhg's body with his own blade. "You just murdered my brother, and you think I'm going to let you inside this castle? Not a hope in hell. Good luck getting out of Tearmann alive, you traitorous bitch." The creatures behind him stepped forward, murderous eyes trained on me.

"Give me my sister," I said.

Rían shook his head. "She's *my* fiancée."

"Rían, please. I need to bring her back to end this bargain."

Couldn't he see that I'd had no choice? That if it had been up to me, I'd be the one lying dead in the grass?

Rían folded his arms over his chest. The blade in his hand gleamed like his boots. He opened his mouth to say something but closed it when Fiadh stepped forward. The dark waves of her magic swelled around her, spinning and climbing the walls, searching for a chink in the invisible armor.

"If you don't want me to turn my sights on you, little Rían," Fiadh crooned, drawing a nail down the invisible barrier, "I suggest you give the pathetic human her sister."

Rían's face paled. The creatures behind him glanced at one another and started whispering. With Tadhg gone, Rían was the rightful ruler of Tearmann, and he was being forced to choose between my sister and his people. A muscle in his jaw ticked, and his blue eyes narrowed, but he flicked his wrist, and Aveen's coffin appeared between us.

I glanced over at Tadhg's body, then back to Aveen.

She didn't *need* his life force. In a few months, her curse would be broken. If only there was a way to return it to Tadhg.

"Hurry along, girl. I don't have all day," Fiadh grumbled, her nose wrinkling as she peered into the coffin.

My sister's hair and the ribbon at her waist fluttered in the breeze.

I stepped closer to the coffin, but also to Fiadh. Aveen's cold hand felt heavy as I lifted it in mine and squeezed, saying hello and goodbye. With a deep breath, I drew the tip of the dagger across her palm. At first, nothing happened. Then Tadhg's blood dripped down the blade and into the wound, and a line of deep red appeared in the broken skin. Aveen's face lost its waxy gray sheen, and the black of her lips slowly faded to a delicate pink.

The light from the dagger flew between her lips, and I heard her suck in a breath.

I'd done it. I'd saved her.

Tadhg's body loomed in the distance, the price of this victory.

"Our bargain is complete." Fiadh stepped forward and held out her hand. "Now, give me the dagger."

If only I could change the way this story had ended.

What was I saying? I could change this. I had the dagger; all I needed was the courage to take back control.

I adjusted my hold on the hilt and plunged the blade into Fiadh's gut. Her piercing scream rattled the castle walls, and she stumbled back, her pale hands covering the gaping wound. Black blood seeped between her fingers, dripping into an onyx puddle on the cobblestones.

If it had been an ordinary dagger, it wouldn't have killed her. But this was a cursed dagger, created to steal life from immortals.

"You scheming bitch!" Fiadh lunged for the weapon still in my hand, but I was quicker. A nightmarish black mist emerged from her wound, stretching and writhing toward me. The first tendrils hit the emerald, and it began to glow brighter and brighter.

More mist poured from Fiadh, coming faster and faster as she stumbled forward and fell onto the cobblestones with a vicious curse.

I hurtled for Tadhg's body. If I could reach him in time—

Pain ripped through my chest. Something warm and wet trickled down my nose. My movements slowed, like I was wading through tar. Only three more steps. Only two more steps. Only—

Coldness settled into my bones, and I caught a glimpse of Fiadh's sneer when the bloody dagger clanged onto the cobblestones.

The world tilted, and my head slammed against the unforgiving ground. I tried to breathe, but there was no air in my lungs, only liquid fire. My hands searched the ground, landing on the hilt. My fingers shook as they gripped it. I knew I was dying. The only way to save myself was to use the dagger on my own hand.

With every ounce of will I possessed, I stretched toward Tadhg's open hand, but he was too far—

Aveen screamed my name as my eyes drifted shut.

There was too much pain. I wanted it to go away. I wanted the whole world to go away. There was movement and screaming and cursing, and somewhere, someone was crying.

Something warm touched my face.

Something cold touched my lips.

And then my heart stopped.

35

There once was a girl from Graystones,
seeking a cure for death.
She met a witch and begged for help,
but instead drew her last breath.

36

BREATHE.

I couldn't

couldn't

couldn't breathe.

My lungs had been replaced by stones. Darkness surrounded me. I'd been swallowed by an inky black pool of frigid water. My stone lungs anchored me to the bottom of whatever abyss had claimed my life.

Breathe.

BREATHE!

A crack.

There was a crack in the stone. I tried again, and the crack expanded to a fissure.

Breathe Breathe Breathe

I felt the stone cracking, breaking, crumbling, until my lungs could finally, *finally* expand and contract and I could

breathe.

My tongue had turned to ash, and air burned my newly formed lungs, and I was on fire, burning from the inside out. Why did this hurt so much? Breathing shouldn't be so painful.

I changed my mind.

I didn't want to breathe. I wanted the comfort of the cold, ruthless darkness.

Something touched my forehead. A wisp. A cobweb.

"Your senses will take some time to return," said a muffled female voice. The owner of the voice drew me upright and pressed something to my lips. "Drink."

Water dribbled down my chin, but some of the ashiness subsided. The glass was taken away. I whimpered, shocked when the harsh noise broke free from my chest. The glass returned. This time my tongue cooperated, and water doused the fire.

"Can you open your eyes?" the woman asked.

I wasn't sure I wanted to.

But the quiet question left me peering between my lashes at smudges of light and darkness, shapes and colors.

"Very good."

The room around me was unfamiliar, not opulent but open and airy. White drapes around the bed undulated with the breeze blowing through the open window.

The woman turned away as she refilled the glass from the crystal jug on the bedside table. Her blond hair cascaded in ringlets down her back. Then a pair of brilliant blue eyes met mine, set in a face I'd known my entire life.

"*Aveen?*"

Her smile was the same. I had missed her smile so much.

My sister's arms came around my shoulders, tentatively at first. It wasn't until she crushed herself against me that I believed she was real and not a figment of my imagination.

"Oh, how I've missed you, sister. Every day without you has been torture," she said in my ear.

"Without *me?*" Her hair fluttered when I huffed a harsh laugh. "You were the one who decided to kiss the bloody Gancanagh and spend four months in the underworld."

Aveen pulled away, and her smile faltered as she started fussing with my hair, spreading the glossy curls over my shoulders. "I'm so sorry, Keelynn. For everything. But mostly for deceiving you."

She had sacrificed herself to get me what I wanted and she was the one apologizing? It was I who should be apologizing to her. "And I'm sorry you thought you had to die for me to find happiness."

"Don't be daft." She smacked my shoulder, the hit barely registering against my useless limbs. "It was my choice, and I'd make the same one all over again. There was no way *I* was going to marry Robert. And I can't say I'm sad that you didn't end up with him either." A laugh. "The bloody Gancanagh. You would win the heart of the Prince of Seduction."

Tadhg.

My own heart broke.

If only I'd been enough to save him. The backs of my eyes burned, but there was no moisture in my body for crying.

Aveen's lips pursed into a perfect pout as she glanced toward the door. "Speaking of Tadhg, I'm surprised he's not in here already. He's been unbearable waiting for today to arrive."

"Tadhg's *alive?*"

When she nodded, my heart gave an answering thump.

He's alive.

He's alive.

He's alive.

"How is that possible? He was dead. I killed him." And then the witch killed me and—*Wait.* How was *I* alive? I remembered Aveen shouting and had assumed she had used Fiadh's life force to resurrect me. Had they sacrificed someone else to bring Tadhg back?

Aveen's mouth flattened. "Rían brought him back with the dagger. And then Tadhg kissed you."

Tadhg kissed me? Why couldn't I remember?

Hold on.

If Tadhg kissed me—"Are you saying I've been gone for an entire year?" No. It couldn't have been that long. It felt like I had just closed my eyes.

"A year and a day," Aveen confirmed, pressing a cool hand to

356

my forehead. "Do you want more water? When I woke up, I was desperately thirsty, and I was only gone a few months."

I nodded, unable to find my words.

Aveen retrieved the glass and held it to my lips. I hated feeling like an invalid, but my hands refused to work. I drank until it was gone, wishing I could fill the emptiness growing in my heart as easily as I could quench my thirst.

What would happen when I saw Tadhg again? Could he find it in himself to forgive me for killing him? For not being enough to save him? And I'd been gone for over a year. What had he been doing in the interim? What if he'd found someone else? What if he was in love with her?

"I see our guest has returned to us," said a voice from the doorway.

Aveen turned and smiled at Rían. "It's about damn time."

"Good to see you looking so well after your stay in the under-world, Lady Keelynn." Rían executed a courtly bow, his black-on-black attire impeccable.

I didn't bother speaking to him. The memory of the terrible things he'd said to me at the castle gates was too raw. Aveen had said he'd saved Tadhg in the end, but he could've done something *before* I stabbed him. But that was a problem for another time.

"Aveen, I've held him off for as long as I can." Rían inclined his head toward the hallway. "If you want to keep the castle intact, I'd suggest you catch up with your sister at dinner."

As much as I didn't want my sister to leave, I needed to speak to Tadhg. Aveen hugged me again, kissed my cheeks, and told me that she loved me. A throat cleared from the doorway, and when my sister pulled away, I saw Tadhg standing in the gap, his green eyes shuttered and white shirt surprisingly unwrinkled.

My stomach fluttered. He looked the same as he had a year ago. I wasn't sure why I had expected him to look different.

Aveen pressed her forehead against mine and gave my arm a reassuring squeeze. "Good luck," she whispered, rising and gliding to the door. After exchanging a quiet word with Tadhg, she and Rían both disappeared down the hall.

Tadhg stepped into the room and shut the door.

And waited.

Why wasn't he saying anything?

Surely after a year and a day he had *something* to say.

"I see you're alive again," he said finally.

That's it? He had died, and I had died, and all he had to say was, "*I see you're alive again?*"

"Yes. I'm alive again."

He stepped closer but stopped before reaching the foot of the bed. I hated that his expression was so unreadable. With his teeth scraping his lip, he shifted his weight from one foot to the other. "Death isn't a very pleasant experience, is it?"

"No. It's not."

A tiny black-and-white bird landed on the windowsill only to fly away again. It sounded like someone was dragging something in another room. Somewhere, a door slammed.

Then, more silence.

The longer the silence stretched, the more I felt like crawling back to the darkness. How could he even stand to be in the same room as me after what I'd done?

Tadhg's fingers tapped idly against his hip. "Can you walk yet?" he asked, his eyes raking down the blankets covering my bottom half.

I tried moving my legs, but they refused to budge. Wiggling my toes didn't work either. "No."

Tadhg nodded as he rubbed the back of his neck. "Right. Um . . . Well . . ." He huffed a humorless chuckle. "You'd think I'd be ready for this. I've had a feckin' eternity to prepare."

I could only sit and wait and hold my breath.

"Right, so. First and foremost, I would like to apologize." Wide green eyes met mine, filled with glistening regret. "I should have revealed who I was the moment we met and let you run the cursed dagger through my black heart outside the Green Serpent."

If he'd done that, we never would've gotten to know each other. He never would've fallen in love with me. Did he regret everything? Of course he regretted it. I had *killed* him.

"If I'd accepted my sentence, Fiadh wouldn't have tried to kill you twice, and you wouldn't have been forced to marry me, and you could've gotten Aveen back right away and . . ." His gaze dropped to his wringing hands. "I'm so sorry."

How could he think this was his fault? "Tadhg, I'm the one who's sorry. If I hadn't made that bargain with Fiadh, none of this would've happened."

Tadhg's expression hardened, and he stepped forward. "If you hadn't made that bargain, we never would've met. And that is the one part of this mess that I do not regret."

I heard the words, knew they must be true, but they didn't make any sense. "How can you say that after I killed you?" Could he truly forgive me that easily?

"I killed you too, so, I suppose that makes us even." The barest hint of a smile crossed his lips, but it was gone just as quickly.

I stared down at my hands, paler than ever from a year of death. I had killed him, and he had killed me, and now we were both alive. "What do we do now?"

"That's up to you."

Up to me.

Just because he had forgiven me didn't mean he could find it in his heart to love me again. And I couldn't remain in Tearmann knowing he would always be searching for someone new to break his curses.

"If you wouldn't mind me staying a week or so, until all my faculties have returned and I've had a chance to catch up with Aveen, then I will leave." I would need someone's help to cross the Black Forest, of course. Perhaps Rían this time. I wouldn't mind watching him get stabbed to death.

"Is that what you want?"

If I could have lied, I would've said yes. It was what I wanted. Because Tadhg deserved someone better than me.

"Y—" My head started to pound. "Y—" *Dammit.* "No. It's not what I want."

"Then stay with me."

Stay with me.

It was what I wanted more than anything. "How can you stand being near me after all that's happened?"

Tadhg's head tilted, sending his dark hair tumbling across his forehead. "Because I love you."

This had to be some sort of joke. *The ring.* He was wearing the ring. "Liar." It must be a lie.

Tadhg took off the ring and tossed it onto the mattress. The emerald caught the sunlight, sending green sparks across the coverlet.

"I love you, Keelynn."

"Even after all I've done, you *still* love me?"

"Desperately."

I swallowed, but the tightness in my throat refused to ease. The mattress dipped when Tadhg sank onto the bed at my side. He reached a tentative hand to brush his thumb across my lips. "I know you don't love me," he said, the quiet resignation in his voice breaking my heart, "but I think I love you enough for the both of us."

I know you don't love me.

But . . . what if I *did* love him?

True love was sacrifice, putting someone else's needs above your own.

True love endured every trial, every curse.

What if that thing that had been unfurling, stretching, coming alive inside of me had been the revival of my own heart?

"I love you," I whispered, the words slipping through my lips with an unsteady exhale.

Tadhg's swirling green gaze searched mine. His tongue nipped out, wetting his lips. "How can you lie?"

It wasn't a lie.

I glanced down at the emerald and smiled.

I loved Tadhg.

And he had been cursed long enough. We both had.

"Keelynn, look at me. How did you break the——"

I stopped his question with a kiss. Tadhg tried to pull away, but I caught the back of his neck and refused to let go. His lips were as cold as I remembered and just as intoxicating, tasting of almonds and sugar. I breathed him in and found his tongue, and he shuddered and groaned, and still I didn't let go.

His lips began to warm, his mouth growing hungry and insistent, and then he crushed me into the mattress and took and took, and I gave and gave until Tadhg broke our kiss to drag in a ragged breath.

When I found my voice, I asked, "Did it work?"

He pressed two fingers to the pulse at my neck and smiled. "You seem to be alive, but I could be dreaming."

He had a point. This could all be a fantastic, beautiful dream. "Lie to me," I said.

Keeping his weight on his elbows, his chest brushed mine as he whispered, "I hate you," against my neck.

"Again," I said, drawing his mouth to mine so I could taste his sweet lies.

"I have been so happy without you. I never want to marry you again. I have absolutely no desire to lift up your skirts and sink between your thighs."

I slipped his shirt free of his breeches, reached for the buckle on his belt, and said, "I hate you too."

The
End

PRINCE OF SEDUCTION

A MYTHS OF AIRREN NOVELLA

JENNY HICKMAN

Prince
Of
Seduction

CHAPTER ONE

THE LAST TIME I KILLED MY BROTHER, HE'D REEKED OF BURNT flesh for a week. But if Rían didn't stop smirking at me, I was going to throw him into the fire and hold him there until the flames robbed him of his final breath. *Again.*

I laid across the settee the way I always did this time of night, bored out of my feckin' mind, wishing there were something to do in this castle besides endure Rían and Ruairi's relentless optimism.

I hated this room almost as much as I hated Rían. Thankfully, the darkness muted the lavish furnishings, gaudy gold curtains, rugs, and floral tapestries. It had been at least two hundred years since it had been decorated. I couldn't remember who had been responsible for the travesty. Certainly not me. If it were up to me, I'd torch this room and everything in it. Including Rían.

"What's it going to be tonight, lads?" Ruairi asked from the drinks cart beneath the window. The bottles clinked together as he read the labels. "Wine or puitin?"

I said "puitin" at the same time Rían said "wine."

I hadn't a head for either, so it didn't really matter. But puitin would make me pass out faster, and then I'd be back to another day of slogging through problems. Executions in Airren occurred every day now. No matter how many times we had advised our people to return to Tearmann, they always refused. With my jurisdiction ending at the Black Forest, there was nothing I could do to save them short of starting a war.

And the last war was still too fresh in everyone's minds.

Ruairi returned with a tray of six glasses, three filled with clear puítin and three filled with green faerie wine.

My stomach roiled. Tonight wasn't going to end well, and tomorrow was Friday. The last thing I wanted was to sit and listen to my people squabble with a hangover.

He set the tray on the small table between my settee and their two chairs and took a seat. When I made no move to reach for either glass, Ruairi picked up the puítin and thrust it into my hand. "Stop moping about and have a drink."

"I haven't had dinner yet." Which meant I'd be on my ass after a few sips. The two of them could drink the entire bottle and still be up for devilment.

Ruairi raised a black eyebrow. "Yer point?"

Rían sniggered, swirling a crystal glass in his hand. The rings on his fingers glinted. "I have a brilliant idea."

"No." When Rían had an idea, it usually landed one of us— or someone else—in the underworld.

Ruairi kicked the settee's leg. Puítin spilled down my shirt. "I want to hear what it is."

"I said, no." I didn't have the energy to die tonight. Plus, Eava, our kitchen witch, had made blackberry pie for dessert. Before Ruairi had shown up unannounced, my plan had been to eat enough of my dinner to appease Eava, then stuff my face with pie.

Rían sipped his wine slowly, as if savoring it. What was there to savor? It tasted like licking the bottom of a bowl of rotten fruit.

I gulped my puítin, loving the way it scorched my throat. The fire was better than feeling nothing at all.

"Ah, go on, Tadhg. It's a good one this time," Rían said, taking another sip. Firelight played on the reddish tones in his short mahogany hair.

"Go on, then." It would take less time to hear him out than to argue.

From his waistcoat pocket, Rían withdrew three scraps of paper.

The Golden Falcon
The White Stag
The Green Serpent

"Each of us selects a pub, and we see who lasts the longest inside. No glamours and no wards. Ruairi, you can stay shifted as a human to make it fair. Tadhg, you can shift into—oh, wait. Never mind."

The crystal glass shook in my hand. *Dammit,* I wanted to kill him.

"Winner takes all," Rían finished.

Rían's gambling had gotten worse since I'd killed Aveen. Idle hands and all that nonsense. He needed to find an occupation beyond irritating me, since bedding his way across the island was off the table.

The second gulp of puítin burned worse than the first.

Those three pubs were the most infamous in all of Airren, infested with mercenaries who murdered Danú for sport. And my younger brother wanted us to spend the night in them? Not a feckin' hope.

"I'm in." Ruairi withdrew a black medallion from his waistcoat pocket, threw it atop the scraps, and guzzled the faerie wine. How did he drink that shite without gagging?

I shot my best mate an incredulous glare. He was always the first to add to the pot, even though he never had a hope of winning. The problem was that he had more money than sense and eternity on his hands.

"I'll pass." The blackberry pie was calling my name.

"Well, I'm in." There was a flash of gold as Rían withdrew something from his pocket and dropped it onto the pile.

The pair of gold triskelion cufflinks, gifted to Rían by our father, were his most prized possession. I had tried for a century to get him to bet them, and he'd always refused. His dark eyebrows lifted in silent challenge. The bastard *knew* I had no choice but to accept. It wasn't about the money. It was about beating Rían out of something he loved.

I ripped the button off of my own black waistcoat and added it to the pot. I'd sit in whatever pub I chose until morning if it meant winning his cufflinks.

Rían grinned as he folded the scraps. He shifted a bowl from the kitchen, dropped them in, and held it toward me, a mischievous glint in his blue gaze. "Let's choose where we're to die tonight, shall we?"

I inhaled a deep breath, closed my eyes, and stuck my hand into the bowl.

The Green Serpent

It would be my luck to pick the worst of the lot. And it was across the entire feckin' island from Tearmann, so I'd have to waste a considerable amount of magic getting there. Before I was cursed, I could've made the trip fifty times in a night, not a bother. But now? I'd be lucky to get home.

I snagged the glass of faerie wine and finished every last rancid drop. If I was to die tonight, I was going to die drunk.

The Green Serpent reeked of rot and sweat and stale drink. And I was fairly certain the mercenaries trading pooka claws at the table next to mine had bathed in shit.

I kept my head down, knowing what would happen if they caught me staring. Their whispers rattled through my head; they were as aware of my presence as I was of theirs. Wearing the enchanted kohl had been risky, but I refused to come into this hell hole without it.

For the moment, I was relatively safe. I was reading, after all. How threatening could I look with a book in my hands? The humans appeared more interested in drink than in me. It wasn't until they got deeper in their cups that they'd begin plotting how to kill me and divvy up my parts.

Death was tedious, and finding the bits when I got back was always a feckin' nightmare. The last time it'd happened, it took me a fortnight to locate my thumbs.

"Like I was sayin', yer Lordship," Oran said, a spark of greed lighting his pinpoint eyes, "if ye just gave us half, we'd be able to buy enough port to turn a tidy profit." It looked as if he'd put on a stone since I'd last seen him, and there was barely enough greasy, gray hair left to cover his head.

Every time we met, I had this overwhelming urge to force my magic into his oversized gullet and watch the life fade from those tiny eyes. It was nothing less than he deserved for trying to swindle me out of more gold, but there were more pressing matters at hand. Like not getting my head severed by the axe sitting next to the mercenary glancing at me from over his shoulder.

"I'm not giving you anything until you pay back what you owe." He'd already borrowed a small fortune for his smuggling venture. Unfortunately, he was one of only a handful of men willing to supply Tearmann with drink. I could've shifted all of it straight from the ships, but the damned treaty my father had signed forbade it.

"If I could pay what I owed ye, I wouldn't be askin' fer money." His grimy fingers wrapped around his flagon, and he raised it to his thin lips.

Oran was a leech.

I wouldn't put it past Rían to have told him I was here just to make me lose. After all, if I killed him, the other humans would take offense.

I glanced toward the broken clock on the shelf.

Four past eleven.

I'd already been here for two hours. Was Rían still out, or had he returned to the castle? Ruairi wasn't a contender. He couldn't come back from the underworld, so he'd be gone at the first hint of trouble.

On the other side of the room, the main door opened.

This was the type of place where ignoring that mundane detail could end in death. Everyone else seemed to know that too, as the boasting and swearing came to an abrupt halt.

A woman came in, her face hidden within her cloak.

I'd known my fair share of female mercenaries, but the way she walked, all perfect posture and swaying hips, pointed more to her being an escort than a cold-blooded killer.

One of the *actual* mercenaries across the way nudged his friend, nodded toward the woman . . . and grabbed a handful of her ass.

White hot rage clouded my vision.

I knew what it was like to be touched without consent. To have people take from you what you didn't want to give. This woman— escort or not—deserved the right to choose who touched her.

Brown hair. Leather vest. Crescent-shaped tattoo on the right forearm.

The vile bastard wouldn't leave this pub of his own volition.

The woman stumbled forward, and her skirts swirled when she twisted toward him.

"Ye've a fine arse 'neath all them skirts," the man slurred. "Five coppers fer a ride."

Her hood lifted a fraction. Instead of responding, she threw back her shoulders and stomped toward the bar. The men around her grew rowdier, but no one else had the bollocks to do anything but shout lewd suggestions and gesture to their dicks.

Sorcha emerged from her flat in between the two pubs. She was smart enough to keep the glamor in place on this side of the wall. If only there were something to be done about the scar her husband had left when he'd used a hot iron to brand the poor selkie.

And these humans thought we were the monsters.

"I wonder if you might be able to help me," the woman said, her voice surprisingly husky. Her posh Airren accent was too refined for an escort. "You see, I'm looking for a man—"

"Pet, I've been lookin' fer a man in this pub fer forty years," Sorcha said, limping toward the bar, "and haven't found an honest one yet."

"A man to help me get to Tearmann," the woman finished.

"Why would someone like ye want to go there?"

Why, indeed? I flipped to the next page in my book, hoping to catch the girl's response. Humans knew better than to try and enter our territory. No one could hope to survive the Black Forest without an escort. And even then, it didn't guarantee they'd make it.

"I need to find the Gancanagh."

Shit.

The smile fell from Sorcha's weathered face. "These men will rob ye blind. Best be gone with ye and get the foolish notion of findin' the Gancanagh outta yer 'ead."

Sorcha's eyes flitted toward my table before shifting back to the girl.

Perhaps the stranger hadn't noticed.

Shit.

The girl in the cloak was looking at me.

Don't look at me. Look at Oran.

Squeezing the book in my hand, I focused on the names listed on the weathered pages instead of the way the woman's shadowed eyes grazed over Oran and the drunkard passed out on the table to settle on me.

"Please," the woman said, turning back to Sorcha. "Surely you can recommend *someone*. It's a matter of life and death."

She sounded desperate.

But there were only two reasons a woman came looking for me. And I wasn't interested in sex or death tonight. I wanted to beat Rían and celebrate my victory with pie.

Oran nudged me with his boot.

I kicked him in the shin and kept my eyes on the book. The man who had assaulted the mysterious woman slipped from behind his table, adjusted himself, and started for the bar.

It only took a flick of my wrist and a few whispered words to get his companion to tackle him. I kept the book in place with one hand and hid the other beneath the table.

One. Two. Three.

Three hits to leave his head lying in a puddle of his own blood.

If my magic had been at full strength, I would've turned him to ash.

Sorcha flung her hand toward the door. "Get outside and wait. I'll see what I can do."

"Thank you. Thank you so much." The woman gave Sorcha a coin and pivoted on the heel of her expensive boot. The bloodied body on the floor blocked her path to the door. I held my breath, waiting for her reaction to tell me something about who she could be. Faint, scream, or—my personal favorite—fan herself with her impossibly pale hands.

The woman didn't do any of those things.

Those pale hands fisted at her sides as she lifted her boot and kicked him. Twice.

Feck it all, I think I just fell in love.

The mercenaries shouted riotous cheers, none of them bothering to help the man dying on the floor. The woman sauntered toward the exit, threw open the door, and stepped into the night.

Oran jabbed me with his elbow. "That girl was lookin' fer ye."

If he touched me again, I would have his hands. "Was she?"

His bushy eyebrows came together. "Didn't ye hear her say it?"

Why was I destined to be surrounded by pillocks?

Sorcha stared at me from behind the bar, a look of pinched irritation on her face. She probably thought whatever the woman wanted was my fault. But I'd never seen her before. Still, it would help no one if I didn't at least speak to her. If she wanted the same thing every other woman before her had wanted, I'd have no choice but to oblige.

That was a problem of my own making, and I wouldn't drag Sorcha into it.

Still. A matter of life and death? That seemed rather dramatic.

"Go and get her for me," I told Oran. "Bring her around back." There was a second pub that catered to the Danú at the rear of the building where it'd be safer to speak.

The broken clock said it was a quarter past eleven. And from the glassy-eyed stares being shot my way, I figured I'd worn out my welcome anyway.

Oran's eyes widened, but he didn't budge. "Ye can't expect me to go fer free. Not all of us can pull coins out of our arses."

I should have made him shit a few coppers for his insolence. Instead, I collected a coin from my pocket and shoved it into his grubby palm. He clattered to his feet, then pushed past the mercenaries and out the door.

"What do you say, old man?" I kicked the drunkard beside me. His eyes didn't open. "How'd you like to be my puppet?"

The bloodied man on the floor let out a low groan, reminding me there was one last thing I had to do. I set my book aside and shifted the mercenary's axe into my hand. When I stood, my stool scraped against the floorboards. I could feel the eyes on me as I stalked forward and stooped next to the man with pain-dulled eyes.

"It's time you learned to keep your hands to yourself," I whispered, adjusting my grip on the heavy axe. Using a tendril of magic, I stretched his crooked arm toward me. Fighting was useless, but he tried anyway. Stools clattered to the ground when the mercenaries shot to their feet. I aimed the blade at the man's wrist and let it fall.

ACKNOWLEDGMENTS

As always, the first people I need to thank are the readers who picked up this book. Thank you. And in case no one has told you this yet today, you're amazing.

My husband has been taking up my slack for years in hopes of me "making it" so he can finally realize his dreams of becoming a pool boy. Hopefully this book will bring us one step closer to that goal. I love you, Jimmy and cannot wait to see you in a Speedo.

My children, Colin and Lilly, thank you for being so good at watching screens so Mommy could get work done. You both mean the world to me even when you're being monsters.

Hi Mom. I know this book was racier than the last few, but I hope you enjoyed the story and my improvement all the same. Megan, thanks for devouring my books and saying they're good even when they're not. And Dani, thanks for helping me embrace the scandal.

Phyllis & Shay, thank you for babysitting my children so I could "write another one."

Miriam, thank you for being my go-to Beta and for loving this story as much as I do. And Krysten, thanks for shouting about this book via the inter webs, creating a spectacular playlist and vision board, and being a genuinely amazing human.

The editing goddess also known as Meg, you continue to bring my stories to a whole new level. Thanks for making it sound like I know what I'm doing.

Elle, Candace, and everyone at Midnight Tide Publishing, thank you for being so wonderful to work with. I'm thrilled to be part of the MTP team.

ABOUT THE AUTHOR

Jenny is the founder of the PANdom and a lover of books with happily-ever-afters. A native of Oakland, Maryland, she currently resides in County Tipperary, Ireland with her husband and two children. As much as she loves writing stories, she hates writing biographies. So consider this the "filler" portion where she adds words to make the paragraph look longer.

ALSO BY JENNY

The Myths of Airren
(NA Dark Fantasy Romance)

A Cursed Kiss

A Cursed Heart (2022)

A Cursed Love (2023)

Prince of Seduction (2022)

Prince of Deception (2023)

The PAN Trilogy
(YA Sci-Fi Romance with a Peter Pan Twist)

The PAN

The HOOK

The CROC

MORE BOOKS YOU'LL LOVE

If you enjoyed this story, please consider leaving a review.
Then check out more books from Midnight Tide Publishing.

THE CASTLE OF THORNS
BY ELLE BEAUMONT

To end the murders, she must live with the beast of the forest.

After surviving years with a debilitating illness that leaves her weak, Princess Gisela must prove that she is more than her ailment. She discovers her father, King Werner, has been growing desperate for the herbs that have been her survival. So much so, that he's willing to cross paths with a deadly legend of Todesfall Forest to retrieve her remedy.

Knorren is the demon of the forest, one who slaughters anyone who trespasses into his land. When King Werner steps into his territory, desperately pleading for the herbs that control his beloved daughter's illness, Knorren toys with the idea. However, not without a cost. King Werner must deliver his beloved Gisela to Knorren or suffer dire consequences.

With unrest spreading through the kingdom, and its people growing tired of a king who won't put an end to the demon of Todesfall Forest, Gisela must make a choice. To become Knorren's prisoner forever, or risk the lives of her beloved people.

Available November 3rd, 2021

THE BONE VALLEY

BY CANDACE ROBINSON

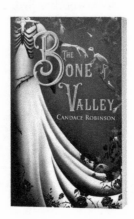

He's a lover. She's a thief. A magic bond like no other will tie them together.

After the death of his parents, Anton Bereza works hard to provide for his younger siblings. Love has never been in the cards for him, especially after desperation forces Anton to sell himself for coin. And he has no idea that, beneath the city of Kedaf, lies a place called the Bone Valley.

When Anton's jealous client plots against him, he is cursed to spend eternity in a world where all that remains are broken bones. There, Anton meets Nahli Yan—a woman who once tried to steal from him—and his cards begin to change. But as the spark between them ignites, so does their desire to escape. All that stands in their way is the deceitful Queen of the Afterlife, who is determined to wield her deadly magic to break Anton and Nahli apart. Forever.

Available October 13th, 2021

CPSIA information can be obtained
at www.ICGtesting.com
Printed in the USA
LVHW112158090822
725593LV00018B/333

9 781953 238498